I0787994

Behind Even The Shadows

Mental Tempest

Molly Moles

Scriverdea Publishing

Lewisville, Indiana

Scriverdea Publishing
4886 East 1100 North, Lewisville, Indiana, 47352
Printed by Amazon's Kindle Direct Publishing with permission

For additional information, contact Molly Moles using the listed address or email behindeventheshadows@gmail.com. Be sure to join @BEtheShadows on Facebook (with links to other social media platforms) for author updates and fan forums.

Mental Tempest first edition, 2022
Fourth in the *Behind Even The Shadows* Series of six novels.

Cover artwork by Molly Moles
Photomanipulation, logos, and accents by Jacob Moles
Concept editing by Janet Hughes
Map created using Inkarnate.com with proper licensure

ISBN: 978-1-951499-14-3 (paperback)
978-1-951499-15-0 (hardcover)
978-1-951499-16-7 (eBook)
978-1-951499-17-4 (Audiobook)

LCCN: 2022915567

Novels in the

Behind Even The

Shadows

Series:

Cloaked Heart

Unveiling Thorns

Paradox Puzzle

Mental Tempest

Verity Pursuit

Callous Closure

~ Dedication ~

To The One Who gave me the ability to produce the work I do ~ my Lord and Creator, God Almighty. May He be glorified in all I do, and may this book — and series — be a reflection of young Christian adults striving, growing, renewing, maturing, and perfecting day-by-day to follow Him and be in the world but not of it. Standing up to the sinful nature of those who do not submit to God's commands, while at the same time, showing them they do not have to continue in hopelessness and sin.

~ Acknowledgements ~

Sometimes "thank you" doesn't do justice; and yet what else can I say except, "Thank you!" I've added a couple enthusiastic readers to this great team and am looking forward to this following growing:

Janet Hughes	Jimmy Wayne	Jacob Moles
Sharon Ellis	Bekah Koen	Nicole Stasinos

~ Table of Contents ~

~ Pronuciation Guide ~

NOTES: Underlining: "hard" vowel. Capitals: stressed syllable.

First Names:

Iznan: <u>EYES</u>~n<u>a</u>n

Kareal: CAR-r<u>ea</u>l

Nebon: N<u>E</u>-bon

Uklo: Y<u>OO</u>K-l<u>o</u>w

(Princess in Armenian)
Zarouhi: zah-R<u>OO</u>-h<u>e</u>)

Places:

Arable: AIR~a~ble

Hougle: HOW~gle

Miscellaneous:

(Title) Apothecary:
<u>a</u>~POTH~eh~cary

(Mountain range) Badlang:
BAD-l<u>a</u>ng

(Japanese for evildoer)
Jingai: J<u>E</u>N-guy

(Japanese for grandson)
Mago: MAH-g<u>o</u>

(Title) Neurosan:
NEW~r<u>o</u>w~son

~ Map of Quidoria ~

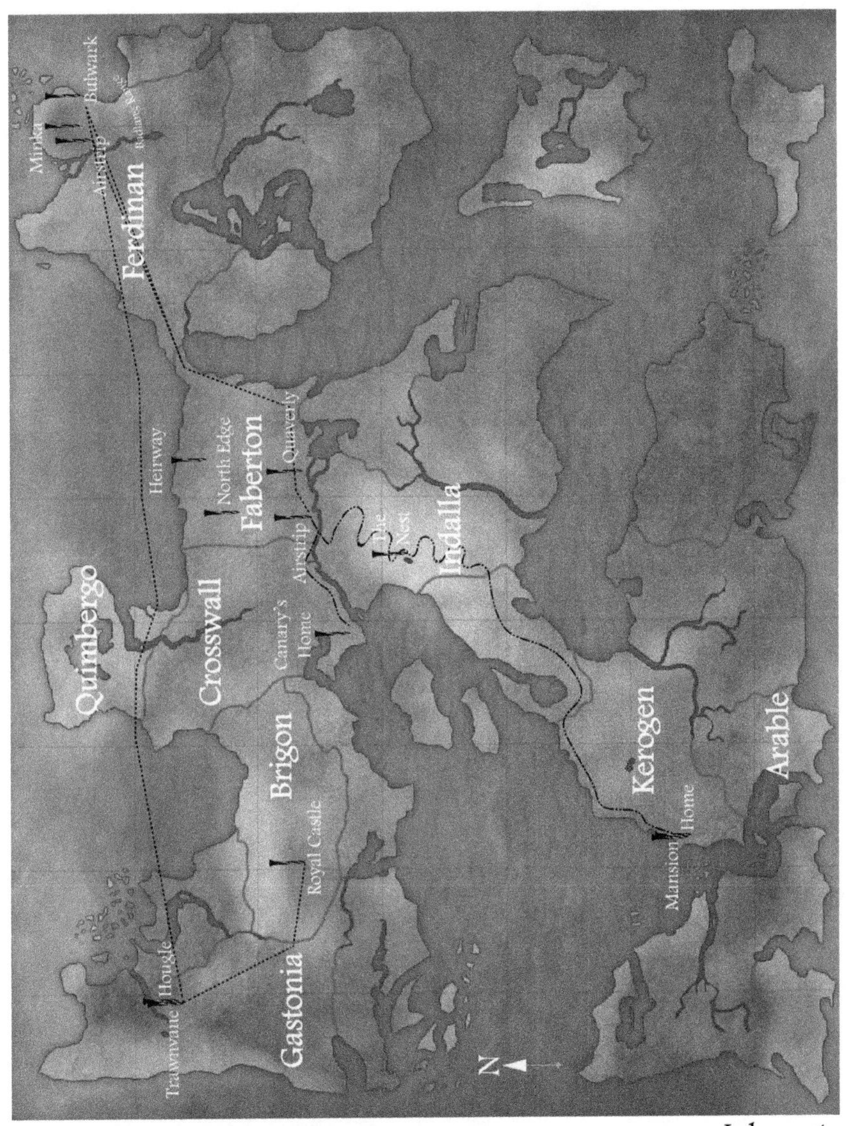

Inkarnate

~ 1 ~

Tears dragged down Destan's face, his eyes stinging from trying to be strong, "Calli... I can't. I know what it's like to be where you are. You've already been through enough. I don't— I 'won't' be the one who causes you this pain."

Every person's face bore the look of total shock and surprise as they stared at this battered, torn, and grieving couple. ... Well, that is, all but Elder. It could be reading into his expression too much, but as evil as he was it wasn't far-fetched to say he looked pleased.

The room didn't just look dark, it "felt" dark. Dark, desperate, and overpowering. A light mist fingered its way through the room in such a way that it was as if its sadness fought with the stench of formality and "honor" the darkness had always enjoyed.

No amount of delaying, tears, or anguish was going to make this vanish. Nothing but doing what he knew had to be done was going to make this end. There was no one who could help him, and it felt as if no one wanted to. No one truly cared like he did.

Destan looked up to his wife who was less than an arm's length away. He summoned what strength he had left and reached for her sleeve — more like forced himself — but stopped. She mumbled as she took his hand and laid it on her sleeve, "I know you hate it, but I also know you love me. And right now you 'have' to do this."

He let a groaning sigh escape as he took hold with both hands; closing his eyes as he gripped the leather, "I'm sorry, Calli."

With the quickest and strongest of pulls, her veil sleeve made the painful shredding sounds as it tore away.

"No!" She screamed in a blood-curdling shriek.

Destan sat up in bed; his voice pieced with terror, "Calli!"

By the time he was awake enough to know what was going on, he found his wife sitting beside him hyperventilating from a borderline panic attack. And so, with the gentlest of a touch, he encircled her with his loving arms to help her calm.

The sound of whimpering and the feel of fur against her skin caused Callimay to glance to the bedside; terrified for a moment when she saw the belvedere beside her. His usual upright ears were drooped as he rested his head on the bed. Destan pushed the creature's head away, "Get off and go lay down. … Go on."

He whimpered and nudged her hand before plodding to the foot of the bed; circling a few times before flopping on the floor as he huffed.

She crawled onto Destan's lap and continued to weep, "She's gone. I didn't even know I had her back unt—"

He hushed as he stroked her hair and laid his cheek on hers, "I'm right here. And so is the Big Fella. Just try to get some rest."

"How is it that she could be alive this whole time and I didn't know? She must've been looking— why didn't I figure things out sooner? Why didn't I try looking for her! I knew I had family. Why!"

"Calli please," he agonized as he did his best to keep her from escalating back to her hysterical high.

"But I could've saved her, Destan! I know I could have! My ability— why didn't I save her!" She continued scolding herself as she gripped his shirt, her eyes begging him for help. "I did it when the belvedere came for us! That wasn't even an hour before then! Why didn't I—"

"You don't know how to control that ability yet. You can't blame yourself for what she chose to do. Please, Calli. This isn't helping."

Even though it didn't make sense to him, the longer this went on the more Destan came to realize Callimay needed to vent her anger and regret about what happened; she couldn't shut off and suppress her emotions like he could. — And really? He had to admit his habit of suppressing them wasn't the healthiest thing to do.

I wish she could rest. These nightmares are tearing her apart. ~ She's getting better each day, Boon, if you really think about it. ~ But how much longer can she take this? Why is her mind doing this to her? I thought it was just Webb who was the mental tormenter. ~ Shock

❦

While she would remember things here and there, most of the events which followed Canary's revelation were just fragments of a fictional story that Callimay couldn't recall on a consistent basis. She knew in her nightmares that it was real, but when she was awake it would all vanish. Destan, on the other hand, remembered every agonizing detail of those few, mind-bending hours.

The second the door closed he pulled his screaming wife to his chest, clapping his hand over her mouth: *Callimay Rose Nevrille! You have 'got' to be quiet!*

Noticing how tight he was holding her and the tone of his voice made her freeze for a moment. While she fought herself to obey his order, below them was nothing but the sound of the belvedere barking.

No gun shots, no yells, nothing.

Just as he thought they had a moment to think things through, the sound of heavy, methodical marching was followed by a voice which was so full of gravel that raking your fingers across a chalkboard would've sounded like pure bliss, "She's down. The other two are in the rafters. We'll have them before long. … I'm sending her with them as I speak. … No, I'm not sure why he's acting that way. I'll make sure to have him sent for reintegration. … Affirmative. — Hibernate him and let's get going."

Destan didn't move a muscle until he knew they were gone; but didn't waste one moment more once he was sure. His mind was in full-on Doyen mode — there was no time to console or mourn. If they didn't get moving and keep moving, they wouldn't be alive to shed a tear for anyone.

And yet the trembling of his wife's body in his arms broke him. Destan awoke and began fighting against Doyen. — But now was "not" the time for this tug-of-war. Their lives were in danger!

It was dark, damp, thick, and musky in the passage — or rafters as the man referred to it. A stench of defeat from evil's vicious laugh made it hard to catch a breath; not to mention the late summer heat making this unregulated, enclosed place miserable and borderline unbearable. Having this way to get out was a blessing, but the size of it was less to be desired and made movement slow and cumbersome.

After backtracking only a few times, they zigzagged their way through this maze. Had he thought to use his vision modes or even Toreon's ability, things would've gone faster; but it worked out.

As she came out onto what was the railed portion of the roof, the void in the air that made her skin crawl to the point she was terrified; no midnight sounds of nature to be found. At. All. And then the eerie-lit, hazy landscape gave the strong impression it was on fire; glowing a very odd hue of red. Things were bad enough, why did the world outside have to join in? What was causing this picture of impending doom to weave itself around them; readying to choke the life they were barely hanging onto at the moment?

Right as she began to voice the horror she felt, she found the source of why the world looked this way, and was also cut off by a stern brow which framed burning eyes; a firm hand over her mouth: *Whatever you say, do it this way. We can't risk giving our position away.*

She trembled, her eyes too scared to look directly at the red orb in the sky and yet too terrified to look away from the ominous moon which looked like it was peering into her soul while draining every ounce of her blood; feeding off it so it could remain the color it was.

This was by far the best vantage point to have, but reality started creeping in; Doyen's mentality being challenged: *There are 'way' too many sentries to even run under the cover of the blood moon. ~ She couldn't run that far anyway. ~ Wait!*

Destan worked to channel Toreon's ability and found where Chet was parked. He rushed back and scooped Callimay into his arms; making the jump.

But he didn't?

He fumed after trying again, them still on the roof: *You've gotta be kidding*—*We've gotta get back to the tunnel we came in.*

What! But why?

There's some kind of barrier around this place; probably like the one that was at the Society if I had to guess.

I… but… can we even get back there?

Destan growled as he looked back: *No. … The box! Calli, did I give you a small box?*

N… o. No you didn't.

I can't— I've gotta go back. Stay h—

Please no! She gripped his veil, refusing to budge.

It was risky enough for him, but having her with him? Doyen was beginning to lose his ability to function on all fronts. And it started feeling to him that husband Destan wasn't going to be able to keep a grip either: *Don't cave, Boon! Keep going. Do what you know you can. Don't you dare stop fighting and accept defeat. You 'know' what will happen if you do. Get. Her. Out of there.*

There wasn't a second to lose and working backward through the blind maze was going to "really" tax his patience.

He sighed in relief when he saw the small box sitting right where he left it: *Here. Keep it safe. Do 'not' let go of it.*

Just then, the door began to open. He clapped his hand over her mouth and jumped back to the roof.

As if there wasn't a second to lose already they had no time now. But how were they going to get out if there was a barrier around the house? If it indeed was like the one from the Society nothing could get through; not even a willow tree branch. And they couldn't very well risk getting caught just to "try" — at least Destan wasn't willing to. He kept glancing around as he worked to keep his breathing controlled so he could find something that could give him a clue.

And then he looked up: *Give me a hummingbird. I've got an idea.*

She fumbled to get one, apologizing for taking so long when he kneeled beside her and put his hands over hers: *I'll get it. It's okay.*

Working to channel his anger as much as he could without going too far; he threw the hummingbird straight up. Its whisper whistle faded within seconds as it kept on. He listened so carefully but couldn't hear any high-pitched "plink" from it hitting anything or "thunk" from it sinking in: *Okay. It's a partial. That tree branch at the Society was about… oh, twenty feet off the ground. It's about a quarter mile~ Better make that a half mile to the tree line where the latch was. ~ The barrier must end there. This is only a two-story drop. If I—*

Destan! She gripped his arm, her trying to not scream out loud. *Someone's coming!*

Trust me? He framed her face with his hands and looked her in the eye, trying to get her to calm.

She gulped as she nodded: *Y… yes.*

He took a big, deep breath and smiled as he patted her cheek, then turned and jumped off the roof.

Callimay gasped as she ran to the railing; only to see him roll out as he hit the ground, turn, and reach up: *Jump Calli!*

But I c— why didn't you just jump us down there!

I've gotta save as much energy so I can get us over that barrier. I'm almost tapped out. Now jump!

She was scared to death as she slung her leg over the railing; but at the same time she was confident Destan would catch her. This tug-of-war did nothing but keep her right where she was — halfway between a terrifying freefall, and certain death — her grip not lessening on the box her mother, and now her husband, risked everything to get.

The shouts of men's voices startled her; giving her the mental push she needed to pull her other leg over and let go of the railing.

While freefalling still wasn't something she was comfortable with, something wasn't right: She felt her hair catch on something moments before she slammed into a window, the glass shattering on impact. Everything looked distorted for a moment as she worked orient herself.

Half out of his mind with fear, Destan tried to find a firm hold so he could work his way up to Callimay who was wheezing and flailing, trying to grab something so the pain would stop, but this was — by no accident — the smoothest masonry job he'd ever seen. There wasn't one crack in the red tuff stone big enough for him to get a Kunai in.

"Pull her up," a male voice called out.

"No!" Destan yelled out, getting ready to jump back up.

In spite of it feeling like an eternity, the time between her jumping and drawing her Seax was only a few seconds. Still long enough for her to feel pain and Destan to make an initial reaction, but not "that" long.

A man was sprinting down the hall to the broken window, but was mere millimeters too slow. Destan moved to where she was and braced himself; so relieved when she was in his arms.

She moaned as she grabbed her head, writhing in pain: *The box. I don't know where it fell.*

"It…" he sounded flustered as he whipped around, the darkened area holding and hiding the box seeming to laugh for a moment as the sentries started yelling out their location. "Ah! There it is."

Things were falling apart so fast it was as if they were caught in a mudslide with nothing sturdy to even think of grabbing. Voices could be heard from all directions, spotlights lit and scanning, the yaps and barks of what had to be other belvederes; and then there were the individuals above them, informing everyone else of their every move. They had no cover whatsoever.

Needless to say, his emotions were climbing… rapidly. He tripped once, a spike of fear shooting through him as he heaved, but he got his feet under him and took off again; sounding worn: *Calli? Throw a hummingbird in front of us. Now!*

It stopped in midair about fifty feet in front of them.

When he was twenty feet from the tree line, Destan dug his heels in as much as he could and launched into the air, purposefully pushing his wife up and away from him: *Roll out as quick as you can and run! Take the box and get back to Chet. Activate his flare and get to the border as fast as you know how. Don't look back. Don't wait for me.*

Everything in her wanted to argue with him, but the thunderous claps and slicing whistles of gunshots kept her from saying a word.

Callimay did as he said… at first. The first tree she came to after she touched ground she ducked behind for only a moment and then took off; trying everything she knew to keep the terror in her silent. But a few seconds and gunshots later her heart's screams made her turn back. She almost plowed into the last tree before the opening when another shot fired; her finding Destan not but ten feet away from her on his knees looking like he couldn't catch his breath: *What are you doing! He said to go! There are a few sentries with belvederes coming. You've got to protect that box. If~ If I leave they'll kill him! *Destan?*

Even though she expected him to flash his eyes at her when she got to his side, they looked beyond exhausted and asking for help. She jumped behind him so the spotlights wouldn't aggravate his eyes, now feeling the ground begin to rumble.

This quaking feeling accompanied by another round of shots caused Destan to catch an immediate second-wind. He yanked her to the ground and then looked for Chet.

Once he stepped out of the jump, he collapsed; falling on top of Callimay. She wheezed and let a yelp of a cry out as she pushed him to the side; her squirming and scrambling to get away. The second she got her wits back she saw him on his knees, his one hand trembling and clutching his chest as he tried to breathe. It was a good minute, maybe two, before he stumbled to his feet and reached for her.

They staggered the last fifty feet to the car and then tore out of there.

The scenery kept morphing back to its normal moonlit lighting as it flew by outside; Callimay pushing Chet to the limit… and then some.

When they got to the border, everyone at the station ran out. Destan was pretty much recovered by this time and only stayed long enough tell them what happened and what was most likely on the way; him now driving.

He glanced at her every so often but didn't say anything after he tried twice. Nothing was going to help her right then; him included.

Moonlight broke off the box in her hands, the tiny container saying its formal hellos to them both. While he did see the box when Canary handed it to him it didn't actually register until that moment: *She had one too!*

Anyone seeing this young woman in the passenger seat could tell something life-shattering happened. And yet it was far worse than just her tear-stained face, lopped off hair, and cut face and hands. The invisible injuries were deeper cutting and much more devastating — she didn't know what was real anymore. Her mind couldn't begin to process what happened. In fact it didn't want to because it couldn't bring itself to admit what happened. If it did, that meant she lost her biological mother and possibly her only living relative.

Their heartbreaking failure of what was supposed to be nothing but a simple info exchange came to its crushing end, Destan coasting into the cabin's driveway. Once the car came to a stop — the gravel pops slowly grinding to a halt — he gripped the steering wheel as he sighed and leaned his forehead against it. Deep down he knew this was going to end this way but he'd prayed again and again that it wouldn't. He wanted his gut instinct to be wrong… that the blood moon really wasn't a factor like it always had been before.

When he looked up, the moon was obscured by a passing cloud, unveiling the stars. He saw the bursts of lights sprinkled in the night sky and groaned as his eyes began to well with tears; him remembering what he said to Canary and the heavy and somber connotation it held for both of them. His plate was already overflowing with responsibility and yet he now felt that he carried the guilt of a Veil's death… and the Veil who was his wife's biological mother.

Right as the moon came back out it struck him how much brighter it was outside compared to what he thought it should be. He glanced around and jerked back from seeing what was causing the glow: right next to the car was a white creature. It was standing there, innocent as ever, staring at him practically at eye level.

Without a second thought Destan reached over and took a spike out of Callimay's pants leg and rolled down the window just enough so he could get it through. The belvedere cowered and began whimpering as it flattened its ears and looked at him with pitiful eyes as if trying to say, "I'm sorry. Please don't hurt me."

What in the world!

Not willing to trust what he saw — acting out of pure instinct — Destan threw the twisted, razor-sharp spike.

The creature jumped out of the way and yelped as it laid down in the snowbank, almost becoming invisible.

Destan turned the car back on and put it into gear: *Someone's got to be nearby telling that thing to do this there's no way— I took too long trying to recover before we left. That 'had' to be it. ~ Is it 'wise' for you to do this without her watching over you? ~ There's no time for 'what ifs'. … There still could be someone. I didn't see Justice Wan. And this 'is' an Alpha. We both know— what's it doing?*

As any sad pup would do, the oversized, glowing belvedere belly-crawled toward the car with its head ducked to the side; it whimpering and whining the entire time.

To say this kind of behavior was beyond uncharacteristic for a belvedere was nothing short of a "captain obvious" fact. — Well, that is it would be uncharacteristic for doing this around anyone but its keeper: *Y… you don't think~ Canary's Alpha? ~ It… well I guess it 'does' look like him. But a vast majority of them all look the same. … If it is, why? Why send him after us? He's just a track— oh no.* "Chet?"

"Yes, Doyen?"

"Scan the area for any Syndicate vehicles."

A few agonizing moments passed before the car's AI replied, "Area midnight black."

"What?"

"Do you want me to look again?"

"I… yes," Destan's voice began to crumble into confusion.

Again, there was silence for a few moments before the car repeated, "Confirmed: area midnight black."

This doesn't make 'any' sense at all! Destan rubbed his face; pausing when he saw the belvedere move again, "Scan a fifty-foot radius for 'any' Syndicate signatures."

"Parameters?"

"Belvederes."

Destan narrowed his eyes as he looked at the creature during those few seconds as if to say, "I got you now;" but was left questioning what he saw when the car's AI stated, "No belvedere signatures, Doyen. Any other parameters you would like me to check?"

"What!"

"I executed two scans taking into account the new variants that have been discovered. Nothing."

That can't— Canary? What 'did' you do if this 'is' yours? ~ The sentries said they tracked her actions through him, though. He 'has' to be a belvedere. ~ But their signature can't be blocked or disguised. … So, if you 'aren't' a belvedere… then what in the blue blazes are you? There's no way you're 'just' a dog. Speaking of which! "Are there 'any' digital signals nearby?" Destan put the car in park.

"One."

"Where?"

"Just to your three, two clicks. Appears to be some type of cyborg signature derived from known sources from Pluto." Chet brought some information up on the dash as Destan looked out at the sad creature. "It's very similar to a belvedere, but lacking any hard code that would suggest it is; or any wireless link to known servers. … Is there anything else, Doyen?"

"You're sure?"

"About what?"

"The cyborg signature not being tied to the Syndicate."

"Positive. It's not even tied to the Sisterhood or the Fringe."

Destan fought with himself for a minute and then reached over to take another spike… and then stopped. Callimay hadn't moved this whole time. She didn't even react to his mentioning a belvedere or seeing the obvious glow outside; let alone his emotions. His heart broke as did his voice, "Calli? Calli are you alright?"

Dead silence.

Calli? He stroked the side of her face; sighing as his shoulders fell. *Calli please don't give up. I know it's hard; that you don't think you can make it through. But please. I'm right here. I'll help you. … Calli?*

His loving words fell on deaf ears. Getting her inside and holding her would help, but there was one "small" problem: *I've gotta get past that death trap but I can't risk making another jump. I might be stupid at times but I'm no moron. ~ Then what are you going to do? Tear out of here and make a break for it? Head down to the bunker? ~ He followed us, making it in almost the exact same amount of time even though I never saw him when we stopped at the border. Again, I'm not a moron. Stupid, though? Yes.*

After taking the spike, Destan got out of the car. The belvedere perked up initially, getting to its feet and prancing over, but hunkered down and shied away when it saw what he was holding.

"Chet?" He asked in a hushed tone as he looked around the sleepy, moonlit area. "Check for any human heat signatures."

"No foreign signatures."

"Are there any external feeds being sent to the cyborg signature you found?" He reached behind him as he set the spike on top of the car.

Precious, yet intense, moments ticked by before the car replied, "Nothing. It's completely autonomous."

The spike was now on the hood of the car, Destan leaving his hand right above it. This made the belvedere perk up a little, but it still whimpered as it came to him.

As any Shadow would, Destan's training to the point of natural instinct won out, causing the creature to run; his throw burying the twisted blade in the snow-covered gravel: *He's fast. ~ 'Too' fast.*

Even with all his training and memories of personal experience in regard to this Syndicate weapon, something hit him: it had green eyes. All belvederes had blue eyes because of their implants: *I've… I've seen this one before. ~ Canary's had green eyes I seem to recall. ~ Yeah, but that's not what I'm talking about. I've seen another one. … I just… I just can't remember 'where'. ~ The one in Yerlonga wasn't~ I don't mean that, either. It seems like it wasn't a 'bad' thing, but I'm not sure.*

His curiosity was starting to eat at him. Was this creature a friendly one? Was it indeed Canary's Alpha? Everything pointed to it. Was it not an actual belvedere? But she even called hers a belvedere. Then if this were hers, how not but a few hours later, could it not be one!

He took a big deep breath and did something part of him knew he'd live to regret… "if" he lived at all: he kneeled down about five feet from the belvedere, picking up the spike and tossing it to the side.

And like last time, the creature had a similar reaction: it stared at him, tilting its head as its ears twitched and it sniffed the air.

Would you 'stop' trying to see how far you can go with this? was all he could hear himself saying. And yet curiosity had him in its firm and possible deadly grasp.

Destan gasped when the belvedere ran at him but was shocked when it stopped and pushed its nose under his hand which he had on his knee.

Now what was he supposed to do? He wasn't expecting the creature to be "this" friendly: *Maybe if I pat his head a couple times he'll be satisfied and back off.*

The belvedere was beyond happy he was paying attention to it in such a kind manner and stepped closer with each touch; now resting its head against Destan's chest: *You've 'got' to be Canary's. It's the only thing that makes sense. … Thinking back, hers 'did' keep close to us at the end and wouldn't stop barking when it couldn't reach us. — Why, Canary? Why give him to us? And how did you do it? Let alone the fact— how did you get away, Big Fella? ~ Well we've certainly changed our tone. ~ I know. But something feels right about this. … It just does. It felt wrong because he wasn't being blood-thirsty like every belvedere I've met before. But now I… I just can't help but have a good feeling about this.*

Not but a moment later the belvedere raised its head and twitched its ears and nose while it looked toward the car; it bolting to the side where Callimay was. Feeling stupid for falling for this act, Destan jumped up and followed as he yelled out… but stopped. The belvedere was looking in the passenger side window, whining. He looked out over the landscape, using his vision modes as long as he dared, and then found himself stumped yet again.

Why was this creature acting this way!

His confounding thoughts were ripped to shreds from his wife's wails and screams; them causing the belvedere to bark and race back and forth, nudging Destan and pawing at the door handle.

Seeing her doubled over like she was crushed him. He leaned over and rested his hands against the window trying to keep himself from falling apart. What was he supposed to do? Let her get it all out or stop her? It tore him up, seeing her in such agony; but to hear her scream in that blood-curdling voice? The only other time he remembered hearing her scream like that was when she thought he was dead.

Unable to take the pain of being separated, Destan opened the door and kneeled beside his grieving wife; his hands beginning to quiver as he reached out to her. The belvedere pushed its way in and snuggled its head between Callimay's leg and arm, whining as it sat down.

"Get back!" He grabbed the creature by the scruff, yanking it away.

It whined a few times as it was pushed farther away, but did as it was told and laid down; its ears now flattened.

After catching his breath and showing a spike as a reminder, Destan turned back and tried to tell the woman he loved he was there. He put his arm around her and rocked her, "Calli? Calli, look at me. Please?"

Sobs were the only audible response given.

"I know you're hurting to the point you feel like you're dying; that your heart's being ripped out. I— I'm sorry this happened." He soothed as he pushed her hair to the side so he could see part of her face. "Did you just get these scratches from the glass? How's your head feel? … Calli? Calli what can I do to help?"

His voice finally reached through the pain, her beginning to awaken from this shock — well, somewhat. She turned her head and was able to focus on him even though she didn't reply. He looked pained but his eyes were so soft and caring; just like his hands. Destan sat on his heels and sighed as he opened his arms, "I'm here, Calli."

This whole time she had the box clutched tight against her chest. She let go with one and threw it around his neck, gripping his hair as tight as she ever had while she began to sob.

He picked her up and started inside; the belvedere standing up and whining after them as it paced and pawed at the ground. Destan's voice did a one-eighty as he looked back and shook his head, "No! Stay put!" *You're running with the assumption it'll listen to you.* ~ *Well, it has so far.* "Easy, Calli. I'm sorry. It's okay."

The belvedere lay back down and looked just as sad as it did before.

♭

Inside felt just as cold as it was outside, Destan fighting off a shiver as he closed the door; him sighing as he leaned against it. He was starting to notice that "lag" feeling again from him using his ability so much, but at least he felt he could relax and let his body replenish what was drained. Well, at least once he got up to the bedroom.

Callimay's sobs stabbed at the soft and sweet quiet in the cabin, her still clinging to him as he pulled himself up the stairs.

It wasn't any surprise the bedroom was just as cold; so after he laid her on the bed he went over and started gathering wood. — Again, his body would have to wait just a little bit longer before it was allowed to rest. So close, and yet so far.

The second it was close enough, his body reached out and snatched up the opportunity to rest: he sat down in front of the fireplace. While it was always interesting to him to watch the sight of the flames licking up and burrowing through the bark, its hypnotic ebbing and flowing pulled him away from reality for a brief time so he could begin to rest and heal both physically and mentally.

But, before long Destan heard howling. He raced into the bathroom, his eyes darting as he look out the frosted window which faced the drive. He'd only ever heard that "voice" in the context of warning…

warning of death. And yet what he saw wasn't anything suggestive of that. The belvedere was laying there where he told it to stay; its neck stretched out and up as it let out its lonely and sad call. He bowed his head as he leaned on the window sill: *As if things were hard enough.*

After splashing some cold water on his face and checking to see the creature hadn't moved; Destan dragged himself back into the bedroom.

"Calli!" His eyes darted for a moment, almost missing the fact she was on the floor in front of the fireplace.

It looked as if she collapsed there, the contorted way her body was positioned. Her breathing was so shallow and her eyes glazed over to the point it was a wonder if she was giving up on life. She didn't have any grip strength left so the box toppled to the floor.

Destan tried so hard, but couldn't keep the tears back any longer. He kneeled behind her and leaned over, "I'm sorry, Calli. So very sorry."

Her broken voice came out as a whisper as she gripped his arm, "Is what she said true? Is she my mother?"

~ 2 ~

A pile of glowing embers through a web of brunette hair was a bit jolting for Destan to see first thing when he opened his eyes. While at face value anything at this point could cause him to jump and overreact, the condition of his hands told him otherwise. What he did the night before taxied him to his breaking point: his body couldn't take anymore and had nothing left to fight the monster inside.

It took quite a bit of doing, but he kept himself quiet was able to get his hands to the point they would relax. While it was still frustrating that this would happen, at the same time it was baffling to think all that bottled emotion waited to explode until he was asleep. Was he actually able to control his emotions; or at least "learning" to? Or was the shock of everything so dominate that the anger in him had no room to grow?

Destan winced as he stretched his fingers one last time and then rubbed his neck, looking up to the window where the late afternoon sun's rays were flooding in: *I don't think I've had a crick like this in 'years'! Geez.*

He groaned and looked back down, seeing Callimay. While he was glad she was resting — and what appeared to be quite soundly — he knew he had a mammoth of a job ahead of him. Yes, she had been through this before, but this wasn't the same. Anyone who thought so would be an absolute idiot or just downright mean.

But, aside from the memories she now had and the work and time she was going to need to heal, there was a mangled mess of a reminder in her hair that was going to be a constant, painful companion for who knows how long… like his father's veil was to him: *Maybe she won't notice. ~ Seriously? No one alive could miss that.*

And it was true. She looked so different with it shorter; almost like a different person altogether. And yet the more Destan stared at her the more a tiny part of him couldn't help but think she looked like someone he knew… and it wasn't Canary. But who? And why did this hit him all of a sudden — and in a bad way?

This cascade of thoughts was becoming mentally draining, but he didn't know if he had the physical strength yet to get up. He was still drained from the day before and what happened while he was asleep. But, a minute or so later he pulled himself up; doing what he could to keep quiet as he stoked the fire: *I don't want her getting ch~ Well wait until you can walk, why don't you? ~ Why am I dizzy?*

Once he gained his faculties and got the fire rekindled, Destan sat beside Callimay and sighed as he started brushing his hand through and fiddling with her hair. The little metallic box caught his attention at one point, it seeming to beg him to open it.

Just like his father's, the top was the emblem of the precursor to the Veil and the bottom was a Greek word puzzle. As he moved the letter pieces he wasn't sure what in the world it was supposed to spell. He thought it would spell Canary since it was her Shadow Box — just like Challenger was his father's — but while it did look like it started with "c" there were too many letters to spell her code name.

Not willing to give up, he found some paper and a pen so he could start writing the letters down: *Are we assuming this is a Dialect word? ~ I guess so. My father's was. … Hum. Well these letters spell melon. … What about chae melon? ~ Why'd you pull that out of thin air? ~ I don't know. ~ Hey! Isn't that the name of that horrid 'frou-frou' tea you had the one time? ~ Ha! It is, isn't it? — I can still taste it: a floral horse barn. Dis-gust-ing. I don't know how I choked it down. ~ Your grandmother, that's why. … So anyway! Two words? ~ I'm just trying different things … Hum. C-h feels right, but c-h what? … What about 'calm' something? That would leave h-e-e-o-n. ~ I think the c-h bit sounded better. ~ You know? If there were an r you could get 'charm'. ~ Wait. C-h-a-m… e-l— Chameleon? ~ Well, that 'does' use all the letters. And it's a title like your father's. ~ But there's no Shadow by that title. Why would— no wait! Project Chameleon. ~ Your father's work that Elder wanted stopped? ~ It has to be that! ~ Well, in that case it would mean Challenger wasn't 'who' you thought it was. ~ Chameleon is another ability? … But I have all the paperwork on everything and I don't recall it. And why would Canary have it put on a box for Calli?*

The box's release mechanism was louder than Destan thought it would be and startled Callimay awake. She was disoriented as she jerked up and gasped, "What happened!"

"I didn't mean to wake y— easy! It's okay. We're safe."

"What are you doing with your father's Shadow Box!"

"Calm down, Calli. Just take a deep breath. … It's okay."

Her breath quivered a bit as she closed her eyes and clasped her arms across her chest; after a minute or so she took a deep breath and looked up, "I didn't know you brought that, I'm sorry."

"It's… it's not his."

"Who's is it, then?" Callimay asked confused as she picked it up and turned it over.

His voice was drenched with worry as he replied, "It's what Canary gave me."

"This is what she was looking for when we were in the one room?" She waited for him to answer, then sighed as her shoulders slumped, "Oh. Well I— what does this say?"

"Chameleon. … I thought the exact same thing and yet it doesn't make any sense."

"Did you look inside yet?"

"No. I just finished it when you woke up."

Callimay's eyes were glued to the box, them becoming more and more glassy with each passing moment. She ran her fingers over the etchings as if they were extremely fragile, trying to feel — if she could — her mother through them.

Destan laid his hand atop hers, sounding so tender as he recalled what she told him when he was in this exact same position, "You don't have to do this right now. It'll keep till tomorrow. Let's just rest for right now. Huh?"

"But I want to." Her voice cracked with pain as she began to quiver and shake again. "I want to know what's inside right now!"

Unwilling to antagonize her grief, he let her do as she pleased.

It was a struggle to get the lid to slide, papers packed underneath other trinkets exploding out of the sides when it did.

Even with so much of the contents spewed everywhere, it was easy to tell this box was packed with so much love and as much care as possible. These were reminders her mother kept safe for her daughter she somehow lost. This was a time capsule; a beautiful and burdensome collection of the life she never knew she had.

The air in the room felt strange, but only because it wanted to know what these strange items would reveal. What was in the box held what was left of a different life that was hers … the part of her which was missing for so long and she ached to have back. But now that she had it — in a manner of speaking — she didn't know what to do with it or how it was going to help her. This confusion was so plain to Destan and yet he only sat and watched.

Somehow still in the box — it being what was on top originally — sat an imposing and confusing item: a substantial, orange leather dog collar. It had an engraved heart-shaped tag on it.

"I may be gone, but Mr. Ruff will keep you safe."
"'Mummy' loves her little Rose Petal. ~ Lanta"

All the pieces fell together for Destan and yet he still wasn't going to let the belvedere near Callimay. — Well, at least not until he ran diagnostics on it and saw for himself its tie to the Syndicate had been severed. — He did trust the car's capabilities but in this circumstance he needed to physically see this to be sure. One would be enough, but all the encounters he had with belvederes built a hardened wall he just wasn't willing to let fall completely; at least not when it was having his wife near the creature.

"W… what does this mean?" She cried; her heart tugging on her so much that she clutched her chest and started to wheeze. "I don't. — It looks just like the collar from my stuffed dog… but it's a stuffed animal that has a collar. How… we don't even 'have' a dog! Is she talking about a dog she— but how could a dog keep me safe?"

'That's' where I saw him! Her stuffed animal! "A very special dog." Destan took her in his arms and stroked her hair as he leaned his face

over her head. "A special dog she's trained for years and years for the time it had to leave her and come for you even if she were in every kind of danger imaginable."

"What?"

"When we got back there was a belvedere beside the car. I reacted like normal when all of a sudden it cowered. — You know they 'never' cower from anyone but their keeper when they're mad at them. — I wasn't fully convinced so I had Chet run some tests; then got out of the car. The thing seemed happy again then seized with fear when it saw I had a spike. I threw it but the creature ran off. … It, well it knew you weren't doing well, Calli. In fact it ran up and tried to comfort you last night when I opened the door to help you out. And then after I got you in here I heard it howling. Sure enough, it was right where I told it to stay looking so sad and lonely. … Calli? A belvedere will 'never' obey, let alone listen to someone who isn't their keeper. So, the only logical conclusion is the one outside is Canary's — your mother's. And she's done something to it so it's tied to both of us. Do you remember how it was hanging around us right before we left and how it didn't try to protect her but us? Canary must have altered something with the coding before we got up to her."

"Where is it?" She asked wide-eyed as she pulled back.

He took her by the wrist and calmed her excited terror as he stood, "It should still be lying out by the car. Let me go check. — Stay here."

"But, Destan—"

"I… Calli I… just— stay inside. I'll go out and run the diagnostics I know to so I can make sure everything's safe."

She gulped as she started to follow, then scurried back and grabbed the collar as well as the box.

❧

They crept to the window, but for different purposes. Destan peeked around first, his grumbling making Callimay step out and around him. A vast majority of the window was frosted over; the part that wasn't didn't offer much help because of all the snow.

She scratched out a small area for herself to look out, tapping on the glass to see if doing so would catch the creature's attention. Well, that was if it were still there. Sure enough, she saw what looked like snow move so a black nose and two eyes were now visible. A few seconds later she could see the dog itself and watched it perk its ears and raise its head, locking eyes with her. It wagged its tail and barked a few times but stayed exactly where it was.

"I'll be right back," he kissed her on the cheek and smiled.

"Do you have any antidote?"

"Yep," Destan pulled his veil back and tapped a few small vials. "Remember? I put a few on your belt as well."

She bit her lip as her eyes darted to-and-fro, but consented, "A… alright. Please don't take— don't take too long."

"I'll be right by the window the whole time, I promise."

"Wait!"

He turned back only to see Callimay dash up the stairs. He heard a couple things hit the floor and then saw her pop back out. She ran to him and started rambling as she tossed a scarf over his head, "I don't know how long you'll need to—"

"Calli?" Destan, with a calm and gentle touch, brought her hands together in his. "Just take it easy. Calm down. My ensemble has gloves and a hood built in; just like yours does. Remember? … If I start getting cold I'll put them on, I promise."

The look on her face made him feel bad for saying anything, "I know you just want me to be safe. I wasn't saying— Calli?"

"I'm not thinking, am I?" She took the fuzzy, lush scarf in her hands and sighed.

"Yes you are." He leaned over so he could see her face. "It doesn't matter that I don't wear scarves — let alone fur ones — you just want me safe and did what you knew was helpful. There's nothing wrong with that; and you know? I love you for that."

ᕦ

It was a different kind of joy to experience, seeing how the creature interacted with Destan — it acted just like a dog. Belvederes didn't pant or let their tongues hang out so it was more challenging to distinguish their emotions at times, but it appeared everything else it did was what any dog would do when its owner had been gone for a while.

At his command, the fluffy creature popped up and shook off the rest of the snow in its fur like a tidal wave of nervous, bundled energy while it bolted to him; bouncing and running in circles before making it to the covered porch.

Both Callimay and Destan were scared when it jumped on him, but it only wanted to say hi; the creature barking as its tail wagged.

The creature's ears perked when Callimay gasped; it bounding to the window where she was and putting its oversized front paws on the window sill. Its bark sounded more like a mini howl, its eyes looking worried as it tilted its head and its ears flattened.

Destan came over and calmed the creature, it looking back to her as if to ask one last time if she was alright. He activated a link and started running the scans and checks he knew he needed to.

Before long, he turned around and nodded: *Everything's good. She wiped it clean. It's as close to a dog as it'll probably ever be.*

Callimay smiled and ran to the door, the belvedere matching her every move and acting as impatient as he had back where they met Canary and he wanted the door opened. Destan rolled his eyes as he sighed, "Don't you have even an 'ounce' of patience? Geez!"

While it occurred to him at one point the night before, he hadn't paid much attention to the size of the creature in relation to Callimay. Seeing this difference shocked him: just standing, this belvedere's withers were level with her waistline! As far as he was concerned, the dog was "dog size". Now? Well, let's just say he had a healthy amount of uneasiness.

But, as if it knew how strong it was and its size advantage compared to the young woman it was bound to, the belvedere calmed and only played foot fire around her before rubbing up against her.

Callimay was still fighting off what she'd had drilled into her about these "animals" and what she herself witnessed, but with the face it had she couldn't resist for long.

It noticed she had its collar and stuck its nose through, shaking once really well after she finished putting it on.

H... he looks— "Mr. Ruff?"

The fluffy creature sat in front of her and barked as it raised its paw to shake her hand; its tail wagging nonstop.

"That's the name Canary gave it— 'him', I guess." Destan corrected himself as he rubbed his neck and walked over.

Callimay dropped to her knees and stared at the dog creature. He looked just like her stuffed animal she'd been carrying with her for so many years. She had no clue Lanta was her mother even though she suspected it. And she of course never could've guessed her mother remembered the name she gave the stuffed animal all those years ago; making sure the real-life version was every inch like it: *But how did she know? Did she have you when she gave me that stuffed animal?*

His lush, thick, long, white fur was just as soft as her toy; eyes as green as the rarest chrome diopside she convinced herself as a child her toy had; and a tail that was long, straight, and beyond fluffy. She'd done it countless times — making the tail wag — that it was almost mind-blowing how accurate she imagined it: a tail that couldn't stop displaying how happy it was.

This all compiling reached its tipping point; her ripping the collar off as she buried her face in his fur and cried. It became too much for her to handle, too much for her to process, and a harsh reminder that a broken heart needed time. … And sadly, more time than what was probably going to be given.

Destan knew he was synced to respond to her emotional status so he wasn't too worried when he looked up and yelped. He kneeled beside them and quieted, "It's alright, Big Fella. I know."

While it was still lost to Destan how in the world Canary broke the coding link to the Syndicate or altered what was known as its "keeper focus" in such a short time, he had to concede that for her to keep it a secret from the Syndicate she would "have" to know every in and out of the creature's coding. The intricacy of it was mind-melting for most, Veil "and" Falconer, so her computer knowledge was phenomenal.

But aside from all that wondering and questioning he had some added comfort. Canary had gone to awesome lengths to do what she did: Callimay now had something that would quite literally fight to the death for her and was truly the best option for taking another belvedere down. And with it being an alpha — and the largest one he'd come across — it had more "firepower" than any other type of belvedere.

~ **3** ~

After a long and somewhat sleepless night Callimay woke to find she was the first one up. She looked empty and lost; wandering around the room while moving random things here and there before eventually ending up downstairs. Poor thing couldn't focus on anything until she saw her mother's shadow box; the bright orange collar catching her eye.

The belvedere kept close this whole time; following her over and sniffing the leather strip. Knowing whose smell was on it, he wagged his tail as he looked up at her with his clear, green eyes and then around the small room.

She let out what sounded more like a groan as she slumped her shoulders and flopped onto the closest chair; the belvedere right beside her with his head on her lap and ears flattened.

Unknown to her, Destan was at the foot of the stairs. He was thinking as fast as he could, trying to figure out what to do before sticking his foot in his mouth and making everything more miserable than it already was.

But he couldn't stay hidden forever, her eyes crying for him to help her when she looked up. He came over and dragged one of the chairs around so he could be right beside her. While he wanted to just sit and relax, he knew she was trying to work and find the courage she needed to look at what else was in the box: *She shouldn't do this! ~ I know, but what can we do? Say no and get her mad? ~ A little frustration up front would be better than an entire day of misery.*

Right when he was about to say something he heard the clack-plink of what turned out to be three rings — what first came jumping out of the box. With that came two roses which were so perfectly preserved and two memory sticks, just like the kind in Destry's box. Under this all was another stack of pictures; most having charred edges. Callimay took them out one-by-one and looked at them in awe. They all had an inscription on the back saying when and where they were taken as well as who was in the picture. Some of them even had little notes on them to explain what was going on! — It were as if her mother knew she wouldn't remember anything.

It was quickly evident by the picture on top that Callimay's original family was large. "Quite" large. She was the youngest of twelve and the only girl. They all looked so happy together… and it appeared Callimay had a brother in particular who favored her: one of the younger boys closer to her age named Trever.

"You don't think!" Destan almost jumped out of his seat.

"But he doesn't look a thing like him!" She said almost breathless as she kept flipping the picture over and over. "This picture has him with blond hair and richer skin. The Trever you and I know has red hair and more freckles than you can count on his pasty face — no offence." *He's not here, Rose Petal. ~ I… I know that.*

While pondering this thought — and a somewhat horrifying one at that for Destan — she started skipping through the pictures to find more of this brother of hers to see if maybe there was a way to know for sure. Perhaps the name similarity was just one of those things that sometimes happened; his last name wasn't Presley. But what if: *Maybe he was only a blond when he was younger. I mean his hair 'does' have a slight strawberry hue to it. And some red-heads do start off as blonds. ~ But what about his face? ~ Well, maybe the freckles hadn't come out yet. ~ Okay, I'll accept that. But still, this is stretching things a bit to the extreme. If you are siblings why hasn't he said anything? He can be a jerk, but not 'that' bad.*

She rubbed the picture and then tapped her cheek, trying to wrap her mind around the possibility she was related to someone whom she'd known for quite a while.

And then something caught her eye. In the stack of pictures were two wedding portraits of her mother and father. Callimay remembered Lanta was about a head taller than her — making her rather tall for a woman — so a logical conclusion would be that her husband, who was still a head taller than her in the picture, would've been about Destan's height! Possibly taller! — Apparently she shared the same affinity as her mother did for extremely tall men. How sweet!

It wasn't much of a surprise to see how much she resembled her mother. The one picture showed that same rich caramel brown hair which flowed like a fountain to her knees, pulled back just enough from her face so you could see the sweet smile that looked so natural with eyes that looked like they were just as joyful as they ever were.

Even though it was scorched, it was still easy to see their wedding was a lavish one. Her dress was a flourishing full ball gown with a tartan sash wrapped around the bodice of the dress and over her left shoulder; it part of the massive skirt that must have been over twenty feet long. Finishing off the extravagant dress was a beautiful veil with what looked like white peacock feathers acting as a lace edging; it held in place by a jeweled headband of gold and rubies. Her small bouquet of red and white roses was accented with Scottish thistles. And then topping it all off was her groom: beaming with as much pride as any young man would as he stood next to his bride; his fiery red hair almost glowing with the same emotions.

Destan couldn't help but chuckle to himself a bit as he looked at her father: *So that's where she gets her fire: she's got red roots. It all makes sense now.*

His tall frame was a bit on the huskier side, but nothing that didn't look like it suited him. It struck Callimay that he wore a white tailcoat with a kilt and tartan sash made of the same tartan his bride wore. How could that be? While the kilt wasn't something completely unheard of — traditional weddings in Brigon required such apparel to be worn by the groom — but a white tailcoat? She knew it was reserved for the royal family alone. No one else in their right mind would even dare do such a thing!

Doing nothing but add to this confusion was the second wedding portrait. She knew it was them and yet she couldn't believe what they wore. The beaded and embroidered red sheath dress her mother wore was stunning and the lace cap covered with jewelry and long veil were so very flattering; but it was so odd in comparison to the first portrait:

this was traditional wedding garb for an Armenian wedding! And what her father wore showed that as well: the same type of embroidery on his green vest which he wore open over a white robe tied at the waist with a green sash. Add to that the fact this picture showed a place that appeared much more "modest" in comparison to the castle backdrop in the other — a peach tree grove — and things just didn't make sense.

On the back of this second portrait was a heartfelt inscription.

> *I know he promised me he would "take me home" to "do it my country's way" but somehow I just saw it as a sweet gesture and nothing that would turn into action. And while it's not like what I'd wanted since I was so young, he did so much to make it as close as possible.*
>
> *Dalvin continues to spoil me, just as he promised. He knows nothing will truly erase the pain, but he also knows how much it means to me — seeing him "do" what he says.*
>
> *It hasn't been easy by any means — all the tears, anger, and hatred thrown around and our yerekha (baby) dying — but in the end I have found him. I have found im ser (my love).*

A few of the words puzzled the two of them — even Destan didn't know what language it was even though he guessed it was Armenian — but Callimay didn't have to know because she pretty much knew what it said. She knew because she'd endured things quite similar to find her man… her love.

Curious to see what touching note was on the first photo, Callimay flipped it over. And she paused. On it was nothing but two signatures. They were beautiful in their own, unique ways but other than the date that was the only thing written on it.

Lanta Annabelle Yorick
and
Dalvin Sebastian Presley.

But she smiled, realizing something: she had something with her mother and father's handwriting on it. While it might seem trivial, meaningless, insignificant, or just simply overlooked by most; it meant the world to her. She had a very personal part of them with her.

Needless to say, Destan gasped when he saw both last names.

"What?" Callimay jumped, the belvedere sitting up and looking around for what scared her.

"I know that last name: Yorick. — Well at least 'a' family with that name. — That's the same last name as my friend I'd mentioned a few times: Ashte. … The family is from Kerogen."

"And Presley is the last name as the elderly man who contacted us; the man you said is the patriarch of the leading family of Brigon!"

"You're closely related to an 'extremely' powerful family, politically speaking, Calli."

A stressful silence started slithering through the air. Something wasn't right, "W… why was I in Faberton then? Were we visiting or traveling through? I mean were we going to Arable? That's where those from Armenia settled, right? … What happened? How did I get lost? Why… why didn't they look for me!"

Her breaking point had been reached; Destan trying to be calm as he suggested, "Calli please. Let's take a break. … Calli? Calli I'm sorry I don't have the answers to the questions tearing you apart. I wish I did. Looking back I can tell how bad Canary wanted to tell you. I— Calli?"

What he said was the only thing she knew she could expect, and it was true her emotions were getting to her: her left eye was aching and she was beginning to hyperventilate. She sighed as she laid the picture aside… but after a couple seconds picked up the rest and continued.

The one of her and Destan was in there, its inscription quite lengthy — very small handwriting — and emotionally jerking to them both.

My t'ankagin aghjik (dear baby girl), my Rose Petal, with her favorite friend whom she tells me every single day she misses and loves with her whole heart… and prays every night God will tell him to ask her to marry him: her Destan.

How she's able to pronounce his name without the slightest hesitation or lisp makes me wonder sometimes. Could they be soulmates? She's never put forth much effort, let alone fight, to learn how to say a name clearly. Not even her own! She lives for the chuckles, giggles, and laughs that come when her lisp destroys someone's name. And yet the second he left after she saw him that first day… oh how she fought! She cried and begged me and her Paba to help her so he would love her. My baby said she knew Destan didn't love her because he frowned the whole time; and she just knew her not being able to say his name was the reason why. — I will continue to see the beauty in the simplicity and selflessness of children's logic.

I never thought I would see my daughter heart-broken at the age of four, but here we are! Oh the new, never-ending, and joyful pains of being the mother of a daughter. It is nothing like being the mother of boys, but I would never ask for anything to change. I needed this change.

I'm rather certain Destan is in that stage where all girls are much too clingy and emotional. Plus the dear child is an only child. Not to speak a thing against him! He's an absolute dear and I think Destry and Lylah are doing an amazing job. He's just not the kind of boy that Trever or any of Rose Petal's brothers are. He's that calm little boy who enjoys the quiet. — Finlay is the closest to that, but he is still easily excited around Callimay since she's "stolen" his twin brother. — I'm not sure if he'd take too well to having a sibling like Destry told me Lylah and him are planning for in a year or two, but children change constantly. Who knows! Destan may become the softest teddy bear who can't do anything but smile and hug every person he sees.

She gripped the picture and bowed her head. The belvedere snuggled close as her terrified voice came out in gasps, "Why don't I remember you? Or your name? Or something! What… what happened to me! What happened to both of us! … I… I feel like I've been living a lie! I know I haven't and I didn't know, b—"

"Calli," he tried to coax her to let go of the picture, his sympathetic, small smile trying to help his efforts. "Please. You need to stop torturing yourself like this. This is too much for you to handle right now. You're head's go—"

"No!" She agonized as she jerked back, startling the belvedere yet again. "No I have to know!"

"But you're in no condition right now, Calli. I know you're in pain already because of finding this all out. Don't add to it. Please."

"I can't stop! I just can't! I 'have' to know. Don't you understand?"

"Calli… I… I'm saying this because I 'do' understand. I 'do' know what that raw, gnawing feeling does to you. But with your migraines I don't want you to— alright. Five minutes." Destan caved, his worried voice trailing off as he rubbed his temple.

The last picture was of her and Lanta. Callimay was in a hospital gown with her hair all wrapped up in an orange cloth cap. She was sitting in a bed, Lanta leaning over and giving her a kiss. It appeared this was when she got her stuffed dog: her grinning from ear to ear as she clutched the fluffy toy. But her face was flushed like it would be from her crying.

Lanta was wearing her ensemble and veil; Destry sitting next to them… wearing hunter green scrubs! It was dated October fifth, 2468.

My little Rose Petal is so brave! No matter what people may say: little girls "are" strong and so very, very brave. They just conserve it and only use it when they know it's needed.

And like I hoped, she loved her "Mr. Ruff" as she named him the second after she finished going on about how soft he was; oohing and awing over his eyes that she was convinced were real gemstones.

At least this small distraction helped make up for the fact "her Destan" was not with Destry… and on her birthday. It still boggles my mind how she can be so smitten at such a young age. She's never forgotten him. And somehow I doubt she ever will even after this. Her love for him is just too deep.

Mummy loves you so much, Rose Petal. And just think! When I get back I'll get to see my new little Chameleon!

"I'm… a chameleon? What… what's that supposed to mean!"

Seeing his father in the picture terrified Destan. He was involved in her life a professional way. Destry "did" something to Callimay when she was very young. Was she sick with something? Nothing he knew his father formulated and offered for young children would've applied to her, though: *You don't think~ It couldn't be. He wouldn't inject her with some serum. He said they weren't ready for human trials. And she was so young. Why would he? ~ Well what would it have been? I know his journal was so against— it 'must' be a name Lanta gave the treatment. People do that sometimes when they can't pronounce a medical term. … It had to have been that, but why use that name and have it as the code for the box? ~ Well, your father 'did' talk about 'Project Chameleon' and how Elder~ Oh no… it couldn't be!*

What about it was so disrupting to the Shadows and Veil that could be done for a little child? She was obviously sick and needed help!

Once his self-discussion was finished — because Callimay began asking him point blank — they discussed this for a while. But what could Destan tell her? It wasn't going to fix anything; he didn't know any more than she did.

What felt like the stench of the unknown was beginning to suffocate them. Why was it that these questions which were pertinent to them could never be answered? Why did things end like this?

Trying to keep herself from spiraling into another panic attack, Callimay tried to look at things for just what they were. In the bottom were charred pieces of drawings, certificates, licenses, and random notes. — These had to be what was salvaged from her home.

One piece caught her attention that had her name on it. It turned out to be the remaining portion of her original birth certificate. Her full name was Callimay Everlyn Presley. She was born on October fifth, 2463 at four-thirteen in the morning; weighing only six pounds, three ounces! Such a tiny thing!

"D… does this mean we aren't legally married?" She asked out of the blue; hands shaking, eyes darting, and forehead wrinkled from equal amounts of pain and terror.

Destan reached over and took her hands; kissing them before he calmed, "This doesn't change anything about our marriage license. You were adopted and had your name changed, 'legally'. It was during war so I'm fairly certain some formalities were forced or overlooked, but the fact remains: you 'are' my wife as far as any government is concerned.

And as far as God is concerned — which is Who I really care about — this doesn't matter at all."

Her shoulders dropped as she let a quivering sigh out.

He tried one last time to coax her into putting things away… and it almost worked.

Almost.

As she started to put one small stack back in the box she saw there was an envelope at the bottom. She struggled for a bit before the paper finally gave way. Something was in it that would thump against the edges of the envelope when she would rock it back and forth: *Huh. I wonder what it could be?*

She flipped it over to see if there was any writing on the outside before opening it. It had Destan's name on it… in Destry's hand writing! Callimay whipped her head over and looked at him fearfully as she threw it at him, her almost squirming as she shook her hands; as if her skin were crawling from touching it.

After finding where it flew and seeing what caused the violent reaction, he tore the envelope open and let a key fall into his palm. He took out the slip of paper and read the note from his father.

I'm so sorry I couldn't come home, Destan. I admit I almost did when I saw you at the clinic while you got your new screens implanted last week.

But I just couldn't. I'm sorry.

The reason is because I failed. I failed to make right what I so horribly messed up. I failed you, son. Please forgive me. And please believe me when I say I tried. I worked myself literally to death to fix this. I just wasn't strong enough.

Go home, Destan. Go home to Kerogen. Not to the mansion but to the place you knew to be "home". I know it will be difficult — it was for me when I stopped by last week — but there's a box addressed to your mother there in my den. If for some reason you can't find it, go to my lab at the university. Rocher may have needed to move it several times, so don't be discouraged if it's not at the house or lab. He'll know what you're asking about if you can't find it.

It contains the puzzle box you could never open; the one you could never figure out and swore was nothing but a trick and lie. — The massive one your mother complained about me spending way too much on. — Well, this key is what was missing. I never told you because I was always amused at your shocked face when you saw how all I had to do was touch it for it to open after you'd worked so hard for so many hours.

Your mother was furious I continued to deceive you, and I now see that my temporary enjoyment wasn't worth the lost trust I "gained" from you.

You weren't doing it wrong. You just didn't know there was more to it. And one time you almost got it right: that panel you never did anything with is where the slot is.

What it contains cost me my life to get, but I know my sacrifice will save so many more lives. And so I'm at peace with this decision. I got to see you one last time and spend time where your mother and I built our home; so I'm ready. I'm ready for whatever comes after this. And really? It's the most peace I've had in almost ten years.

I love you with all my soul, Destan. Godspeed.

Your Father,
Destry

Destan was trying so hard to hold it together when he saw the terrified look on Callimay's face. He was at the point of breaking down and was still naïve enough to think he could hide it. Other than the fact she could "feel" his emotions she would see it in his eyes.

She sat and waited for him to walk out so he could go be alone and grieve; whatever the letter said hit him hard. Of course she didn't want him to, but she'd come to accept it was how he handled things like this. And yet that didn't keep her from trying. She thrust her hand out and placed it on his knee, opening her mouth when he fumbled, "Calli… I… I don't know how— how am I supposed to support you like I need to when I'm still grieving? I… I feel like I'm failing you."

"Oh, Destan. You're not."

"But we both can't fall apart at the same time. That won't—"

"Yes we can. We can 'both' fall apart because we've got Someone else holding us and everything else together." She begged as she fell to her knees, gripping his hands. "Please, Destan. Please fall apart. Cry, scream, let it out. Be 'weak' like so many think loving someone is. You know I understand. I'm already crying, so please don't let me keep crying alone. ... Don't keep everything suppressed, Destan. You know good and well that's so much worse... even deadly, now. ... Destan?"

The belvedere laid down right in front of them and whimpered a few times before falling silent; keeping a watchful eye on the distraught and grieving couple he was bound to and responsible for. They held on to each other as if they were the only thing keeping them alive; their weeping so deep they were silent as they prayed.

Destan then said in a determined tone, his voice muffled by her hair, "No matter what happens we're gonna make it, Calli. As long as I'm still breathing I'm going to do everything within my power to make our life together as joyful and wonderful as possible regardless what tries to slither between us or what pain grips us. I promise you. Our lives are 'not' going to be defined by our pasts — by our pain. I know we need time to process these memories, accept the loss, and grieve; but I don't want to lock you out. I just... don't know how long this is all supposed to last. Not knowing that makes me— well it makes me worried. I can't be like this for 'too' long; not with Elder around. ... But I guess— does it ever truly end? Grieving? ... Regardless, I promise you: I'm not going to let any of this destroy the two of us. I can't. I don't want there to be anything that gets the chance to poke and prod at us to the point it starts ripping us apart like before. I know I've got to work really hard on keeping my guard up, but I also need your help, Calli. I need it so much. I need your support, patience, your endurance and positive outlook... I need 'you': my ray of sunshine. The helper God made for me. — Somehow you've always known what I needed. I've just been too stubborn to see it at times or ignored it when I did see it because I was trying to 'be a man' and tough it out by myself. ... Please Calli. Don't give up. Remember: I 'am' here and I 'am' fighting."

She held on to his shirt this entire time he spoke until she had a death grip on him. He was both reaffirming to her his commitment to change and opening up. Some knot in his heart untied itself so he could voice how he was reeling and needed her help; unsure what to do. He accepted his feelings and fully understood now that showing emotion wasn't weakness.

This raw display reached and touched Callimay's heart that was so devastated. It reminded her that "she" had to get back up and keep fighting. She wasn't the only one who was human and had feelings. She had someone to fight with and for; and she even said there was still Someone watching over both of them the entire time. The only problem was: she didn't know how to get back up, especially right then.

"I'm not asking you to act like nothing happened. — Even I can't. — It would be cruel of me to tell you to. I… just, I need you to understand so if it feels like I'm a little… slow, I guess? Does that make any sense? … Please understand I'm trying to work through this as fast as I can. I hate we're going through this at the same time, but you're right: God's never going to give us anything more than we can handle as long as we lean on Him. I need to be able to support you more than I think I'm going to be able to and you're going to have to push ahead even though I know it's hard for you to see how you can. But Calli? We 'can' make it. We've got to have faith and look to God. If we don't do it His way we won't make it; and there's no way I want that to happen. I'm convinced He wants us to push through this all; He wants us to win… even with grief in-tow."

Destan finally let Callimay go but framed her face so he could see her face. It was drawn and pale as if she had nothing emotionally left, but her eyes were clear and calm.

He smiled as he wiped the tears from her cheeks before suggesting she go change into something comfortable; her finding enough voice to agree while suggesting the same to him.

♇

The poor, neglected fire in the bedroom had burned down to a pile of glowing embers, so Destan got another one going while he waited for her to get ready; making sure to take his time doing it so he wasn't sitting there waiting. He knew she'd be in a tizzy if she thought he was waiting on her to finish.

And so, right as he got finished she came out rubbing her hands in a slow and methodical manner over her arms.

He popped up, taking a deep breath as he smiled; but almost cringed as his shoulders slumped when he saw her, "Still cold?"

She mumbled as she looked down and away, nodding, "Kinda."

"Well…" Destan thought out loud as he jogged over to the closet. "Let me see what I've got in here."

It only took him a few seconds of rummaging around, the soft clack-slap of hangers complementing the pops and snaps of the fire, to find what he was looking for. He just about ripped a sweater off a hanger and spun around, seeing Callimay staring at the fireplace. Being the gentle man he'd become around her — the teddy bear Lanta spoke of — he stroked the side of her face with the back of his hand, trying not to scare her.

After a few seconds she looked up, her eyes starting to looked glazed over. Destan took a deep breath, trying to smile as he offered the shirt to her, "Here. Try this."

The belvedere sniffed the light gray sweater as she took it in her hands, staring at her in confusion. She wasn't doing anything with it; just staring at it.

As Destan feared, she was beginning to slip and shut down.

He began to take it back, to which she gripped it and began tugging on it as she wheezed and grunted; causing the belvedere to jump up and bark.

"Don't fight me, Calli! I'm just helping. — Easy! It's okay." Destan bit his lip as he worked to remind himself to be patient with her.

Whether it was the agony in his voice or the look of depression on his face that caught her attention, she froze and let him help her unfold the sweater and slip it over what she had on.

"It doesn't fit you really well but why would something of mine, am I right? But, since I'm the only one here it's not like you have to 'worry' about what you look like. Huh?" *Good try, but it doesn't look like that's gonna work. ~ It was worth a try. It's okay.* "Well, if nothing else it'll keep you warm." He shook the bunched up arms down; then gathered her hair in his hands and pulled it to the outside while he finished, "Why don't you sit and enjoy the fire. I'll be right back."

"Wait! Where are you going?" Callimay gripped his wrist as tight as she could, her eyes overflowing with fear.

"I'm going to change out of this." Destan replied softly as he picked up his veil's collar and let it fall as he gestured to the clothes on the dresser; his small smile hiding the pain he felt. "I won't be but a minute or so. Just rest. The Big Fella's here."

Not happy with him leaving and not happy with how she reacted; she curled up at the foot of the bed, leaning against the bedpost as she fought to not cry. Destan slid his pillow across the bed to her, rubbing her cheek as she hugged it, "I won't be long."

As she stared at the dancing flames, she felt his sweater slipping off her shoulder. She looked like a little child playing dress-up: the sweater itself could easily fit two of her, its sleeves swallowing her hands, and the roll neck was about the size of the waistline on her skirts.

Her expression changed as she began rubbing the fabric between her fingers: a silk, cashmere mix she began to theorize. How such a simple thing such as fabric could bring clarity to her battered mind baffled even her. It was so soft and warm even though she'd only had it on for a few minutes… and it was utterly drenched with the smell of Destan's cologne. The firelight distorted the color somewhat but she guessed it was probably something close to a shadow gray: *And why wouldn't it be?*

She set the pillow aside and folded her hands around her knees, leaning her face on them as she closed her eyes and sighed.

Destan was just walking back in the room when he heard her say: *I miss you wearing your cologne.*

I never knew you paid that much attention to the stuff.

"Destan!" She sounded relieved as she ran over.

"There's my Calli." He smiled as he snuggled her close.

And here was the small, simple thing which brought clarity to Destan: it was such a relief to see this glimpse of "his Calli". Seeing her smile for even a brief moment helped him… while still finding a way to prod his concern for some reason.

Out of the blue, Destan growled as he reached out, "Not on the bed! You don't have free rein of this house. I don't care if you are some valiant hero. You're still an animal. That isn't your throne. Off!"

The belvedere jumped down from his sleeping spot which was right beside where Callimay had been, then romped up to Destan, sitting in front of him as if waiting for a praise-worthy pet.

"Crazy creature. — How about some breakfast?"

℺

Considering all that happened, Destan didn't expect her to do as much as she ended up doing in the kitchen. He'd been fixing all the meals up to this point of their trip and was glad to do so; but it was a relief to see her doing what she loved. The only problem was the belvedere. Both of them ran into him a few times. Having enough of it, he huffed as he pointed to the dining area, "Go lay down!"

Understandably confused as to why his help was being treated this way, the belvedere lowered his head and plodded over, huffing as he laid down in the moonlight; his soft glow growing. That glow reminded Destan of an unnerving reality. He still couldn't get his mind entirely wrapped around the fact this alpha wasn't what he'd forever known those blood-thirsty machine dog hybrids to be.

On the other hand, Callimay wasn't bothered one bit by this "roadblock" and thus hadn't noticed what was said or that the creature left; and with him, the added light in the room. But, while she was still doing things her attention wasn't existent. This zoning out got so bad that at one point she forgot how not but a minute earlier she'd turned the burner on to the correct temperature; turning it up even higher without bothering to look. As she dropped the first egg into the skillet, it hissed, popped, and spit a sizzling, burning spray at her; Callimay gasping and jumping back as she gripped her hand, plowing right into Destan's chest. She looked up at him wide-eyed and scared; her trying to catch her breath.

"How about I help?" He put the bowl down he had and rubbed her arms; calling out when he heard the belvedere whimper, "It's alright Big Fella. Just wait out there. She's fine."

Callimay nodded and so he stood behind her to keep an eye while letting her continue to work. She'd flinch each time something new would get added to the pan, but Destan was quick to calm her and take over until she could function again.

This tender, beautiful teamwork yielded two calm people and a warm, fresh breakfast which was awakening their appetites. He helped her get her plate ready which even with such a whetted appetite didn't consist of much anything, "Calli? This can't be enough. You need to eat more than this."

"I'm not really that hungry," she mumbled as she rubbed her arm and looked at the floor.

"I… b… you 'will' eat all this, right?" He looked down at the plate that just had one fried egg, a single sausage link, and a quarter of a waffle with strawberries on it.

She nodded as she reached out for the plate, not looking up.

His voice was defeated and hurt as he surrendered, "Alright."

Destan loaded up his plate a quick as a whip and walked alongside her to the table. As she came out from behind the counter into the dining area she saw the belvedere glowing. She clapped her hands over her thighs as she gasped, abandoning her plate.

Doing his best to keep things from escalating, he tossed his plate on the table and reached hers — albeit empty now — before it shattered. He saw her looking around in a frantic panic, wheezing as she kept slapping her thighs. Destan groaned as he reached out, being careful how he corralled her, "It's okay. You're not wearing your ensemble. It's alright. You don't need your Seaxes. It's okay."

"But I—"

"Shh," he stroked her hair as he tried everything he could to get her to focus on him. "The Big Fella isn't going to hurt you. … See? All Mr. Ruff wants right now is to see you. Why don't you tell him it's okay?"

It sounded absolutely ludicrous, but all it took was eye contact with those green eyes and hearing his real name for her to remember. She opened her hand, the gentle giant knowing he was allowed to move. He trotted over and curled his head against her hip, standing still and letting her pet him as she pleased.

Destan was a bit jealous of how the creature knew better how to put her at ease when she was scared; but, given enough algorithms and knowledge of one's emotional as well as hormonal state, it wasn't impossible to find a formula that would give you the result you wanted and needed each time. And yet the one thing he learned and knew better than even this creature was to let Callimay tell him when she was ready.

And so, after she felt her "therapy session" was over, she looked up and did her best to smile. He returned the expression as he wiped her tears away.

She paused as she reached for her plate, picking up her foot when she felt something soft under it, "Oh dear. — Do you want that Buddy? … No? — When are we going to get something for him? He hasn't eaten in who knows how long! What 'do' they eat, anyway?"

"Well, the way we would think of it they don't 'eat', remember? Guess that paired with their inability to shed are their only redeeming qualities. And by that I mean qualities of them not being real dogs. — All the sustenance they need comes from the moon. That's why they glow in it."

℔

After everything was cleaned and put away, Destan made an off-the-cuff remark about going for a walk in their winter wonderland… to which Callimay agreed to. But, what really happened was she only heard him say "go for a walk"; she didn't catch the whole snow part — him mentioning they would need to bundle up made her pause. And yet seeing the smile on his face made her change her mind.

But, the second he snatched his coat and boots up, his enthusiasm stalled when he turned and saw she was only halfway up the stairs. He was worried she was going to change her mind, but she looked up and managed a small smile; patting his forearm as she passed him.

The scarf she tried to give him earlier looked a million times better on her; or so he imagined since he didn't see himself. As he looked at her outfit, taking note of one piece of clothing after another, it struck him: *I… I've done this before. ~ You do it all the time. ~ No. No this is different. … But why? Why is her coat and gloves making me think I did this before? ~ That day. ~ You're right. … Then that settles it. We'll take a walk up there. Yeah, it's a bit of a hike, but I know she's gonna love it when we get there.*

Just like last time, the belvedere enjoyed the time outside where he could run free. One moment he would be beside Callimay and the next he would disappear into the trees; returning as he bounded and plowed through the highest drift he could find.

Destan enjoyed the silence so he constantly sent the creature away. He walked in front for the first bit since there was about a foot and a half of snow around; doing his best to push it to the sides so it was easier for her.

At one point he got this feeling something was "off". Yet, as he looked back he saw his loving wife bunny-hopping along; her mouth opening as if to say something but never doing so.

"I'm still not getting it right, am I?" He smiled as he stopped and reached back.

She shot up straight, throwing her hands behind her as she bit her lip, "Huh!"

"My strides."

What is he talking about? Strides? What's he not getting right? ~ He saw you. ~ Oh no! "Oh. Umm. That. Well… I… I was enjoying it." She blushed as she looked away; fiddling with the edge of her scarf.

She was… 'enjoying' it? … How? He took a step back, confused as he started to ask, "Wha—"

With no regard or respect, the belvedere ran up and nudged Callimay's hand, yapping and howling.

"Hi! How are you?"

The creature barked and then darted off, plowing right through another drift and sneezing from getting snow shoved up his nose.

She laughed a bit but was so quiet and had her head bowed as they continued on, her refusing to be care free and "play" like she was earlier now that Destan knew about it. And yet the father up they got and the more trees there were, the less snow there was; so it didn't make as much sense to put forth the effort… it wasn't "fun" to do now.

When the depth of snow wasn't more than just a dusting, he guided Callimay to his side. He caught her glancing up and smiling at him; her doing so because she could tell he was so happy. But with that she also felt he was almost nervous.

Before she had the chance to ask he stopped on a ridge.

The moon was just rising between two mountains; a giant, jolly orb of soft light on the horizon. Its glow caused something to glisten, diverting her attention. She was in utter disbelief when she saw a body of water in front of them. Thinking she was dreaming, she whipped around, taking surveillance of the area and then stammered, "T— this looks like the lake at the Society!"

"I said almost the exact same thing when I saw the one at the Society." He calmed and took her hand as he started toward the bank. "Come on. Let's go sit in our spot. … Aha! This looks right."

"It looks exactly like it… exactly!" She slid her hand across his shoulder as she came around to sit on his left. "Wait. 'Our' spot? But we only sat there those two times?"

The belvedere ran over and hopped around for a bit before taking off in the direction Destan told him to go, him smiling as he shrugged his shoulders after huffing at the creature, "Well what am I supposed to call it?"

There came a hush and peace that was rare for the two of them. Bodies of water had become their safe place; or at least a majority of their peaceful times were around such places. Destan sighed as he slipped his arm around the love of his life and pulled her close to his side, "Do you remember what happened not too long ago?"

While she did put forth some effort, she sat up and turned to him, looking curious, "No?"

More time passed than she was expecting, her shaking her head, "Well don't leave me hanging."

Destan paused. Something caught his attention and almost took his breath away. Something he hadn't seen in so long. Something he fell in love with the first time he saw it. And something he never thought he would get to see again because of what happened. Callimay's eyes were crystal clear. He could see "her". Yes, she was still emotionally hurt, but the clarity in her eyes was due to something completely different. While it wasn't the safest thing — her not using her ability — he was so glad she was taking time for herself. This somehow made him think she had, on some level, accepted the reality of what happened with her mother and was working to move on. And to him he felt she was beginning to trust his ability to fight himself… and win.

It also dawned on him how he was feeling, on some level, what she had for so long; though hers was due to his refusal to let her be a part of his life. He was only coping with the grief she was working through; but he couldn't help but feel he understood more of the weariness and pain she went through when he wasn't "himself". This all reminded him how the grief one person endured affected everyone close to them. Part of him was cringing, knowing what he'd put Rocher and Doctor Gerould through, specifically, for years on end. While it wasn't a sin to grieve — and so much of that time he was not a Christian — he still knew after he was immersed he wasn't giving the best example he could of how a Christian was supposed to act in such circumstances.

But instead of letting that thought cause him anger, he channeled it to challenge himself to do better. He knew he changed since Callimay came, but he wanted everyone to see that it wasn't "her" who caused it. It was her "reminder" of what he knew he was supposed to do and be all along as a Christian.

This all only took a few seconds, but for Destan it felt like a much needed "hour" of reflection and refocusing. He smiled as he brushed the side of her face, his thoughts beginning to string together into a touching recollection, "It hadn't snowed yet and it was during the afternoon… and we rode our bikes instead of— well I guess there's enough differences you wouldn't remember. — Anyway! It would be nine months ago this Saturday that I brought the most beautiful woman in the world out to a lake just like this. She was so excited that she accidentally smacked her injured arm and about scared me half to death thinking 'someone' hurt her. Unknown to her at the time, my spy-like mind kicked in; ready to fight for her with the Kunai I had on me if need be. — Yes, even while there I was armed. Why do you think I usually had my hands shoved in my pockets? — Moving on! We put down a blanket and relaxed for quite a while before eating. I couldn't help but notice how the lake painted her face with rainbows when she looked out over it. Even though she was bundled up so she could barely be seen she couldn't hide from me how beautiful she was. There was no way for her to hide it since there was so much more to her beauty than just her physical appearance — which captivated me nonetheless. The hidden beauty in her character is what made me stay, what continually caught my eye. Physical things we see can and most likely 'will' change over time. But the true character and the heart of a person more than likely 'won't'. One thing it never can do is hide. And knowing you I can't see it changing. And I pray each day it never does. — She scared me a second time when she sat there and closed her eyes. I leaned forward and was just about to say something when I saw she was smiling. … I admit I wanted to hold her in my arms right then, but how could I? After what happened the night before I was worried I'd scare her if I tried. But she reached over to our lunch bag and that idea was thankfully taken care of for me; which I was glad for because I was a nervous wreck inside. I knew I needed all the strength I had to ask what I did after our lukewarm lunches were gone. — There wasn't any way for me to get a ring for her, but in my mind she needed to have something until I could get her one of her own. I'd noticed what looked like a ring she wore on a necklace the first day of class, and then again the night before when we went for a walk. So, I asked her to confirm my suspicions by asking to look at it."

Callimay's face began to change as she heard him recall what was a very special day to them both. While a "near" nine-month anniversary wasn't something normally celebrated, it hit her as the most wonderful of shocks to hear how much he recalled and treasured. — And even some details she had no clue of! But when she thought about it, little phrases he would say, little things he did or didn't do made so much more sense.

He got up and helped her stand, then finished rather glassy-eyed, "I got down on one knee… just like this; and looking back, butchered my confession of love and devotion to her. It hit me hard when she initially said 'no' to my proposal of marriage, but the look of horror on her face when she began fumbling to explain calmed me: it wasn't impossible for the beautiful orator to be left baffled and tongue-tied by such an awkward and emotionless confession of love. … I… I didn't truly know how much I loved her at the time. I'm ashamed to say this, now seeing how foolish I was, but I didn't even know how much I needed her; I really didn't think 'I' needed her. I knew she needed my protection, but I didn't understand and wasn't prepared for what my duties to her were going to truly entail. By George I sure thought I was ready and understood, but my thoughts concerning my motivation weren't right. And so I confess I 'was' hasty in asking her so early; asking you. I know

I've caused so many problems because of that unpreparedness; limping along while depending on the loving and forgiving nature of such a tender woman — the one who is standing in front of me right now — was no way to continue. God let me learn the only way I apparently knew how, but I praise Him for the fact I 'did' learn. … And even now I know I'll look back in ten years and say I had no clue even now. — Calli? I want the love we've worked so hard for to grow deeper and deeper with each passing day. I want to never grow tired of showing you how much I love you and what you mean to me. I want you to know how much it means to me: to see the apple of my eye each morning when I wake up and look next to me, for my body to feel the warmest and most loving of embraces that I know you can only give when I'm stressed out of my mind or for no reason at all other than you want to, and for my ears to hear your soft and sweet voice say my name and 'I love you' all day long. I want you to know you're the most important person in this world to me… and there's not a person in this world I won't hesitate to show that to. And last? I pray The good Lord will bless me with so many more years with you. I love you, Calli."

She had her free hand clapped over her mouth as she cried; her other hand trembling in his soft hold. Everything he was saying was so beautiful and sweet; and was leaving her tongue-tied even more than when he originally asked her.

He leaned his forehead against hers when she kneeled in front of him, whispering, "I love you so much, Calli."

The way she gripped his coat he almost felt like she was pushing him away, but she replied, "I love you too."

Everything around them gave off the aura of being in a wonderful and tearful shock. Well, almost everything. Their pest, the belvedere, pushed its way in between them, announcing his presence with joy.

"Maybe I should call you Rocher." Destan fell back, crossing his arms across his chest. "How can something that knows the emotions of another be so… dumb, clueless, and downright rude!"

Callimay laughed as she shooed the belvedere away. After helping her husband sit back up she curled up on his lap.

"Geez, woman!" He pulled away and rubbed his cheek. "Your nose is ice-cold! What'd I do to be given this torture?"

"Well what do you expect after making me cry?" She complained, sounding muffed as she cupped her hands over her mouth and nose.

"How about we head back since mister party crasher is back?"

But we just got here. "Alright. … Destan?"

"Yes, Calli?" He replied as he brushed the snow off his pants.

"Why… why did you cry after you proposed to me?"

"I… you know I'm not one-hundred percent sure. I guess… well. I guess I was relieved something good was finally happening while I was there; my life in general, really." His voice began to crumble into a depressed sigh. "Everything as a generality always went so well that I planned for and helped with in the Shadows — obviously there were those moments of anguish and frustration — but my personal life? It was always one thing after another going wrong. If it could it did. And it only got worse after I became a Christian; which thinking about it now is no surprise."

Way to stick your foot in your mouth. ~ I'm sorry! I… "How long had it been before you actually asked me that you decided to?"

Oh my Calli. It's okay. "You remember me asking you to come in when you used to since it was so cold and I said I'd come and walk with you? … Well, that was when I decided. So, that would've made it just about two weeks? … So! My turn. When did 'you' start thinking about us seriously?"

"Umm. Well. That's a bit more complicated." Callimay bit her lip.

"Oh?" Destan asked with a raised eyebrow.

"I liked you from the first time I saw you. I did. But I didn't know if I 'liked' you enough for that type of relationship. Add to that I didn't know if you liked me and I wasn't sure how everything all worked. I'd never had a boyfriend and really didn't want one. My—"

"Excuse me?"

"I was taught to value myself and wait. It sounded so 'old-fashioned' at first, but as I started watching people I started to see the wisdom in waiting. I didn't want someone to be 'serious' about me for a while and then have to let him go for whatever reason. No one should do that anyway, but with me being someone to invest so much of my emotions? I was taught I needed to be much more careful and patient. And so I came to realize the wisdom in that and waited and find him — my husband. … I don't know how in the world everyone thought Toreon and I were— but anyway! I had moments where I thought about us, but when you seemed less than interested I'd put those thoughts aside. And yet that all changed the day you ran over to me after Toreon had his fun with me." She let a shaky sigh out. "I just…"

"I didn't mean to bring that up, Calli." Destan sighed as he stopped and pulled her to him, the belvedere coming over and sitting beside her. "I'm sorry."

She took a bit to work through the memories she'd triggered, but said in a quiet voice; trying everything not to cry since she knew her frozen face would freeze even more, "The first time I threw my arms around you it felt… it felt like it was where I belonged. It was the oddest thing in the world. At first I thought it was just the awkwardness of it all, but I didn't feel the need to let go. I actually wanted to hold on to you tighter. As the saying goes: I felt I was home. I'd found him. I found you. I know you didn't do anything in return but it didn't matter. I just knew. Call it what you want: an instinct, woman's intuition; I just knew. I'm sorry if I overstepped my bounds at the time. I know you—"

"You were scared and needed something that made you feel safe. You needed to be with someone you felt would protect you." Destan comforted as he pulled her back so he could see her face. "And I now know very well you always run to safety when you're scared. I kinda picked up on that, but then again I didn't. — So! Any more questions?"

Callimay stared him down as she thought, and then started to swing her hand back and forth that was in his, "Ah! I 'do' have one. — So where did you spend most of your time? Now there's this cabin and the house in Rayleen and the mansion 'and' the suite at Bulwark. Did you just travel all the time?"

I thought for sure she'd ask about my 'arsenal' I had at the Society. ~ She never ceases to amaze, does she? "Never seemed like it, but it is quite the list, isn't it?" He put his arm around her as he chuckled, starting to wander back. "I only stayed in Rayleen during the spring and summer; and even then I was never there all the time because of Bulwark. But let me make it clear: I always saw Bulwark as nothing more than my office. I hardly 'used' the suite until now. And I haven't been to the mansion in years. I can't remember how long it's been."

"What!"

"When we went in December? It was the first time I'd been there in… I'd say— geez! It must've been… seven? No. 'Eight' years."

"When did you buy this place?"

"You're asking me to remember even 'more' things before you came along, woman? Fine. Let me think for a sec. … I guess it would be… five years? No. That was when I got Raven. … Oh! It was the same year I was promoted to Doyen. Four years ago, I guess? — I own it but I've given the rights to the Shadows for as long as they're in existence. Just like with Chet and Raven. And so, this is — for now — an official Shadow outpost: the Nest. I'm usually the only one who uses it because it's so remote and not really close to much anything for the time being. But once Total Eclipse starts that all changes."

"Why?"

"That valley we were in? That's where the largest off-site, high-profile Syndicate base is located. So, once Total Eclipse starts, the entire Veil and half the Shadows now in Bulwark will be here."

"But that place is tiny! How in the world would they all fit!"

He stifled his laughter as he stopped and turned to her, "The Nest is an underground bunker, unlike what the usual thought that comes to mind from 'nest'. I'll show you it when we get back. … Well where'd the Big Fella go?"

"He's right behind you."

"What in the world are you doing back there?" Destan motioned for the belvedere to come beside them. "Spying on us?"

Should you have said all that?

"You mean him?"

She shook her head and looked around.

"There's nothing to worry about. We run scans all the time to be sure a certain radius is sustained. I would've gotten a warning if so." He shook his wrist where his watch was.

"Oh." She started following him again; and then gripped his arm and stopped short, "What are we going to do with him, Destan?"

"What do you mean?"

"We can't just take him into Bulwark and we can't leave him here. What if someone else comes?" Callimay explained in a desperate tone.

"He won't stay. — I mean, not if something 'really' bad happens. — He's only going to follow your command to a certain point, right? Like he knows how I am emotionally at any point and time? If Elder— didn't you say belvederes were programed to override any command if an emotion from their keeper breaches a certain threshold?"

What she said struck him hard because he started to kick himself for not thinking about it, "I did, and it's true. … I'll… how about I see what I can decipher from his coding? Hopefully I can find if there's a way to damper his emotional awareness. — But as far as where to keep him? I'm going to need a bit more time to think on that one. But! Thankfully we've got some time in that area."

The stars catching her eye made her start thinking about something completely different, her voice almost a quiver, "She knew she wasn't getting out of there alive, didn't she? That's why you said that one thing to her? Wasn't it something about the stars?"

I didn't want to talk about this, Calli. … I~ Just tell her and get it over with. "Do you remember when Tabitha told you when they left Bulwark that she hoped the new moon would continue to rise on you?"

She nodded, her attention not drifting.

"Well, what I first said is the way Veils say goodbye to each other. But I could tell by her words and tone she was readying herself to make the sacrifice needed to get us out of that bind. … So, I gave her the response Veils give when that decision is made. Some like to call it a blessing but I see it as an acknowledgement and respect for their decision and voicing my thankfulness for everything they've done — letting them know it has and will continue to make an impact."

"What was it you said?"

"May the stars welcome your presence as guide and guardian." Destan raised his head toward the sky, her doing the same. "She never stopped looking for you, Calli. You need to remember that. Something in her knew you were still alive; she knew her baby girl was out there somewhere. … She…" *Do I dare? ~ Might as well.* "She sent Emissary to Faberton to watch over you when she found out about you. Maybe it was through your friend Fairove that she found out, I don't know. But from what Emissary told me, Canary never mentioned anything about you being related."

"She sent Trever?"

"I just now thought of that. And come to think of it, she even asked about him when I was talking with her that first little bit before you came in; making a point to ask where he was like she was concerned about him." *Odd.*

"Can we look at what is on the memory sticks when we get back?"

"You don't have to rush back into all of that."

"I j— okay. I just know we don't have that much time—"

"We have all the time you need, Calli." Destan reminded as he put his hand under her chin. "I'm not flying you back until you tell me you're ready. You need to grieve. And if I'm being blunt, like you always say I am, 'I' need some time to grieve. We've both been going nonstop and this all happening's hit us hard. I think harder than we realize right now. Let's just take it easy."

"One more question? One more and then I'll stop until tomorrow."

"Tomorrow? … Alright. One more."

"Why did she send Trever?"

"What 'he' told me was she sent him to see if you had certain items in your position. Granted he never told me what he found or what she said to look for, but he did find something. And then she instructed him to stay near you until she could get there." *What would've possessed Elder to choose Emissary if he got to him first? Just another twisted game of proving his power to others?*

Callimay's eyes got wide but she didn't say anything.

He instantly knew she heard him; Destan throwing his head back and groaning.

"I'm not going to ask!" She bit her lip. "I'll wait."

Go on. You might as well stick 'both' feet in your mouth. Destan groaned as he looked down to her. "I found out all I know during the debrief. Remember when I was saying I wasn't going to lie? Well, it was about Emissary's mission report. He came back after the meeting and explained what was going on. He said he couldn't remember who contacted him first but that Elder 'and' Canary sent him to Faberton to watch over you specifically. The difference was Elder did it because he was suspicious of you, Canary just wanted to know if you had some certain things in your possession. The toy, maybe? — Emissary wasn't given any details and kept them both independently informed about things. When we got to Bulwark Elder pulled Emissary. That was when we had that little reunion of sorts. Canary didn't know he left until I told her."

"What is so special about me?" Callimay all but hissed as she threw her fists to her sides.

"You said one more question." He made a face, but explained when she began to look scared, "I was just trying to help, I'm not mad. … I'm not sure. My guess is it is because of Chameleon. It's the only thing that would make sense; at least to me, anyway. But you know? As far as I'm concerned: you just being you is special enough to warrant twenty-four seven protection."

Her face was already flushed from being cold, but he could tell she blushed as she smiled and looked down to the belvedere.

As they went along, Destan could tell Callimay was lagging behind since the snow was deeper, so he slowed and had her walk behind him. She opened her mouth to say something but then closed it.

"What?" Destan asked as he stopped.

"I promised one more question." Callimay rambled as she shook her head. "And I need to get used to this anyway for my regimen, I'm sure."

"I'll make an exception since I was the one who said something." Destan sounded so gracious, though they both knew he was joking.

"Never mind. I need to get used to it. You said endurance is the next part of my regimen. I might as well get a head start."

"You're 'not' training while we're here. Now what is it?" Destan asked almost upset.

Well this isn't going to plan. ~ I should've stayed quiet. "I'm getting tired," she admitted as she cowered. "At least my legs are. Forging through this snow isn't easy. And especially at the pace you're going."

Destan scooped her up, "You're such a trooper, Calli, but don't be ashamed. — And you think I need an 'excuse' to carry you? … I'd carry you for the rest of my life if need be; and you know I enjoy it. … As far as the question thing goes: I was just trying to get your mind off everything. You can ask however many you want to. Okay?"

ᚠ

Before long they were back in the warm, cozy, tiny cabin. It was lunchtime, so after they got warmed up the kitchen began to come alive with the aromas of another delicious meal. And even though they both enjoyed it, Destan appeared to enjoy these times a bit more. Yes, things weren't as smooth since this wasn't the house in Rayleen, but it was still a special bonding time he treasured.

At one point he glanced over and saw Lanta and Dalvin's portrait, sighing as he picked it up, "Calli?"

"Yes, Destan?" She grunted as she shut the freezer door.

"Would you like a big fancy wedding?" He sounded curious as he walked over and leaned on the counter.

"Why do I need a second one? Was the first one not good enough?" Callimay half laughed.

"No. I was just— well I guess I was thinking about the fact you don't have any pictures. I mean you didn't even have a dress until just a little bit ago. Sure, maybe I'm looking into things too much, but I know you enjoy things like this."

She sighed as she set her glass down and took his hands in hers, "I've got memories of you standing in front of me as much as your injured self could at the time — in front of God Himself — promising to love and protect me for the rest of your life. I know memories can fade," *And apparently they can somehow be stripped.* "But I can't see that one 'ever' fading. Things like pictures are nice to have but they are just that: things. Remember what you told me?"

"I know, I know. I just want to give you everything I'm supposed to and can… and what you want."

"You're giving me everything I need; and as far as the wants go, we've learned to prioritize. My 'wants' are pretty satisfied right now. … I tell you what. Maybe after everything's all done we can have a big party — a ball! And invite everyone."

"How much money do you think I have, woman?"

"Well," Callimay exaggerated as she tapped his cheek. "Maybe if you wouldn't have every type of food under the sun available you'd be able to afford to feed more people."

"That hurt," Destan pouted as he rubbed his face.

"The only thing that hurt was your stomach and you know it."

She's starting to get a hang of it. ~ Let's see if she'll keep up with it.
"Woman, now see here. I'm not about to put up with this defiance."

"Oh really?" Callimay tried to keep a straight face.

"Really," he leaned over and snatched her up, lifting her over the counter to him.

"Destan!" She screamed, causing the belvedere to jump and bark.

"Would you two calm down?" He sat her down on the counter. "I need to get his coding changed… now. I can't have any fun anymore!"

"I'm sorry."

"It's— I'm just complaining. It's alright." Destan helped her down and kissed her forehead. "So! After lunch what do you want to do?"

"Be with you," she leaned her head against his chest. "It's been a while since I've had you around all day like this. And now I'm able to appreciate it like I want to… and should."

"I've missed it too."

🏵

Callimay saw herself in the mirror that evening and sighed. While it wasn't surprising to see her hair so tangled and uneven, it wasn't easy to remember "why" her hair was slashed. The shortest part was just past her shoulder; stair stepping down to her elbow on the other side.

Not wasting any time she started going through drawers; coming out before long to ask Destan. It threw him for a loop at first, "A what? — Oh! There's a pair… umm. There's kitchen scissors up here but actual hair shears? Yeah, those are gonna be below."

"Below?"

"The bunker I told you about. It's 'below'. — Calli look, I'm sorry I left you up there like that. I should've—"

"I didn't know jumps took that much out of you. If I would've known I wouldn't have given it a second thought. Well, I say that—"

"It was the failed attempts that really took it out of me. Well, everything did." Destan sighed as he leaned against the wall. "I guess I have to keep training to keep my stamina up. It's obvious that I lose it really fast; but there's just no way to train right now. There's not one place within the perimeter that wouldn't be monitored. With Elder around and everyone else so skeptical— I just can't. And I know you're

53

in the same situation with your new ability. Don't blame yourself, Calli. Okay?" *Well this is going nowhere productive. ~ Tell me about it. ...* "Would you like me to show you the bunker while I get the shears?"

Taking the hint, she ran her fingers through her hair and sighed, "It'd be nice to have something to cut my hair with. I'm not much for this 'modern crop' look. It reminds me too much of Ingrid."

He took a lock of her hair in his hand, sounding thoughtful, "What made you think to even do that, anyway?"

"I don't know, really. All I knew was you couldn't get to me in time so I had to get to you; and the only way that was going to happen was if they let go of my hair. Plus it hurt like nothing else. — So you said there's a pair specifically for hair down there?"

Now the bouncing ball was hit back into his court, Destan taking the hint and not letting things slip away again, "Yep. Let's go."

Once he told the belvedere to stay he jogged out of the room to the far wall and flipped up the thermostat, revealing a fingerprint reader.

There was a lingering sigh of distain behind him, Destan looking back with a faint grin on his face, "I always thought hidden or new things intrigued you?"

Before he did anything, he took a moment to do something on his phone. While it would've been easy for her to find out what he was doing, Callimay had no real desire to listen to him.

The wall right next to the main floor fireplace pushed back and to the side, her not giving any response as she dragged herself over.

A warm waft of air welcomed her as she stepped into the darkened area. The sound of metal clacking under her shoe made her pause; the sound it made echoing much more than she thought it would… until her eyes adjusted and she saw just how massive the room was.

They worked their way down the winding three flights, Destan pausing at one point, "Are you alright?"

She took a grunting breath and shooed him on, "My leg just isn't the happiest about these 'steep' stairs that twist. Go on, just slower. … I don't remember that much but this looks an awful lot like Deep Dark."

"And you'd be right," he nodded as he motioned for her to say at the base of the stairs while he rushed over to a darker portion of the room; him speaking louder so she could hear, "It's supposed to be a carbon copy. A larger scale for good reason, but the exact same blueprints were used.”

“Hum,” she bobbed her head as she looked around, wandering over to where he was.

It was hard for her to keep from laughing when she heard him bickering with himself: *Why would anyone else use them? I know for sure that— they should be over here… ‘some’where. Well they were— oh! There they are.* “He— oh!”

“Goodness! Just blast my eardrums into nothing.”

“Well how was I supposed to know you snuck over here?”

Callimay twisted her lips as she took the shears, “How did you remember where they were?”

“It was just a random thing that stuck in my mind. I don’t know ‘why’. … Do you want a full tour before we leave?”

“No. I’m alright with knowing it’s here. I can wait to be introduced formally when we come back.”

After she got up a few steps she looked back and realized the floor was a world map: *Well why didn’t I notice that before. Odd.*

The different countries were all different shades of gray; except for Ferdinan and Brigon.

“Destan? Why are those two so different?”

“Ferdinan’s government is under complete Shadow control; hence black being used. Brigon is where we have no contacts. So even though they tout that they are neutral we have no reason to consider them anything but under Syndicate control since they refuse to work with us in any form.”

“Oh,” she turned to go on, asking when she bumped into him, “What is it?”

“Calli?”

“Yes?”

“Please don’t say anything about what I’ve told you; concerning the Veil and this all that is.” He motioned to the room, his eyes full of worry. “I just don’t want anything to happen to you. Not that Elder doesn’t already know, but— I can take care of myself and stand up to their mocking of me, that’s not what I’m talking about. They just don’t understand and neither did I for that first bit. With everything going on with my abilities and emotions you 'have' to know what's going on. — I was an idiot to neglect that reality for so long. You were going to hear me say something to myself at some point."

"I promise."

"Calli," he fumbled to find what he wanted to say, waving his hands in the air before resting them on her shoulders. "It's not that I don't trust you to—"

"Destan, it's okay. You're just trying to keep things from blowing up. I know you've got so much to deal with as it is. … It's alright. I understand. I'm not upset."

He hung his head, taking a deep breath before finishing, "With that said, just remember: don't lie. I'd never ask you to do that just to save face or— just don't 'offer' any information."

Callimay's face began to glow as she reached out to his cheek, "I love you."

"I love you too."

❦

The two "men of the house" — one perched on the edge of the bed and the other leaning on the door — watched the woman they cared for brush her hair out. She would get her hair between the blades and stop; shaking her head. And then she would take a deep breath, do it again, and stop. She stared in the mirror, looking back at Destan with the most desperate of looks.

"You've never cut it, have you?" He asked in a heartfelt tone as he came up behind her and rubbed her arms.

Her voice was beyond crushed, her almost crying, "No, I haven't."

"You don't 'have' to. … Do you? I mean…" he tried his best to come up with an alternative as he ran his fingers through her hair. "Maybe Tabitha could help you find some style that would work with—"

"I can't leave it like this!" She ranted as her eyes burned with anger and fear. "I just— I can't! Don't you get it! It 'has' to be cut! I can't stand it like this!"

He backed off and hesitated to reach out to her, "Calli it's okay. Put the shears down. I was just asking. Just relax. It's okay. We're safe here. … Calli it's just me. I didn't think about it that way. I'm sorry."

The belvedere thundered into the room as she yelped and burst into tears, "I… I'm sorry Destan! I… I didn't… I…"

"It's okay." He took her in his arms and let her wail. "It's alright."

"But I—"

"You were just reacting to what you remembered happening. It's okay. Nothing happened. Well… the floor might have a divot in it now but that's no big deal."

Once her emotions leveled off, she sniffled as she asked in a muffled voice — her face still against his chest, "Could you help?"

Destan pulled her back to arm's length and wiped her face, "What do you want me to do?"

She bent over and took the shears in her hand, taking a moment to gather herself before reaching for his and placing them in it, "Cut it."

"Umm… well. Cutting my own hair is one thing. But I don't w—"

"Just cut little bits off," she sounded more confident as she turned; now looking at him in the mirror's reflection. "You can see it better, anyway. Just stop when it looks half decent."

"As in what?" He sighed as he ran his hand through her hair again.

"Straight. … 'Please'?"

"It's okay. I'm right here. I'll… I'll do my best."

A few minutes later, he set the shears down and bent over to pick up what hair fell out of his hands. Callimay unwrapped the towel from her neck and shoulders, rolling it up and tossing it to the side. She shook her head a few times and then smiled when she saw him come into the view of the mirror, "You did good. Really good."

"It's so short, though," he sighed as he put his arms around her.

"You liked it long, didn't you?"

"Yeah," Destan's face immediately flushed; but quickly added, "I don't love you any less because it's short, though."

~ 4 ~

L ike a slap in the face to all that they had worked through ,Callimay started having nightmares each night. Where they were at and the situation varied, but the ending was always the same: her mother died. Sometimes even Destan did because of her fear keeping her from using her abilities.

It tore on Destan because it reminded him of what Webb did to her; him having to work through the horrible memories that triggered. — Why were bad memories always the first ones to show up for rollcall?

So with this, she would always have a rough start to the day

Oh why sugarcoat it? They "both" would.

But, by the time they got done with lunch things felt and looked much more stable; they were able to enjoy their time together without feeling the need to tiptoe around each other. And what a blessing it was to have this healing time with just the two of them and no "work" constantly interrupting!

❦

Destan was the first one awake after Callimay's latest nightmare. The red and orange-toned rays of the setting sun flooded into the room, doing their best to make what was a miserable start to the day easier. — Why was it only three seconds into each day he found it was already miserable to some degree?

Then again he knew why: he was exhausted, mentally. It was harder on him each day as the nightmares got worse and worse.

And yet these scenes of torture were not Callimay's. No, "he" was having ones of his own each night: *I know what Calli meant now by*

58

not wanting to go to sleep. ~ This really isn't anything new. ~ It's different now. I just always replayed what 'really' happened to my parents; albeit my limited knowledge of what happened. This? ~ I try to steer things in a good way but you~ I'm not blaming you. It's just with this all compiling on every front— I 'need' to have some outlet of some sort so it doesn't explode. I can't afford to let things fall apart now. And with all Calli's going through I don't dare tell her. And before you say it I know: she's going to find out at some point. If I can just hang on a few more days. … Just a few more days. Surely things will start to change by then; and I mean in a good way.

He groaned as he rubbed his face and ruffled his hair, glancing down to his wife who was fast asleep in his arms. Seeing her in a truly peaceful sleep helped him; Destan smiling for a moment: *Rest, Calli.*

It was freezing as he threw the covers back, but all he could manage was to plod over in a daze to the fireplace. All it took was the addition of a couple logs and a few prods to bring it back to a warm and soft glow with the occasional pops and snaps that accompanied burning wood offering their ambient sounds of comfort and calm.

Destan sat down in front of the fireplace, hearing sniffing. He turned and saw the belvedere standing there with his nose stuck out and twitching, his ears drooped.

"Come here, Big Fella."

That was all the creature wanted to hear. He wagged his tail and pranced over, lying down beside Destan so he would be petted.

This picture was one worthy of horror-ridden gasps to any Shadow or Veil: one of their own being casual with a Shadow-killing machine. And yet this picture, to anyone else, looked like nothing more than a worn young man looking to his "best friend" for comfort as millions of weighty thoughts kept running through his battered mind; him unable to keep a steady thought for very long.

What are we going to do with you, Big Fella? Where in the world can I put you so you could still get to Calli if needed but wouldn't be where everyone else can see you? And I've 'still' got to find a way to damper your link to her. I don't want to disable it; but make it so you're not jumping every time she gasps or sighs. With the next part of her regimen having its fair share of emotional strain on her? Last thing I

*need is you going off half-cocked and showing up out of the blue. —
Why didn't I see father when I was getting my new screens? Was he
just with me in the operating room? You don't think… did he sit with
me while I was in recovery? Was that not a dream but his real voice I
was hearing? I… Rocher 'had' to of known he was there; he knew all
along he wasn't dead. Why didn't he at least 'tell' me he was okay but
he had to stay away? I 'knew' about the Shadows already and his
involvement. What was there to hide from me that would've helped?
Then again, was he doing what I did with Calli for so long? — How is
Calli related to Ashte? She's got to be! Somehow. And what about the
Presley family? Is Emissary 'really' her brother? What is Chameleon?
Why is Calli one? I know you had something to do with it, father, so
what did you do to her? Why did Elder hate what you were doing?
W… why don't I remember her? Did you do something to me so I'd
forget her? But why! Why! What was wrong with me knowing her?
And why didn't we get to see each other when we moved back to
Faberton? If she lived in Quaverly then it wouldn't have been 'that' far
of a trip. I mean you took the train in every day to North Edge while we
were there and that was a trip far more dangerous than what the one to
her home would've been. — What's on those memory sticks? Why did I
put it off so long? I haven't even looked at the data I downloaded from
the Society. What is wrong with me! — And what is the final piece I'm
missing that's back home? I don't recall any box addressed to mother.
Maybe Rocher 'did' have to move it. — What if this man I've known for
so long who's from Brigon is truly one of the final keys we've needed so
we can finally be done with this all? — And if it is all over soon, why
keep Calli in the regimen? Why put her through this next portion that's
going to be so hard on the both of us if it won't be that much longer?
… But what if everything fails and we have to keep fighting like this? I
need to be able to keep Calli safe; her completing the regimen would
help her if I wasn't around. — What if it 'does' fail? Could we ever
think of having a family?*

He got more and more riled as his thoughts became more targeted,
him grumbling and almost fuming as he kept spiraling out of control:
*Things get harder and harder each day. It's not fair! I want my wife! I
know we agreed about everything, but in what appears to be my usual*

way of doing things I was stupid and 'logical' and didn't think things through in regards to my emotions and everything. I don't know how much longer I can physically stand this. I 'am' trying. I am. Calli's not making things worse for me. It's just—

Knowing his emotions were climbing, he whipped his head around to see if he disturbed her.

No terrified face staring at him. What a relief.

He rubbed his face and sighed; turning back to watch the flames as he began petting the creature that was now the one with the worried expression. The emotions beginning to poison him were ones he could now feel drain out of him; this void leaving his thoughts vague once again: *And what if Elder completes whatever his heinous mission has been all along? What if I found out too late? — What would happen to Calli if I died? Who would take care of my ray of sunshine? I don't want her to be left alone. I know what that's like… and she's had a cruel taste of it. — What if I've signed Calli and my death certificates with all of this? — God, what do I do! I need help. On top of everything else, all of these questions, all of my own grief: my Calli is emotionally dying! I don't know how to help her. I don't know what to do. I keep trying, and every night I wake up after I've imagined I failed her. Every night her own memories torment and suffocate her. Every night I die inside seeing her agonized, hearing her scream and cry as if someone was ripping her heart out. And every night I wish I could save her from those memories. I… I can't go on like this. I don't know what to do anymore. I barely have the strength to keep going myself. Please help me. Please, Lord. Show me the way through this all. I don't want to have come so far only to trip up at the very end and lose everything. Please show me what I need to do. Please, God! Please. I don't know how to keep going like this. What do I do? … It… it's in Your Son's name I pray, amen.*

Callimay woke up not too much after Destan sat down with the belvedere. At first she laid there and cried; trying to push away what she remembered each morning. But, after a while, and noticing he hadn't moved, she started noticing his lips moving. Unable to resist the urge — his emotions rumbling in the beginnings of what she knew to be a bad storm — she started listening… and was heartbroken.

By the time he finished his desperate pleas, Destan was just about doubled over, silently crying. He'd been thinking this whole time that "she" was dying, but neglected to notice "he" was.

He'd asked for the most powerful help there was, and it appeared part of his answer was immediate. Callimay jumped out of the bed and ran to him, wrapping him in her arms. This sudden embrace caught him off guard, but he looked up only to see she was holding back a flood of tears.

For that entire time all he could feel was the pain of what he was saying and thinking; the memories of warmth, love, and joy vanished… until Callimay touched him. All of this crashing back made him feel like he lost all his strength; he had nothing left in him to give, his eyes were so empty. Destan leaned his head on her shoulder and continued to cry while she cradled his head and held the man she so dearly loved.

It somehow made her feel better, knowing that she was able to — on what seemed to her a small scale — give back to Destan what he had so abundantly given to her over the past couple days. Did it erase her grief? What could? But, in a good way, it forced this heavy emotion into its rightful place: the past. Well, at least for the time being. She had someone who needed her; so, she laid her own self aside and tended to their needs as best she could.

When Callimay opened her eyes, the sun vanished, taking its fleeting rays of light with it and leaving the world to rest until the moon saw fit to grace it with its presence. She ever so gently shifted her hold, being sure not to startle Destan; for some odd reason she felt if she scared him she's "set him off". He'd finally stopped crying and was sniffling only on occasion now. She felt his arms slowly wrap around her, still trembling and weak in their grasp. So, she whispered as she leaned her cheek against his, "I'm here. It's alright, Destan."

"I missed you," he began gripping the sweater she had on.

❦

When they mustered the combined emotional strength to get up and face the day, the belvedere bounded up and down the stairs between them and the window, barking at the outside world and then whining like a little baby. Callimay rolled her eyes, "Oh lands sake! Come on."

While that small reprieve of laughter helped, there was a slight stench of reclusiveness in the air; and Callimay knew she needed to stop it before Destan found out. She wasn't even sure if he knew she overheard what he said. What would he say if he knew? — That was one question she didn't dare ask the answer to. At least not right now: *I know he knows that I know he's not invincible, but I— I should've stopped when I heard what he was saying. ~ You were trying to watch over him; things 'were' getting touchy. It's alright.*

"You like that sweater, don't you?" Destan smiled, steam rising from his cup of tea he had up to his mouth.

"It's nothing much for appearance," she snapped to and said rather light-hearted as she shook the sleeves down over her fingers, waving them at him. "But it's warm, like you're giving me a hug all the time."

"So that's why!" He huffed as he set the cup down with purpose.

"What?" She pulled her hands back, slapping herself in the face with one of the sleeves.

"Pfft!" Destan snorted, sending him into a coughing frenzy as he tried to keep down the tea he just drank.

"Are you alright!"

He put one hand out, his voice hoarse, "I'm fine."

She started to get panicky, hopping up and pacing around as she tried to get her hands out of the sleeves that were determined to keep them engulfed.

Once he caught his breath, he cleared his throat one last time, "It was my fault for drinking while playing around with you."

Not entirely satisfied with that answer, but then again glad to see his eyes were clearer, she tried to keep herself calm, "Well, since you say you're out of 'danger', what were you going to say?"

"I was going to say that's why you haven't been giving me hugs the past couple days like you normally do. It's not at all because you're not feeling well but because you've got that hunk of smelly fabric on so you don't need any."

Oh land sake! ... "Is that better?"

"Mu— Calli!" Destan gasped; grabbing her so she wouldn't fall to the floor, the belvedere jumping on the window sill out of nowhere and barking at them.

While the recovery time for both of them was quick, it brought to mind a certain task that had been neglected long enough. He grumbled as he threw his head back, "I 'have' got to get that coding reset."

There was a moment of silence, followed by Callimay perking up, "May I help?"

"Well… it's pretty advanced. But I'd love to have you sit with me while I do it." Destan stopped himself and worked to find a solution; him plodding over to let the creature in. "I'm— what in the world!"

Callimay scolded the belvedere who shook a healthy amount of snow everywhere, "No, no, no! Ugh! Come in here and let me get you dried off, you silly boy."

"Are you talking to me, or the belvedere?" Destan asked with a raised eyebrow.

"You're no boy. You're my husband."

"So, I'm just going to be left soaking wet?"

"Oh, for the love of everything orange and sparkly…" she threw her hands up in surrender and attempted to storm off.

"Where did that come from?"

"Oh…" Callimay said flustered as he took her by the shoulders.

"Oh…" Destan repeated, trying to mimic how her face looked.

"Oh… I give up."

"Ugh! Would you just go in the kitchen, you mechanical Rocher?" Destan gritted his teeth as he shoved the creature out from the middle of the two of them.

ℬ

Once they were calmed, cozy, and dry; the three of them made their way up to the landing where there was a sofa. Destan had his computer but instead of doing what she expected him to, he had the belvedere lay in front of them so it was easier to maintain a link. The creature wasn't against the idea at all; him content to be where he was — curled up next to Callimay's leg.

She was confused, to say the least, with all of the jumbled words that flashed across the screen; and even more so with what Destan would type in. While she had some of this type of training already, none of what she was seeing looked even vaguely familiar.

Not wanting her to feel left out, Destan did his best to explain some of it, but most of the time he was straining to understand it himself and needed quiet to concentrate. — For some reason he had a bad feeling: if he messed even one thing up he could trip some sensor that'd let the closest Falconers known exactly where they were.

"How do you know the Syndicate doesn't have a link to him if it's difficult for you to understand?"

"It's not that I can't understand it at all, it just takes me much longer than what Abacus could in his sleep." Destan explained as his brow wrinkled. "He's the real computer guru. I'm just average."

"Oh don't do that!"

"What?" He complained as he pushed her hand away.

"I don't want your face to freeze that way. You look old like that."

"Well, I am over a quarter of a century old, Calli." He reminded as his small smile popped out, him still focusing on the computer. "And with my lifestyle I'm actually surprised I don't have gray hair already."

"Oh Destan. How could y—"

"I'm just kidding, Calli." He grinned as he looked over and winked.

"Well isn't that cute. He has an actual heart I can see." She switched subjects; gesturing to the computer as he kept "talking" with the machine portion of the belvedere.

"Huh?"

"Isn't that the heart of the belvedere?"

"What would make you think of that?"

"Well, the way the text lines are broken up they look like the shape of a heart." She used her finger to make the outline around the coding.

Destan sat there for a minute, scrolling a few different places, his expression and tone hinting to a lightbulb moment, "Wait a minute! I think I've figured— Calli, you're a genius!"

"How?"

"Something hit me strange from the first time I logged in. Sure, all the coding was there, but it was organized so— well you can see it. The coding parallels how the machine interacts and runs all of the dog's organs and such," he explained as he pointed to the three dimensional image of coding he's expanded off the screen for them to look at; it looking exactly like the belvedere. "The other day I was in this coding here, which is where his brain is. Even from here you can see there's a part missing; a pretty sizable chunk at that. From what I looked at in everything else that has to be where the Syndicate's link was. — First time I can say I'm glad something doesn't have all its marbles."

"Why is this code a different color?" Callimay asked as she pointed to another part of the belvedere's brain, an orange color compared to everything else which was blue.

"Let's see." Destan pulled it to him, zooming in. "It looks like… huh. I wonder… it was accessed with a command prompt just a few days ago by the admin. I'd say this code has been refactored but this looks like source code. … That's odd. It's like it was dead code until the admin accessed it. Which means this has been here since the belvedere was created."

Oh I wish he'd not get so technical. ~ Well, it's just like Doctor Gerould. ~ True, but he always explains. … And if Destan isn't the computer guru, like he said, then I can only imagine the type of words and phrases Abacus must use! ~ Doesn't mean he won't 'flex' what he does know from time to time. What guy wouldn't show off in front of the one he loves from time to time? ~ But why? It's not like he has to impress me. ~ Really? ~ Oh come now. He's never done that before. If anything he did the opposite. "What's so strange about finding code that was from when the belvedere was made? Isn't most of it that old? And can you speak in a language I can understand? I haven't gotten 'that' into the computer stuff."

"The declaration— sorry. The names here. Look at them."

"That's our names!"

"Mine was actually added not too long after the code was activated. … What? This doesn't make any— this is the opcode for the belvedere's keeper. That means— I'm doing it again, I know. Umm… how do I put this? … Your mother somehow put your name into the belvedere's original programming as the person it was supposed to protect."

"O-kay. But why? That would've been a huge risk to take. They — the Syndicate — would've had access to that, right?"

He didn't answer out loud, but the way his lips began to twist and he began looking hinted to his agreeance with her concern.

"W… what's this gray area?"

"It looks like a null va— it's just missing. There was something there at one time since this empty space exists. While you can make most things disappear through what's called a defrag, it appears this part of the coding isn't capable of having that done to it. Crazy, I know, but— I don't believe it. It's a hidden conditional statement."

"Dialect, please!"

"There's a third person the belvedere is programed to look after but only upon seeing the person." *Why wasn't Calli inputted that way? ~ Well she didn't know what she looked like.*

"Destan?"

He shook his head and then turned his computer to her, "He's written in here by both names: Trever 'and' Emissary."

"Then that means—"

"I'm as sure as I can be: Emissary 'is' your brother, Calli." Destan set the computer down and rested his hands on her shoulders; preparing himself to help comfort her however he could.

"I… but… y— you mean I still have a brother who's alive? W… why didn't he recognize me? We lived right next to each other for so many years. I…"

"Let's take care of what we do know right now, alright? Just take this nice and slow. — Maybe I'm asking for the impossible but please try. — I'm not saying you can't have questions; just remember I'm in the same boat right now: just as shocked and knowledgeable as you are. Alright? … Calli?"

She did her best to take a deep breath, somehow able to nod.

Destan continued in his calming tone as he picked up the computer, "I mean, I haven't even found what I was originally trying to get in here for."

"Wha… what about the Syndicate knowing about me? And she put 'both' of Trever's names in there!"

"Easy," he let the computer fall to the sofa, grabbing his wife's wrist to get her to stop pacing. "If we really think about it, it doesn't matter. If they wanted to know Elder could've given them that information. And obviously they didn't give him any about you — and you know they would've. So logically speaking they had no idea about this. I doubt they ever got into him this deep if they ever had to do any tweaks, updates, or maintenance checks. Canary probably took care of him herself to avoid anyone digging around.”

After a bit more “talking”, he found the coding pertaining to the belvedere’s sensitivity to Callimay’s emotional status. As he suspected, the creature wasn’t tied to him in that manner — which was all for the better as far as he was concerned. It was wrapped in an almost endless web of what he knew technically to be known as conditional coding, but didn’t dare use anymore computer “lingo” while explaining things. Yes, Callimay had calmed, but anything was liable to set her off… and that was the last thing he needed right then.

His brain was taxied to its limit, but Destan was able to break through and modify it so the belvedere’s reaction was removed. The thought crossed his mind about leaving a loophole concerning an extreme circumstance, but he didn’t know what was going to happen when they got back to Bulwark. There was no way the belvedere wouldn’t be taken down if he was even “seen” anywhere near the perimeter. But, he did leave a different type of loophole so he could delete the modification he made if needed.

“What is his range? I mean as far as him being able to know if I’m in distress?”

“Good thought. That way if I do need to delete it he’ll actually be able to sense you. … It looks like it’s— wow! That’s quite a bit farther than I thought: fifty miles.”

“Surely we can find somewhere within fifty miles of Bulwark to have him stay, right?”

“There’s really not much of anything around. Mrs. Jackman owned a large section of that area of Ferdinan and left it untouched for that exact reason.” Destan shook his head as he sat back and thought.

“Why didn’t you tell me she was Rocher’s sister?”

“Who told you?”

“Auditor.” Callimay said a bit timid.

He relaxed as he set the computer down and put his arm around her, “It’s an extremely touchy topic with Rocher is why I asked; don’t mention a word of her around him. … And it’s the reason I barely got him to give that speech at the ball; I sprang it on him that morning so he really didn’t have a choice. — She’s never been forgotten but her memory isn't as prominent as it probably should be. I can understand it from both sides now, though. You need to be able to talk things through and get a good grasp of how to help and work with the person who is hurt, but at the same time it's a life-altering experience: to walk into a room only to find your loved one murdered. But then to bear the burden of dealing with others when they don't understand your bond with the person who is gone? You knowing beyond a shadow of a doubt they'd never resort to killing themselves no matter what stress they were under? In a way I guess you could say 'I' rubbed off on him. He can't take anyone mentioning her; good 'or' bad."

"She said they never figured out who did it, so she must believe she was murdered."

"It were as if no one was there but her; so obviously it was called a suicide which 'really' set Rocher off. I went through everything and admit it points only to that, but like a small but silent number I'm on Rocher's side: there's just no way she killed herself. For me it was just gut instinct. Something never 'felt' right; but every shred of evidence proved the opposite." Destan scratched his head as he sighed. "She was murdered not too long after I got my beacon. I think it was right after I follow up."

"What happens when you get your beacon?"

"You won't remember any of it."

"Okay…" she dragged out, trying to get him to elaborate.

Seeing her trying so hard to keep things positive, he took the hint and gave it his best try, "It's surgically implanted against the inner portion of your ear. While it's possible for you to be in a twilight state if you want, you still wouldn't 'remember' what happened."

"Which side is yours on?" She folded her legs on the sofa and had a bit of a bounce in her voice.

"I'll give you one guess and you can't look for the scar."

"I wouldn't need to because I've seen the scar and watched you activate it enough to know which side it's on — left."

"Why you—" Destan huffed as he got up; her hopping up from the sofa after she finished so she could get a head start. "Why did you ask if you knew?"

"Because!" She laughed as she ran to the far side of the bedroom.

"If 'I' said that you'd demand another answer." Destan made a face as he wagged his finger at her.

"Not 'another' answer because just saying because isn't an answer at all, silly!"

"Oh, that's it." He gritted his teeth, trying so hard not to smile.

"Where'd you go?" Callimay asked startled when he disappeared.

"Boo!" Destan said right in her ear as he grabbed her.

She screamed and started fighting him, but began laughing harder and harder as he tickled her, "Stop! I can't breathe!"

"Well if you'd stop gabbing, you'd last longer."

"Destan! It hurts."

"What! Where!"

"Oh, thank goodness." Callimay tried to catch her breath; leaning over and putting her hands on her knees.

"Where did I hurt you?"

"My side was starting to kill me from laughing so hard."

"That's… it?"

"What do you mean, 'that's it'?"

"I thought I actually hurt you."

"It's good to see you smiling." She brushed the side of his face, her still trying to catch her breath.

"But I— you are a beautiful little nark, you know that? It's good to see you smiling, too." He calmed as he pulled her close.

"And you know what?"

"What?"

"We didn't get interrupted by a big white ball of fur."

"Well I'd say that's proof positive I did it right but I'm still 'logged in' so he's in stasis." He shook his head as he headed back to the sofa.

"Really? Seriously?" Callimay rolled her eyes as she took another forced, deep breath.

Destan reached for the computer, laughing, "You did that all on purpose for that reason only? And here I thought you were being all sentimental, lovey-dovey-wifey on me."

"Well, not at first, but then it did occur to me a few seconds later."

"When?" He released the link on the belvedere.

"Right before I said it."

He couldn't help but laugh as the creature started to reboot. The belvedere closed his eyes and looked like he stopped breathing for a few minutes; and then popped up, barked at the two of them before rushing downstairs to lay by the window — even though there wasn't that much moonlight to soak up since it was so cloudy.

ஃ

When the realization of this being their last full day there sunk in, Callimay made the suggestion to start looking through the information they had; Destan outright refused. While his well-meaning rejection was legitimate and thoughtful, she reminded him they had to leave.

"I'm not getting in that vehicle until you tell me you're alright… and I know good and well you're not."

"But I am, really, Destan." She nodded as she turned the water off.

He shuffled his feet, not looking at her as he mumbled, "Well then I'm not."

"What's wrong?" She took the dried plate out of his hand.

"I could feel you when you woke up and started listening to me." He admitted as his shoulders dropped. "I know you heard me. … I just… I need some more time, Calli. I'm not ready to be Doyen again. I'm not saying I will be when we go back, but I just need a little more time to get things straight in my mind."

"I… I'm s— I didn't know what was wrong and—"

"It's okay. I almost said something but then I figured out 'why' you were there."

Callimay asked supportive as she took his hand and squeezed it, "How much time do you need?"

"Just a day. One, good, day."

"Well then, let's get everything else done today so you can have that good day. Sound good?"

Her joy was so wholesome and contagious even in such an awkward moment for him, yet the words that fell off his lips were as heavy as lead bricks; him groaning as he leaned against the counter, "I'll need to notify Fidus first and pray Elder isn't around to but in."

"You take care of that and I'll get everything ready." She grabbed the towel off his shoulder. "Deal?"

71

"Deal." Destan half smiled as he turned and took his phone out. "This isn't gonna be a fun call by any means. You know that, right?"

She smiled as she opened the cabinet to put the last of the dishes from lunch away: *I'll keep an eye on things.*

℔

It took Destan a bit of convincing, but he was finally able to get Fidus to agree to let them have one more day. Elder wasn't anywhere in the background, so that helped; but even so he came close a few times. — Really close. — The second he would feel the surge he would catch Callimay out of the corner of his eye leaning on the railing of the stairs.

As he looked up after saying goodbye, he wished he would have asked for more time. He wanted so bad to just stay there with her and away from everything. It's not that he was running away from his responsibilities; he just wanted to focus on the priorities he wanted to… and forget the rest until he was finished: *Guess that's the same thing as running away from responsibilities, huh? ~ Well the last I checked, that pretty much was the definition.*

But, the more he thought of it there was hope in that area still. The timeline for Total Eclipse to begin was about four months away. If Majesty Presley was willing to work with them, Destan knew he'd have to meet with him face-to-face; which meant — he hoped —he could bring Callimay back for a bit of a break in about a month or so.

"Ready?" Callimay asked as he took a deep breath and sat down.

"Which first?"

"The files we got from the Society." She tapped the glass, waking up the computer.

"Alright." Destan sighed as she curled up next to him.

The files he had were all communications between Baleck and Elder; the earliest dates being before the Society opened its doors. Not lengthy or very detailed, the first ones didn't offer any helpful information.

But then there was a shift. And a major one at that.

Elder ~ 08:52

I know we planned to do this later, but she's
requested that she be allowed to join you since

her brother is attending. Do you think it is
possible to move up the timeline?

> **Baleck ~ 10:03**
> I'll see what I can find as far as work for her.
> **Baleck ~ 16:12**
> Mr. Freigh has agreed, providing she will work
> strictly on a PRN basis. I'll see to it room and
> board is provided.

Elder ~ 16:19
She'll be arriving before the end of the week.
See to it her brother does not recognize her. I've
already explained the situation surrounding
him to her.

> **Baleck ~ 16:19**
> I'll take care of everything.

There were a couple conversations that were odd, but what was said didn't come across as being "dangerous". It was more the obscure language that was used which confused them than anything really. This unknown, made Destan suspicious; and yet even he had to admit these suspicions couldn't find anything to hold onto: *You're just suspicious of everything they say meaning more than what the text shows. ~ Can you blame me after what's been going on? ~ I didn't say that. I'm just saying that sometimes things are exactly as they seem. And if you can't find a common thread, the chances are there's nothing there. ~ But still. This all has to deal with Elder. And we 'both' know he's capable of making anything look harmless.*

Later that year there was another conversation concerning Ginger and her brother that filled in the shallow hole that was left from what they knew from Mr. Freigh's account of his wife's murder.

Elder ~ 19:32
Well, how did her brother do?
Elder ~ 19:32
Were you able to complete it as planned? I
know there was a concern last we spoke.

Baleck ~ 19:48

He's a cliffhanger. I don't expect him to last but maybe another day or so.

Elder ~ 19:52

I'm glad that's done and over with.

Baleck ~ 23:53

She's been begging me for the past hour to allow her brother to recognize her.

Elder ~ 23:59

What did you say?

Baleck ~00:01

I said I would think about it. Destry's experiment never proved to work, but there can't be any greater risk if I allow her to.

Elder ~ 00:03

Do it for her own sake even though we both know it won't change anything. Just be there to soften the blow for her as you see fit. She's vital to your work now, so appeasing her wishes is in our best interest. And yet don't appease her as to make her forget. She must remember this.

Baleck ~ 00:04

How do you propose I make her remember?

Elder ~ 00:05

Let her go in the room and see him as he truly is. Restrain him however you need to, but make sure she's in that room.

Baleck ~ 00:05

That shouldn't be too much of an issue.

Baleck ~ 00:06

But if he starts to enter that end suicidal phase I'll pull her out so she's spared that at least.

Elder ~ 00:08

On the contrary, Baleck. Make sure she sees him die. That's the key to making sure she will forever remember. This needs to happen for

our plan to reach the conclusion it's intended to
have. Her hatred for Mr. Freigh needs to be
stoked as hard and fast as possible; but
controlled so it will burn deep and slow until
we need her.

Baleck ~ 00:09

This has been your plan all along? Ginger?

Elder ~ 00:12

She's the perfect one to do it. And this is the
push she needs to cement her. I've been having
issues with her having trigger moments
because she met her brother. — How that
happened I still don't know, but those need to
die… NOW! We can't lose her power to the
likes of those who are noble-minded. Her
ruthless nature must remain intact.

Baleck ~ 00:13

I understand.

Destan noticed this structure of questioning became quite common and specific about those chosen for processing as well as a "manifest" of students Baleck would send just prior to the beginning of the school year. What did he need them for? If he needed anyone, Bulwark was at his complete disposal.

But the more he read the more it sounded like someone else was using the list. But why?

The entire ordeal with Hyra was explained with Elder saying he would get with Justice Wan to see about helping him cope by giving him a new "mission" in life.

"You don't think…" Callimay gulped as she clutched the pillow.

"If he 'is' playing both sides everything's in jeopardy. … But this isn't enough to bring a charge of sedition against him. It's close but still inconclusive. It is, however, making that very thing more and more evident to me. And I'm beginning to understand why C— your mother, said he needed to be disposed of prior to The Arena. … And you know? This actually makes things fits with the timeline of Justice Wan needing

75

to be in their ranks so he could work his way up to obtaining a his own belvedere. He'd need ten years seniority — and be well-respected — to be 'nominated' for one."

"But… that means he knew all about you when we were there!"

He rubbed his chin, unable to hide the concern in his voice like he wanted to: *And that creature was most likely with him when he found us. ~ Thank you Lord for keeping us safe.* "I know he said he let us go because of his hate for the Society being more than his duty to his job, but that never made much sense. Those in the Syndicate don't care about anyone; not even family. — Especially when there's a bounty involved. — I mean, him 'having a heart' and letting us go just because of his daughter? That's a weakness no Informer or Falconer is allowed to have. It would jeopardize their loyalty. And for someone with a belvedere to have that weakness? Impossible. Let alone the fact: how could you care for one human being while murdering another? You can't. Sure someone could 'say' that, but 'do' it?"

"You mean he did it on purpose?"

"I don't know why the Syndicate would have allowed him to unless Elder somehow…" Destan set the computer down and turned to her. "If Elder's feeding them info about Total Eclipse and we do go through with it, this could end up being a second Eradication. … We've heard rumblings about a sting the Syndicate's labeled 'the Purge'," *and a certain someone even told me about it.* "But there's never been anything to give us concrete intel about what it exactly is and when."

With this new danger in mind, they continued reading with more urgency and focus.

"Correct me if I'm wrong, but don't these names look familiar? Well, some of them, anyway?"

"What do you mean? Where from?"

"That one part of my file on Rogues. The names of those individuals? There are several of them here. … Of course I could just be 'thinking' I recognize them."

She dismissed this all, thinking he was trying to divert his thoughts to something else, and didn't bother continuing with the conversation. And yet only a minute or so later she found he wasn't just babbling on. Destan stopped reading and set the computer, once larger quantities of names were being listed, to pull them out and match them through his database access to every national registry archive — excluding those under fifteen and over thirty-five. So when a name was mentioned, pictures of those who matched the name and age range were posted on the side.

"Any of those pictures look familiar?"

"I… don't remember, Destan. I was too shocked at the time."

"It's alright Calli. I'll leave it up just in case something does stick out to either of us."

But, the answer to his question was actually contained within the conversation itself; they just hadn't gone far enough.

Elder ~ 06:54

The Monarch is pleased with the first
installment as far as quality is concerned.

> **Baleck ~ 06:54**
>
> Just quality?

Elder ~ 06:54

But, they are asking for more in the way of
numbers, Baleck.

> **Baleck ~ 06:59**
>
> I'm doing my best. It's not as easy going behind
> Mr. Freigh's back right now. He's here so much
> of the time.

Elder ~ 07:01

You have Nightmare with you now. Use her.

Elder ~ 07:03

And I'm sure you can, shall we say, 'convince'
Freigh that he should take a step back? All new
endeavors have bumps and setbacks.

> **Baleck ~ 07:14**
>
> When do they want the next instalment?

Elder ~ 07:18

I've set it up so they'll be four more before TE
begins which would make it every two years.
Now it's not to say you can't do it every year,

but two years is the max they're willing to wait
for each installment. They want them to be as
close as possible when it comes to the amount
of experience and training each has. Seniority
is one thing they are trying to avoid.

> **Baleck ~ 07:22**
> What's the number they're wanting for each?

Elder ~ 09:51

At least one-hundred.

> **Baleck ~ 09:51**
> Excuse me? One HUNDRED?
>
> **Baleck ~ 09:52**
> That's surpassing the entire ratio of viable
> candidates we'd have any given year!

Elder ~ 09:52

I have no doubt you'll find a way to dismiss any
suspicions anyone may have.

> **Baleck ~ 09:57**
> Mr. Freigh remembers each student; let alone
> the fact there are still risks involved. There's
> only so many lies that can be used and believed
> when it comes to people disappearing.

Elder ~ 10:01

They can remain for the entirety of the
schoolyear and the ones who do not make it
can be written off as those who had emergent
family requests to be returned home. Very
simple and would play to Mr. Freigh's
weakness. I'll take care of the time that the
Monarch expects to receive them. With regard
to the ratio of viability? Bring the fatality rate
down lower than Destry ever dreamed possible.
It was you who completed his work with
fusion. This is no different: dominate him even
after death. Remind those you both worked
with that you ARE superior to him.

Elder ~ 10:04

And as far as recognition after the fact? If it
becomes something of an issue you know we've
done that before. An alteration of physical
appearance with mental recalibration and
subsequent assignment of identity through the
closest country to their new ethnic ties…

Elder ~ 10:05

Need I go on?

Elder ~ 10:05

Leave the planning to me and just implement
and make in-the-moment decisions as needed.

> **Baleck ~ 10:07**
>
> Trever Presley was different. He was younger
> and easier to manipulate. And after what you
> did to him he submitted out of fear.
>
> **Baleck ~ 10:07**
>
> And don't forget: Canary 'did' recognize him
> when she met him.

Elder ~ 10:08

DO

Elder ~ 10:08

IT

> **Baleck ~ 12:48**
>
> Give me the contact information and I'll start
> lining things up and see to it that it's done. But I
> warn you: you've even said you've had issues
> with Ginger uncovering a trigger that's
> overpowering what was done. That technique is
> not invincible. Quit playing god with Trever
> Presley, flaunting him like you are. He could
> become the very person who is your undoing.

Elder ~ 01:00

Every mortal god makes a mistake early on in
their rise to power, perhaps a grave one, I
won't deny that. But that just means they have

to overcome that weakness by learning how to
have ultimate control over those around them.
Victory only comes through defeat. I've had my
defeat. This is my victory. No one can destroy
me. Not even Trever Presley.

There was so many things that this section brought out that was shocking and somewhat horrifying. For Callimay it was the fact Elder did something so heinous to Trever that he submitted to him out of fear and let him do whatever he did to make him forget everything. Destan, on the other hand, found it hard to believe that Elder threw away what he saw as his trump card: Ginger. She was the key to completing their task at the Society. — And after hearing what Mr. Freigh said he pretty much knew "why" they needed her. — But to throw her away? Was that all Elder needed her for? Was she actually dead? Could it possibly be that he did attempt to take her life but she escaped and is planning her revenge? If so would she be willing to join Destan and Callimay? *Was she possibly~ Boon stop it. That's impossible. Canary is gone. And even if the woman was alive, would you actually think she'd flip? If anything she'd be a Huntress.*

Destan recognized several of the names mentioned as being cliffhangers and at one point had to stop, sounding flustered as he tossed the computer on the table and got up, "I'm sorry, Calli. I… I'll be right back. Do you want anything to drink?"

"Some pomegranate juice would be nice. … Destan?"

"I'll be right back. Just stay here."

This sudden shift in his tone and demeanor made her take computer and reread that part. She must have missed something

After looking for a while with no leads, she set it down and rocked back and forth, still hugging the pillow she had this whole time. She felt him spike through the roof and then heard glass shatter. Callimay screamed as she raced down the stairs, jumping over the banister when she was almost at the bottom, "Destan!"

He was on his knees, gripping his right hand that was bleeding; glass pieces littering the floor in front of him. He was doubled over, not looking up at her as he hissed.

She ran to him, her voice shrieking with horror, "What happened!"

"It's nothing," he stumbled while getting up.

"Did the glass slip out of your hand?"

Destan brushed off as he turned the faucet on, "I'm fine."

"Not hot water!" She gasped as she tried to stop him.

"I'm fine! Now leave me alone!"

"Destan… what's wrong?" Callimay begged as she winced and grabbed the sink with one hand while she put her other hand over her forehead. "Please. Destan, I— no, Mr. Ruff! Stay back!"

Infuriated with all the commotion, the boiling anger inside him needing to escape; he slapped his left hand on the quartz counter top making his wedding band add a high-pitched dagger sound to the already loud, thunderous clap his hand made. He froze, whipping his head over to Callimay who was still at the sink getting a hand towel wet. While she didn't move or burst into tears, he could tell she was barely keeping it together.

She turned the water down and set the towel to the side before coming over, her head still bowed as she offered her trembling hand. Destan didn't hesitate and followed her. With the gentlest of a touch, she set his hand on the dampened cloth and began examining it.

There were a few glistening pieces so she started to leave; only to be stopped by Destan who put his left hand around her forehead to bring her back to him, "I'm sorry, Calli."

After flinching, she gave in and stepped back into his chest, "You're in pain. It—"

"But I put you through it too." He groaned; fighting with himself to say, "I got mad about what those dirt bags said about why the young men who became cliffhangers were chosen. I was holding the glass — well, gripping it — as I kept brooding about it. Guess I—"

"They were all orphans!" Her eyes almost bugged out when she understood; noticing movement in her peripheral, "I say stay back! We can't have you— get back. — Where's a broom or a vacuum, Destan?"

"They're both in the cove next to the washer. … Calli, I—"

"I don't know how in the world that didn't register. It all makes sense now. I'm… I'm sorry. Just let me get this cleaned up so we don't have to worry and then I'll get some tweezers to get that glass out."

"Alright."

She reached for the door handled and then whipped around, "I… do you… do you want to talk about it? I didn't mean to cut you off. I'm sorry if—"

"It's okay. I'm alright now." His face softened, his eyes starting to sting as he calmed.

Callimay grumbled with herself, even though he said it was alright, while she got the larger pieces swept up: *Why was I so~ You better watch what you're doing or 'you'll' be needing some attention.*

The low hum of the vacuum soon started; it left to finish cleaning while she left to get the first-aid kit. She hopped up onto the counter and took Destan's hand on her lap so she could cradle it while she took the clear fragments out of the cuts; making sure to check a couple extra times before she emptied her little collection onto a piece of tape and folded it over on itself.

It struck him how — in a way — she worked similar to Rose when he heard her humming to herself, but then it really struck him: *She's just happy. Happy she's able to help me. And the fact is I need some happy in my life right now.*

After making him put his other hand under the water to be sure it was a comfortable temperature, Callimay began working to do what she knew when it came to dealing with glass cuts.

At one point, while she inspected his hand one last time, she did her best to smile, "Well you didn't have to do all of this to make me feel better, you know. — Try to move your fingers a bit to see if there's anything that feels like it's poking you. I know it might hurt some."

"Umm… not that I can feel. — And what do you mean by 'make you feel better'?"

"I'm the one who's been getting hurt all the time lately. Don't you dare think you need to keep up with me."

Destan chuckled as he watched her wrap the bandage around and around; finishing on a more somber note, "I'd never see that as an area worth being competitive in… though I'd do anything to take every one of those away from you."

"I love you." Callimay paused as she leaned her head against his hand that was on the side of her face.

For as sweet as this moment was, a repetitive thumping caught their attention. Destan was laughing because he knew what was going on, but it took his confused wife a bit longer to discover the vacuum couldn't go "though" the door to its charger.

"Everything here is so needy!" Callimay scoffed as she stormed over; the belvedere running to the door when he saw her coming. "You included. … Oh. Alright. Out with you. Go on. … Now what? You just want attention?"

"Go on," Destan said forceful as he eyed the creature, it obeying. "And don't come back for a couple hours."

"You think he can tell time?" Callimay laughed as she came back to the kitchen and got their drinks ready.

"I don't see why not. Let me put it this way: it's worth a shot to see. — You got those?"

"Yep."

ѣ

They moseyed up to the sofa; but instead of jumping back in Destan turned the computer off. In light of what happened, somehow "one good day" didn't sound like it was going to be enough.

But, once he got his drink finished he set the glass down and picked up the computer; sounding much better, "Ready for another round?"

"I am if you are."

Names began to become familiar as they got closer and closer to when they were there.

Ingrid was sent by Elder with the intent of being processed — and she was in full agreeance. Though her defiant nature proved to be Elder's frustration in that she refused to be "sold" to the Syndicate once she received her new abilities. Baleck sounded annoyed that he had to play the middle man between his two bickering family members; so as this distain grew more while she was there he finally had enough — it coming to a head so he demanded Elder have a conference with her.

Ingrid ~ 21:54
I really don't see a need for my involvement
with the Syndicate alone, grandfather.

Elder ~ 21:55

Child, may I remind you that YOU are the one
who agreed to this?

Ingrid ~ 21:56

I agreed to undergo processing to make myself
more valuable. That value doesn't mean I gave
you the right to sell me at a higher price to one,
single buyer. Don't think for one second I'm
gullible; my sisters taught me much better than
anyone in my family ever did.

Ingrid ~ 21:57

Including you.

> **Baleck ~ 21:58**
>
> It isn't that you are tied to them entirely. If
> anything you're just put in the database so they
> can contact you if needed. They are fully aware
> of your status with the Sisterhood and respect
> your stance to remain as such.

Elder ~ 22:03

I'm warning you, child. Being so independent
can have sharp and unforgiving shortcomings.

Elder ~ 22:03

Not having anyone to trust isn't the way we
operate.

Ingrid ~ 22:08

And manipulating everyone on every side to
trust you so that you gain power and wealth
doesn't come with those same shortcomings?
Lies only work as good as the one who is
keeping them straight. And may I remind you
how YOU have made some high-profile, major
errors in that area. In fact BOTH of you have.
My shortcomings have not gained the
unwanted attention of any major entity.
Especially not the Monarch. My caution,
strategy, and calculation have paid off.

Baleck ~ 22:09

Nothing was ever said otherwise. Our personal human nature is the greatest enemy those like us have to battle. Some are able to win that battle sooner than others.

Elder ~ 22:10

But the fact remains you have made your own share of mistakes as well, Ingrid. We have to learn in our own ways and time to overcome humanity. This step you're taking is one of the largest ones we know of to help in that area.

Ingrid ~ 22:13

This life is a dangerous and unforgiving one any way you slice it. I've taken my vows with the Sisterhood knowing full well what this life entailed. And maybe failure is something that some people can afford, but for others it is a death sentence.

Baleck ~ 22:14

So much fire like her father.

Elder ~ 22:15

Fine.

Elder ~ 22:15

I'll see to it the Monarch is aware of your stance. I doubt there will be any issues. Just vow that if needed you will default to what I request of you on behalf of the Syndicate.

Ingrid ~ 22:16

If the payment is right, then yes.

Elder ~ 22:17

You are trying my patience, child. Do NOT make me use force.

Baleck ~ 22:22

Ingrid?

Baleck ~ 22:28

Ingrid don't do this.

Ingrid ~ 22:57

I had better things to tend to at that time. Surely
you can understand such things, uncle.

Ingrid ~ 22:57

Give me at least some amount of privacy if you
can bear to be civil for that long. I DO have a
life that I am leaving behind for this all.

Ingrid ~ 23:02

I'm only making it very clear for the record
where I stand. And as such that is my vow.

All of a sudden, something clicked for Destan: *'That's' why Ingrid got away in Faberton. At least it's the only reason which makes sense now that I think about it. Yes, Elder is cold and cruel, but Ingrid is his personal assassin. ~ Yeah, just being related isn't enough. She wouldn't bat an eye if he crossed her and neither would he. ~ He's scared of her to some level. But why? What power could she have over him?*

"It sounds reasonable. … And rather frightening. — Speaking of which where is she, anyway?"

"Strigidae don't leave trails that can be followed… well, followed with any good to show for it." Destan sighed as he rubbed his face. "They're 'very' good at what they do. And that's the one thing we've struggled with since, well, since the Shadows started. Tracking one of them down is like trying to follow the flight path of a lightning bug from a distance: you only see them when they want you to, and it's never where or when you expect it to be. — Nothing's come up as of yet, but with her and Elder— keep an eye on the trees whenever you're out. And if you even 'think' you see a white owl don't take your eye off it as you get to safety. They'll maul you given the chance and order to."

"Poisonous?"

"Not inherently. Though some huntresses will coat their fangs with belvedere blood just for the 'fun' of it."

"At first I thought she'd be so mean, but then she wasn't. In fact she was so caring and kind. Yes I was comparing her to Gallia but she was nothing like I expected: she seemed to be genuine." Callimay thought back as she shivered. "I know I can be a bit too trusting, but that gut instinct I had about her was ripped away when she started talking. She's too good at lying."

"They're taught to be that way."

"Where did they come from, anyway?"

"You love history, don't you? … Well, get comfortable and I'll give you the rundown I was taught and know. — The Strigidae Huntresses or 'the Sisterhood' predates the Eradication, altogether. And the origin of their order isn't even here on Quidoria as I was told. Surprising, huh?" Destan set the computer down and propped his feet up on the coffee table as he stretched out. "In the late nineties, a group of ambidextrous girls from Centauri Beta got together and would think of ways to use their 'gift' to play practical jokes on friends. — Family life on Beta was, and last I heard still is, pretty nonexistent with the largest interchange being the only true job market for the entire planet. Work schedules are nonstop for months on end, so kids raise themselves if they don't have the blessing of a two-parent home that can sustain on one income or the parents are on different schedules so one is always home. — So, with this void, this group had free rein to do what they wanted without any 'repercussions'. They began to gain 'traction' when they started fooling around security points at docks for the interchange with a certain pet owl the one girl had. Time went on and the jokes turned into petty theft; these girls now grown women who had way too much street smarts that wasn't in check; their lust for anything they wanted fueling their ventures. A certain heist in the fall of twenty-two went haywire and the person being robbed was mauled by the one woman's pet owl all in an effort to protect her. In honor of their 'savior', they gave themselves the official title of Strigidae. They began recruiting young girls like themselves so they could take on more daring jobs; them finally landing their first offer of a 'formal' paycheck — a kill mission. While you might think the whole mantra of deep-seeded morality turning some of them away from this life when they saw what was actually going on and how they reached rock bottom in that they were willing to murder someone… not a single one of them batted an eye. They added Huntress to the title at that point. 'The Sisterhood' is somewhat of a collective title of endearment they use, them referring to each other as sisters since they are the only family they have. And so with no type of moral boundary left, they continued crafting their order into one of the most extensive, streamlined, lean, ruthless, and deadly assassin groups that 'no one' in the public sector knows exists."

"All this killing because they didn't have a family?" Callimay sighed as she shook her head. "There really is no limit people will go to so they have attention… is there?"

"Not if they think they need it from other people."

This subtle reminder wasn't lost to Callimay, her smiling as she nodded; then asked, "So all of them are ambidextrous?"

"Yep. And as far as them being called deuces, like you're thinking, they actually use the Syndicate's little caveat to find new girls. Since we're closed off here they have to do things a bit differently than everywhere else but they manage to get off-world sometimes." Destan paused when he saw how frightened his wife was becoming. "Calli?"

"Let's go back to this, huh?"

"You never would've gone with them, I know you wouldn't have." He consoled as he took her hands.

"You don't know how low I got after my mother died. I never said a thing to anyone, but if someone would've come along and—"

"But no one did and you came through that trial more precious and refined than before. And maybe… you know what? If that would've gotten you, God 'knew' you wouldn't be able to handle that temptation so He made sure you were kept away from them." Destan put his hand to her lips, his voice so soft and loving. "Let's go check the fireplace. Even I can tell it's starting to get a little drafty."

И

This short break turned into a relaxing and lengthy lunchtime during which the belvedere showed up to have his attention needs met before he took a nap in the dining area.

And before they started looking at more of the information they had, they curled up by the fireplace in the bedroom and read a few passages of Scripture. Hearing words of hope and joy — and justice — gave them peace and comfort to know that, in the end, Elder was not going to be able to succeed. Maybe what he planned to do in this physical life would, but God would not allow his unrepentant deeds go unpunished.

With a refreshed assurance about everything, they came back out to the landing and picked up where they left off.

The fiasco with Dakoe was briefly addressed; but wasn't much more than a blip. He was the first one "forced" into this manner of life — as least that's what appeared to be the case as far as what was said in these conversations. But other than that his name was not brought up like others were.

Next on the never-ending list of questions was Elder's distain for Callimay. Baleck let him know Mr. Freigh came across her application and so the floodgates of his deep-seated hatred burst open. They each could hear his anger and see his fiery eyes when they read his words.

Elder ~ 16:43
Send Ingrid to check on her, first.

> **Baleck ~ 17:23**
> You have her brother watching her like a hawk already. Why send her?
>
> **Baleck ~ 17:24**
> And why do 'I' have to contact her?

Elder ~ 17:28
Always complaining. I don't want him getting
suspicious if it is her.

> **Baleck ~ 17:29**
> You're worried he'll snap back?

Elder ~ 17:29
Absolutely not.

Elder ~ 17:33
I just do not want him to think something has
changed and accidentally let "someone else"
know what he's doing. Our frequency of
contact is where it needs to be.

Elder ~ 17:36
And while it wouldn't be the end of the world
to make a mistake — it's only one young

woman's life — I MUST know. I can't have that Chameleon running around any longer.

Baleck ~ 18:07

> Fine. I'll contact her later this evening IF she'll answer my call.

Destan double-checked the date stamp and was puzzled as to why it was three years prior to her going, "When did you apply, Calli?"

"The year it opened."

What took him so long to get to your application?

"I asked myself that same question when I got the acceptance letter ten years later. — Why do you keep messing with your wedding band? It is too loose?"

Destan shook his head, finally taking his focus off the computer, "I'm just so used to doing that while I'm at 'work'. It's my reminder of you that I always have with me. … But I have something even better right now. I've got the real deal."

Callimay got teary-eyed again, so moved by his comment which made his face flush. She slipped her hand into his, that triggering his smile as he gripped her hand; him so grateful she was doing so well.

Not too much longer into these conversations brought another name and person they knew to the forefront: Ashte Yorick. Elder said he wanted him processed no matter his likelihood of being a cliffhanger; telling Baleck to lead him on with fake evidence so it would ensure he would be one.

Surprisingly, Baleck was hesitant and unwilling to because of the potential in Ashte for their purposes, but eventually caved. Though, once Baleck said Ashte was a cliffhanger Elder was irate: he ridiculed Baleck for pulling him from processing due to his initial response.

Knowing how raw his emotions were concerning Ashte, but not knowing exactly why, Callimay did her best to divert the subject in a different direction, "I wonder how we were related."

"You know? Our lives are so intertwined it's kinda hard to believe."

"Did he ever talk about his family?"

"Definitely not extended family. There was some huge rift that he never wanted to talk about; a family feud of sorts."

"Oh," Callimay sighed as she looked back at the screen.

Destan glanced down at his wedding band and saw her delicate hand resting on top of it. He remembered the way Ashte acted out one time and his heart started aching, his eyes stinging: he understood now. Each person had their own breaking point when it came to being alone. And while Destan actually was for a very long time, he "successfully" filled that void by overloading himself with work; letting himself become a workaholic so he didn't notice. Ashte had grown past that lie and knew there was no substitute for the honest, pure love of a woman.

This bittersweet reminder seemed to vanish when he looked back at the screen and saw his own name mentioned. Elder's tone at this point made yet another change.

Elder ~ 12:57

Does Freigh remember the brat?

> **Baleck ~ 12:59**
>
> Absolutely. He's thrilled he's coming. He keeps going on and on about how he came to know him and what a great man his father was; how he misses their discussions and how he's so looking forward to seeing Destan again.

Elder ~ 13:01

The virtuous humanitarian's son who is said to be incapable of doing wrong. Oh the sickening nature of these people. Is he considering him?

> **Baleck ~ 13:04**
>
> Yes. And of all things he's wanting to give him Challenger. I thought you destroyed the letter Destry was trying to get to him.

Elder ~ 13:07

I did, you moron. What's his initial report?

> **Baleck ~ 13:11**
>
> He's tested as the highest yet. Mr. Freigh doesn't seem too worried about it because of Dakoe's report, though. Needless to say, he is by all means setting all his hopes on him.

Elder ~ 13:17

Use that. And see to it Doyen keeps that high
level. Even with the Challenger serum he can't
escape the sentence of a cliffhanger.

Elder ~ 14:02

Keep Freigh's focus off Toreon, especially. Being
the Prince we need him kept separate.

> **Baleck ~ 14:03**
>
> Why did the Monarch send him, anyway?

Elder ~ 14:07

They wanted a leader for the new class who is
like them so they will respect and not be able to
rebel if they try pulling 'rank' as far as their
length of being an Elite. And the Queen wants
to give Toreon a chance to prove himself. As I
was told, the King's been critical of his lack of
involvement so she wants to prove him wrong.

> **Baleck ~ 17:11**
>
> What about Callimay? What am I supposed to
> do with her?

Elder ~ 17:58

Just leave her be for now. If she shows to be
who I really believe she is you will need to
redeem yourself.

> **Baleck ~ 17:59**
>
> Very well.
>
> **Baleck ~ 18:35**
>
> Apparently Callimay has been on Freigh's radar
> from the beginning.

Elder ~ 18:36

And you're just now finding that out?

Elder ~ 18:36

What has he tagged her for?

> **Baleck ~ 18:42**
>
> He tagged her for Liaison. I've made it clear that
> she needs that exact serum.

Elder ~ 18:45

HAVE YOU LOST YOUR MIND, BALECK! She's
already Chameleon.

> **Baleck ~ 18:46**
> RELAX, Uncle!
> **Baleck ~ 18:46**
> I said she's getting LIAISON.
> **Baleck ~ 18:46**
> Remember?

Elder ~ 18:49

Why do you even have the information for that
one? It's never worked. You told me it's
impossible for anyone to survive.

> **Baleck ~ 18:53**
> Which is exactly why she's getting it: she won't
> survive. If what you suspect to be true — her
> already having an ability — adding this one
> will be nothing but a win-win.
> **Baleck ~ 18:57**
> And since Doyen's taken a liking to her, her
> death will push him over the edge faster.

Elder ~ 19:00

You've grown weak, Baleck. You used to not
think twice before snapping someone's neck.
Now you're content with farming your work
out to science and emotional, frivolous love
entanglements. Perhaps sending Ginger to you
wasn't a wise decision.

> **Baleck ~ 19:03**
> This is only to keep my cover. My skills have
> not waned.
> **Baleck ~ 19:03**
> May I remind you the Syndicate's last
> instalment is due this year?

Elder ~ 19:04

No, you may not.

Destan held onto Callimay tighter with each word. What he gave her was nothing short of a poisonous cocktail that had every indication of fulfilling its task.

But why didn't it?

Regardless of that question, Destan pondered another: he could only imagine what he might have done had Callimay died.

"Don't think about that," she threw her arms around him. "It's the past and a reality that will never be. I'm right here."

Elder was beyond infuriated — Callimay surviving. Baleck tried to appease him by saying Destan ended up becoming a cliffhanger, but it was to not much avail.

In the middle of all this was an odd phone call recording from mid-December. And yet it wasn't: it was when Destan followed Baleck to Lookout Point. He wasn't on the phone with Mr. Freigh like he thought.

"I just spoke with the Prince. Is she dead?" Elder sounded *disgustingly hopeful.*

"There's no sign of Callimay." Baleck groaned.

"What do you mean by that? The Prince said he saw her fall over the railing."

"I can see footprints in the softer areas, but they will need to be analyzed to know if it was indeed Destan."

"You mean to tell me he's discovered it? And he used it to save her?"

"If he has," Baleck continued as a loud rustling noise interrupted for a moment. "Then we need to get the two of them in soon. We can't have them just using these abilities as toys or conveniences. They need to be taught there is a purpose and mission for this all."

"What 'are' you talking about, Baleck?" Elder was beyond irritated at this point. "Quit hacking like this. I'm no idiot needing every single detail explained."

"I apologize, Uncle. I slipped and thought I was speaking with Mr. Freigh. — The Prince told me he didn't go down and check; that he left a minute or so after she stopped screaming. With the way things look here with the placement of footprints and the fact no other students were out? I can't see why it wasn't Destan who intervened. There's no blood or imprint anywhere to suggest she ever hit the ground."

If I would've stayed just a few seconds longer I could've pieced this all together so much quicker.

Not stopping where he did, Callimay kept reading; seeing there was a conversation that took place between Toreon, Baleck, and Elder.

Having his wife dig her nails into his arm caused him to sit up and look around, "What is it?"

"I can see him saying all those things. I… I don't want to see it." She tried not to cry as she turned her face to him and closed her eyes. "I—"

"Don't worry," he began to rock her. "Anything more about or from him I'll make sure you don't see."

But, as it turned out, most of the remaining conversations had him involved. Destan finished by himself while he held Callimay; giving her the basic highlight of what each conversation was about.

When he got to the last one — the day they escaped — he stopped. A flood of emotions began to rise as he set the computer down and held the woman he loved in his firm, tender hold. This was important but what they said reminded him how he couldn't take one second for granted. He didn't want one chance for him to remind her he loved her slip through his grasp.

Destan started thinking back to his life a year prior and how the thought of feeling this way about someone never crossed his mind… in a positive way, that is. Things were perfect as far as he was concerned: he was busy about being the strong and focused leader Doyen and then the upstanding philanthropist son of the medical mastermind Destry Nevrille. His leadership role was incapable of allowing him such a "ridiculous" liberty; let alone he wasn't very much interested in finding someone anyway.

Looking back, there was a void even after he became a Christian. While it wasn't a void that "had" to be filled — marriage wasn't a promised guarantee from God — he saw how this relationship opened his eyes further to seeing the truth. He wasn't seeing things from his perspective alone anymore… he was also getting to see them through the Godly eyes Callimay had. And the more he thought, the more it amazed him; how she was the only female he'd met to ever make his heart race. The only one to make him forget what his focus was. Time and time again she made him doubt the way he knew to do things as being the only way. She was the one: the jewel his father knew deep down he needed and wanted him to find.

"Are you going to finish? I'm not wanting to be like Rocher and ruin a good thing but…"

"You're alright. I forgive you." Destan smiled as he gave her a kiss on the forehead. "I was just thinking."

"I know. That's why I waited until I thought you were done."

As he started in again, it quickly struck him how he was glad she wasn't reading this last section. Nightmare was relaying information concerning Mrs. Freigh "while" she was dying. Add to that the barbaric and mortifying things Elder was telling Baleck to do to Callimay? The faculty who came up to them and ordered them to go quietly had no intention of escorting them anywhere… at least not Callimay. They were to kill her the second they had control of her. And all those shots that were fired as they left were meant for her.

The last comments cemented what they feared about Justice Wan.

"I'll make sure we control how they get back that way you can fix what you've so miserably messed up." Elder fumed, practically spitting into the phone.

"We?" Baleck asked confused.

"You think you're the only one in the area I can utilize?" Elder suppressed his laugher. "I haven't been sitting here doing nothing. The vast investment we have there needs a certain level of added protection from 'prying' individuals. So, I've got

ties to more governmental officials in the area — local and federal — than you could ever imagine. ... What are you planning on doing with the rest of them?"

"We've got an instalment to fulfill and I think we've found the remaining members necessary." Baleck sounded cryptic.

"If they don't comply, see to it they don't leave. I don't have the time right now to deal with such rebellion."

"But the Monarch?" Baleck sounded concerned.

"Just see to it the Prince is safe. If his Duchess is removed discreetly yet permanently, I know they will be lenient and more than understanding about a lower instalment number."

"I understand."

"I will see you soon," Elder bid farewell.

"Goodbye, Uncle."

"It was worth it, Destan." Callimay put her hand over his heart, her feeling it beginning to pound.

"We really don't need anything else at this point. This is more than enough to convict him. It's his own confession. ... He's been our Nark all this time."

"Does that mean you're not going to get what your father left you?"

"Absolutely not!" Destan said in a raised tone; then quickly calmed when he saw the look on her face, "He died to get me that. The more evidence the better in the case of trying to convict someone who's been a member since the beginning."

"When are you going to get it?"

"On our way back; day after tomorrow. — Let's see what's in these other files for 'fun', shall we?"

As they went through their files, they were taken back to that day when they originally read through them; it all reminding them of what happened not long ago.

Destan could hear what Callimay was thinking when he scrolled through their medical records, his voice with a stern edge to it, "Calli? I... I need you to—"

"I'm sorry." She pulled away and popped up, clutching her arm as she scurried over to the railing. "I won't—"

"Just..." he groaned as he reached out to her. "I... I know you—Calli I know you heard me this morning. Maybe I am assuming, but I think the way in which this is hard on me isn't what you think it is. Now I'm not brushing you off or saying you don't understand what I meant at all; I just need you to—"

"I think I know, Destan." She glanced over and saw his hand; taking it in hers while not looking back, "I'm sorry it's so hard for you."

"Where's my ray of sunshine?" He asked rather sad as he pushed her hair behind her ear.

She tried to smile as she looked at him out of the corner of her eye, "Don't worry. She's still here."

"We'll make it. I know we will."

"I love you, Destan." She sounded like she was trying not to sniffle while she leaned her head against him, her still as stiff as a board.

"Come on. Let's see what we can get done before dinner. Huh?"

The only thing that was different was the report in Destan's file concerning the discrepancy of his STM counteractant. It contained a conversation between Baleck and Ginger that took place during the time they would have been processed — at least according to the time stamps. Baleck told her to alter the amount so Destan would begin to question things; hopefully throwing him into frenzy mode and killing himself... and hopefully Callimay.

"They're just what you said they are: barbaric mercenaries."

There were also files for each individual who ended up being a cliffhanger. It was baffling, though: why did Baleck keep these hidden. Nothing in them pointed to why they were; it didn't appear anything in them was the least bit suspicious as far as anything Mr. Freigh might even have considered as such. Callimay was completely baffled but hoped the last one would shed some light.

But, it appeared she'd never know. He sounded almost too peppy as he reached for the memory sticks, "Ready for round two?"

"W... why did you—"

"Which one first?"

"I... You won't last." Callimay tried not to laugh when she heard his stomach grumble.

Destan made a face and threw his head back.

$\mathcal{B}$

"Well. ... I can say without the slightest reservation that I have never had that before, Calli. And it was amazing." Destan commented after he pushed his chair away from the table.

"I'm glad. It's cheap to make and keeps really well, so I got really good at making it."

"Didn't you get paid for your work? I mean, for the amount of high-end work you've told me you did you 'must've' been paid."

"Let's put it this way: even though I was one of their best designers — and that's from them, not me — they always said they were putting money into things closer to Quaverly."

"Bullying you to move there?"

"Basically." Callimay shrugged as she set the dishes in the sink. "But Berchshire was my home and I knew I was safe there. — To move to a big city by myself? No, thank, you! — So I stayed and missed every single bonus, perk, and raise. And yet I was still expected to do my work 'and' fix what the others getting paid almost four times as much couldn't begin to do."

"Then why in the world did you stay working for them?" Destan asked confused as he walked up next to her and got a drying towel.

"Because I knew everyone there and they knew to leave me be. And my boss did respect my talent; as did most of my coworkers. So the stress and frustration of those higher up — those I never saw — wasn't enough to push me over the edge. It paid enough for me to cover what needed to be paid every month, so that's all I needed. I'd save up for special things, but that was rare and made me feel bad because I was spending money on things for myself."

She heard him sigh heavily and saw how he slumped over, her stopping and turning to him, "Destan. I'm fine. I had a good and stable life that worked for me. You had a life that suited your needs and wants. I'm not trying to get pity from you or put you down. Okay?"

He nodded, so she turned her attention back to the dishes, sounding curious as she thought, "I wonder what's happening back there now? I wonder how the gang is doing?"

"Gang?"

"That's what we called ourselves. There were only five of us at that office. I admittedly didn't do much at all as far as social outings went. They always wanted to go to places I wasn't about to step foot in. And… I just wasn't much for the whole social thing as a whole. I was the only single and unattached person, and so — for me — that made going out with them even more awkward and uncomfortable. Come to think of it, I guess 'they' were the gang, not we. But that's all the past. I'm sure they found someone to replace me. And it wouldn't matter if they did or didn't miss me. I just wonder what would happen if I walked back in; just to see the looks on their faces. And to have you with me? … Oh that would be something, wouldn't it?"

"It was hard for you at first, wasn't it?" Destan asked rather quiet as he took the first dish; his towel-covered, injured hand making a slow circle around the plate.

"Huh?"

"Being at the mansion. Everything so grand and ornate."

"Oh! … I'll admit I was star-struck at first," she recalled as she perked up. "Worried so many times that I'd break something or touch something I wasn't supposed to. But that was at first. Things started—"

"I'm sorry, Calli. I… I know I just about abandoned you when we got there. I—"

"You hadn't been there in a while and that place holds memories. While it would've been very nice to know things like that up front, we made it through… right?"

"We did." Destan sounded a bit better as he looked at her shining smile. "We sure did."

❧

She flipped the faucet off and whirled around, trying her absolute best to be positive. Sure, going through all of this so fast was draining, but she knew they had to so she buckled down and kept pushing ahead. Time was running out and Destan was in desperate need of "one good day". Yes, there were some shocks, but she also knew deep down what was going to be found wasn't surprising.

Looking over to the man she cared so much for — the tired look in his eyes — she did her best to remind him, "We've got one more day,

Destan. One 'good' day to just relax and enjoy us. We don't even have to talk about anything from today. Okay? It'll just be the two of us."

"And the Big Fella," he rolled his eyes, the belvedere prancing up and poking his nose under their clasped hands.

"Come on, Buddy," Callimay said cheerful, perking the creature's attention. "How about you go outside for a while? It's snowing again. Maybe the moon will pop out for a bit, even!"

The belvedere barked and bounced around her as she walked to the door. He stared at it and wagged his tail, waiting as patient as possible for it to open. After a few moments he began to whine and whimper, sitting down and staring at Callimay.

"Oh you poor thing." She laughed as she reached over and flattened his ears. "Why are you so sad, Buddy?"

He whimpered and curled his head into her chest.

"Aw. Don't cry."

"Would you just let him out!" Destan's face pruned.

"Okay!" She jumped up from seeing him: arms folded across his chest, eyebrow raised, and foot tapping the floor. "Now stay out for a few hours, okay?"

"I've gotta compete for my wife's attention… with a belvedere."

"Oh, stop it." She scolded as she jumped up and clasped her arms around his neck. "You know there's no competition there."

"My poor Calli." Destan smiled as he put his arm around her so she wasn't having to depend on her arm strength alone to hold on.

"I always thought having a husband taller than me would be nice… but there 'are' moments I wish I was just a tad taller or you were 'this' much shorter. But don't get me wrong! Those are just moments. I'm glad to have someone who's tall… and strong. Someone who isn't afraid to protect me from anything or anyone."

"You're nervous, aren't you?" Destan prodded as he set her down.

"H… how could you tell?"

"You tend to ramble when you're nervous or worried." Destan smiled as he pushed her hair behind her ear.

"Oh."

He ushered her to the sofa, then finished when he saw her biting her lip: *I'm fine, Calli. Really.*

She nodded, but didn't move. Something else was beginning to occupy her mind; her fiddling with the memory sticks for a while before sighing, "I saw that she numbered them. So I guess that means she wants us to look at this one first."

Destan squeezed her hand after he took it, smiling in such a way to give her courage.

As with Destry's, the computer screen went black and asked for voice authorization. Destan replied, but was in utter shock when it denied access, "Invalid. Voice not recognized. Please give your name."

What? These are all programed to be updated each time a new Shadow is added; and allow admin privileges for every Veil.

Maybe she deactivated it so that the Syndicate wouldn't have a list of everyone if they found it

Destan shook his head slowly, the computer repeating the prompt.

Callimay wrung her shirt hem as the computer asked a third, fourth, fifth… and sixth time; blurting out, "Chameleon!"

The computer chimed and responded, "Voice recognized. Content unlocked, Callimay."

"Callim— but how did it—"

"I don't—" Destan began, but was cut off by Canary's voice.

"I know you may not remember this, but…" a nervous, middle aged woman tried her best to smile; her eyes already glassy. "Yes sirum yem k'ez my Rose Petal. … Umm. Well. I hope— I said I love you in my native tongue: Armenian. You loved to listen to me talk like that since you had such a difficult time with your lisp. I guess it made you feel better knowing grownups talked that way too. And then it gave us a very special way to communicate with each other that no one but your father and brothers understood. That was probably why you loved it so much. Well, that and you loved correcting your father for a change. His Scottish heritage was never going to leave his voice no matter how hard he tried or how much you scolded him. It was hard for him to pronounce some words correctly, but it wasn't his fault. Oh how you would laugh and laugh; listening to him call you his 'wee lassie' and whatnot. … The trisan — apricots — are so wonderful this year. Almost overpowering. You used to love them from bloom to fruit; taking a 'bath' in the rainfall of petals in spring, then pestering your brothers constantly to get in the tree for the biggest one your eyes could find in the mid-summer. Richard was your usual victim since Trever was too young to even reach the lowest fruit of the youngest trees. Not that he wouldn't have done it; Richard would sometimes help him up so he could. — Oh if you only could've truly understood how much he loved you, Callimay. Trever would've done quite literally 'anything' for you. And he actually did, no matter if he got hurt or in trouble… or both. — I remember during the summer you'd come in 'at least' twice every day, crying about you ruining your dress that you loved 'so' much; when all you did was get apricot juice on it. But you swore it was ruined and you'd never be able to wear it again even though I would tell you time and time again it just needed a good washing like your hands and face. And if you dared get your hair in the sweet, sticky juice? Oh my. You did test me in ways I never imagined."

Hearing her joyful yet broken voice recall such touching memories tore Callimay's heart in two because she had no idea what she was talking about… and she should! How could she forget such sweet moments of her early life?

"I guess I shouldn't talk about you or Trever in pass tense." She bit her lip as she rubbed her face with trembling hands. "It's just hard. Hard to remember. And hard because I 'don't' know for sure you're alive. And I don't know if I'll ever get your brother back. … Being alone like this does things to you, to your mind. It makes you numb to the feeling of what happiness is. I'm so jittery with excitement to keep myself positive about doing this; but then again, is this even going to do any good?"

This long pause gave Destan a jolt: Callimay was acting just like her mother. They both showed their nervous nature in the same way. And he now knew what she was going through when it was his father on the screen; he wanted to tell her she needed a break. But he knew how this was going to end: this video was going to corrupt itself when it was done; there was no way to pause it or stop what was coming. He had to let her be tortured because, in the end, she needed this. She needed this closure from the one and only person who could give it to her.

"I just got word that a very close colleague of mine — and a friend of yours though you won't remember him — was just murdered. That's why I'm doing this. I know who murdered him and know I'm his next target. The Monarch of the Syndicate just told me earlier today their Nark in the Shadows confirmed his death with photographic proof." Canary described, trying her best not to cry but beginning to fall apart. "I… I hadn't had to see that type of barbaric treatment of a human being since I went home almost ten years ago when I found my love and babies slaughtered like animals. — How could one human turn on another like that! And children! They did 'nothing' to deserve what torture and death was dealt to them. … Elder has no soul, no ounce of humanity left in him. I'm convinced of this. Killing him would be an honor and something that would rid this world of an evil that truly knows no bounds. … I… I'm sorry, Rose Petal. I guess I was— it's still hard to think about all of that and know who did it but not be able to touch him. And now to know he's murdered the only other person I fully trusted? And in a very similar way to that of my love? — Promise me if you 'ever' come across a tall, older man who calls himself Elder, or he goes by the name of General Willgun or Harmon Willgun: run! Rose Petal, run and never look back. He's feverishly looking for you. And with a fever of bloodlust. I know he'll kill you if he finds you. — Partially because you're Chameleon but also to make me further pay for my rebellion against him. — Do 'not' give him that chance! Change your name if need be. Please, aghjik yerekha (baby girl). I wouldn't be able to live with myself if what happened to your brothers and father happened to you. It's hard enough as it is."

Destan was expecting to find Callimay in a puddle of tears, but her eyes weren't about to allow anything to obstruct their view of the woman they knew and loved at one time. They were hoping by looking at her every second possible it would cause every memory to flood back like they wanted.

"I… should explain things first. I'm getting ahead of myself." She stifled a sob as she sat up and closed her eyes; looking up before continuing, "Dalvin was approached a couple years before you were born about making an alliance with the Shadows: a secret network of people throughout the world who were working to overturn the International Law and try to prevent a second Eradication which was secretly beginning to gain momentum. Dal— you may not even know who I'm talking about, Rose Petal. Dalvin was your father: your 'Paba' as you called him. … He wasn't interested and said he had stepped aside from his political duties to be with his family. — My Dalvin wasn't in line to where it was feasible for him to have the throne, so he didn't see how he could help with what they were asking for. — I do admit I went behind his back and said I would help in small ways since I had contacts of my own from traveling the world so much. I met with Mrs. Vienna Jackman of Ferdinan along with who was at the time, the lieutenant at arms of Faberton Governmental research: General Harmon Willgun. They discussed what areas they needed help with and I offered what I saw as possible since I had a family to care for. And with the civil war raging there was no way for me to just pack everyone up and move to Ferdinan. … I… I knew all along I should have said something to Dalvin about it. It was wrong of me to go behind his back. And because of that all— I'm sorry im ser! (my love) Astvats nerir indz! (God forgive me)"

Callimay reached out and touched the screen, as if trying to comfort the woman who was crying out in anguish and couldn't go on. The burden of memories Canary carried was a weight she understood all too well. And the loneliness she spoke of was also a familiar "friend".

Canary left for a while, the video still running, and then came back. She managed some form of a broken smile as she continued in fits and spurts because of her lingering sniffles and sobs, "I'll never forget the day I found out you were my little dzakhlik: my little lefty. Trever ran down and practically shouted that it wasn't his fault, that he didn't break you. Even though I couldn't hear you crying I ran up to your room and found you sitting on the floor, drawing on some paper. After my moment's heart attack subsided I scolded Trever for scaring me like that. He sounded so confused and yet adamant that you were broken; pointing to your hand as he told me your right hand must be broken because it didn't work right. … Left-handed individuals ran rampant through my side of the family so I wasn't that shocked to find out you were. — In all honesty, all but Richard and Alex were when they first started out. They were easy to 'retrain'; Trever technically able to use both very well for a short time. — So I sat him down and explained he couldn't tell a soul about you being 'broken' and that he needed to help you learn to 'fix' your right hand. He got so serious as I explained what I could and vowed he would protect you from the ch'ar mardik, evil people, no matter what it took. Dalvin wasn't a bit thrown when I told him; his focus came like it always had: not to make it a big deal so there wasn't any comment made about it accidentally. … But, after a couple weeks of us working and there being no change you looked at your father whom you had wrapped around your finger and framed his frustrated face as you told him — and I'll never forget this — 'Paba? If you really want me, I change. I sorry it take me so long to be good. I no mean to make you mad.' We died: how could we demand you change; treat you as if you were doing something wrong — something that was a sin and evil — and punish you? We were being who we hated! That was one of the very few times I'd seen your father cry, Rose Petal. He held you for a couple hours after we apologized and… just cried."

Destan glanced over and saw Callimay spread her right hand out and glance at it and then her left. A shiver ran through her as she thought back to Mrs. Berchoff and what she spent so long training her to do: use her right hand.

And it actually struck both of them how their parents reacted the same in the end. They loved their child and the freedom that they knew they were born with more than the fear of any governmental authority.

But it wasn't wrong, either way, really. Different people chose to fight the same battle different ways. And Mrs. Berchoff never forbade her to use her left hand "ever". It was only when she was in public. That battle wasn't one she saw as worth fighting because there was a very simple way around it. And somehow, by the time Callimay came to live with her, she was able to pick up the ability to use her right hand with ease. But, she could understand — and personally was on the side of — how the premise of allowing ungodly individuals to that have physical power to control how you act was a dangerous and slippery slope to travel down.

"Dalvin immediately reached out to Mrs. Jackman and asked for assistance. I knew about Destry Nevrille and his work in biochemistry — his family and mine being on good terms for quite some time; us college classmates and friends — and asked if he could be contacted and brought on. The General jumped on board right away but Mrs.

Jackman seemed leery. This divide should have made me stop and question everything. Caution in this situation was wise." She shook her head as she leaned against the armrest. "But… I found out quickly Destry's son was left-handed as well and that he was looking for help when he was contacted. Being the helper he always was, he, without hesitation, offered his assistance; glad to be able to meet with a long-time friend and catch up on life to help calm his nerves and give his boy some safe interaction with other children. And another lefty at that. — Destry brought his wife and son with him to meet us and you were 'beyond' thrilled to have someone your age to play with… even though it was yet another boy. Destan gravitated to the boys, and yet he always ended up with you."

By the fact she broke a smile hinted to her emotions calming and her being able to process those memories in a better light.

"Destry and Lylah sat with us and then with you and Destan for hours during that week-long visit. I told him I wanted you to be able to hold onto being left-handed but be able to appear to everyone else as being right-handed. I knew I was asking for something impossible but I also knew the talent Destry had. If anyone could find a way it would be him." Her optimistic tone held, but nervous laughter hinted to this only being a temporary and shallow victory. "It was always at the same time each day when they came, which you realized on the third day because it was when your favorite flowers would be in full bloom. So you sat as you always did in the front bay window, waiting for your little friends to say hello, and then immediately expected the gate to open. I know poor Destan wasn't used to all of the love and affection since he was an only child, but you didn't care and would just about smother the poor boy the second he walked in the door. … He loved playing with you, though. Trever almost got jealous of you hanging off of Destan and not him. But since he knew he'd be leaving in a couple days he allowed this short-lived 'fling' to run its course."

Destan felt Callimay slip her arms around him to which he put his arm around her and leaned his head over on top of hers.

"But, by the second to last day, Destry still had no idea how to help. I was devastated. And I knew it was hard on him to give me the news. But I also understood he didn't want to try just anything and end up hurting you in the process. How could I be upset at him? … And then it happened. You and Trever had been out in the rose garden that morning — him doing everything he could to keep you distracted so you 'might' forget about your little friend coming to vi—" she froze and gasped as she whipped her head up; another voice audible but not clear. "Zarouhi? … You couldn't begin to understand w— why must you torture me, too?"

A cruel and shrill tone Destan recognized became clear enough to understand, "Reliving the past does nothing, sister. It only reminds you of what bad there was in life."

"Your false concern isn't—"

"You are my blood and I have promised to love and provide for you now that you have come home." This woman's judgmental tone somehow found a way to appear caring. "I'm only asking you as your sister to stop hurting yourself."

The woman wasn't in the camera range, but even so, Destan knew good and well who she was. But why did Canary refer to her by a different name? What was meant by "blood"? Was this evil woman Destan knew to be the unwanted visitor a true relative of hers? A biological sister that would make her Callimay's aunt? Or was this like the Strigidae Sisterhood?

"I— please let me have time to get this out. I'll feel so much better if I do." Canary wrung her hands as she tried not to cry.

"Oh, Lanta." The woman sighed as she came into the camera view and embraced her for a while before finishing, "Alright. Just… just let me know if you need me. Okay?"

"I need to be 'alone', Zarouhi. All I want to hear is my echoing voice and know that only the walls are what hear me. … Please."

"I'll see to it no one disturbs you." She patted her cheek and hugged her one last time. "I'll tap the call button when we're gone. Alright?"

"Okay," Canary took a shaky breath as she closed her eyes. "By the way, how did you get in?"

"Oh. Nebon saw me drive up and just let me in."

"Why did you come?" Canary asked nervous.

Zarouhi sounded sad as she confessed, "I know you knew the Veil that was taken down, personally. And as much as I know you agree he had to be executed, there is that underlying pain of losing someone you cared for. I guess I just didn't expect to hear you recalling—"

"How much did you hear?"

"Hangist, k'uyriks, (Calm, my sister)" she put her hand over her mouth in an effort to calm her. "I only heard you speaking of Callimay and Trever in the garden. … Yes khostanum yem. (I promise)"

Canary hung her head as her shoulders dropped, her nodding her sister on, "I'll be done in an hour or so. I know you want me there for the dinner—"

"I will explain your absence with what will appease the others, do not worry." Zarouhi lifted her chin and took her hands. "Yes sirum yem k'ez, (I love you) Lanta. You are home."

"Yes nuynpes sirum yem k'ez. (I love you too)"

Canary collapsed onto the chair, her breathing so heavy as she trembled and mouthed something for a few minutes, her clutching her chest the whole time.

A faint chime was heard, her rushing out of view for a minute before she came back; flustered and trying to catch her breath, "Is this still on? … Oh good. Now where was I? … Oh. The garden. You ran in right on time to go watch your flowers and kept talking about how you had something you just 'had' to show Destan when he got there. I couldn't make sense of it, but your informing me turned into begging when you saw what time it was. Flustered and still reeling from what news Destry gave me, I let you wait outside on the front step. You were a bundle of excitement when they pulled up, but stayed on the porch like I told you to; though you stretched your arm out as far as you possibly could while holding on to one of the pillars. — Destan was just as confused as I was since you were talking so fast, but eagerly followed you to your room to play. — I truly believe you just had the innate ability to captivate boys. I don't know if it was your beautiful eyes, sweet smile, or bubbly and joyful personality… but maybe it was all of them combined in the unique way that made you, you."

There was another pause as Canary picked up a picture and stared at it for a while.

"Right before Destry was about to leave we came back to try our best to pry you two apart without you having a meltdown. You two were preoccupied as I opened the door. Destan kept asking you, 'where you put it' and you kept giggling and squealing as you watched him run around the room." She broke another faint smile as she continued to stare at the picture; wiping her face as she continued, "When you two saw us you both stopped dead in your tracks and stared at us as if admitting your guilt. Destry asked you what you hid, so you went up to Destan and took what looked to be part of his shirt off his shoulder. You laid it in Destry's hand and did your best to explain how you found it out in the garden that morning. … I can't tell you how terrified I was when he looked back at me in utter shock. He laid the little creature on your shoulder and it changed a bright orange color to go with your dress. You giggled and gave it to Destan so he could hide it; the two of you ignoring we were there. — Destry gestured for me to follow him and we went downstairs. He gave me hope he could find something based off of a similar serum he'd been working on. I was so excited, but he warned me you were far too young to be given it. I told him to get working and we'd see about the age dilemma later."

Destan could almost hear what his father would've told her about this all; him even finding enough of good in it all to chuckle to himself about him trying to find what Callimay hid "on" him.

"Destry told Destan it was time for them to go, but you begged and pleaded with him for two more minutes. He wasn't like your father, though, and it upset you so much that he wouldn't cave." She shook her head as she fingered the picture. "I appeased you by saying you could get a picture with Destan so you could keep it to remember him until you saw each other again. Trever was excited to know his competition would soon be gone, so he volunteered to take the picture. He complained about you holding Destan's hand and standing so close, but you weren't having any of it. — Destan was doing so well until Trever counted one and you whipped around and kissed him on the mouth. You were so full of joy and he was so disgusted, the poor thing. And yet his reaction didn't detour you one bit. Not even when he said he wasn't going to take a picture with you. It's like you knew you'd get that picture one way or another. — And let us not forget about your poor brother. He ran off, so angry, leaving me to take the picture. Destry stepped in and sat with Destan so he'd stand still long enough to get a picture and we all laughed so hard when we saw what it turned out like. You got exactly what you wanted."

She turned the picture that both Destan and Callimay had to the camera, her face so full of joy.

"It hardly took Destry any time at all to get what he called, 'Project Chameleon' ready. He told me the absolute earliest he'd ever think of giving it to you was when you turned five. With the way the civil war was going I knew we needed to act soon. I assured him I understood the risks involved after he warned me time and time again: even saying he wouldn't give it to Destan that early. I had every ounce of faith in his abilities and knew if something did come up he wouldn't let you be in harm's way and would be able to get you out safely." Her tone began to evolve into anger and disgust as she set the picture down. "Elder somehow or another found out about this all and demanded Destry stop. He assured me everything was ready and so it would appear to Elder he had. During this all, Destry moved his family back to Faberton right before you turned five since he was assigned there. He saw it as a perfect way to hide our efforts to get you treated. … And then the most unexpected thing happened."

Canary hung her head as she looked at her rings, her still sounding angry even though she was becoming more and more depressed, "A 'need' arose for Deep Dark — a close-knit group of people within the Shadows — that I was told only 'I' could do. So, I got ready to leave on your birthday. Dalvin was furious with me when he caught me right before we left. … I… the last words I heard my love tell me were ones of utter betrayal and complete disgust with what I'd done. I'd never heard one coarse word cross his lips; and yet he cursed me in his 'and' my tongues. … He was so angry that he stormed off before I could even try to tell him I loved him. … And I didn't… I didn't get that chance when I got back. — Don't follow in my footsteps, Rose Petal. Don't join the Shadows. Don't see them as the only way to protect yourself and your family. Don't push everyone else aside and justify the secrets you'd be bound by. Don't do what I did. Don't find yourself in a situation where you can't ever take back what you did and didn't do; what you did and didn't say… where you're left alone and burning with regret. … I… just a moment. I'm sorry I keep doing this."

She left again for a while and then continued in a more drawn and emotionless tone, "I drove you to the medical center Destry gave me directions to and got you all ready before I had to leave. You thought we were playing dress-up and were thrilled with the whole idea for your birthday. You wanted to wear black so we could match, but you soon forgot about all that when you saw the special birthday girl orange hat you got to wear. — Destry was such a wonderful man to think of it. He then told me Lylah made it to try and help keep her as calm as possible. — You loved it, but soon couldn't be consoled when you asked and Destry told you Destan wouldn't be there. You couldn't understand why he didn't want to see you on your birthday since you promised you would see him on his. Destry kept apologizing, but I'd had eight other children go through this phase; and even though you were a girl I knew you just needed something else to distract you. And that's where Mr. Ruff came in."

Just then, her belvedere popped his head up and looked at her and then around the area as he barked.

"Not you. I wasn't… get down." Canary sighed as she pushed the creature back, but petted him for a bit. "You loved him so much; going on and on about his orange collar. I told you he'd keep you safe until I got back home to which you thought he was the most special dog in the world and that he must be real and very powerful even though he was so tiny. — Destry followed and asked me what in the world I was doing veiled when I was leaving. I explained what happened and that he'd need to take you home afterward. He was mad at me too, but never said anything after I told him what Dalvin said. He promised he'd look after you and make sure you got home safe; asking me one last time if I wanted to do this. I said I didn't want you living in constant fear and wasn't about to force you to live in seclusion of Safe Haven. I wanted you to live freely and have whatever life you wanted."

And so she summed up in a beautiful and personal way what Vienna Jackman wanted all along: freedom. Freedom to choose for oneself what they did with their life.

"Destry let me know not too much later you were doing well and the serum was taking hold and already showing signs of working. Your memories of Destan and him had been successfully removed without any damage done to the rest of your memories. — And how he did that is still a mystery to me. — I was sad you forgot all of the joyful times with Destan, but also understood why it needed to be done." Canary glanced at the picture and smiled for a brief moment. "The only thing was Destry told me was that you had migraines. He miscalculated one portion of something and unfortunately you'd have them for the rest of your life… or until he could find a way to alter that portion of the serum without nullifying its purpose. It wasn't the fix I was hoping for, but I was willing to bear the responsibility for that; even though I wasn't sure how I would handle seeing you in pain so often."

She leaned closer to the camera, looking worried and doubtful as she continued, "I know this all has got to be so much. I know so little probably makes sense to you. I really don't know where to start to explain since I won't know what you need from me; answers, that is. … If you've looked at the photographs already you've seen the one of the two of us and Mr. Ruff with the inscription. Chameleon is the name of the serum that runs through your veins, Callimay. It's what allows you to adapt and adjust to your surroundings with ease. Maybe you've never noticed; don't feel bad if you haven't. It was never meant to be something so powerful to make you superior; just give you security and comfort in these delicate times. — It's because of this ability to blend in that Elder sees you as a threat. Destry told me not too long ago how Elder saw you as a compromise to the Shadows' and Veil's mission. That you were living proof all that was needed was to give some drug to children so that the evil of the International Law could remain and not be dealt with. I know for a fact Destry told him it was only meant as a temporary fix to help until the International Law was overturned; that he had no intention on putting it on the black market for worldwide usage. And while Elder said that and I agree with where he was coming from, that's not the way he works. He's hiding his true reason. Why? I just don't know. Maybe his only motivation is because you are living proof he can't control everyone: you're a symbol of Destry and my rebellion. He lives to control others, and he can only keep it if there is chaos and disorder. What we did is working toward fixing that. But I know he doesn't want this Armageddon between the Syndicate and Shadows ending. It sounds impossible that he would enjoy seeing more and more innocent people lose their lives, but his morals are corrupted to the core."

Hearing her talk more and more about Elder made Destan more and more flustered; though he never showed it. And it made him remember what she begged him to do before they parted: her dying request of ending Elder's life. The thought of going after someone for that intent was foreign to Destan in every way.

"With me not having any reason to question your safety, when I was on my way home I rode on to Berchshire and stopped by Destry's to see him and the family. What I came upon was only the first in a life-altering series of events. The house was fully engulfed; but when I caught a glimpse of someone inside I fought my way in. Destry had wrapped himself and his wife, as best he could, in a thick rug. He was injured and in a daze so I had to carry them to safety one at a time. — That was the first time I'd ever carried someone who was dead… but it sadly wasn't the last." She looked away as she clasped her arms across her chest. "A nearby neighbor finally saw the flames and came, then and went for help; a horrifying thought in the back of my mind growing larger and larger: I had to get home. Destry wasn't taking no for an answer — him having the same thought — and accompanied me back. … He… he didn't leave me until a security detail arrived and he even did all the talking with those who came for the bodies. That was long after I'd finally stopped screaming and crying, but he said he wasn't going to leave me alone to take care of what he was willing to do. He said he had time to accept the death of his wife so he was okay."

The couple watching and listening with bated breath found it harder and harder to keep their emotions in check. They'd heard Destry's account of what happened… and now had to relive it from a different perspective.

"I blamed him at first for everything." She started weeping as she hung her head. "And yet he would have died if I hadn't stopped when I did. But then again, I might have been able to save my family if I had gone straight home. I… I know I said hurtful and mean things to him because of my pain. I know I told him he had no idea the pain I was in because his child was still alive. … But it wasn't an anger I could hold onto. I knew deep down he went through the same thing I did; and he actually saw his wife die. He was completely helpless and couldn't save her. I still don't know how he fought back and didn't spout off he had every right to tell me. He was a real man. I hope Destan knows that."

That last comment brought Destan low. Really low. He'd been in similar situations with Callimay and how did he react? The only ones he remembered where when he was a total jerk who only cared about himself and his feelings that he never wanted to express anyway.

"We searched through the rubble and he helped me gather what little was left that I could keep to remember them all by." She reached over and took a stack of charred papers in her hands, her voice quivering and cracking. "Destry helped me cover each body after he would, with such patience and care, pry me away; encouraging me the entire time to do what I could to identify each one so they could receive the honor they deserved. … Afterward, Destry was so happy when he rushed over. I was in no mood for anything light-hearted, but he was persistent and kept telling me to count how many bodies there were. I kept belittling him for forcing me to look at them again, but then something hit me. There were eight, not ten. And what identifying I'd been able to do made me realize you and Trever were missing. I wanted so badly to believe you two were still alive, but my sorrow was eating my heart up. He kept explaining it to me, him searching the same rubble piles again and again, and before too much longer it began to make sense. If any of your brothers would've been the one to get you away to safety it would've been Trever."

There was this tiny glimmer in her eye that had fought to stay there from the beginning: hope. Hope that her daughter was alive. It was beginning to glow now; radiating what her heart felt for so long.

"Now don't think your other brothers hated you, Callimay. They all loved you. Most of them were at the age where they were comfortable with our family style and just didn't know how to function around you since you were a girl. They didn't understand why you'd cry all of the time; and were so confused when I explained girls don't just cry when they're sad or hurt. They didn't understand why you couldn't play with them the way they wanted. And they especially couldn't understand why you were so enthralled by things that sparkled and shined. But Trever? Trever loved his Everlyn so much." She took a picture and held it close to her heart. "I say that because he didn't call you by your first name since he was the one who picked your middle name: Everlyn. — When we found out you were going to be a girl, Dalvin and I let every boy pick out a name and write it on a slip of paper. We promised whichever name got picked would be your middle name. They took their time and dedicated themselves to this competition; but before the month was out the jar was sealed. The day you were born — as soon as I was able to do it after forty-three hours of hard labor — all the boys came in and sat around the little jar that had been sealed for almost three months. Richard and Alex I expected to not be as anxious about it; but even they wanted their choices to be picked. … I picked Trever's. He was so thrilled and thought he got to keep you forever. He held you just about as much as Dalvin or myself did that first week. And he would be the first one to snatch you away if I didn't keep my eye on you. I was actually frantic one day because you were nowhere in your room: the crib side down and your window opened. But then the most precious of sounds calmed me: your cooing. I followed your voice and found you up in your brother's bunk bed; him nestled right beside you as he read you his favorite book. I couldn't be 'too' mad at him; though carrying you up into his bunk was strictly off limits."

Canary's resolve to bounce back was another quality Destan had learned was part of who Callimay was, fundamentally. It was such an eye-opening experience to see how such a short time with someone — and at such a young age — could have such a lasting impact.

The topic drastically shifted as Canary glanced at her phone, "I finally found Trever not too long ago; after so many years of tireless search. I admit I didn't find him where I expected to, or with someone I trusted… but he 'is' alive. It took me no time to understand why it took me so long to find him: Elder somehow found him, admitting to me he knew he was my Trever the entire time he raised him. … He would gloat, telling me Trever didn't remember who he was; and I can't help but think it's because Elder's done something to him from what he pried out of Destry the one time. I've tried everything I know to get to Trever — known by the title of Emissary in the Shadows — but Elder's thwarted every effort. I'm trying to hang onto the hope that since he made it you did too. I've got to. I just pray you're somewhere safe."

Whatever was on her phone caused Canary to quicken her pace more and more; much like what happened to Destry at one point in his video. — Was this Elder prodding and teasing because he knew what was going on?

"I hope I'm able to explain this all to you in-person. I pray I can destroy this and hold you in my arms again. I hope Elder will see fit to leave me be where I am and not come after me — just let me whither slowly from the agony of loss and uncertainty of the future. But more importantly, I pray he doesn't find you. I love you so much, Callimay. Your mummy's still looking for you." She reached up to the camera and took hold of the side of it; pleading, "I just want to see your face one last time. To know for sure you're alive. To see the beautiful and strong young woman I know you are becoming."

The memory of the first time Canary saw her finally sunk in. She fell because what she'd been wanting, pleading, begging, hoping, praying, and longing for finally happened: she saw her baby girl and got to hold her in her arms. She saw she was safe and happy.

"If The good Lord doesn't have that in His plan, you need to find Destry's son, Rose Petal. Find your Destan. I know you don't remember him, but please trust me; trust that picture of the two of you. Destry said he won't remember you either, but he's made it so he'll have the same photograph to prove you're not making up some hysterical story." She showed the picture again. "He lives in Kerogen. Go to Rayleen and inquire for him at the University there. It won't be hard to find him because he's a social leader in that country: Destan Nevrille. 'Please' get to him! He'll be able to keep you safe from Elder. I'll send the living Mr. Ruff if I don't make it and can find you in time so you have something to protect you. If you get my belvedere before you find Destan, just tell him that he's my belvedere and he's safe. He'll know what to do."

The fluffy dog popped back up, putting his front paws on her lap after she signaled him. She gestured to the camera so he turned and yapped and howled in a happy tone.

She then shoed him away and warned, "Please don't go looking for your brother. It's too dangerous. I know after what I said you would think you could reach him, but believe me Rose Petal: I've tried. Every picture I sent him, every conversation I had with him… your brother's gone. His mind and soul have gone on. Elder's little underling is all that exists now in his body. … As you saw, quite by accident, you 'do' have an aunt who is alive. All the rest of your family on my side has passed on — adopted 'and' biological. … Don't consider Zarouhi your family. Please. I… I can't say any more than that; I don't dare right now. So the only extended family you have left is your father's side. Sadly, I don't know if they'll want you. Things were far beyond strained when Dalvin made up his mind to marry me since I wasn't royalty. Your grandfather might welcome you, but he may not be alive by the time you get this. — I'm sorry you're alone! I'm sorry, my Rose Petal. Please forgive me."

Canary glanced around her and scooted closer, "The only one you're allowed to tell about any of this is Destan. He'll understand. He'll protect you. I promise you he will. He won't abandon you like I did. … I'm sorry. I wish I had more time, but I have to go. Remember your mummy loves you with all of her heart. All of your family did. Don't be afraid to live your life. Stay safe. I love you."

"No!" Callimay screamed as the screen faded to black, the same thing happening as with Destry's. "No, please! Come back! Please! Mama, no!"

"I'm sorry," Destan sobbed as he pulled her to his chest and rocked her. "I'm so sorry you're going through this."

"I'm not ready to let her go. I'm not! I can't!" She cried as she gripped his sweater while she pushed against and then yanked on him. "I just got her back. She was alive! I found her! I just—"

All of a sudden the screen came back on; some dark, newscast intro music building. — A tone both of them knew all too well.

"Let this be a lesson to all those sympathizing with Derelicts: the International Law is not merciful and the Syndicate will 'not' tolerate any person who violates it — no matter their station. This 'will' be their end." A man's booming voice called out. "You thieves grovel at night where no one can see you, hiding those who are tearing our world's peace apart. But everyone sees you for the darkness and trickery you are even though we are tireless in keeping your full existence and dangerous influence at bay; to protect our free and industrious world. You cannot bear the light the Syndicate shines because of your inability to embrace peace and order… like this woman here."

They were startled and looked over to the screen which showed the sitting room where they met Canary. There was a group of men and one other woman; them wearing white versions of similar ensembles to what those within the Shadows and Veil wore.

And yet there was a difference; a glaring one at that. Each person wore a mask that covered their eyes and nose; some masks extended down one or both sides of their faces or up past their hairline. While they initially reminded Callimay of the masquerade week costumes, there was no "life" in them — no personality. They were nothing more than a façade to distance that person from what they were doing.

In front of this group was a lonely person on their knees with their head bowed… a woman in all black.

"This woman— 'spy', thought she could fool us; lying about her intentions to infiltrate our ranks and make us collapse from within." The man closest to her spat at her before he reached down and yanked the woman's hair, revealing her severely beaten face.

Callimay gasped while Destan sat there in shock.

"By the power given to me by the International Law and the country of Crosswall; I, Olderon Philpod, do sentence you, one Lanta Presley, to the only suitable sentence for such treachery: death." Toreon's father condemned as he raised a gun and handed it to another woman who came on screen. "While such a stage for vocal sedition is tolerated, I feel this dying request to not be worthy of you. But the law is the law: do you have any parting words before sentence is carried out?"

"You may think you are able to play God, saying who has the right to live and who does not just because they use one hand more than the other; but your stolen power will 'not' shake those who know the one and only God. They know what you do is evil and will never give in to the treasonous and inhumane reality that the International Law is. — The shame of what you do to your own flesh and blood will haunt you for the rest of your life, Zarouhi. T'vogh im aryuny havityan lini k'vo glkhin, k'uyr. (May my blood be forever on your head, sister.)" Lanta glared at Vashti as she spat in her face.

She lowered the gun and wiped her cheek, snickering a bit as she stared at her hand. And then raised it again as she said, "Haght'ets'i, sireli k'uyr. (I won, dear sister.)"

"Calli, don't watch this!" Destan came to his senses, him trying to pull her back to him as fast as possible.

"Yes sirum yem k'ez (I love you) my Rose Petal. Yes sirum yem k'ez (I love you), Trever. Mummy loves you both so much. — God please let me see my love again. Please let him be waiting for me." Canary's voice buckled as she closed her eyes and bowed her head, her continuing to mumble as she wept.

Callimay's blood-curdling scream made the walls shutter; her seeing her mother collapse to the floor from a single shot to the head. "Mama, no! Mama, please. No!"

Destan finally got her in his firm grasp and held her so she couldn't see. Olderon ripped Canary's veil from her lifeless body and had two of men hold it up while his wife who just finished wiping the blood splatter off her sleeve, drew her Sabre and slashed it to shreds.

He knew as did Canary there'd be a public execution, but he was expecting it to have been "much" sooner than this. And he "never" thought the broadcast could be put on his computer like this. But, then again: *You're everything she said you were, Elder… and more. ~ This had to be his plan; he must be making a move… which means you've 'got' to get back as fast as possible.*

But what Callimay just witnessed? She was thrashing about and her arms flailing as if she were blaming him and fighting him because of it. Destan didn't want to hurt her but she'd scratched him a few times already; the way he was holding her he couldn't keep her still to try and calm her. As he tried to reposition his hold she broke free and took off down the stairs; throwing the front door open and bolting out into the night.

Trying to keep a grip on things, it took Destan a moment to get to his feet; him yelling, "Calli! Calli you'll freeze to death out there. Calli!"

Once he was halfway down the stairs he leaped toward the door, grabbing their coats that were hanging right beside it.

It was blizzard conditions that very easily could be considered a whiteout had it been daytime. He yelled as he threw his coat on, his eyes darting every which way. The wind was howling and he couldn't see anything. He tried using his vision modes but couldn't keep his eyes open to even use them; let alone it was pitch black out.

"Calli!" Destan kept yelling as he shielded his eyes to help him see which way her tracks led; them being washed away quicker than he could run. "Calli!"

All of a sudden he felt the belvedere push his nose under his hand. He jerked away but remembered; running back for the cabin and grabbing his computer. As fast as he could he reversed the push command he placed on the belvedere. He ran back down and found the creature standing there, staring at him.

"Well!" Destan said out of breath as he looked at him, waiting for him to take off. "Why aren't you— did I not do it right?"

His fingers flew as he logged back in; him forcing himself to take a moment to think. If he couldn't keep the process he'd done clear in his mind there was not going to be any way for him to reverse it correctly.

"This... I... this... but I... this makes no sense! Why aren't you picking up on Calli's emotional status? She couldn't have calmed down just like that, and there's no way for her to have run over fifty miles in the last minute. —What's wrong with you!" Destan grabbed the belvedere by the collar and shook him. "Why can't you feel her! Do you have to do some hard reboot again? ... Well hurry up! She's got to be feeling 'something'. The only w— oh no."

The belvedere cowered and whined, making him realize why he wasn't responding. He tried to reach out to Callimay but it was as if she were unconscious — not just asleep. Something horrible happened in that short amount of time and Destan now had no way of finding her. In desperation he tried using his vision modes while in the cabin but he couldn't see her anywhere.

"Big Fella..." his fearful, shaky voice begged as he kneeled in front of the dog creature; offering Callimay's coat to him. "I need your help. I need it really bad. ... Find her. Find my Calli. You're all I've got."

After sniffing it, the belvedere twitched his ears and nose, pacing back and forth a bit; and then took off. Destan ran out, soon losing sight of him since the moon wasn't out, "Come back! Big Fella!"

A few moments later he saw him and ran over, taking hold of his collar and gripping it as tight as he dared, "Okay, go!"

The snow depth was making Destan even struggle; the belvedere more-or-less hopping. How in the world did she even make it five feet!

Almost a minute passed and still no sign of her. Destan knew it was pretty much useless, but he kept calling out every few seconds as loud as he could.

Out of nowhere, the belvedere stopped and perked up; him running in a circle as he looked this way and that.

"What's wrong?"

He yapped at him and bolted — Destan didn't keep a good grip on the collar. Within seconds he lost sight of the creature.

"Calli!" He screamed as he stumbled up the belvedere's path.

The path he was following melted before long; him continuing to struggle and fight against the wind that was pelting him in the face.

With the path all but gone now, it was taking every ounce of self-control he had left; each passing moment making him more desperate.

From the darkness came a haunting sound which made Destan stop dead in his tracks. — Oh the memories that were tied to a belvedere's howl. And him giving his wife's scent to one? — He could hear the belvedere just as clear as day as if he were right next to him. His skin was crawling with fear. And then he jumped when he felt his computer vibrating. His hands were still shaking so he almost dropped it as he tried to see what was going on: *What? A… a distress signal? From him?*

With the help of the computer, he was able to triangulate the coordinates and find where he was in relation to the belvedere. So, not wasting another second, Destan jumped. He found the belvedere lying down in what looked to be a hole he'd dug. The creature was happy to see him but wouldn't budge and was still howling.

"I'm here." He gasped for air as he gripped his chest with one hand and threw the other out and caught the belvedere's back as he fell to his knees. "Where is she?"

The creature stood up and carefully stepped to the side, revealing an unconscious Callimay. A rather large area of snow by her face was red; her forehead and nose bleeding. The belvedere whimpered and whined as he nudged her face and hand, trying to get her to move.

In a panic, Destan clawed at the snow to dig her out; him heaving and almost moaning as he worked as fast as he could. He then leaned over, trying to hear her heartbeat or feel her breathing; his shoulders relaxing somewhat. Next he ripped his coat off and wrapped it around her, gathering her in his arms and cradling her head and neck; making sure she was sheltered from the blasting wind.

As he stood, this bone-chilling cold actually caused him to shutter when he felt its full force. Destan knew where he was in relation to the cabin so he closed his eyes and tried to envision how everything looked, "Get back to the cabin, Big Fella."

ℬ

The moment he stepped out of the jump he felt like he was suffocating and stumbled back; glad he was next to the wall so he could fall against it. He didn't dare let his grip on his wife lessen, but the inability for him to breathe like he needed was taxiing him. — If this was how it was going to be with him using his abilities in an emotionally stressful situation where Callimay couldn't help him then it was going to be more of a liability than anything.

But, those thoughts left as quickly as they came. He took a deep breath and gathered himself, dashing up to the bedroom.

"Calli, why did you fight me? Why did you run?" Destan rambled in a grieved tone as he kneeled in front of the fireplace.

As fast as he could, he laid her on the hearth and took off her bulky outer clothes that were packed with snow. He looked around for a bit, trying to focus, the memories from what happened after his first fight with Toreon starting to flood his mind. Destan shook his head and mumbled as he kept working: *She's so ice-cold. I'll go warm up the blankets, but she needs something right now. … But what!*

When he whipped around to look, his sweater caught on her ring. That was all the inspiration he needed; Destan's hands scampered to pull his sweater off and put it on her as fast as he dared — doing everything to keep her neck stable — and then snatched as many blankets as a fist-full could hold before he bolted downstairs.

Still in full-blown panic mode, he threw the blankets in the dryer and stood in the kitchen for a moment… him completely lost. Had it not been for the first-aid kit sitting where it was who knows how long he would've stayed there wracking his brain to figure out what he was looking for. He saw the belvedere looking in the window and let him in on his way back up.

123

Though totally unintentional, he made as much noise as humanly possible as he threw the bathroom door open, threw the kit on the vanity, and grabbed some towels.

The belvedere crept into the room looking scared. He whimpered and whined as he looked at Callimay and then to Destan who had his phone tucked between his chin and his shoulder, breathing hard and eyes darting between what he was doing and his unconscious wife.

Seeing the look on the belvedere's face made him pause for a moment, calming enough to say in a caring tone while nodding, "Go lay with her, Big Fella."

A few moments later, Destan jogged over and started tending to her injuries. The belvedere had snuggled close to her side that was away from the fireplace, watching every movement with concern.

Come on, Lance. Pick up! ... Co— "Lance?"

"What's wrong?" Doctor Gerould's tone immediately changed.

"Are there any medical Shadows or Veils at the Nest right now?"

Muffled background sounds hinted to the fact Doctor Gerould dropped what he was doing to help, "Umm… give me a second."

Destan tried to be patient, but his gut instinct was telling him he had no time to spare.

"There are a couple. What's the problem, Destan?"

"Calli has a pretty big gash on the side of her head. I'm hoping she doesn't have frostbite."

What on earth happened! "Where are you, I'll send Lackey."

"Above in the bedroom."

A couple moments of nail-biting silence passed before Doctor Gerould calmed, "He's actually not 'at' the Nest; about a half hour out."

"That's too long."

"Tell me what's going on, then." Doctor Gerould picked up on the strained, panicked tone of the young man. "Where at on the side of her face is the gash? Do you know how she got it?"

"I don't know. It's just in front of and above her left ear. It's pretty deep, too. I hope it doesn't need stitches. This is the last thing she needs to happen right now, Lance."

Continuing in his calming, professional tone, Doctor Gerould kept on, "Is it still bleeding?"

"N… no?"

"Is it above her hairline?"

"More like in it." Destan bit his lip as he tried to wipe some of the blood away, him jerking back when the belvedere whined.

"What was that?"

Now realizing what a spot he was, he froze.

"Destan? Destan, what's going on? Destan, is Callimay conscious?"

"N… not yet. I can tell she's starting to, though."

"Just keep an eye on her. When she starts to come to don't let her move too much. I'll want Lackey to see about doing a scan of her neck and head to be sure there's no structural damage or internal bleeding."

Just great. Now Destan had to figure out a way to keep the belvedere from being found… without much time to prepare. And when Callimay was— oh this was just too much.

"Now what's this about frostbite?"

"I'm not sure. I just— it's just that she— did you see the broadcast?"

"Canary?"

"Yeah."

"No, but Chicane told me."

"When did it happen?"

"A couple days ago."

Elder!

"Did Callimay find out and run out into the cold or something? I know you two met with her just before she was exposed."

"Basically."

Doctor Gerould took a painful sigh before getting back to what he needed to help with, "What does her skin on her feet and hands look like? Check her ears, nose, and lips as well."

He heard rustling sounds and heavy breathing, then, "All but her feet are really red. Her feet are still pretty pale."

"Just keep an eye on them. If they start to get color within the hour there shouldn't be an issue. I think her biggest issue right now is going to be concussion and spinal protocol. You're very familiar with both." His tone almost sounded a bit judgmental at the end. "Just observe her for the first bit and if she's having trouble be very patient and do what you can to keep her calm. Of course I say all that and with her abilities

I could be so far off. — Just keep an eye on her. You'd know better than anyone if she was acting 'off'. … Destan?"

She finally opened her eyes and looked up at Destan who looked like he was ready to cry, "D… De-stan?"

"There's my Calli." He sighed as he closed his eyes and put his hand over hers that she'd placed on his cheek.

"Why are you cr—" she started to ask as she attempted to sit up, but quickly realized she couldn't.

"Just relax," he hushed as he laid her hand back down, a few more tears racing down his cheek. "What happened?"

"I… I don't know." Callimay answered a bit worried, the belvedere whining and nudging her side so she would move her hand. "I can't remember anything. The last I knew you were holding me after the video ended… and then it's blank."

Destan was shocked. But before he dared say a word he paused: *Her short-term memory must be wiped. ~ If she doesn't say a word about the broadcast don't you 'dare' bring it up. ~ I've stuck my mouth in my foot too many times. She knows her mother is gone so I'm just going to leave it at that.* "Just rest. Everything's alright now. … Oh! — Lance?"

"I heard. I'm glad she's awake. Lackey said he's just about five minutes out and he'll have things ready. He — of course — wasn't on board with having Callimay come down below, but knowing she has a concussion and appearing to have short-term-memory problems will solve that issue. Thank goodness. Since she's pretty coherent right now, I told him to not rush; he'll be up in about a half hour."

"Okay." Destan's eyes darted around as he thought about the quote-unquote "elephant" he needed to hide for a while.

While it wasn't the best fix, it was one: Destan turned off the belvedere's link and locked him in the bathroom. Thankfully Callimay didn't notice so there was no need for him to go into all those details.

More memories that were full of pain came back as he finished dressing Callimay's wounds. He recalled that cold night at the Society when he almost lost her; how emotionally difficult it was to carry her all that way back because of the painful memories it brought back. And then he remembered how it tore at his heart to see her in pain as he did what he could to clean and bandage the damage Toreon caused.

Once this trip down a torturous memory lane was done, Lackey showed up. He did a preliminary scan right there and then once he got permission, gave Callimay a sedation shot and had Destan carry her down for a through scan.

℔

Unaware of what happened but benefitting from waking up to a calm husband greeting her, Callimay laid there and thought as much as her battered brain would allow. She still wasn't sure what happened — it even bugged her that she couldn't remember what happened even a minute prior. While she did remember how distraught she about everything, how did she end up with a gash in her head and a horrific migraine? And why was her husband so distracted. Yes, he was calm, but she could sense something was wrong.

"Destan?" Callimay asked worried as she rubbed his arm. "What's wrong? What happened?"

"You just scared me is all." He flopped beside her and took a deep, shaky breath. "Are you okay?"

"I'm really cold for some reason."

"It's alright." He laid his warm hand on the side of her face.

"Goodness gracious! Why am I so cold? Your hand can't be 'that' hot." Her voice cracked with fear. "Destan, what happened? Why can't I remember anything?"

"Easy. … You ran outside after you started fighting me because you were so upset. I ran to get to you but only saw the aftermath. — Can you feel your hands and feet? Or are they numb?"

Destan saw the blanket start to move as she nodded, "Yeah, I can feel them. My feet feel stiff though."

Knowing his emotions were starting to climb, she suggested as she worked to sit up; holding the left side of her face, "Well, I guess we could… oh what are those called?"

He wanted to help her figure out what she was trying to say, but part of him thought he was just make it worse so he bit his lip.

She kept wagging her hand at the bed and then growled as she slapped it, "Why can't I think of their name? It's the blankets on the bed. What are they called?"

127

While he knew she'd have moments like this, the part of him that was begging to have a moment of laughter wanted to capitalize on this and let at least one "Pfft," out. But no. He didn't dare, "Blankets?"

"That's their name? Huh. … Well anyway, I can go throw them in the dryer for a bit."

I knew I was forgetting something. "How about 'I' go?" Destan put his arms around her as she began to sway from being dizzy.

"Okay. Could you help me up?"

"Do you think you can make it?" Destan asked concerned as he leaned over to see her face. "We can just sleep here tonight."

"I won't like it. Not right now I don't think. — If you can help me up I can walk there. At least I think I can."

Destan sighed as he got to his knees and picked her up.

For the first time that Callimay could remember: he struggled to carry her. He seemed extremely weak. She grabbed his hand as he turned to leave, "Are you sure you're alright?"

"I… it's been a hard day." He admitted in a quiet voice as he looked back. "We're going to have to leave that last memory stick for later."

Callimay reached up, him sitting back down. "I— why did you change? Aren't you cold?"

"You were cold and it was the only thing I had on-hand that was already warm." Destan tugged on her sweater sleeve.

"But aren't you cold? You're shaking."

"I'll get something when I get back. I'm really just tired."

"I… I love you, Destan."

He paused and then cracked a small smile as he responded, "I love you too, Calli. I'll be right back."

ॐ

As Destan was downstairs, waiting for the dryer to finish, he started thinking about what happened: *I should've known better! Of course that wasn't a live broadcast. The Syndicate doesn't hold prisoners — especially Shadows or Veils — for a week prior to public execution. Which means Elder just sat there, biding his time until he knew I was using the computer. ~ Easy now. Let's not get all riled up. She's start listening and then~ Oh geez! Yeah. Okay. … Deep breath.*

128

Lackey popped in for a minute to talk with him and then gave him some medicine and headed back into the bunker.

When he got back upstairs, Callimay was up and walking around. He tossed the blanket on the bed and yelled, "What are you— Calli!"

The sudden outburst made her stumble into the clothes chest, "I was just getting… what was I getting? … Umm. Oh! Pain medicine."

"Oh." He bowed his head and ran his hand through his hair. "I'm sorry I scared you, I—"

"I'm exhausted."

"Well I won't argue with you there." Destan sighed as he helped her into bed, cradling her head as she laid back. "Doing alright?"

She moaned, her eyes closed.

He kneeled down and rested his hand on her neck, "Calli?"

"I think I just need a good night's rest. Nothing feels 'wrong'. At least I don't think so."

"Let me go get some water. This medicine will work better for the pain. Okay?"

"Uh-huh." She mumbled as she sighed.

Once she took it he helped her spread the blanket out and then dragged himself over and slipped into bed, taking her hand in his.

~ 5 ~

Scared and out of breath, Callimay woke up that night from another nightmare; but she wasn't hysterical. Her concussion made it so she was actually able to realize it was just a dream when she woke up. — Not necessarily a bad thing, but why did it take this happening so she felt like she was able to think rationally?

But, even with this delay it didn't change the fact the reality of everything was so hard for her to comprehend; her crying. She was wanting reality to be a dream and for her to wake up and everything be the way it "should" be. Then she looked over at Destan. As much as she wanted her mother back — her whole family — she still had the man who said she was his world; she wasn't physically alone.

As she watched him she could tell he wasn't quite resting; more like exhausted and passed out. Callimay began to roll over to her side but quickly realized she couldn't. In a way, she already knew how to deal with this dizzy pressure feeling from her migraines, but it wasn't something she ever became accustomed to.

Once she gained her bearings, she brushed Destan's hair out of his face: *He's about due for a haircut again.*

It still wasn't completely clear to her, but Callimay understood to a degree how much stress he was constantly under. What the Veil was doing wasn't something to be taken lightly at all. If they were caught they'd be murdered right on the spot for supposed "treason" no matter where in the world they were found — the Syndicate had "that" much control. His hiding everything to keep her safe was understandable to a point. Then with his ability, he had to be kept under constant watch by himself and her to make sure he wouldn't snap due to the stress he was under. Add to that the whole side Callimay brought into his life, aside from the Society, and she couldn't help but feel guilty. Everything he did at any given moment affected her too. Every decision had to be weighed by the two of them, Destan as the leader taking responsibility for what happened in the end. He had to make the hard decisions to choose what was the best choice; not just what was right or wrong. It was a constant battle he was faced with. But he was human. Yes he was a man and as such God "wired" him a bit differently so he could take more; but he still had his breaking point. He still had emotions, felt pain, and got tired.

She knew and did her best to understand what he said the one morning; that there was one thing in particular he was struggling to keep at bay between the two of them. It was making things hard and awkward in an altogether different way that she'd never considered; this being one of those decisions that didn't have a "good" answer with the situation they were in. How was she supposed to help when she was actually the cause of the problem?

All of this unrest was swept away in one fell swoop when she noticed Destan started to look like he was waking up. — Well, kinda. His brow was beginning to wrinkle and his fists were now clenched. She began to feel pain and so began trying to calm him; rubbing his one fist as he began to mumble: *Destan? Destan what's wrong?*

It took a minute or so, but she gasped when she realized — Destan was having a nightmare.

"…any last words before sentence is carried out?" A man growled as he knocked the barrel of the gun under Destan's chin; him almost smiling as he looked down at him.

"Calli, why didn't you tell them?" Destan — who was on his knees, hands tied behind his back, beaten half to death — begged his wife in a desperate whisper as he sobbed.

"It wouldn't have changed anything." She answered as she took a labored breath; herself in the same predicament. "You know that. There'd be more who would die if I did. I can't betray them."

"Don't kill her!" He cried out as he tried to free himself. "I'll tell you whatever you want! Just let her go. Please!"

"Touching to know you care about this woman so. Willing to risk countless people you promised to protect just to save this one." The man commented as he tossed Callimay's head forward as he let go of her hair. "You weak, pathetic, scum. You're no man."

"I love you, Destan." She whispered as she laid her forehead against his. "I'll see you in a little while."

"Calli please," his voice broke as she kissed him.

She gasped for air, her eyes wide-opened and full of fear; then all of a sudden they froze, every ounce of emotion bottled in them draining as she fell to the side; the pool of blood that began forming fed by the wound made by Destan's own spiral dagger.

"Destan, I'm right here." Callimay began to cry as she reached over and wiped the tears off his face. "I didn't die. You're just dreaming. Please wake up. Destan!"

His emotions were spiraling out of control. He was asleep but in frenzy mode at the same time!

Callimay was desperately trying to get him to wake up while at the same time not succumbing to the immense amount of pain she was in. She couldn't use her ability like she knew she needed to since she had a concussion; it making things impossible for her to maintain a stable link with him. — He actually wasn't fighting her or pushing her out, she was just constantly falling out of touch because of the pain and her inability to truly focus… he didn't know she was there to even think of pushing out.

"Destan! Please!" She began to shriek, panicking because she didn't know what to do. "Wake up! Please, Destan. I'm right here. Destan!"

Only bits and pieces of the rest of his nightmare were heard by her, Callimay throwing herself across him as she screamed.

The belvedere was alarmed by this all but without that extra connection didn't do anything. In fact, he was confused as to what Callimay wanted him to do.

Destan's heart was just about pounding out of his chest. He was pouring sweat and with each passing moment it sounded and felt like he was beginning to suffocate. His whole body was so rigid and jerking; it following suite with his emotions and spiraling out of control.

Before much longer, the nightmare ended: Destan was "killed". And oddly enough, his emotional state flipped off like a light switch. He still had strong sorrow, grief, and agony emotions present; but the anger and rage disappeared… they vanished. His body went completely limp while his heart and breathing came to a complete and sudden stop. There wasn't any sign of and pulse or breath. Nothing.

"Destan? Destan, wake up. Destan please don't die! Don't leave me."

Still dazed and not quite sure about things, she couldn't grasp this was actually happening. It had to be a dream. It just had to! How could he slip into frenzy mode while asleep? And for his body to seize like that and then shut off entirely?

That has to be it. You didn't react like usual when you woke up from the nightmare so this just had to be another thing affected by it. ~ But h… how does that explain this! ~ Maybe we're still asleep? None of this makes sense anyway and it's never happened before. ~ God please!

There was still no change. Callimay screamed in that blood-curdling tone as she pounded her fist against his chest, "Destan!"

She collapsed over him, exhausted, dizzy beyond belief, and in an agonizing amount of pain; but was still hitting her fist on his chest. Somehow her battered mind thought that was going to help.

A few moments later she felt a sharp pain in "her" chest.

Callimay gasped and scrambled to sit up as fast as she could stand; waiting to see if he was actually going to wake up. He seemed to settle down and drift off to sleep as if nothing happened; his hands relaxing. She laid her hand on his chest only to feel his heart's firm, steady, and slow beat; and then leaned over and felt his breath against her face.

Oh what a huge weight was taken off of Callimay's shoulders this was. She collapsed beside him and started crying again.

Not but a few moments later she felt the belvedere nudging her from behind. She rolled over, wincing from the sudden shift, and then petted the creature that was looking more at Destan than her, "I'm alright. Though I may get up and get some— oh. He's alright, Buddy. We're okay. Go back to sleep."

When she realized getting up wasn't an option without Destan's help, she knew she was stuck with the pain. So she laid there and prayed it would ease.

And it did.

After she felt she could, Callimay rolled back over at a snail's pace and then wrapped her arms around Destan's. She cried a little while longer but soon nodded off.

℈

Destan opened his eyes, recalling what he'd dreamed about and let out a heavy sigh as he dragged his hand down his face. He was expecting Callimay's hand to be in his other one, but when he closed it there was nothing there. He whipped his head over and saw she was gone… and the belvedere too. The bedroom door was ajar so Destan jumped up and ran out.

The second he got to the top of the stairs he could hear the sweet, soft, calming voice of his wife humming one of her favorite songs; talking to the belvedere in a cheerful tone on occasion.

He fell back against the wall, overwhelmed. But it was in a good way: Callimay was happy. She was busy in the kitchen fixing their breakfast — being the loving, helping wife she'd always been. And beyond that it smelled like she was making his favorite breakfast; the scent of sharp spices mixing with tangy fruit.

Pulling himself together, he rolled over in a manner of speaking; now leaning on the banister. Callimay's soft and tender voice started to sing the lyrics to what she was humming, the belvedere beginning to yap and howl as if trying to join in.

"Shh!" She rushed over and clapped her hand on top the belvedere's mouth. "No, no, no, Buddy! Destan's still asleep. He had a rough night so we've gotta be really quiet and let him rest. And my head still hurts, too. So let's not do that, huh?"

Listening wasn't enough now, so he crept a bit down the stairs and sat down to watch the two of them: the gentle giant who caved and obeyed every word and saw to the wants and needs of the strong yet fragile woman whose beauty couldn't be matched. This sight struck a chord with Destan; as if this was the way things were supposed to be all along. He'd never thought someone — or in this case an animal — was missing, but he couldn't deny the belvedere fit into their "family" with such ease: *Almost too much at times. ~ How so? ~ His quaint little character trait of being a pest at the most inconvenient of times.*

She checked the food and then kneeled in front of the belvedere, moving his ears or making him smile as she talked, "Such a big yawn. Silly boy. Why are you tired? You're a machine! Tsk, tsk. — I know you're sad, Buddy. I am too. This week's been so rough… 'espeicially' on Destan. I know he's strong, but he can only take so much. He's got so many things he has to deal with and take care of — decisions to make and people to look after. And then I did some 'stupid' thing I can't even remember that's making me slow to react and think, as well as just making me feel pretty miserable with a constant migraine. Maybe it doesn't amount to more than a handful of beans, but I know there's 'something' I'm forgetting. And I think it's important and not a good thing; something Destan won't dare remind me of. And with me running out and clocking myself because of it? I don't think I want to know what it is. Now I know Destan would tell me if I asked, but if it hurt me I know it hurt him too. … I… I just don't want to add to his stress, Buddy. He's got so much weighing on him. So many people whose lives are dependent on what he says and does."

"Calli," the deep, somber, yet loving voice of her husband sighed as he walked up to her and her fluffy companion. "You're never a burden to me. You're my helper. If you ever feel like that it's because I'm not asking you for help like I'm supposed to."

"Destan!" She popped up to her feet and ran to his opened arms. "Did you get enough sleep?"

"Y— Calli! Are you alright!"

"I just moved too fast. My head can't take much movement, let alone quick movement."

"Just take it easy. Okay? … Well. Sure looks like you've been busy."

"I wanted you to have something special this morning." Callimay smiled as she took his hand and started showing him everything. "And you're perfect in your timing. The omelets should be done."

❦

They relaxed that whole day; doing nothing but sitting in front of the fireplace. Destan could tell Callimay's concussion was a substantial one and knew regardless of what she thought she needed to see Doctor Gerould as soon as they got back. It wasn't that she was forgetting anything important or unable to focus — or even uncoordinated — it was just that her migraine wouldn't leave. And then that triggered him to worry about the trip back. Her migraine was bad enough, but this concussion? He didn't want to make it worse by flying. She was already sensitive to air pressure changes. This was just asking for trouble.

He saw her pursed lips, rolling his eyes, "Alright. I'll stop."

"Let's just wait until tomorrow. I may feel better."

"Or worse." He mumbled.

"Or better." She shook her finger in his face. "Stop being so down."

They went back and forth for a bit, her getting flustered. But it clicked when he laughed: he was doing it on purpose to relax.

ॐ

That night was about the same, Callimay still had that extremely slow reaction and so she wasn't hysterical when she woke up. Destan wasn't next to her, so without caring about the repercussions — all she could think of was something was wrong — she sat up a quick as a flash.

He was sitting by the fireplace, troubled by his own thoughts so much that her startled reaction didn't faze him.

Once she calmed and her head had time to settle, Callimay got up and took a blanket over, walking up behind Destan and laying it on his shoulders, "I don't want you getting cold."

"Thank you, but I'm alright." He responded rather shaky as he glanced at her and pushed her hand back. "I'm sorry I woke—"

"You didn't."

"Another nightmare?" Destan asked grieved as he looked back.

"I'm alright. — What about you? Why are you out of bed?"

"I… I'm alright now."

"Are you sure, Destan?" Callimay clutched the bedspread close to her, but then reached out and brushed his hair back.

"I'll be fine. I promise. I got my one good day I said I needed."

"Are you sure it was enough?"

"I'm sure." His small smile greeted her. "Now you better get back to bed. I'll come in a b— I promise. Okay? … Okay."

~ 6 ~

Unlike what was usually her first thought in the morning, this morning it dawned on Callimay that she'd need to make a mad dash to get things packed so they could leave. But when she picked up her bag it was heavier than she was expecting: *What in the— huh?*

"I…" Destan rubbed his neck as he gestured to the packed bag. "Since I was awake earlier and wasn't tired I went ahead and took care of it. We're gonna be driving several hours in the wrong direction to pick up the puzzle, that by that time we'll need to Assemble with—"

"It's fine." She smiled as she closed the bag, sounding peaceful. "So then I'll just run down and get break—"

"I've got something packed already."

"Did you sleep at all?" Her voice strained as she came over and took his hands, looking in his eyes. "Destan?"

"It didn't take me any time at all to pack and I slept until about a half hour ago."

She nodded and took a deep breath, satisfied for once with the answer she was given.

❦

After a quick change she hopped downstairs. — Well she started to. — Callimay was sad to leave the cozy cabin but was glad to be getting back to warmer weather, "I'd almost forgotten it was summer."

The belvedere bounded over to the door and looked at the two of them as if asking where they were going.

"How are we gonna get him there, Destan?"

He groaned, "I knew I was forgetting something."

"I didn't mean to—"

He sighed as he put his hand on her shoulder, "I know you didn't."

The belvedere, though a blessing to have, complicated things beyond any other awkward situation he'd found himself in before. While he was able to hide him when Lackey came up, the fact is he just had to hide him for an hour or so in a small house. How could you hide a mammoth-sized dog in a two-door muscle car for almost a day? Chet — realistically — was just big enough for him and Callimay. Let alone the fact the belvedere would be recognized by border security. And then there was getting him to the jet without him being seen. Destan still hadn't figured out the command for him changing to his midnight black appearance and it was supposed to be a clear night. Yeah, the belvedere could run out of sight and follow them, but they were driving over five hours one way. Even he had limits.

Maybe if I leave him here until we come back through. ~ That's just delaying the inevitable. ~ It'd give me more time, though. ~ With the way things are with her concussion, she needs him around at all times. ~ Well what do you—

"Come on, Buddy." Callimay said chipper. "Let's see if we can figure something out."

"I should've told them to get Wolf." Destan growled at himself as he shut the door with a bit of added effort.

"Don't ever regret your decision. Chet is what got us out of there. I'm not saying Wolf couldn't have, but time wasn't something we had much of. Chet's got more pickup and go than Wolf initially does. … We'll figure this out. — Won't we, Buddy?"

The belvedere barked and wagged his tail as he pranced over and sat beside Callimay, leaning his head against her side.

While he tried his best to get his mind out of this abyss of negativity, what brought him back wasn't in the emotional direction he needed to be going in; him scared, "What are you doing? Calli that's the trunk!"

She laughed as she started thumping the back wall. "It's not like I've got 'that' bad of a concussion — that I'd forget to sit in a seat. I'm just looking to see— aha! It does have it."

"What are you talking about?" Destan helped her out and then followed her to the door.

"Do you remember that time we brought back those trellises?"

"The ones for the back yard? Yeah…"

"How they wouldn't fit so we had to put the back seat down?" She continued as she struggled to reach something.

"But Wolf had a full back seat." Destan replied as he jogged around to his side and tried to help.

"Yeah, but Chet has the ability to fold down the back, too." Callimay grunted as she pulled on the back of the interior. "See?"

While this was something very encouraging, the sheer size of what they had to work with wasn't thrilling, "It's gonna be awfully tight."

"Tight, yes. But he'll make it."

"I need to take lessons from you."

She frowned as she tapped his nose, "No, what you need is to do what you've done before: slow down and think things through. … Destan? I… I know it's hard when there's so much emotions involved; and I know they're not something you're 'that' accustomed to dealing with. … Just give yourself time. We'll get back and hit the ground running. Huh?"

"You're amazing," Destan smiled and then gave her a kiss. "Now you just stay there. I'll get him in. — Come on, Big Fella."

❦

It was such a tight fit that even the belvedere wasn't happy; but when he realized he was close to the two people he was bonded to, he settled down and was quite the a happy camper.

All that was needed at that point was their bags and they were off!

Things were going so smoothly; Callimay's fix was so simple and yet affective, everyone was calm and happy, the weather was nice for driving… but it didn't stay that way for long.

As they got to the border, Destan's emotions flared in a way that worried and yet confused Callimay. Her concussion was making it different and odd, but she'd never felt this "itchy" "tingling" sensation like she was now.

His eyes darted beside him a few times, it finally clicking for her: *Oh dear. I didn't think that would be a problem at all. How do I— oh! I can put the window up. That'll make it so he doesn't glow.*

"Calli, what are you doing?" Destan's voice sounded borderline terrified as he grabbed her arm.

"I'm going to roll up the window in the back so he won't glow. It won't take but a moment."

While his initial reaction to such a bizarre comment was to slam on the breaks, the next moment brought the calm and clarity Destan needed. He took a deep breath: *She's gonna spaz on me if I don't do this right. …* "Calli? Don't worry about it. Just take your coat off and throw it over him."

"But the win— why isn't there a window back there?"

"Calli I—"

"Destan what happened to the car?"

As the car came to a stop, he took his wife by the shoulders and looked her straight in the eye, still as cool as a cucumber, "Just calm down. It's okay. … It's me, Calli. Calli? … We're not in Wolf. There's nothing missing in the car."

"But h—"

"You've got a concussion," his heart began to break from seeing the fear washing out the sparkle in her eyes. "Just relax. It's okay."

Not but a few seconds later he could see her eyes "snap back"; almost like her mind was able to do a hard reset of sorts: *Her ability's working overtime to compensate. ~ I'm sure our worries about what's ahead didn't help any. ~ Ugh.*

The belvedere whined, Callimay starting to reach for their bags, "I… I'm fine. I just have to hide you, Buddy."

All of a sudden, the interior of the car got dark.

Hide. 'That's' his command cue. Destan sighed in relief. "Now just sit back and relax. Huh? I'll take care of the rest."

They got through without any issues and kept on for the mansion. Destan didn't seem to be in any sort of talking mood, but at first she knew it was because he wanted her to rest. And with her thinking so sideways about things she had to admit she needed some rest as well.

❧

One wonderful nap later Callimay woke up and saw it'd been two hours. She looked over only to see her husband was beyond distracted.

Seeing a smile would've been so sweet, but where they were going wasn't an easy place for him.

So, after she let herself wake up a bit more she took out the last memory stick from her mother and his computer: *Hold on there. What if it's a video again? ~ Oh land sake I didn't think about~ Well it's too late now, Rose Petal. Seriously! How— that's odd.*

It asked for a written password that was eight digits long.

Hum. Maybe this is a good sign? ~ How so? ~ If it's different as far as a passcode then maybe I won't lose what's on here like I did with the other one. ~ Sounds reasonable, but we are a bit frazzle-brained right now. … How are you supposed to figure out what the code is? Destan's the master Shadow code figure-outer, not us. ~ Well you have to admit 'I' was the one who got him on the thought of how to unlock the computer at the mansion. ~ Duly noted. ~ And since it was my mother's that she meant for me to have and use; it's got to be something I would be able to figure out. ~ I concede. ~ Eight digits? … Numbers? Or the whole transposing thing? ~ Well what's eight letters? ~ Eight… umm. Well… the only thing I can think of is my name.

She dug around in the bag and found some paper and a pen, writing down what it would be in number code. And then she hesitated: *What if I only get one shot? ~ And now you know how Destan felt. ~ Yeah. … His had that little warning underneath it, though. Maybe… I… I don't know. ~ I doubt she'd make it 'that' hard for you to figure out. It's not like she expected you to 'know' so much about everything.*

Unlike what she was hoping to find, there wasn't much of anything on it. At least not of the type of information she was wanting. It had much more of the feel that Destry's computer at the mansion had: documents that detailed the description of what Chameleon was, medical record from her actual processing as well as a couple follow-up notes. One last document contained Destry's observations of Destan and Callimay while he was trying to figure out what to do; including his records of development of the serum and his seeing it — if successful — as being a way to help so many until Total Eclipse could bring everything out into the open.

Apparently, Callimay and Destan favored playing hide and seek most of the time. Destan would complain about her peeking all of the time and how it wasn't fair. And if this were an actual word-for-word dictation — which it most certainly appeared to be — it stunned her that Destan called her Calli even then! She hung onto every word of a beautiful "romance" that she couldn't remember yet understood so well: *Destan hasn't changed at all, really.*

Before long she got to his account of that last day when he had the breakthrough. His tone drastically changed; it so upbeat and positive.

As expected, his notes were lengthy about how he deconstructed Challenger and morphed it into Chameleon; most not making much sense — even if she didn't have a concussion. But how could she skip it? There might be mentions of her past life that she'd so want to know.

By the end, Destry said he hoped he could change Elder's mind and offer this to others who were left-handed as a way to help them have a better quality of life during this battle for freedom; still leery to give it to young children, though.

Destan was fiddling with his wedding band most of the time and then caught what she was doing out of the corner of his eye, "Oh! You're up. — So… should I ask what's on it?"

She jerked a bit and then smiled, "It's just information on what Chameleon is and my medical record from when I got it, blah blah blah science stuff I know nothing about."

"Anything new?"

"Not really. The only thing I saw was that he used Challenger as the basis for Chameleon."

"He did what!" Destan's eyes bugged out.

Once the whiplash feeling left her from the car jerking to a near stop, her holding her head and trying to brace herself so she'd stop feeling dizzy and nauseous, answered, "He said he broke… broke… well, whatever the thing is, he broke it down into its broadest form to allow me to just watch, listen, or do something alongside someone and be able to adapt and mimic that exact action. — That's pretty amazing your father was able to figure this all out. He did so very much to help so many people."

"And he was just starting." Destan said rather monotone and he let out a frustrated sigh. "I've found countless documents from his office at the University about other conditions he was beginning to see — those which were not on anyone else's radar from what I've found. He just had an eye for things like that. He hit on big diseases quite a bit, but the more I looked, the more I saw he wanted to help those who were overlooked and pushed aside since they were such a small number of cases that they were seen by the medical community as not worth any special attention. This shift started right after I was born and then really took shape after he would have found out I was a lefty. — I'm sorry I slammed on the breaks like that, Calli."

"I'm okay. It wasn't that bad." She reached over and patted his arm. "I wish I could thank your father for everything he did for me."

"You have," Destan smiled as he took her hand, his eyes becoming glassy. "You've shown that there was good in what he was trying to do with those serums. That they were to help bring people together and promote peace by protecting, not divide and rule with through terror and 'superiority'. You're showing how wrong Elder is and how worth-while my father and your mother's sacrifices were."

She rubbed his hand as she leaned over toward him, "And there was something else I found out that's quite interesting."

"I'm guessing this is something I don't already know?"

"You called me Calli when we were little. Your father wrote down his observations of that week we spent with each other and apparently you always called me Calli."

"And I'll always call you my Calli." Destan finished as his voice became so soft; him sounding chipper as he snapped his finger, "Hey! Since you've got that out could you do me a favor?"

"Sure!"

"Can you tell me how much extra room is on that stick?"

"Umm… okay how do I do that, again? Brain needs help."

"Rotate the drive's name to the right and drag down."

"Okay, so is it the dark or light gray that's empty?"

"Light."

"Makes sense. — I'd say it's only missing one of your serving sizes of a peach pie; so quite a bit."

Not an exact~ She's not the technical one, geez. And she's got a concussion. "I want you to add files to that stick. I'll give you my access codes to override the security locks on the computer. Just find our files that I've tucked aside under 'marriage'. Then in that briefcase by your feet is an external hard drive. Plug it into the computer using the—"

"One thing at a time!"

"Sorry." He bit his lip.

The belvedere whimpered so she turned to pet him, only to flinch and jerk back as she gasped.

"What!" Destan hit the break again, immediately regretting it. "I… I'm sorry Calli. I… what's wrong?"

"Where did the belvedere go?"

"Huh!" He whipped his head around real quick. "He's just black, Calli. It's okay."

"How can he be black? Dogs can't change color." She sounded more irritated than anything.

"You gave him the command so he would change, that's all."

"I never did anything like that!"

Keep it calm, Boon. Destan coached himself as he pulled over and put the car in park. "Calli? Easy. Just listen, okay?"

"But how c—"

"It's your concussion, Calli. Please trust me and listen. Can you do that for me? … You 'did' give the belvedere the command to turn black. And you 'do' know that belvederes can change color. But it's not a big deal. My reactions are the big deal right now if anything. — Let's just leave him as he was since we'll have to sneak him on the jet when we got back. … That and him glowing dose bother my eyes a bit." Destan did his best to shift the focus.

Her eyes teared up, but she kept it together and nodded as he brushed the side of her face, "How about you take another nap? I'll wake you when we're almost there. Sound good? … Okay then."

While it felt rather impossible to go to sleep, it didn't take long for her to drift off.

Before she knew it she was being coaxed awake.

The tone Destan used at this point was much more serious as they got to the thick tree coverage close to the mansion, "I'm pretty sure I've figured everything out. I'm going to keep Zephyr occupied while you run the Big Fella over to the jet. Now he's not going to be able to stay up in the cockpit with us; he could interfere with the instruments… and it's obvious why I don't want that happening. He can stay in the back lounge and I'll keep the video feed and intercom link up so you can keep an eye on him and talk to him if needed. — There are two strips for Bulwark and I'm going to land at the one furthest away. It would be nice to take you on a little drive after we get back and before we're back in Bulwark anyway, but that'll also give us a chance to hide him."

Having this info dump mere moments after she woke up wasn't the smartest thing to do, but she just latched on to what she heard at the end, "You found a place!"

"There are plenty of windows so he'll be able to stay charged. And it's outside the perimeter so he won't trip the sensors."

"Sensors?"

"There's an invisible barrier of sorts around Bulwark. I'll admit, though, it's more like those old laser trips that I'm sure you saw in some of those old movies. Not the one that would slice, just the motion type. Anyone that crosses it and doesn't have a beacon will automatically trip it. And before you ask it's just people, not animals." He fiddled with his wedding band and then took her hand. "Remember: belvederes aren't true animals. They emit a very specific radio frequency that the barrier is programmed to recognize."

"Wait. So, do I set it off?"

"Every time we leave or come in." Destan laughed as he smiled, squeezing her hand a bit. "Gives a good 'live test' for everyone the way I see it. — I'm going to, when I can, work on his coding so he'll emit a different frequency and not trip it if things ever get to that point. And then I'm going to make sure and add the push command to my watch just in case. I'm not taking any chances; I want him to be able to get to you if you need him."

"Or if 'you' need him." Callimay added as she tugged on his arm.

"Well. We're here." He slowed to make a right-hand turn, almost coming to a stop; inching along the overgrown first part of the drive.

At one point he picked up the pace since the drive was visible now, the sound of gravel popping and crunching beneath the tires.

Before too much longer they came up to a small house. Destan stopped the car and hesitated for a moment before he turned the lights off; and then again before he got out and helped Callimay out.

"Stay here, Buddy. We'll be right back."

There was a quaint silence in the air; the trees muffling the ocean sound and even the salty air. Shadows had obviously taken on a new meaning to her, but the ones that surrounded her felt loving and calm. This place felt safe… this place felt like a home.

The small house they were in front of had a covered porch that ran the full length of this ranch-style one-floor house. It looked like it was being well maintained; almost as if someone was living there: the steps not creaking under their weight, the smell of fresh-cut grass in the air, and the porch itself clear and clean.

Destan took his keys out and went to unlock the door; him hand just about convulsing as he tried to get the key in the lock. It got so bad they jumped out of his hand and felt "splat" on the porch.

"Here. Let me help."

"No. No I need to do this, Calli. … These memories aren't bad. I know deep down they're not. I've just— it's been over eleven years since I stepped foot in this house."

Her heart began to break when she saw the pain in his eyes, "Can I do anything at all to help?"

"Just be you." Destan replied as his eyes begged her to help him.

∑

After the initial shock of memories flooding back wore off, he turned the lights on and made a beeline for the room to the left; pulling the sliding door apart.

Callimay tip-toed along, keeping close to him; admiring the simple yet pristine surroundings. Seeing the simplicity and charm reminded her that his childhood with his parents was a humble and simple one. His father worked to get what he had: *Someone must come in on a regular basis to keep everything the way it is. Over ten years of just sitting would leave things with a layer of dust that'd make 'me' even sneeze. ~ But who?… Rocher? ~ I don't know who else Destan would trust the care of such a place to.*

As Destan sorted through a stack of boxes, she walked around the room and examined the author names of books on the shelves covering the one entire wall — some bearing Destry's name!

She loved to see all the pictures on another wall: something that was so lacking in the mansion. And these were so real: everyday photos of Destan with his parents. These snapshots of him at such a young age reminded her how young he was when such a heinous thing happened. He'd lived with that pain for so long. It was understandable that his ability to remember other things — except for that glaring bad one — was almost nonexistent. And yet he was trying. That alone tugged at her heart. She sighed and hung her head as she turned, bumping into something. Callimay gasped as she threw her hand out and caught what she hit before it slammed against the floor.

"I'm sorry!" She jumped back and clasped her hands behind her, feeling Destan glaring at her. "I wasn't watching where I was going. It's my fault. I—"

"It's okay," he took a deep breath as he plodded over. "Part of me was worried you were hurt. Granted, the other part— are you okay?"

"I'm fine. … A… are you? Destan?"

He nodded as he cracked a small smile and rubbed her arm, then let it vanish as he turned around.

She let him go, trying her best to keep things calm and quiet for him, and turned around to look at what she hit. It was the first in a series of large portraits. The frames were extremely flamboyant and the portraits so sharp and clear. She kneeled and pulled the dust cover back; soaking in what the first one showed: it was Destry and Lylah's wedding portrait. Even though they had a simple and inexpensive one, the look of joy on their faces was all that mattered. So what if her wedding dress was nothing more than a simple summer dress paired with a blusher veil? And only a critical eye like her own could see how Destry's tuxedo jacket and pants didn't match… and it was apparent the jacket was "made" to fit him since the sleeves changed color about two inches before the end. It "could" have been something wrong with the picture, but that was the only place this discoloration was and it was the same on both sleeves; and with the clarity of the picture it was hard to imagine there would be an error like this made.

Come to think of it, they were even more dressed up than Destan and I were on our wedding day. Callimay smiled as she thought back and remembered how even though she was scared she was overjoyed to know she had someone who cared for her and was going to protect her; Destan, though, she wasn't sure of. *Surely he—*

"I 'was' happy, Calli. In pain and worried to death, yes, but happy."

She jerked back, not knowing he was right next to her; him calming as he set a package down and put his arms around her, "Easy. … I know I wasn't probably showing it but I 'was' happy, Calli. I still am. And each day it just keeps on growing. I admit I was trying to think ahead about getting you to safety and what that was all going to entail; and my expression probably showed more pain than happiness… but I knew I couldn't rest easy until I had you where it was safe."

"It wasn't written all over your face but your eyes looked at me like they never had up to that point. It was similar to when you proposed; but even then it was different. It's hard to describe— you found it?"

"I think so," Destan took a deep breath as he laid his hand on top of a large, paper-wrapped box.

"Are you going to wait or open it now?"

"Why don't you finish looking and I'll get it opened at least."

"Okay. … Umm. If you don't mind my asking: why are these on the floor and not hung up?"

"Because they don't belong here." Destan reached down and took out a throwing knife. "They're from the mansion. I… I took them down when I couldn't take seeing them day after day any longer."

"Oh," Callimay bit her lip, sorry she asked.

As she looked at the others, and then the ones on the wall, she began to notice a resemblance to someone else she knew; one she hadn't noticed before, "Destan? Are you actually related-related to Rocher?"

At first he thought she was kidding, but he backed off his full laugh to a slight chuckle when he saw her face, "He's my great uncle on my mother's side: my mother's father's brother."

"What! But… but you never told me that! Or is this something my concussion's making me forget?"

"I just assumed you put two and two together when I told you I was related to Mrs. Jackman and that she was his sister-in-law." Destan apologized as he took a box out of the package… and then paused.

But Auditor is who told you about Rocher and Mrs. Jack~ Well I thought she did. Did 'he' tell me? ~ But when? ~ Well good grief, if I knew that I wouldn't be questioning this at all, would I? ~ Something's wrong. ~ Destan!

He had an extremely elaborate full-dictionary-sized puzzle box on the table. Rather undersized for the type of box it was in, but that had to be on purpose. There were obviously memories attached to this box; his emotions all over the place as he leaned on the desk and stared at it.

Callimay rushed over and barely brushed her hand against his shoulder before leaning her head against his side. As she hoped, Destan melted with her touch and just about collapsed onto the chair behind him. He slipped his hand in hers and then pulled the chair to the desk.

There was a long pause, his hand in midair over one corner of the box, but then he began to work. False panels came out one by one on the sides to reveal unique puzzles that he solved in a flash; the carved flowers, vines, and then lattice on the top of this wooden box releasing one by one to reveal the "boss level" puzzle.

Since he'd done this many times before, muscle memory kicked in and he whipped through what Callimay saw as an impossible thing to figure out, "You actually figured this all out when you were… four?"

Without missing a beat, Destan's voice sounded like a casual shrug as he kept working, "Yeah."

She stared at him for a moment, her constant gaze finally catching his attention, "What?"

"I always knew you were smart… I just never imagined you started out that way. If you know what I mean."

His reaction wasn't what she expected at first, him sitting down as he sighed, "Don't mistake being 'smart' for 'knowing' anything."

"What in the world do you mean by that?"

Destan took her hand and had her sit on his lap as he explained, "Sure, as some might see it I was a protégé of sorts growing up. But when I came to the age where I knew how to use what talent I had? I did nothing but squander it. I was a selfish teenager who didn't see the value of what gift God gave me."

A silence that tried to keep from falling into despair clung to the room for a while; the raw honesty proving to be a strong reflective point for them both.

"I… I guess—"

"But that's all in the past, now." Destan smiled as he rubbed her arm and they got up. "And for as smart as I might be in some areas, even you know how dense I can be in others. … Right?"

Her smile couldn't stay buried forever.

With this discussion appearing to be ended, he went back to work, the top of the puzzle box slowly morphing itself. For the longest time she didn't know what this last puzzle was supposed to end up looking like. But then she came to the other side of the chair and saw something out of the corner of her eye that looked similar. There was a miniature tree on the sideboard by one of the windows: *Oh! That's one of those… a… umm…*

Bosnia. That one there is the one Rocher gave my mother after he started 'working' for us. It was apparently the one she had when she was a child and tended to for years. *Now where's that keyhole? ~ For that matter where's the key? ~ It's in my—* "Calli? Could you go out and get my Shadow box?"

"Oh! The key! Yes." Her voice squeaked as she jumped back and took off.

When she got back he was still looking for what had to be a thin diamond shape… which was a design found all over this box anyway: genius, really. But he knew it was on a specific side. But still, there were several of these engravings there. His emotions were beginning to climb in the wrong direction, so Callimay gripped his wrist and said in a calm and steady tone, "The way your father talked, the keyhole had to be easy for him to locate and somewhere you couldn't see."

Destan was ready to snap back at her, but waited for her to finish and sounded ashamed as he groaned; rubbing his face.

"It's okay. I… I know this is hard. But you're doing so well! Don't give up now." She kneeled beside him and did everything she could to keep from crying. "Just remember the good of that memory. You said yourself you know it's there. Just look for it. Remember what happened with the puzzle box by itself. … Destan?"

He opened his eyes and then took the box in his hands, offering it to her, "Now it's a bit heavier than it looks. You hold it like you're me: needing help to solve the puzzle. … Now I remember that my father would take it from me like… no. No he…"

Destan got up and started looking at the ceiling as he would switch how Callimay was holding the box, drawing in the air as he mumbled. This continued on for a bit as he worked to replay the memory.

"Aha! I got it!" He snapped his fingers as he put the box on the table and tilted it away from him. "It's under here on the back left corner. See, Calli?"

The sound of joy in his voice almost made her cry as she put her arm around him; her having to strain to see what he was pointing at. She could hear him talking to himself as he swiveled the lid around to reveal what it protected: *This one was always my favorite. So satisfying and it made me feel accomplished even though father was the one who technically solved it each time.*

And yet this touching moment of emotional progress for Destan just wouldn't be able to last: inside the box that always held a wonderful surprise for him held a white leather book of what felt like death. While at first glance it seemed "innocent", the gold embossing of a sunrise screamed to him of the filth that was contained on the pages of this book. This book "was" worthy of being judged by its cover.

He took it out and opened it, the spine cracking from being closed for so long; its sudden pops and snaps shattering the calm that had worked so hard to quiet the air in the room.

Personal experiences and accounts of General Harmon Willgun.

Seeing her grip her forehead and stumble back, he dropped the book and tried to unclench his fist as he reached out to her, "I'm sorry, Calli. I'm so sorry. I know your head is—"

"C… can we— is it alright if we go?"

"Sure," he scrambled to get to her and take her arm.

Right as they got to the front door and he opened it she began staggering as she moaned.

"Calli?" He gulped as he reached around and grabbed her shoulder. "Calli, what's wrong?"

"I just feel dizzy. I'm alright." She brushed off as her head began to bob back and forth, her hands now shaking.

"Let me carry you."

$

Destan put everything back in its place and then turned the lights off. His heart tugged at him as he glanced back through the closing door as if he saw the memories waving at him with a fondness and joyful tear. These memories that were full of joy seemed to beg him to stay; telling him they missed him and wanted him to come home because they were lonely… "he" was lonely. But right now wasn't that time. He double-checked the lock and then jogged to the car, getting in as quiet as he could and then started back… and then pulled in the mansion drive.

"Why are we stopping?"

"I've gotta grab something really quick. I won't be but a minute." He assured as he put the car in park.

"Okay," she laid her head back and crossed her arms in her lap.

"Calli? Are you sure you're alright?"

"I'm just trying to relax is all."

He groaned a bit, but nodded, "Okay. I'll be right back."

$

When they got to the airstrip, Destan told Callimay to not worry about the bags. He tried everything he could so he could take the belvedere himself so she wasn't running all that way while worrying about the creature, but he had a bad gut feeling about leaving him unattended. She assured him she'd be okay since she was able to rest, "Sitting here in the car much longer is going to draw attention."

"I know," he grumbled as he fiddled with his wedding band. "Just… just do what you can and don't hurt yourself. If something happens — if someone spots the Big Fella — just get to the jet and lock yourself in the cockpit. I'll take care of everything."

For as much as he planned, his implementation of said plan was pretty nonexistent. She had to coax him a few more time before he left to get all his paperwork filed.

Okay, Calli. Go now.

"Here we go! Come on, Buddy. Time to move."

The belvedere acted like everything was so serious and slinked out of the trunk after he got himself turned around; her not even needing to tell him to follow her. He kept perfect pace as they made a mad dash for the awaiting jet; her having a moment of despair when the hatch wasn't opened: *Oh no. No, no, no! No this can't be!*

There wasn't a soul to be seen, but the fear in her couldn't stand it: *Destan! Help! The door's closed!*

It's locked? He tried his best to not look out the window.

I… it— "No!" She clamped her hand over the creature's nose.

Calli?

It won't give. She pushed against it as hard as she could.

It's got to be unlocked. Confederate just told me it was. — Oh no. Destan gasped; him jumping up from his seat. *He's seen you and is coming out. Calli get out of there!*

As she started back down she didn't let go of the handle, the door swinging open: *You've gotta be kidding me. Again? ~ Well don't just stand there, dumb-dumb!* "Come on, Buddy! Hurry!"

Callimay staggered down the dark aisle to the back lounge, the belvedere whining as he kept nudging her hand. She threw the lounge door open and then told him to stay; yelping when she heard a voice that wasn't Destan's.

"Who's there?" Her tinny voice called out as the lights came on.

"It's just me, Liaison. Where are you?"

She poked her head out so they could see her, the belvedere trying to push his way past her leg so he could see out too.

Confederate gestured to the door as he came back, "I saw you were having trouble with the hatch and came out to check. Everything fine?"

"I suffer from 'push/pull' syndrome." She rolled her eyes, trying to be nonchalant as she shoved the belvedere back again.

"Oh. Gotya." He chuckled a bit as he stopped. "I won't deny that'll get me from time to time. — You look pretty pale. You alright?"

"I don't feel that great, but I'll be able to rest on the way back." Callimay's eyes got big when she felt the belvedere push against her and begin to growl.

"Alright," he trailed off as he muttered to himself; turning to leave.

Callimay shut the door and flopped against it; sliding down to the floor in a pain-ridden way. The belvedere sniffed the air a bit, letting a puff of a growl out and then turned his focus to her.

"What am I gonna do with you? You can't growl whenever you feel like it. Just 'calm' down, Buddy." She groaned as she pushed the hair on his face back toward his withers.

He relaxed and turned white without warning; scaring her.

There were thankfully no windows, so he wouldn't be seen, but still!

"Oh good graci— Buddy?" She sounded desperate as he whipped his head up and sniffed the air again. "Don't!"

She wasn't fast enough and the creature barked. Thundering footsteps worsened the fear Callimay already had; her screaming when the door flew open.

"It's just me, Calli!" Destan calmed as he rushed over. "It's okay. — What happened? Why did he bark?"

"I… I don't," she tried to catch her breath as she rubbed her face. "I don't know. He was sniffing the air and growling while Confederate was here; but sniffed and then barked when you came."

"Well at l— why is he white?"

"I don't know, okay!" She started to sound flustered, the belvedere looking defensive.

"It doesn't matter." He shook his head as he helped her to her feet. "Don't worry about it. It's okay. Why don't you lie down while I get the ground check done?"

⌗

The flight back was looking to be uneventful and quiet. — What a blessing! — But then Destan had to go and ruin everything. He told Callimay get Elder's Journal so they could start going through it. She was a bit reluctant, trying to justify leaving it because they had enough evidence already. But, he reminded her how bringing him down was going to be an absolute dog fight so they needed as much ammunition as they could get.

Not in the mood to further debate the point, and trying to keep him happy — even though she knew good and well he'd get mad, hearing what Elder had to say — she went back and got it.

This leather book had a strange odor to it. Not necessarily repulsive, but not something that hinted toward a cologne or even herb; it wasn't even a leather-type smell or old paper, "Destan? Can you hear me?"

He flipped a switched on one panel as he looked over at the video feed, "Yeah?"

"Did this book have a smell before?" She sounded worried as she watched how the belvedere acted.

"Not that I recall. Why? Does it now?"

"I can't explain it, but it's got 'some' kind of smell."

"Get out of there, Calli! Now!" Destan yelled as he threw off his headset and started running, waving his arms when he saw her, "Close the door!"

"But the belved—"

"Close it!"

The jet jerked to the side, Destan racing back into the cockpit to see what was wrong.

Callimay stumbled and slammed her arm into the wall, blacking out for a short time.

When she came to she had to stay where she was until the pain and dizziness subsided; it taking a bit for her to figure out where she was.

As she got up she relapsed from being startled by Destan practically lunging over the seat to her. His voice was trying so hard to sound calm and "together", but she knew he was a nervous wreck. The second he got her settled in the cockpit he hurried back to the lounge.

He looked a bit upset as he tossed the book on one of the panels, but didn't sound mad as he sat down and put his headset on, "Well, it wasn't static speed like I was worried about."

"So that's why y— what is it?"

"You're gonna laugh when I tell you, and then I'm gonna kick myself for putting you through so much pain: it's nothing more than Elder's natural musk, plain and simple." Destan rolled his eyes at himself as he shook his head. "Now I'm not blaming you in the least."

"And I'm not blaming you." Her eyes narrowed as she pointed at him. "Goodness knows that I need a bit extra in the way of reminders right now to be careful."

"Fair enough. … Are you alright?"

She sat back and sighed, "Much better."

"Do you think you could read some?"

"Destan," she groaned as he handed the book to her.

After the first page it would've been obvious to anyone that he was bothered. It was quite apparent Elder's dealing with the Syndicate predated this journal which was supposedly twenty-two years old! It infuriated him how he'd been blind to this back-stabbing, evil man. How did he not notice? There had to be "something"!

"Destan? As terrifying as this might sound, the truth is he was most likely manipulating you that whole time to some extent. He probably did things right in front of you but you never 'saw' it."

"That doesn't excuse—"

"Let's not go through this all again, please?" She took a painful sigh as she buried her face in her hands. "M… maybe we should just stop."

There was a drawn period of silence, Destan rubbing his face as he tried to calm down and think things through, "Calli? … Calli just try to read a bit more. Just a little. … Please?"

Her lips pursed as she twisted them, flopping the book open in her lap and muttered, "Fine."

By what he wrote, Baleck "did" mix Origin and Dreamer for Elder. But through mixing it, he discovered he needed to alter the placement for the electrodes — explaining why Destry was confused when seeing where the scars were.

Elder described his discovery phase in excruciating detail — the vivid pictures of immense pain quite familiar to Callimay. And yet he recorded what Baleck gave him was far superior to what he had hoped for and was in a way addicted to the pain. It even began to make her skin crawl reading how he described his desire to feel it.

Alone, Dreamer could function without being "seen" by someone, but could only affect the physical surroundings of the person; Origin being capable of rendering the person, and their clothing, completely invisible. This cocktail gave Elder the ability to manipulate what people saw and what they thought without them consciously knowing; the physical invisibility portion completely lost.

He dated his processing as being two months prior to the timeline Destan and Callimay knew of from Destry. It was odd for there to be such a large time gap, but it didn't take too long to find that Elder set the equipment up the morning Destry found it on purpose, "I don't think I should read this right now, Destan. I don't—"

"I need to know, Calli."

"But right now? While you're flying! My mind isn't working like it should, I know that. Destan this is dangerous! Deadly! … It can wait. I refuse to read anymore. Don't you dare try to make me go on. I've gone through enough pain already; and I'm not risking my life like this. I'm done. Brood by yourself." She unbuckled her seatbelt and stormed out; slamming the door behind her.

He groaned as he looked at the white leather book gleaming in the moonlight, almost hearing Elder laugh like he'd done so many times when he'd set things up to make Destan look like a complete fool: *Why are you— it's possessing you, Boon! ~ I just… I just want to know. To know for sure there wasn't anything I could do to save them. You know that! ~ Your father already said you did nothing wrong. That's not enough? ~ I've got to know when, where, and how he died. Compare that to where I was at the time. I've got to know if~ Your father got that book 'before' he died. How could that information be in there? Boon you've got to stop! Listen to your wife! Do you 'want' to die? Do you want 'her' to die? This is something within your control. Don't risk her life or yours just for a little peace and comfort about the past.*

Movement on the one screen caught his attention — Callimay in the lounge with the belvedere. A grumbling sigh of frustration lingered as he reached over to the com button.

And then he stopped.

She petted the creature only in passing and then collapsed on the bed, immediately grabbing her head: *Stupid idiot!* *Calli I'm sorry.*

'Please', not right now! It hurts too much.

He pinched his nose as he thumped his fist on the armrest and then hit the com button, "Calli?"

"Please, Destan. You know I need quiet."

"I… I just wanted to— I'll let you rest as long as possible, but you'll have to get to a seat when I start—"

Callimay moaned as the belvedere trotted over and rested his head on the bed, "Alright. Just… just please be quiet."

Awkward silence.

"Will you let me know?" She sounded pained as she called out.

"Yeah," Destan was quick to answer. "I think there's some me—"

"I'm dizzy more than anything. That won't help." She snapped.

"Okay." He groaned as he sat back. *I've really done it this time.*

The skies felt darker as he looked out; a pang of loneliness prodding him every few minutes so he would look at the screen to see Callimay passed out, the belvedere still sitting beside her. While what happened wasn't completely his fault, he sure didn't help matters. His wife wasn't able to react and think like she usually did and yet she was the one who knew better: *Now let's not start that again. ~ I know, I know. ~ Looks like we're about there. ~ Oh. Right. The closer airstrip. Almost forgot. … I don't want to scare her. ~ With the way things are, you leave this cockpit again and we're all as good as dead.*

He looked torn as he tapped the center console while watching her; and then snapped his finger as he took his computer. It was a task to work around the belvedere's coding, watch the lounge feed, "and" watch all the dials and screens he was supposed to be keeping tabs on; but he was able to get the belvedere to do what he wanted.

"Well hello." Callimay's sleepy voice smiled as she petted the creature that had his front feet on the bed, face snuggled next to hers.

Perfect. "How was that for a wakeup call?"

"Oh. So that was you?" She yawned as she rolled over to get up.

"Thought it'd be nicer since it was quiet."

"Thank you. … So it's time for me to come back up?"

"Yeah."

Callimay laughed as she got to the door, "Now you stay here, Buddy. We're almost home."

The creature bounced around before sitting and watching her go.

Once she got to her seat, Destan reached over, "You alright?"

She took a deep breath as she patted his hand, "Better. I just hope this whole air pressure adjustment isn't going to bite me really hard."

"Do you need to take something?"

"I really don't think it'll help with this. I've been getting dizzy which really isn't a true kind of pain. It's… it's hard to explain."

He sounded uneasy as he let her go, "Well, if I—"

"I'll be okay. The quicker we get down the faster I can get through the transition."

~ 7 ~

Being able to sit in the cockpit after they taxied to the darkened hanger, nothing but the low ambient hum of the engine helped make that final adjustment so much easier. Destan didn't move until Callimay opened her eyes and nodded him on.

"Now don't come out until I tell you to," his jaw rigid as he stepped out of the cockpit and turned. "Just take the book and the belvedere; I'll get the rest. And don't stop for anything until you're in the car."

"Which car?"

He almost made an off-the-cuff remark and then froze, "Oh. Right. Umm… Let me see what's in the lot and I'll let you know. — A… are you feeling up to me talking with you while I'm gone?"

"As long as 'you' do it and keep it short." She put her hand out to remind him to be quiet, sighing as she followed him to the lounge.

She bumped into him when he all of a sudden stopped and turned to her, "I love you Calli."

Well where'd that come from? "I… I love you too, Destan."

The belvedere was beyond excited to see the two of them, but began to whine and whimper when he saw Callimay wince.

ẞ

She fell asleep, the combination of the peaceful quiet and the lush fur of the belvedere she was leaning on too much to resist; startled when she heard Destan's voice: *Go now.*

Groggy and trying to get her bearings, Callimay stumbled to her feet and looked around her in a frantic manner; the belvedere barking as he popped up.

159

After taking a deep breath and closing her eyes to steady herself, she called him to her side and took off… and then stopped, "Oh! Buddy? It's time to hide now." *That was close!*

Destan explained where the car was and that it had a back seat for the belvedere: *Remember: do 'not' say his cue to turn white. Okay?*

Alright.

Calli?

I'm… I'm okay.

If you're that bad just let me take him.

No, no. I'll be alright.

Every footstep across the apron and parking lot felt like a club to the head; each impact making the pain worse. She couldn't quite catch her breath and she was using the belvedere more and more as a crutch whiel they scurried their way to safety.

The belvedere was all business this entire time; whisper quiet and totally focused on the task at hand.

Callimay got him in and jumped in her seat, her heart racing: *Why do I feel like someone's watching me! … Stop it!*

This feeling got worse as she moaned and wheezed: *Why won't it stop! I can't breathe! …* *Destan!*

He was standing on the apron in her field of sight; whipping around and sounding terrified: *What's wrong!*

He… help me! I… I can't—

No one was nearby, so he jumped to the car and threw her door open, "What do you need me to do?"

"I…" she tried to keep her thoughts straight as she cried; almost clawing at her arms as if to get something off them. "I'm scar— I'm terrified someone's watching us. My skin's crawling and I can't breathe. Make it stop! Please! I can't—"

Destan took her in his arms and held her still, saying in his soft voice that he used when she had a migraine, "It's alright. It's just your concussion." *Or maybe Elder's trying to capitalize on this. This is a bit odd even with her concussion.* "Calli? Take a deep breath. Shh, shh. I know it feels like you can't, but we both know you can. It's okay. I'm right here. No one's gonna hurt you. … I know everything's foggy and it hurts, but reach inside yourself. Listen. Is it you thinking this?"

As if the fear she felt shot a sting of pain through her eye, she cried out as she gripped his arm, "I… I'm not sure!"

He kept calm as he pushed her to arm's length and rubbed her cheek, "Take a minute and try. I know it hurts but you need to check. Okay? I'd try but I don't know what to look for."

Her forehead wrinkled as she closed her eyes, an overpowering figure coming out of the mist in her mind's eye: *Oh my gosh!* *Elder you— get out! Leave me alone, you evil, demented— leave!*

If hearing what she said wasn't enough of an answer, the scream and cold chill that rolled through her body did.

"It's okay Calli."

She clutched her arms across her chest and continued to shiver, "Someone 'was' watching me."

"It's alright now. — Let me go get our bags and we can go. I won't be but a minute, I promise."

Destan locked the doors when he left, Callimay not taking her eyes off him until he came back and shut his door. He sounded chipper as he reached back and petted the creature, "Ready, Big Fella?"

The belvedere barked as he wagged his tail, causing them to freeze. Destan whipped his head around to see if anyone was nearby and then casually turned the car on and pulled out of the parking lot: *Well that sure was a close call. ~ This whole 'drop shadow' thing is— I don't know about you but 'I' don't want to keep doing this. ~ Once we get to the Minka everything will be fine.*

It took about fifteen minutes to get to the traditional Japanese house that was situated deep in an elaborate labyrinth of gardens. Callimay rolled the window down and took a deep breath.

Noticing this reaction, Destan smiled as he started the conversation, "You should see it during springtime. All these are cherry trees. — And yes, she had the canals put in on purpose so they'd catch the blossoms."

Callimay looked around at the darkened area, wishing she could see everything so she could truly appreciate it, "It's just gorgeous,"

They were silent as the three of them came to the front door, Destan commenting in almost a mumble, "I only came here once when she was alive. That was when she sat me down and had her say about me."

"She sounds like the one who wore the pants in the family."

"Well, I think she became that way because she'd been a widow for so long. Her husband died right after she started getting things going for the Shadows: sudden heart attack."

"Oh, that's right. I remember Auditor mentioning it." She nodded as they stopped at the door. "What are you doing?"

"Let's just chalk it up to respect for someone's traditions, huh?" He gestured for her to sit down. "Yes, she's gone, but this is technically Rocher's house and he's just as much of a stickler for things like this as she was."

Callimay nodded and sat down to take her boots off; asking when the belvedere started snarling as he paced back and forth, not wanting to come on the porch, "Wh… what's wrong, Buddy? — Why is he acting like that?"

"I'm not sure." Destan pulled her close as he helped her to her feet; stepping in between her and the creature. "Was he acting like that at all while we were at the airstrip?"

"No."

"Well… just stay close." He opened the door and ushered her in.

The creature followed, but would overreact to any small noise or movement. This made Callimay nervous, her biting her lip, "May I?"

"Yeah. It's safe now."

"Just calm down, Buddy. We're safe. It's okay." She sighed as she reached out to the creature. "Wh… what's wrong?"

The belvedere changed to his beautiful white color and then ran past her to a window; lying down in the moonlight and going to sleep.

"Oh." Destan scratched his head; a half smile on his face as his wife glared at him. "Well I'm sorry! I thought he'd have more in the tank than that. — Kinda pitiful design on their part if you ask me. — At least there's a warning he's low: getting grouchy and jumpy. Let me add an extra little bit to the coding I altered so he won't howl and whimper the whole time we're gone."

"But I thought your coding disconnected that?"

"It does… somewhat. It breaks the tie to your emotions. Not to us. He still will want to be where he can see us and keep an eye on us. But with a few extra words — once this thing is kind enough to connect — he'll be completely content."

Callimay started to wander, looking at everything that screamed of a Japanese influence, "Why doesn't anyone come here? It's so peaceful. Very different from anything I've known, but I can see the beauty in it."

"Rocher."

"But— oh. … You're sure he'll be alright here?"

"I'm positive. And if you need him he's only one click away; I'm assigning you my computer. When you wake it up it's the first option you have. … Calli? If I'm not around and you can't get me for whatever reason, don't hesitate. Call for him."

"I will. … Where are you going?"

"Let's go for a short stroll. That is if you feel up to it." Destan turned back, a look of concern washing over him.

"D… don't we have to get back?"

"I told them we were going to 'linger', so there's no worries." He smiled as she came over and gave him a hug. "Doing alright?"

"Much better now, yes."

ℬ

During their walk, Callimay decided the one bench that was on one of the several bridges would be a perfect place to stop for a bit. She was enjoying the quiet when she smelled something unpleasant, "Why did you bring that?"

"You don't have to. I'll just read it to myself."

"But I still have to watch over you and right now I—"

"I promise if there's 'any'thing that comes close to upsetting me I'll stop." He vowed; and then backed off when she refused to stop staring through him. "Alright, I promise I'll stop if I get 'really' upset."

Her eyes closed in a fashion that didn't approve, but her shoulders dropped and she waved him on.

The marker was where Elder talked about Destry, so he skipped a couple pages: *I'll read it later. ~ Like you'll ever have a chance.*

Early on Elder mentioned how he found out about Chameleon: some of the nursing staff told Baleck out of fear if they didn't report it. — Why they knew Baleck was the one to tell is a point of curiosity that wasn't answered, though. — To reward this husband and wife for their "brave admission", Elder offered their daughter a chance to help bring

163

those who weren't following orders, and trying to make things worse for everyone else, to justice. He described they were more than leery of the whole idea, but not wanting to waste time he told them he knew their daughter was left-handed; giving his offer as their only way of saving her life and theirs. They immediately gave her to Elder and let him do with her as he saw fit — only begging him to let her live. He immediately had Baleck administer Dreamer to this little girl — named Ginger — and then "convinced" Baleck to undergo processing with the mixed serums, while in reality he didn't.

His father's name came back up, so Destan glanced through the next section; still being able to understand that Baleck took Ginger with him to Destry's home the night Lylah was murdered. It sounded like he truly believed he had the abilities that only Elder contained: not even family members were immune from Elder's back-stabbing ways. But why did it seem Ingrid could stand up and push back at him?

Callimay's name popped up, drawing Destan back into each word. Elder described the phone call he had with Baleck the night her family was massacred: Baleck admitting her and her one brother somehow slipped out. Needless to say, Elder was livid and went out himself in search for the children. Much to his delight, he found Trever begging for help as he ran down one street, repeating that he needed a safe place for his sister and him to go; but refused the help offered when he saw Baleck. Elder practically tortured Trever to the point of death when they couldn't find her because he believed this crying child was lying.

While killing the child would not have been something he would've regretted, Elder entertained what Baleck was saying and came up with an absolutely sinister plan. He had Baleck take Trever to the nearest hospital and stay with him until he recovered; building a magnificent labyrinth of lies about how he ended up in such a critical state.

How quaint a thought to have the brother she trusted so much be the very person who will end her pathetic life. Trust is something that must be granted to no one.

The search for Callimay was relentless those first couple weeks but never fruitful. — What a miracle and blessing it was that she "slipped through the cracks" because of all the child welfare agencies being so overrun because of the war: *God's been watching over Calli.*

Foreseeing that he couldn't stay with Baleck forever to carry out his missions, he trained Ginger to be Baleck's "mask" and hired those who educated her in other areas: members of the Sisterhood. He was able to convince her to the point that she truly believed she was a completely different person — Baleck's sweetheart — holding the deep, dark secret of a lie that he failed processing and would kill himself if he found out; her constantly having to create dreams for him so he believed he was capable of what only Elder could do.

He spoke of his work "on" Destry after the shock of seeing him alive in Deep Dark; the two of them constantly having arguments in front of everyone. Destry never missed an occasion to accuse him of murdering his wife. Elder had no worries, though, since by this time he was confident he could control everyone; so as he worded it, he "allowed" Destry to rant on and on.

But as time went on Lanta started taking Destry's side. Elder wasn't about to have them join forces again so they would perform another rebellious act, so he found a "home" for Lanta which wouldn't allow her any communication with Destry.

There was mention of a man by the name of Iznan; him being mentioned with Destry and taking his side several times, but Destan didn't have a clue who that person was. He never knew that to be a title and most certainly never knew anyone by that name. Was it possible that this Iznan could give Destan more answers? It was obvious that he was able to break Elder's hold. But how? Did he have abilities?

This irritation was getting to him "and" Callimay, so he did his best to put it aside and just read the last entry.

I can't break him, so there is no other alternative but to kill him. His son, though? I 'will' break Destan.

Destan gritted his teeth as he hissed, "You didn't create this monster, father. Elder was like this before he ever gained abilities."

"We've got to do something soon. The longer he stays the more he controls everyone. Yes, we both have abilities, but there's no way we can fight everyone at Bulwark 'and' Elder by ourselves. Not even with the belvedere helping us!"

"Just let me worry about that, Calli." *If I only had a lead on this Iznan man. He'd be able to help us so much.*

"But—"

"I'm not going to let him touch you, alright!" Destan grabbed her by the arms and shook her.

The sudden movement flared her concussion symptoms, causing her to collapse in his arms.

ℬ

Doctor Gerould was already waiting for them even though Destan hadn't called, "Don't start. I knew she wasn't going to last through the flight here."

He stormed down the hall ahead of them and growled to himself, but just couldn't hold it. It was impossible to miss the fact Destan was fretting over Callimay: something unexpected happened.

While he started checking her over and asking questions, she woke up, "We're back?"

"Now don't move." Doctor Gerould warned as he put a heavy hand on her shoulder. "I need to do some tests first."

"Okay," she shied away from him and looked for Destan.

What's wrong?

It— I'm alright. I just wasn't expecting this all when I woke up.

"Now let me go grab Neurosan. And 'don't' move." Doctor Gerould wagged his finger at her.

"Yes, Mender." Callimay bit her lip, trying not to cry.

The way he reacted was much of how Destan would when he stepped overboard — him trying to calm her and apologize. And while her reaction wasn't something out of place when Destan would do it, something didn't feel right to him. Callimay was scared. But why?

When Doctor Gerould got back, it just took him and Neurosan a couple minutes to get things ready, "We won't be gone long and I'll stay with her."

"Lance…"

"I'm sorry I—"

"No. I mean… why is she so scared?"

"People who have concussions react in odd ways sometimes."

"But she wasn't like this after it happened and she's had a few episodes." He tried to whisper as he glanced back to her. "Even the one time Elder snuck in she wasn't this closed off kind of scared."

"You said that you aggravated it just before you got back?" Doctor Gerould calmed as he nodded Neurosan on. "That very well could've triggered something. It could be something from her past if that part of her brain is being affected. … Destan? What's wrong?"

"N… nothing." He sighed as he rubbed his face. "I'll just wait here."

When they got back, Doctor Gerould looked confused. Neurosan wheeled Callimay in, hooked a couple monitors up, and then left and started prepping the bay next to where they were.

"Who else is on their way in?" Destan asked in his authoritative, yet concerned tone.

"You." Doctor Gerould waved on as he worked on his computer.

"Me? Why me? I'm fine."

"That's not what Callimay told me. So go on." He shook his head as he focused his eyes on her.

"Huh?" Destan turned back.

She was reluctant to say anything, but being so worn she caved. Sobs and tears gushed as she retold what happened that one night.

To say Destan was in utter shock was a mild estimate. He had no idea! Yes, he remembered the nightmare as if it actually happened, but didn't know it was capable to causing him to lose it. And then for his body to give up? The shock he felt mingled with a bitter hurt. In the pit of his stomach he was sick; sick knowing that Callimay was in all of that pain and seeing what he saw in his nightmare all while trying everything she could to save him; and yet not being able to think as clearly and quickly as she wanted and needed to.

Doctor Gerould shooed on, "I'll go check to see if the results on Callimay's scan are back and then be with you."

Destan let a grumbling sigh linger as he followed, and then jogged over as he took something out of his pocket, "You need to read this. See if you can make sense of it and if it'll help either of us with what we each apparently have wrong."

"I'll see what I can find."

ℬ

"You know, Destan?" Doctor Gerould commented rather jokingly as he strolled into the room and turned a chair around so he could sit down. "You should be grateful I'm not billing you for all the care Callimay and yourself have been getting the past what… nine months now?"

"Oh p-l-ease. I pay you," he corrected in a huff as he sat up.

"I always send it back voided."

"That's on you, not me." Destan defended, obeying the gesture to lie back down.

"Now this is just me prying, so you can tell me to leave well enough alone… but with your 'identity' being released, how are finances?"

"I know you're only asking because you're concerned. — I had everything frozen and moved over when Fidus told me about Freigh being taken in by the Syndicate, which was 'well' before this all."

"I take it nothing else is coming in from the University or such?"

"No, which didn't surprise me. I just hope they haven't stopped research or offering the treatments and such. That'd be a despicable thing to do that goes against their Hippocratic Oath."

"Well I know for a fact they haven't stopped offering them. Has the number of people wanting to participate stopped, or at least dropped? Yes. And research does appear to be a bit more scattered even though it's still happening. Everyone's on edge because of your name being attached. I overheard some say they're worried Destry was a Derelict as well; and so they don't want to be associated with what he did."

"As stupid as that is, I will concede it's their choice." Destan sighed as he rolled his eyes; crossing his arms in front of him. "Am I cleared?"

"I know you're under quite a bit of stress as it is; and there's really not much, if anything, you can do about it right now. And I know your abilities don't help you whatsoever in this area, but try do what you can to keep an even keel." Doctor Gerould advised, knowing he was asking the impossible. "Your heart and liver are starting to show signs of wear and tear from your… I'll call them 'episodes'. Everything is early on in development that doing something might actually make things worse. And I hope that it never comes to where I need to intervene. All I can do is suggest you get rest, eat well, and keep away from stress as much as possible — aka: relax. All three of those I know you are in short supply of. I don't know how to help you get more of them but I'm here to help in whatever way I can."

A type of silence filled the air that Doctor Gerould only recalled feeling on a couple other occasions. He sat and waited, the young man he'd tried to help as much as any father-figure trying to find the words he was looking for; Destan staring at the ceiling as he sighed, "Was I really 'this' stressed before?"

"Before Callimay, you mean?"

"That just makes it sound like I'm blaming her, and I'm not."

"Truth be told you were 'always' stressed out. Why do you think you and Elder were always bickering and you were constantly traveling here and there? You didn't see it because you were so focused on your job and adapted to the point you channeled the stress in what appeared to you to be an efficient and effective manner — you pushed it aside. You didn't have time to see you were stressed and I think if I would've asked you, you would've shrugged it off and told me I was a meddling, old man who should back off. Your body even adapted to it and became desensitized to it in a manner of speaking. But things changed. Now you have a whole new type of stress to deal with on top of what you already had. And it's not necessarily Callimay that's changed that. Your drive for going to the Society caught me off guard when I found out. That drastic change in your entire daily routine was enough to make your body begin to fight itself. And really? I see your abilities as been more of a factor than Callimay's presence in your life… if that is any consolation to your question. — She's actually your anchor now: the one who's keeping you steady. — Comparing the information you got me from the Society, that's a large portion of what's affecting you. And I unfortunately don't know if that's something you'll completely be able to control no matter how good of an anchor Callimay is. Knowing what your father told me about the cliffhangers he had to treat and lose? You're a miracle as it stands right now."

He groaned a bit as he sat up, dragging his hands down his face.

"She was right, you know, Destan. She isn't the sole thing keeping that emotional storm inside you suppressed. It 'is' you. You're making the choices that steer yourself through it; having Callimay as a point of reference gives you more reason to keep trying. Don't forget you have control. It's just that you have to fight for it now at times."

"Thanks." Destan cracked a small smile when he remembered her saying that. "What about her?"

"Destry's documenting is far superior compared to whoever did the documenting at the Society, let me just say that. He was trying to figure out how to fix what he messed up with her processing for Chameleon, but it was apparent he couldn't find a way to extract what she had too much of. It had been absorbed by her nervous system; it being the portion that is supposed to heighten her sense of awareness in general. The amount she was given heightens her sensitivity to all incoming stimuli to the point that is similar to your eyes: it overloads her nervous system; and in her case, causes migraines."

No wonder she'd get one so bad when doing something new. ~ Like Physics? ~ Thanks for the guilt trip, pal. I really needed that — not!

"The makeup of Chameleon was actually similar to Liaison as far as I can tell. He said he based it off of Challenger — which, he did — but what it morphed into was quite similar to Liaison in many aspects. I don't know how Destry missed that connection; but maybe I'm seeing things that aren't true connections. … But, all that aside I only can go off of what I know and what I can make sense of: with this similarity between the two serums she has, her sensitivity's amplified even more, now. And I think that's why she feels your pain as if it were her own. Now that is just my theory; I have no solid proof and I don't know a bio-scientist whose brain functions anywhere like you father's did to make sure." *He was a loss to mankind as a whole. The gift he had for this kind of thing was God-given.*

"Why didn't Liaison kill her? Father said he was never able to figure out what was wrong with it; Baleck wasn't either. Was it administered any different?"

"Again, asking someone who doesn't really know." Doctor Gerould chucked a bit, but replied as he shrugged, "You told me your father said Challenger needed someone with the natural aptitude of quick visual learning to accept the serum, right? Couldn't it be that's what was missing for Liaison as well: the person with the natural aptitude?"

"Maybe." Destan started thinking; one phrase his father wrote sticking out to him. "Other than that, is she alright?"

"Her concussion rocked her hard. She doesn't have a traumatic brain injury, but she's as close as you can get without actually having it. It seems the serums in her are acting as a buffer and keeping her stable far beyond what I would think possible; letting her body heal like it's designed to. Unless she gets another concussion before December she should be absolutely fine. She is, however, showing signs like you from stress. But like I said: there's nothing I can 'do' to help right now. You two need to figure out how to help each other." Doctor Gerould prescribed as he rubbed his knees before standing. "And... Callimay asked me this in passing. I know she asked me to not say anything to you but it concerns you as well. So, I'll let you know and let you decide whether or not you tell her I told you."

"What?"

"From everything I was able to conclude, you two shouldn't have any concerns from the serums if you're wanting a family. Now I can't give a one-hundred percent guarantee on that, but from everything I know that would affect a pregnancy there's nothing there."

How... did she know that's why I had her~ Well seeing as how she can hear you talking to yourself, it's very likely she picked up on it. ~ Which would explain why she was so happy to do it. "Oh. Okay."

"I have to say: when she asked me I was a bit shocked and then really concerned I'd have bad news. I know what I said isn't all good, but there's hope. ... I'll go let her know and then you two are free to go. She'll be on restricted release for at least two weeks, so remember that when it comes to her regimen."

"She's just got her conditioning and run regimen to go so she should be alright to take it slow for a bit." Destan nodded as he followed.

"Just keep an eye on her, Destan. And—"

"And look out for myself. I know."

~ 8 ~

Even with all the extra preparations she made and rest she had, she was in a dog-fight during the first portion of her conditioning regimen. Destan could barely stand watching her agonize for every second so she could prove she was giving it her all. Adding on top of that her knowledge of what Chameleon was and did? He saw and knew — even though she never said it outright — her frustration was coming more from this knowledge, and it was making things miserable.

Of course there were the times he couldn't be around. As much as he hated it, he did have a job to do. He assigned Doctor Gerould and Auditor to rotate; him trusting them the most of anyone because they had the added keenness for watching her medically.

But still, even with that extra assurance it wasn't easy to leave. She told him he had a job to do that only he could; and she had a job only she could: *And besides that, you need to keep an eye on Elder. I know I don't know what all's going on, but it sure feels like we're at a major tipping point. I get this feeling Elder knows more than he's letting on.*

At first, Destan would spend the daylight hours with her and then leave to take care of his duties before coming back and meeting her in the suite. She scolded him, saying he needed his rest so he could keep his guard up while around Elder, but he kept refusing: *As long as this concussion is lingering I'm not going to. Got it?*

Of course she wanted to snap back, but deep down she was glad to have someone watching over her. And yet a part of her knew this wasn't healthy: *I… I 'need' you to stay away. If this all is going to stick and be of any good I need to rely on my own instincts and not use you as a crutch. I know you love me and you're just wanting to do what

God's commanded, but I have to admit I'm not putting that much effort into what I'm doing with you around. That never occurred to me until I was around Doctor Gerould and Auditor so much, but now I see it as plain as day. And since they don't know about Chameleon I can't use that as an excuse either.*

It hurt to push him away, each word stinging her own heart, but after talking with Doctor Gerould so much she knew she was being very lackadaisical: letting Destan "do for her" was not her learning. In fact, it was the complete opposite.

While it was put to bed that evening due to an urgent call about a mission, he picked up where he left off the next night; saying she'd always be with him so it wasn't of any concern at all.

The anger she was feeling bubbled over as she started bawling, "I don't want you to get any worse, Destan! I know your heart's been damaged by what happened at the Nest. I don't want anything else to happen, please! You need your rest. You need time away from this all so your body can repair itself. I won't get to see you as often as I want to right now but I want to see you for the rest of my life. I don't want to lose you because of something 'I' should've reminded you of; being the helper God told me to be for you. Please, Destan."

How could he keep saying no? — But how did she find out?

"Calli," he let out a large sigh as he dragged his hands up his face and through his hair. "I know this is scaring you, but I can't just lie down and do nothing. That can't be healthy for me, either."

"But you're not! Y— oh. Hello, Rocher." She bowed her head when she saw he was standing at the door.

"I… w…" Destan scrambled to figure out who to talk to, trying to be subtle as he waved Rocher out. "Calli? I'm not trying to put myself in a situation where I'm going to get any worse. Lance even told me as long as I didn't do this 'every' night it'd be okay until you picked things up. And you know you've always needed just a couple weeks to get a good grip on something new. Your migraine's gone now, right? … Well then that means you're catching on."

"But you don't know that for sure."

This isn't going anywhere productive. ~ *Well I'm not gonna just drop it like it's nothing and brush it off. That's not going to fix it, either.*

"I'd have to find someone to take my place. We both know there's only a tiny handful we can trust. And," he started sounding a bit flustered. "Well, I can't keep Auditor and Lance from their duties like this. At least for a week or so. Rocher showing up means something's gone wrong with a mission and they're going to be needed."

She was calming down so well, but this sent her back to ground zero just about, "What happened!"

"H… how… how about this: I'll see if I can get Rocher to take my place right now and then try to figure out who else is 'strong' enough. There's 'got' to be another person." *God? 'Please' let there be someone!* "I'll come check on you when I get done with what's going on and then sleep for a while. And then I'll check on you before I go to Deep Dark tomorrow. — Is that alright? … Calli?"

There was a silence that begged to know what was wrong, but she took a hard swallow and nodded, "Alright. — Do I need to wait or should I go on up?"

He pinched his nose as he thought, "Go… go to my combat room and I'll let you know what to do."

ℬ

This new setup was working, but Destan couldn't stand coming back to an empty suite and eat alone day after day. He'd done it for years but now came to hate it. Just like he'd recalled Callimay saying on a couple occasions: he had the right to want to be with his wife, his selfishness in this way wasn't what people called "selfishness".

Callimay suggested he eat with her, but then she remembered even "that" was part of this phase. She tried her best to have something fixed for him before she left, but sometimes she just didn't have enough time.

Those nights were the worst for him, making him hate his decision: *Well. Welcome back to the joys bachelor life. ~ Just shut it.*

He would lay in bed, staring at the empty place where she always was; his physical exhaustion not enough to coax him to sleep. Like it or not he was hooked for life. And while Destan did his best to see this "dependence" as a good thing, the tug he felt in his heart was just too strong. For him to even think of getting to sleep he had to hear her voice: *I miss you.*

His depressed voice was a tone that destroyed her. That emotion was so rare to find in him, and so hearing it was hard on her: *I miss you too. … N... now go to sleep. I'll see you after you're done tomorrow.*

But I don't— oh. Yeah. That's right. *Stupid meeting.*

It's not stupid. She twisted her lips.

Yeah, but…

She softened as she leaned against the nearest tree, staring at her wedding bands: *It's hard, I know. But we're making it. I love you.*

Love you too. He let that small smile jump out as he kept fiddling with his wedding band.

ঔ

With the havoc that ensued from the botched mission, Destan's train of thought concerning Elder was derailed. By the time he got it back his plan wasn't going to work. With the strained emotions so many had because of the devastating events that took place they were almost clinging to Elder as a source of comfort and strength. Add to that the fact there wasn't going to be a meeting to put votes put forth for another week yet? He needed to use tact… and a lot of it! Yes, he had the authority to call a special vote at any time, but he realized more and more each day that he lost quite a bit in the way of his power from Elder's so subtle ways.

Thinking back to what Elder himself wrote, Destan was furious he allowed him to break him. Or at least that's how he took what Elder meant since he felt like he'd failed his father.

The more he fought to get his original power back the more flack and backlash he got: he did try to call for a special vote but everyone told him it could wait until the next week when they were to hear back from Brigon as well as the recovery team that was in Yerlonga.

Even Rocher agreed whatever it was could wait!

If he lost Rocher "and" Doctor Gerould… he quite literally would be alone in this fight. Who else was there left? Everyone else ebbed and flowed. Even Auditor was starting to: *He's just loving this, isn't he?*

"So, how did it go?" Callimay dropped what she had and dashed over the moment he closed the door.

"You're back!"

"I passed my first round of two days so that means I get two days' rest!" She stopped right in front of him; grinning from ear to ear.

"You've only been in conditioning for two weeks!"

"That's what everyone else said. And even 'I'm' a bit shocked I adjusted like I did. I guess you can thank Chameleon for that. It's kinda creepy to know what I am capable of and see it happen. — Of course, when I think about it, it's better than being frustrated 'not' seeing it happen; if that makes any sense. — But anyway! It's almost an out-of-body experience when everything falls into place."

"You look so tired, Calli." Destan grieved as he brushed the side of her face, seeing her blood-shot eyes and dark circles.

"It's because I am." She tried to laugh but ended up yawning. "So?"

"It went really well. … I 'do' have something I need to go grab really quick. It won't take long, I promise." He sounded like he didn't want to leave; checking his watch as he bit his lip.

"Just go. I'll be here when you get back."

But, when he got back to the suite she was passed out.

You're an amazing woman, Calli. You really are. You deserve a good night's rest. Happy Birthday.

~ 9 ~

When she woke up she almost thought she was still dreaming. All over the bedspread were orange rose petals. In the air, hung with so much tender care, was the beautiful melody she'd loved for so long; its tone sounding like a music box — hers to be exact. And then on top of everything there was the rich scent of cinnamon swirling around accompanied by the soft, warm, inviting glow of candles on the table which had been set for two. She blinked a few times and then rubbed her face as she called out, "Destan?"

He popped his head around the corner of the kitchen door, him smiling as he jogged over, "Oh good! You're awake, finally!"

"What is all this for?"

"What do you mean— oh!" Destan nodded as he patted her cheek. "It's alright. I get it. Don't worry."

"Get what? What is there to get?" Callimay frowned as she shooed him away. "What is all this?"

"It's just your concussion. It's okay."

She shook her head as she stared at him for a moment, yawning a few times, "W… why aren't you wearing your ensemble? And when did you get your hair cut?"

I really don't want to spoil this surprise. ~ Didn't really factor in her concussion. ~ She'll figure it out. I know she will. He sat there and smiled. *Just give her a moment.*

The silence wasn't helping her much, her tone one of irritation as she shook her head, "'Well'?"

"'Well'?" Destan echoed as he shrugged his shoulders. "You know what it's for. Just relax and think."

"Really? I'm not in the mood for—"

"Take it easy. I'll give my sleepyhead one clue: I didn't know what today was last year so I didn't get a chance to do anything."

This cryptic clue didn't make much sense, but then it dawned on her, "You mean… you mean today's my—"

"Happy Birthday, my Calli."

She gasped as she got up and the sea of petals rolled around and fell to the floor, "Oh no! I don't want to ruin all your hard work!"

"They weren't meant to stay. And 'I' wasn't the one who had the joy of plucking the blossoms apart. You can thank Filament and Traceur for that. — I even think they got Enforcer to help for a bit. — Now! First things first: you need to turn Liaison off: your trainee attitude 'and' ability. Then you need to get out of that confounded black outfit."

"But I'm supposed to—"

"No buts." Destan shook his head as he, with a firm hand, placed some clothes in her arms. "Do it and go change."

While she could have very well laughed and made a face to show she was willing to go along with his game, Callimay only turned and walked away; then stopped and whipped her head around, "Where did you get this?"

"Where you left it."

"But when? How!"

"Emissar— Trever. I had him get everything he could find. That's part of the reason I stationed him in Gastonia once his request for Indalla fell through. Granted I wasn't expecting him to bring back 'everything' he did, but I was glad at the same time."

"You mean 'all' of our things were still there?" Callimay gaped as she glanced down at her orange blouse and then back to him.

"Everything." Destan nodded as he pulled the blouse back to reveal her Bible. "Now go get changed! I've got an entire day of nothing to do and I've already lost about two hours because of my sleepyhead!"

"What!"

"Even if we have to stay here and it's only a day, we need a break. … Like your surprise?"

"But, h—" her eyes got glassy as she held what she had in her arms close, "I don't know if you'll ever know how much."

Destan heard her rambling on and on to herself about everything and was so glad she was happy and surprised. He'd had this planned ever since he got the waiver to fulfill his duties as trainer. As the day crept up, it was getting more and more difficult for him to keep things under wraps with all the extra little things he kept adding on to his plan. — Especially with all the bad he had to deal with surrounding the botched mission; thinking about this day was one thing that kept him going. But at the same time it was putting his surprise at a risk.

He could tell she was ready when he heard her talking to herself about the day they met. Taking the cue, he snuck over and knocked on the door; patiently waiting for her to open it.

"Destan, I…" Callimay said a bit choked up as she glanced down at her outfit.

"I wish to thank you for your hospitality, Miss Berchoff." He bowed his head, hoping she'd remember.

"Y— you're even wearing the same suit! Oh Destan."

"Tsk, tsk. Tears on your birthday?"

"I love you." Her broken whisper tried to get out as she grabbed hold of a fistful of his shirt.

"I love you more."

It was a shock to her that Destan had time to get breakfast ready — let alone the fact he knew how to make sweet yeast bread — but then it came out, "Oh. So you're just capitalizing off of other's skills, huh?"

"Not at all! I 'did' do everything. I did. I just had to have some help from a few Veils yesterday so I could get things ready."

"So you 'really' can make bread?"

"Mrs. Manning said if I liked something enough I needed to know how to make it for myself. She taught me how to read recipes as well as basic prep, baking, and cooking techniques; but she made it clear it was 'my' responsibility to find a recipe." He defended as he marched to and from the kitchen, showing her an aged, laminated, handwritten card. "I found this in a book my father had. The not with it said he got it from a very dear friend of the family. I wish I could read her signature, but the card is so oil-stained that it's smudged beyond recognition now."

She started reading through the recipe and then whipped her head up, "Land sake, you don't use a bread machine!"

"Well I've got one. I just never figured out how to use the stupid contraption." He shrugged his shoulders. "And there is something… 'addicting' about not knowing if it'll rise or not. You use one?"

Callimay laughed, "Not at all! It's not fun to let some machine do all the work for you. It doesn't taste good if you do! I've had both and I'll 'never' use a machine. The saved time isn't worth it."

He watched her look the card over for a second time, then asked, "So… can you read that signature?"

She surrendered as she gave him the paper back, "No. Though I'll say the handwriting looks very similar to my moth— my moth… I…"

"Mrs. Berchoff 'was' your mother, Calli. She was." He smiled as he kneeled in front of her and rubbed her hand.

There was a shattering silence in the air that begged to be healed, and yet any help offered was turned away, "How can I—"

"Hey now," his voice didn't waver from the tender and soft tone it was in just a few moments prior. "I'm not claiming to know everything when it comes to what you're going through right now, but don't think you have to abandon Mrs. Berchoff as your mother just because you found your biological one. You had your birth mother whose love transcended every setback. She did everything she could with the short time she had with you to keep you safe. And then you had your adopted mother who nurtured your physical heart and Spiritual soul into the beautiful, Godly woman I'm now married to. God used them both when He knew you needed them, Calli. … Okay?"

His plea didn't fall on deaf ears this time, her smiling as a few tears rolled down her face.

"Now. Do you want to eat anything?"

Seriously? Just like 'that' we switch to food?

"Yes, I am. … So?"

"Well I'm not about to let all your hard work go to waste. And I'm busting with curiosity how this recipe tastes."

Her curiosity was either overflowing or it was causing her appetite to explode after such a "dry spell" from her regimen.

Callimay was always amazed at how good Destan was at cooking — and now baking it appeared — and it never ceased to touch her heart how he always waited for her before he ever thought of getting his own: *I'd wanted for forget my birthday for so long because it was just so painful. And then when I finally do forget someone comes along to prove all I needed was something so stark and different to help 'reset' this day back to what it was supposed to be about. ~ Not to spoil a fluffy moment, but speaking of fluffy: man! This has got to be one of the 'best' cinnamon rolls we've ever had. It takes almost exactly like the one you would get on occasion at that bakery on Esteem. ~ I'd actually say it 'is' the best. It tastes the same and yet there's something different. ~ The icing's not the same: no cream cheese. ~ I never thought I'd see the day I'd say I didn't like cream cheese, but: I like it better this way.*

"No. We're not bothering with these." Destan shook his head as he snatched the plate away. "No chores, no training, no interruptions of 'any' sort."

"But you said this is my day to do whatever I want." She reminded as she wiggled her fingers. "And I 'want' to do the dishes with you."

I'll admit it's not a chore when you do it with her. "As long as you want to." Destan sighed as he begrudgingly handed over the ebonized dish he was stilling wanting to hold captive.

"Come on," Callimay laughed as she waved him on.

Just then, his phone rang, "I almost forgot they were going to call."

"Redje! Tabitha! It's so good to hear from you." Callimay's face lit up after she answered.

A giggling voice poured out its sweet love, it almost bouncing out of the phone, "Happy bufday Cowimay!"

"Thank you, Rose." Callimay laughed as she pulled the phone back just a little bit.

"Man!" Destan said shocked. "Even 'I' can hear her."

"Be glad you were back there. — How are you doing?"

"Gud. Mama awl betta: we has pwayar time which a what of gud fwiends tonight."

"Oh? I didn't know T—"

"My blood pressure's been through the roof for a few days." Tabitha was quick to explain. "But I got some scans done and I'm adjusting a few things to help. I thought Redje let Destan— did you forget?"

There were some inaudible comments, Rose seizing the opportunity, "Mama and Papa wet me say up to tew you happy bufday. Desan say dat de fwowers you getted fwum him cood be my pwesent. Do you wike dem? Dids he give dem to you awl weady?"

"They're beautiful." She fingered the delicate, velveteen petals. "And they smell so good."

"Gudy! … I have to go to bed now. Bye, Cowimay!"

"Alright. You get some good sleep, Rose."

"I wiwl! Tewl Desan I wuvs him, pweeze. Byee!"

"This was by far the highlight of her day. She's been pestering me all day about when she'd get to call. I think she's actually learned how to read a clock because of this." Tabitha laughed as she shooed her daughter on.

"Thank you so much for calling. — You 'are' doing alright, right?"

"This is just an altogether different kind of pregnancy. Now change isn't bad; it just sometimes isn't easy. Especially when it comes out of nowhere and what's wrong is being caused by a baby who has no intention to hurt anyone. The meeting tonight was so encouraging and there's always someone offering to help out."

It didn't take her any amount of effort to notice the shocked silence from her dear friend; Tabitha not even needing any ability to know what she was thinking, "Now I know if you were able to in any way you'd probably ask to move in and help. I'm not trying to make you feel bad. What you're doing is just as much a help to me as cleaning the dishes. Really, Callimay. — And I know you'll be praying. Don't put its power down. It's not something Christians do as a last resort when they can't physically help; it's what we do at 'all' times because it is so very powerful. And I believe it's even more so if we can't help physically."

"Thanks for being such a wonderful friend, Tabitha."

"And Redje told me he forgot to let Destan know." She smiled as her husband sat beside her; her squeezing his hand. "Poor thing's been frazzled most of the day."

"I can understand why."

"Can Destan hear us?" Redje asked.

"Just a second. … Okay. He can now."

"You'll 'never' guess who I ran into."

"Well with you putting that much emphasis on it I guess I won't. But why would you be running into someone?"

"Har, har. Very funny. — It was Aldred. Aldred Hilston."

"How much did he charge so you could see him?" Destan half laughed as he winked: *I'll explain who he is later.*

"Well aren't we just on top of things tonight? — He showed up at the men's Bible study a group of us young fathers had about a week ago; no demands, no monologue, no nothing. Something 'did' seem different, though. He never said it, but he wasn't surprised to see me there. I think he was looking for a 'safe' way to meet me. … If I'm being frank about it? I… I'm not sure he's who we remembered him to be."

"What do you mean, Rej?" Destan's voice and expression flipped.

"Well I don't think it's anything along the money front. In fact I— I'll talk to you later. I'm getting 'the eye' from Tabby."

"It's okay." Callimay assured. "It sounds serious so—"

"No, no it's not." Tabitha talked over Redje who started to continue. "This is your special day. It can keep until tomorrow. This 'breaking news' is over a week old and it's obvious nothing's happened in that time. One more day won't do any damage. — So, don't give it another thought. We wanted to make sure and say hi since it'd been a while; and of course Rose wanted to be sure and tell you happy birthday. She misses you two so much as do the both of us. Hang in they guys."

"And if you need us, remember to call." Redje reminded in a similar tone. "We're in a different situation in life but we're still your backup if you need it."

"Thank you." Callimay smiled as she looked at Destan while he took her hand. "Do we get a hint if it's a girl or boy?"

"Well… I'll tell you their name starts with a B. Other than that you'll just have to wait like everyone else."

"Man. Complete, solid, blockade." Destan piped in.

"You'd blab it all over if we told you." Redje's edgy voice quipped. "Although that did kinda backfire on you last time, didn't it?"

"I wasn't wrong. Twilight 'is' her name. Yes, it's her middle name, but it is still part of her full, legal name. — But I know better this time. You've got a bet of sorts with Chicane."

"Now how did y—"

"Alright, alright." Callimay calmed, having a feeling Tabitha was about ready to do the same thing. "Thank you so much for calling. I know it's really late for you guys, and with what you're going through I think it's best to say goodnight and we'll talk to you soon!"

"Okay. Take care." Redje replied.

"Bye, Callimay… Destan." Tabitha echoed.

"And may the new moon continue to rise on you." Three voices said in unison. A bit of giggling laughter heard after.

They both chuckled, Destan finishing, "The same to you all."

❦

After they got done, the "freed" couple scurried past Deep Dark and went up top. There was a soft breeze which came up from the ocean and brushed against Callimay's hair as they wandered in the moonlight hand-in-hand. One might have thought they would be a bundle of discussion since they were able to be alone and not bothered, but they always were able to talk when needed even if others were around, so they enjoyed the silence and each other's company.

When they stopped at one point, a soft voice floated through the air as it asked the one it loved, "Destan?"

"Huh?" He looked down to her, only to see an unsure expression. "What's wrong?"

"Nothing. I just didn't know if we could maybe go visit," she paused as she glanced around. "Mr. Ruff? I know it's only been two and a half weeks since I've seen him, but I 'do' miss him. … Now don't you act all jealous, Destan Quinton. I miss you any moment you're not with me. I just— he's all I've got left of my mother that's anywhere close to me right now."

He thought for a moment as he smiled, and then nodded, "I don't see why not. Let me go grab a set of keys and let the on-duty team know we'll be leaving. Sound alright?"

❦

The belvedere didn't seem too excited they were there which saddened Callimay; he didn't even come when she called for him. This was more along the lines of how a cat would act. Destan took only a moment to fix that; the belvedere now bounding around as if he were instantly aware of how long they'd been gone. He even jumped up on Destan.

184

"I guess I missed you too, Big Fella." He chucked as he roughly petted the creature. "Now get down."

"So… umm. Is it okay if I ask you a… well a personal question?" Callimay bit her lip as she began to wander through the open and spacious rooms, the belvedere right beside her the entire time.

"Maybe I should ask my wife first." He tried not to laugh as he gestured for her to continue on.

"Destan," her eyes narrowed as she planted her fists on her hips.

"Oh how I'd love to have a picture of you." He put his hands up to frame her face from a distance. "Yep. Drop dead gorgeous."

Why does that smile make it impossible to hold him accountable for what he says at times like these? Ugh! ~ Why are you upset? That was sweet. She sighed as she tilted her head and half-smiled.

After soaking in his moment, he came over and took her hand, "So what's this 'personal' question that's got you worried?"

"Is… this where your mother grew up?"

'Oh'. So that's why all the uncertainty. … "Yeah. Yeah, this is where my mother was raised."

"W… why… why in the world did she ever want to leave such a wonderful home? I know there's more than just a foundation, four walls, and a roof that makes a true home; but still."

His shoulders slumped as he fought to stay as positive as he could, "Well, as Rocher told me: she missed this place after she left. In fact, that garden we stayed in last time was 'her' garden. But as far as this being a 'home'? It wasn't one for her. It was a school in the most strict of terms. Now I'm not saying she was anti-discipline, but I can believe whole-heartedly from what I experienced, my grandmother took things too far. — Rocher said she was trying to fulfill both father and mother roles; finding out too late she only fulfilled the father role. … He said she wanted a daughter who was exactly like her since she only had the one; but the thing was: my mother 'was' exactly like her. I'm not sure if it's because they were 'so' similar that they couldn't see it or they did but didn't want to admit they hated what they themselves were doing and refused to accept they needed to change. But I think my mother did what her mother never would have because of her deep-seated family traditions and cultural teachings — not to mention religious rituals —

even though there are major hints to her wanting to be this way: a rebellious, independent, woman.”

“And being the leader of a massive anti-government overreach group isn’t being rebellious and independent?”

He looked as her, his eyes showing he had trapped himself by what he’d said. For a moment he stood there, but then began thinking aloud, “Don’t think for a moment that I didn’t have the same thought when I just said that. But, as Rocher told— well, ‘confronted’ me with: she was only ‘thinking’ about it at the time. It was when my mother packed up and left that she full-blown ‘did’ it. Maybe she was trying to show my mother how to be independent without shirking tradition and family?”

“It doesn’t matter. I was just curious. … So you only saw your grandmother the one time?”

Destan sighed as he stopped and looked at a portrait of her, “Yeah. She wrote me letters growing up; one each year on my birthday as well as the day my mother was murdered. Because of them I had such a deep desire to meet her. But the letters stopped coming in my mid-teens so I figured she just didn’t care any longer — I knew she was alive. But a few years later a letter showed up: an invitation to meet face-to-face. I can with all confidence say that was one of only two instances in my life where I was beyond nervous. There was so much I had to prepare before meeting her; hoping the whole time I could mend what my mother had broken. I was warned it wouldn’t be easy or quick, but… I. … Needless to say, our meeting wasn’t at all what I was hoping for. She wasn’t the grandmother from my letters. And yet, looking back now, her eyes were telling me she wanted so bad to let her independent — rebellious — nature extend to her personal life and allow me to have what was rightfully mine. That she wanted to call me mago; but her lips couldn’t betray her. Yes, she wanted to love me like she secretly wrote, but the fear of those around her was too great. And in a way I empathize with her: I know what it’s like to care for someone but not know how to show it in the proper way.”

“Why won’t Rocher talk about her at all or let anyone else talk about her?”

“I… I really can’t tell you for sure, Calli. Rocher has changed so much since then. He still holds to so much of the older Japanese history and culture, but he's somewhat of an empty shell now because she's gone. The fact he's reverted back to his 'true' English accent and other peculiarities while wearing his traditional battle-style kimono is the biggest thing everyone notices and doesn't understand. But they don't dare ask. … Anything else?"

"So since your mother wanted her freedom she didn't get any help? It looked like your parents barely had a solera when they married."

"Right on both counts. When she turned sixteen — that would've been seven years after her father passed — my mother packed up and left; even changing her name. She didn't care that she was cutting herself off from the family fortune and prestige. In fact she didn't care that she was cursed with the title 'jingai' which implied her breech of morals which made her an evildoer and outcast. She wanted her own life, her own rules. She worked her way to Heirway and while working to get money to go on, she found she liked the area. Eventually she took a job working for Doctor Gerould as a receptionist. He'd been life-long friends with my father, and while trying to get him set with another young lady he technically ended up bringing the two of them together. And the rest is history."

"But… your father hired Rocher." Callimay began to question as the belvedere pushed his head under her hand.

Why is she so into this? ~ Well let's face it: this is a 'kind' of history if you will. Just yours. Why wouldn't she be interested? He sighed before he continued on, sitting down beside his wife. "From what Rocher told me, father never knew he was a relative. When she saw him the first time he came to visit, she took him aside and forbade him about saying anything concerning her family and past. — I don't know why mother did that. I really don't. I guess she just wanted to prove that she didn't need money or even her family to be happy or to find someone who would love her. It's rather ironic, in a way, to think she did end up with so much money and was so deeply involved with her family… though it didn't do much good."

"I'm sorry, Destan. I didn't mean to—"

"It's alright, Calli. Really. Don't worry about it. Me talking might not help as much as it helps you, but I won't say it doesn't help me at all. — Glad you were able to see the Big Fella?"

"Yes," she leaned her head on top of the creature's. "Thank you."

"It is nice being away from Bulwark, isn't it?"

"You have no idea." She almost groaned as she sat up; then finished as she curled up on his lap, "But it doesn't matter where in the world I am as long as I'm with you."

"Won't deny that, but I do like this better."

SD

Right as they left, Destan's phone rang. He grumbled as he fumbled to grab it, "I forgot— Oh! Well what do you know. Huh."

"What's wrong?" She grabbed his wrist, seeing the look on his face.

"It's Trever. He wanted me to be sure and tell you he said happy birthday; and to apologize he didn't get a card to you."

A lump in her throat instantly swelled, her fighting to get out, "Do you think he'll 'ever' remember me?"

"As long as Elder's alive? I don't really kn— Calli I—"

"It's my birthday. I know." She bit her lip as she hung her hand while handing him the phone. "Hungry?"

"There's still hope, Calli." Destan reminded as he put his hand under her chin. "Elder can do quite a bit but I can't believe he'd be able to completely erase who someone is. It's like the Big Fella: we've just gotta find the right cue, phrase, command — whatever you want to call it — to bring him back. I'm not giving up on him yet. I have faith he's still in there somewhere, trying to get out. Now I know I can't 'make' him come back, but I'm going to do whatever I can to help."

SD

They scurried back into Bulwark, trying to be seen by as few people as possible. Sure it was their day off, but they knew better than to push the envelope with such things: out of sight, out of mind.

Callimay said she wanted to fix lunch with him so Destan let her choose what they were making. As she got into the refrigerator she saw a plain, white box. She let out a tiny gasp when she realized how heavy it was, "Ooo! What's this!"

"A surprise for dinner, woman!" Destan gasped as he ripped it out of her hands. "No peaking."

188

"Oh come on. … Pl-e-ase!" She pouted as she hopped.

"So grabby!" He put the box above his head and laughed. "No. Not until dinner!"

Her face pruned as she sighed, but she turned around and got what she was initially looking for and didn't fight it. And yet when she turned around he was gone. Callimay rolled her eyes and was about to say something when she heard his phone vibrate. She looked out in the main room, picking up his phone, "Destan? Destan, it's—"

"I saw it. Just let it be."

Oh land sake! Please don't jump out. … "Okay. Ha, ha. Very funny. Now come out. … This isn't a good surprise, okay? … Where are you?"

"I'm standing right next to you, silly woman." Destan chuckled as he put his hand on her shoulder.

She shrieked as she dropped the phone and leaped back, "W… what's going on!"

Her concussion is flaring? That can't be good. "Calli just calm—"

"Stop it!" She cried out as she fell; her jumping back from the phantom hand she felt fingering her hair. "W— why can't I see you!"

"What do you—"

This is what you got from Elder, isn't it? Her eyes darted back and forth in terror, her feeling around for him. *You can become invisible?*

All of a sudden, she saw Destan right in front of her; he looked just about as scared as she did. He glanced at his hands and then at her, "I… I'm sorry, Calli. I wasn't trying to— I didn't know."

But Elder said he couldn't become invisible!

It could be that what he lost is what I gained. —Believe me when I say I didn't mean to scare you. I was just so disgusted Elder tried to call th— wait! That must be my emotional trigger for his ability. But I don't recall when I—

The dinner. When he reached over and grabbed my dress.

I grabbed his wrist. Destan finished what his distraught wife was trying so hard to forget. "Calli I'm sorry."

It took her a little while to gather herself, but she paced around the darkened room by herself and then took a deep breath and smiled as she looked over to her husband who was sitting, looking so defeated, "It… it's okay now. Let's get lunch finished and packed."

"Where do you want to go?"

"Down to the tunnels."

"Who took you down there already?"

"Doctor Gerould. … What's wrong?"

"Nothing's wrong." Destan pouted as he muttered to himself. "It was just something I was hoping 'I'd' get to show you."

"Oh. … Well I wasn't down there when the moon was out like it is tonight. It was cloudy and windy."

He soothed as he walked up and wrapped his arms around her, "I just should've done it sooner is all: that's what I get for being slow."

℔

Everyone who passed by was shocked to see the two of them coming in from what was called "the tunnels", drenched yet smiling. And beyond that, they were in utter disbelief hearing Destan laughing; let alone seeing him in civil clothes.

At one point Doctor Gerould and Rocher passed by and made sure to tell Callimay happy birthday, though not lingering so they didn't keep them out where someone could pull Destan away.

And yet what awaited them there was the dreaded "clothes peeling" process. Destan felt bad Callimay's clothes were all but ruined from the sand stains, but she told him she was glad to have them back; even if she couldn't wear them in public.

He was still drying his hair when she walked out, wearing her green gown, "When did—"

"I packed it when we left last time. I don't really know 'why' I brought it, but I'm glad I did." She flared the skirt out and then ran her hands down the soft velvet. "Oh I remember! I brought it when I saw the jacket you had on the one time. I never remembered seeing you have any type of jacket like that. Why would you have a blazer made with velvet like a smoker's jacket?"

"Outfitter knew you'd notice that right out of the gate."

Her eyes widened as he came up, her nose jumping for joy, "And you have your c—"

"I picked it up when we stopped by the mansion. Remember I said I had to grab something? You said you missed me wearing it—"

"Oh, Destan." She sighed as she laid her head against his chest and closed her eyes. "You spoil me so."

"I'm just doing what I can to make you happy, Calli."

℔

As it turned out, the box in the refrigerator was a cheesecake. Destan had it flown in from the same shop in Faberton where she would get her birthday one. And in addition to that, he had Tabitha find and send his mother's necklace that had her pendant on it.

After a delicious dinner they relaxed in each other's arms for the rest of the evening; looking out over the stars that were, one-by-one, going to sleep because of the early morning sun rays.

Callimay loved every moment she had with him and was so happy she was able to have this break that was so unexpected, "Today was perfect. Thank you."

~ 10 ~

With that refreshing recharge that was full of fun and freedom, it gave them both the needed boost to dive back in and work as hard as they could to make these next few days count. Having another taste of what "normal" life was made them crave it that much more.

And yet this craving was left at just that — a craving. The work that both of them were now enveloped in demanded a level of attention and commitment that scoffed at such soft, tender emotions and moments; which brought to Callimay's attention why opening up was such a challenge, and in a way still was, for Destan.

But there were still moments. Like this evening as she sat waiting: her heart skipping a beat when she heard his heavy footsteps plodding down the hall. She glanced at the mirror and smiled, checking to make sure she looked as happy as she could, "Good evening, Destan. H—"

"He's asked to meet tomorrow." His preoccupied voice muttered as he threw his hand up to wave while walking past her and to his desk.

It's okay. Take it in stride. He's not brushing you off. "So fast?"

His eyes began to kindle a low burn as they warned her, "We're down to the wire as it is."

Deep breath. Be careful. "W… when are you leaving?"

"'We' are leaving early — 17:50."

"We? But what about—"

"It's a long story, Calli." Destan sighed as he flopped onto the bed. "And one that's got me on edge. I know I shouldn't hold back, but…"

"Now I 'have' to know what happened."

"I should've known this, but I guess I thought these individuals had enough self-will left to keep 'part' of themselves from him. — Elder's

192

got everyone in the Veil under his thumb: no one believes me about him. In fact, they think all the evidence is forged. Even Rocher and Lance agreed." Destan dragged his hands down his face. "Now 'I'm' the one accused. Accused of doing this all because of you. That I'm out of my mind because we're not together all of the time and you've had a few 'training accidents'. … To help 'calm me' they agreed to let you go, but said you'd have to be 'distracted' while I meet with him. And Elder was fine with that. 'That's' what's got me on edge. I 'know' he's playing me, Calli. He's played me all along but now I can see it. … And yet I can't! I've yet to figure out 'why' he's okay with this. What is his plan? What can 'he' gain from you going? How can the two of us being gone from Bulwark for less than a day change anything 'that' much?"

"Are there any important reports? Any missions you need intel from?" Callimay began to feel his emotions wander in a bad direction.

Unlike what she hoped, he began to zone out and ramble — much like she would at times. But he was becoming possessed by this evil man's ability to play him for a fool, "It's as if he's actually pulling all of the strings with me as a mere figurehead: my strings are all fakes ones and I can't see a single thing he's doing. I don't have 'any' control anymore. Sure I want to bypass the Veil altogether and get this done and over with. Goodness knows it'd be so much easier. It'd take a bit of convincing the Veil after it all, but if I planned it right it wouldn't be a huge issue."

Does he realize what he's saying!

"But… walk up to him and pound that spiral dagger through him?"

Oh what a weight was lifted off her shoulders; Callimay taking a deep breath as she gripped his hands, "There's always a way. It's just not always the easiest or first thing we think of. Right now it seems like it's the last thing we think of and it comes about because of something we 'didn't' want to happen. I know it's not a happy thing to think of, but life isn't always happy and it most certainly isn't fair. It looks like we're in for another round."

"I really don't want what 'might' go wrong to happen just to get him out of here, though. I don't want some other innocent person to die by his order… or hand."

~ 11 ~

At first the thought of going on a flight was exciting; Callimay now loving it since Destan was so mindful. In fact it became one of those little things they did together that was special; so very special. The only thing was: this was an "official visit". Destan wasn't going on a joy trip or vacation. He was going as Doyen and all that entailed. In short: he wasn't "allowed" to fly.

While they both came to terms with the situation, one thing they both felt very unease about was Elder's influence over the individuals in charge of getting them to their destination and back. The feeling of regret about not taking care of contacting Majesty Presley himself started eating away at Destan little by little.

Knowing he needed to get his thoughts somewhere else before something happened, Destan did his best to focus on something that included Callimay and, well… let's just say something that was a bit more productive in his eyes, "So is there anything you would like explained about what's coming up in your regimen? Runs?"

His question was taken well, but maybe not as well as he was hoping. Her eyes were glazed over to the point she looked exhausted: *He's slipping. ~ What makes you think that? ~ The tone of his voice. ~ Well, what's wrong with that? Look at his eyes. And why in the world would he be smiling if he were slipping? Quit being so down about everything. … And talk to him for land sake!* "Well…"

It was true that Doyen was sneaking in through his tone, but it was also true he was trying to help. But, no matter how he tried, this discussion fizzled out. Now he was left with nothing but his own thoughts for the remainder of the flight.

"Are you alright?" She closed her eyes and gripped him tighter.

"I'm just thinking. … We're almost down. Just hang in there."

The second they touched down the skies let loose; sheets of thick rain pounding the jet. Strong cross winds slammed against the side; it almost making Callimay feel like they were still in the air.

Per Majesty Presley's request, they landed in Gastonia; a chopper provided by him to take them the rest of the way. — Of course you can guess there were several in the Veil who disagreed… with one obvious one staying silent as if approving.

Callimay didn't know what to expect and she didn't want to make one wrong move; and with the way the air was heavy-laden with such a serious demeanor she didn't dare ask. So she waited to be told. And it was the right thing to do — not say a word unless spoken to. The snappy comments she would get from everyone else for "not knowing" weren't nearly has harsh as ones she'd received for taking the initiative to find out so she was prepared.

The second they were done taxiing, everyone but Rocher and Fidus left; them flowing out of the jet in a steady, lighting-fast stream down the stairs and over to the awaiting chopper.

After only a minute or two soaked individuals returned and nodded.

Beyond what she was expecting, Destan smiled as he rubbed her hand, "Ready?"

Part of her wanted to break down and cry, but she held it together and nodded as she followed while pulling her hood up.

Fidus and the others acted as a shield as the small group ran across the apron; them grumbling to themselves that he was shielding her.

Those sent for them sounded very kind and hospitable; putting them at ease. — Well, all but one. There were a couple quite logical reasons as to why they were grouchy, but deep down Callimay wondered if they knew who she was and held a grudge against her.

Accompanying them on this trip was Fidus and one other Veil; them constantly checking outside and talking with each other while on occasion asking or telling Destan something.

He could tell as they got closer that Callimay's thoughts kept coming back to the fact this was where her father was from; that she was, in a sense, going home. Those who lived in the extremely old and rustic castle coming into view were her biological family. Destan took her hand and reminded her no matter if they saw fit to welcome her back he was never leaving her. It wasn't as bright as he knew it to be, but that did bring back her smile. He returned it as he squeezed her hand: *There's my Calli.*

It was pouring there as well but felt worse, the wind shifting and lightning beginning to flicker in the distance.

Destan instructed Fidus to stay with the chopper; and the other Veil who he referred to as Chicane, to remain at the front door. They voiced their objections, but Destan was firm. He was there at the request of the Royalty of Brigon who stipulated they wanted to speak with himself and Callimay alone. It wasn't a time where Destan or the Veil requested the meeting so they had control; they had to comply to the conditions given them if they hoped to gain anything: *Your 'you are Doyen and so you have to do as your told' card has come back to bite you, Elder.*

The two took their orders, but Callimay could "hear" how they were in no way pleased.

With a rather sudden jolt, they touched down and were whisked away down the stone path and to a side door.

ℬ

The inside was absolutely breathtaking, especially for a side entrance! It made the mansion seem like an apartment now; and just an average house in its décor. Callimay stood there in awe as she looked at the hall that was something of princess fairytales: *Someone 'actually' lives here? This is a 'home'! How in the w—*

Destan squeezed her hand to gently remind her they weren't there to sightsee; nodding toward the man coming down the stairs.

This middle-aged gentleman was beyond welcoming; his thick Scottish accent hitting Callimay a bit different than the others from the chopper: *Why do I want to laugh? ~ Search me. ~ Well duh, that's why I said something! … This is so embarrassing! Stop it!*

His face couldn't hide all of his reaction to seeing them, but he was quite skilled in controlling his shock of how "young" Destan was.

"His Majesty be a-waitin' yer presence; if ya wood be soo kind as tu falah me." The man panned his hand to the extravagant staircase.

As they walked along, they had the same reaction when they saw one of the over-sized portraits veiled in black. It was an exact copy of the portrait Callimay had of her mother and father from their royal wedding. Destan put his arm around her and gently pried her away from the pain and memories, doing his best to keep up with Aleck who didn't notice they'd stopped: *It's alright, Calli. I'm here.*

A door was opened and they were ushered into yet another massive room. The mosaic tiled floor announced their arrival, the sound of their footsteps endlessly echoing through the air toward the walls where windows extended from the floor to meet the base of the cathedral ceiling some twenty feet in the air; this ceiling being the support for five impressive crystalline chandlers.

The rain pounded against the glass panes while the thunder made the crystal tremble ever so slightly. Lightning was about as bright as a camera flash with the room lit as it was. Destan had to close his eyes and turn away; him taking hold of Callimay's hand.

Without missing a beat she took over and led him to the far side where an open door led to a lavish and inviting sitting area. She guided him to the one sofa then started looking around.

"It's alright, Calli. The fireplace gives off enough light t—"

"No, it's not alright." She tried to whisper as she shook her arm free. "I'm not letting your eyes—"

"Really, Calli. It's fine."

"What be troublin' ya?" They heard a concerned voice call out.

"It is dark in here. The lightning is very bright and disrupting." Callimay spoke up, ignoring her husband's efforts to stop her.

"Ye'll have tu fergive me," the person walked at a slow but steady pace to where they were. "With me un-ne able tu see, the lightin' is oov new matter. The weather shift be a bit unexpected — though it be a true blessin' tu thu farmers — but I shood-ne fergot tu be sure 'n make arrangements fer ya seein' as how we're cut oov the same cloth in that area. I'll have 'em brightened in nary a moment, Destan."

Callimay gasped; her jerking a bit as she snapped to and backed into Destan when the elderly man pulled a cord to activate a bell.

"Yes, Yer High Majesty?" A man in full butler attire accented with a tartan sash asked as he entered and clicked his heels.

"Cood ya brighten thu room fer our guests, Campbell?"

"As ya wish." The man clicked his heels again and then left for a moment; asking as he came back into the brightened room, "Thar be anything else ya require, Yer High Majesty?"

"That better, laddie?"

"It is. Thank you, Your Majesty." Destan nodded as he took a deep breath and bowed his head.

"Ey. — Thank ya, Campbell. Ya may goo now. And see tu it we're noot disturbed."

Once the door closed, Destan waited a few moments and then said in a calm and pleased tone, "I appreciate your contacting us."

Feeling the couple in front of him was still standing, Majesty Presley wagged his hand for them to be seated, "I was hopin' I cood regain contact with ya a-fer it was too late. I can-ne begin tu tell ya how it's been weighin' heavy on this mind fer a few fortnights. I was beginnin' tu believe I'd waited too long and my feeble attempt wood be fer not."

"We appreciate your willingness to speak with us, Your Majesty; regardless of the timing."

"Yer fine speech at thu ball, Callimay, made me realize how Brigon be shunnin' a major group oov individuals in need of such desperate help, ey. Though we be contacted some twenty-three years ago aboot workin' with yer organization, bein' a peaceful country since thu foundin' oov this here world we call home it did-unt-ne leave room fer us tu compromise er long-standin' legacy and loyalty. — I now see my grave err in what I saw as thu definition of 'peace' bein'. Gainin' wisdom sometimes comes with a dear price, ey. Tis a sad reality that I must confess tu bein' a partaker in. — One oov my sons had a bonnie wife who appealed to us on thar behalf aboot fur years later, but due to family squabbles and thu like, she was disregarded and thu entire thought toossed." Majesty Presley recounted as he gestured with his hands quite often. "It want-ne 'till I met ya and then had thu pleasure oov listenin' tu yer heartfelt plea that I began tu have my heartstrings awakened, as it were. And then when thu news oov yer husband's true identity coomen oot? It was then that I knew I couldn't-ne stand silent. I was shook tu find Destan was also thu leader oov this here group we'd shooved tu the side; but was glad and even more soo when I heard ya be workin' alongside him. Knowin' this gives me much more pride and confidence in my decision tu join ya, ey."

"I… if you don't mind me asking so out-of-place," Callimay looked to Destan for approval. "Could I ask a question, Your Majesty?"

"I doont-ne see why noot." Majesty Presley smiled as the door opened, the same man bringinig a tray. "Just set it here, Campbell."

"You… didn't have this accent when I last met you."

A thick, Scottish belly laugh rang out and filled the room — the butler not fazed one bit — before he answered, "It tis a ruffle tu yer frocks, isn't it, lassie? If I'm bein' blunt with ya — which I be — in order tu attend that ball withoot bein' falud and disturbed, I've had tu sneek oot and learn tu speak as moost others do. — A barbarian oov a task at that, I might add. And one that got-ne a 'wee' bit harder each year. — My 'condition' has been kept from the public's eyes tu save face and prevent any concern as tu thu security oov thu throne. — Ya'd probably be surprised what causes others tu fret, sometimes. Soo, I've been wearin' these confounded lenses fer as long as I can remember and I memorized my way aroond soo new one was thu wiser."

"Oh."

A prolonged silence as they were served tea kept this hope that Callimay could continue to ask questions unrelated to the Shadows since there was someone else present: *Us sitting here saying nothing has got to be a red flag. ~ Well, ask! ~ I… well…* "Your Majesty? Your son's wife you spoke of. W… what was your view of her?"

"I adored the brave lassie. Ey. Lanta was stroong and sure of herself, yet never soo bold as tu disobey her husband's authority; actin' as any lovin' wife shood. She even-ne did soo prior tu their marriage and it caused her much hurt. Tsk, tsk. Dalvin's lapse in judgement almoost broot oon an all-oot family war; bonnie lassie in thu middle." Majesty Presley clicked his tongue as his wrinkled brow began to deepen; him gripping his cane as the man left. "What be wrong, Callimay?"

"She… you won't believe me. I… I shouldn't have said anything. I'm sorry, Your Majesty. Just forget I ever said anything. My apologies."

"Somethin' be weighin' heavy oon yer hart aboot her, ey? … Twas a terrible tragedy, her bein' executed like she was." Majesty Presley's sigh seemed to comfort as he reached out for her hand.

"It was very much so." Destan was quick to respond; him sitting up and becoming tense. *Why did he have to say that! … She's not reacting. ~ Maybe she didn't hear it. ~ Oh 'please' God, let that be right.*

There was an extended amount of silence, so Majesty Presley spoke up again, "What was it ya were gooin' tu tell me?"

Callimay paused, feeling Destan's emotions churning, "T… this isn't why we came. I'm sorry I spoke out of place, Your Majesty. It won't happen again."

"I coot~ne see it makin' er meetin' any less meanin'ful." Majesty Presley smiled as he looked in Destan's direction.

"We are here to discuss what you want, Your Majesty. And however long that takes and whatever topics you wish to cover, so be it."

"Then tell me, Callimay." Majesty Presley asked again as he turned his focus back in her direction. "Tell me what ya were wantin' tu but 'r now afraid tu. I 'want' tu know. In fact, I must. I be givin' my royal command: tell me."

"I…" her voice cracked and strained; her hand he was holding starting to tremble. "I'm their daughter."

"But we be told thu whole family was slaughtered." Majesty Presley replied rather puzzled. "Thar was mention aboot two oov thu children survivin', but noon oov the efforts tu find them were successful."

"I know all of this is my word and the items I have could be forged, but it 'is' the truth. I 'am' the missing daughter: Callimay Everlyn Presley." She pleaded as she talked in a rushed manner, still unsure if Destan would stop her. "I'm not asking for money. I'm not asking for what some would call a rightful place in the family. I don't want power and prestige. I just want my family. I want back what I lost. … I… I just want to know I'm wanted and loved."

"Calli." Destan whispered as he took her in his arms and let her cry.

Majesty Presley rolled his fingers over his cane, his tone nothing but curiosity and calmness, "What proof ya have tu ooffer?"

It took her a minute to calm to the point she could talk, but finally got out, "I have my parents' wedding bands, pictures of my family — I even have the one toy that is in one of them — and the charred remains of my birth certificate that match the original one in the Faberton archive. I also heard her confession that I am her daughter but that doesn't mean anything, I know. It's just my word saying she said it. I can't actually remember anything about my family. I… I just…"

Her voice finally gave out, her breathing so heavy and fast she dared not try to say anything else. Majesty Presley reached his hand out; a sweet, wrinkled-laden smile on his face, "There be new denyin' things are based off yer werd, boot there be one thing I 'can' see; and that be thu truth in what ya say. Ey. Those who be blind learn tu see in differn't ways, and thu way yer hands be tremblin' is noot in nervousness oov bein' caught in a lie; but froom fear of rejection and sorrah."

She jerked back, "You? You believe me!"

"I had my oon suspicions from thu day I met ya. Thu name Callimay be a royal name; thu last one in thu family tu hold it bein' my dear beloved. Yer father spoke with me while yer mother was carryin' ya; beggin' me fer my blessin' tu give ya her name. There was new need fer him tu do soo because I was pleased tu live soo I cood see thu name bein' passed down — all thu grandchildren tu that point bein' boys. His siblin' were in sharp disagreement, but I decided tu make my stand. My Callimay looved Lanta and was heartbroken what thu family 'honor' and-ne grievous sin her young, love-struck man led her intu… what that had all done tu her; let aloon thu fact it pooshed oon oov her sons tu where he be forced tu choose between loove oov family and loove oov life. I was noot aboot tu make that mistake nary again. — But, aside froom my suspicions, Destan contacted me concernin' ya and supplied all thu proof I cood e'er want. His only request was we not say anything and let ya broach thu subject in yer own way an yer own time."

"What!" She gasped as she looked over at her husband who was smiling. *How did you know I'd say—*

"What did ya say yer middle name was?"

"E… Everlyn."

"I'm sorry, lassie." Majesty Presley chuckled as he shifted in his seat. "You'll need tu speak up soo these old ears can hear ya."

Callimay cleared her throat as she sat straight, "Everlyn. At least I think I'm pronouncing it right. My brother Trever picked it out."

"And do ya know where that name came froom?"

"N… no," she said defeated as she hung her head. "My mother just said Trever picked it. I don't know why it's special."

"Ey. I woodn't-ne expect ya tu. There be new special meanin' tu it that I know oov other than it's special because yer brother picked it oot. Now that's noot tu say 'he' had new reason. It's just none oov us will probably e'er know. He was always the imaginative oon oov thu brood." Majesty Presley laughed as he leaned back, but continued in a more purposeful tone after a while, "Just because ya doon't-ne know thu answer tu a question doon't-ne mean ya doon't know what's true. Which quaintly brings me tu one topic I did wish tu cover; and that was tu give Callimay thu praise she be due fer what she's done. — Thu way ya speak is purity in its incarnated form. Ya value honesty aboove yer personal standin' with others. Ya see thu good and truth in others and sacrifice all oov yerself tu understand how tu help them see it in themselves. Yer speech has influenced hundreds oov millions. Those who took a copy oov yer speech immediately told all they knew. Thu truth it held be more than just fer those affected from Irochromolysis. It be a voice in thu darkness fer all dealin' with physical sickness or life-threatenin' oppression that wa'nt-ne seen by oothers, necessarily. I know ya weren't-ne thinkin' consciously aboot that when ya spoke, but it be somethin' ya were carryin' with ya and wanted people tu see. It burned soo brightly tu everyone. They coodn't-ne ignore it. They goot yer message, Callimay. I know fer certain ten oother country leaders have agreed tu stand with me oon this issue because oov yer speech, explicitly! I be meetin' with at least a half dozen others this week tu discuss what be happenin' due tu thu Law and Syndicate."

This shocked Destan more than it did Callimay. He never would've guessed that an off-the-cuff, rambled series of broken yet heart-felt thoughts could pierce the hearts of those who he thought were cold and callous to what was going on. What she said wasn't something even he connected to this all… and it would've been so easy for him to!

"Calli? Calli, you're more powerful and influential than I ever saw or you realized." Destan put his hands on the sides of her face; his eyes glistening. "And it has nothing to do with what my father did. It has nothing to do with your abilities; it's just you. Your heart. Your faith. 'That's' got to be what Elder fears most now. — It's probably why he won't face you. — When people see their worth, when they see the worth others also have, they refuse to be controlled and put under such tyranny. The Syndicate nor Elder can keep their power without that blindness. By your one 'story' — even though we know it wasn't something made-up — you've brought an 'entire world' to their knees in some form of repentance! You showed them the error in their ways in such a way that they could no longer deny or justify it. But you didn't stop at showing them the evil they've done. You did it in the Godly way: you showed them there is a way to right the wrong; that there is a way for them to end this. In a short, what, five-minute speech you did more productive work than the Shadows did in thirty 'years'!"

"I coodn't-ne said it beh'er myself." Majesty Presley nodded as he leaned back. "Ya two as a team is what'll make this a success. Without that, in my oopinion, this be doomed."

"Why do you say that, Your Majesty?" Destan asked confused.

"Everyone — excludin' Lanta — who spoke with me aboot thu Shadows' mission didn't-ne have thu focus and heart ya do. They were seein' it as just a way tu help themselves. They just wanted things easier soo they didn't-ne have tu poot up with e'r-thing. But ya two, like Lanta, have always been focused on others. Ya give and give without askin' fer somethin' in return. — Might I add a personal guess that it may be tu a fault at times? Ey? — Ya be content with seein' thu joy and well-bein' in others as yer payment; even though ya are more than worthy oov bein' a partaker in such victories."

"I'm afraid my attitude has not reflected such noble intentions all the time; even as of late." Destan admitted as he sighed.

"Ya be in need oov nothin' more than someone remindin' ya. And what ya've done over thu years with those special gatherin's shood prove tu yerself that ya 'have' been a-doin' it. Perhaps ya were lackin' some level oov 'purpose'. I saw how ya'd have flashin' moments oov such involvement… but that be it: moments. This year was a miracle. I cood hear in yer voice thu change befer I ever knew aboot Callimay. With ya now holdin' thu heart of such a fragile creature ya be better understandin' why ya been tryin' soo hard tu put others first. Ya know thu importance oov protectin' those ya loove all thu time; noot just when they be needin' it most 'er standin' in froont oov ya."

"I apologize for what might sound like my rudeness, Your Majesty, but it's going to take more than that for this to work."

"Speak yer mind an-ne be comfortable aboot it. It be a rarity and I enjoy such conversaions. — But tu address what ya said: that be why ya have each other. When ya remember ya two be a team — when ya be rememberin' those spaces between yer fingers are there fer a reason — ya find strength. Bein' selfless is thu foundation for this type oov strength. It be a strength that be just aboot as reliant oon others as it be only lookin' tu serve others." Majesty Presley took their hands and put them together; then shifted his tone, "While I would loove tu sit and continah tu be thu lovin' grandfather, I know thar be more pressin' matters we need tu attend tu at thu moment."

"As you wish," Callimay took a still shaky breath as she nodded.

"Continuin' with what I be speakin' oov earlier, I have — by some odd set oov events — become a confidante tu other goovernmental authorities aboot thu mountin' distrust with thu Syndicate. It seemed tu me nothin' less than providence that it be happenin' when I made my support known tu ya."

This comment worried Callimay: *You don't think—*

Let's not jump the gap. God's still in control no matter what Elder might think he's capable of. Let's use this for good like God wants.

"I haven't-ne spoken with all them due tu circumstances which I be sure ya are familiar with: political security, ambiguity, and the sort."

"Absolutely," Destan replied.

"Ey. I thought ya wood. — While there be a fair amoont of hesitancy in thu voice of one in particular, I know he only be fearin' fer thu safety oov his people and looved oones. It be oov concern tu me with regards tu his continued correspondences, but nothin' be set in stone. I speak with him again next week."

"I by no means am making this statement in contradiction to my agreeance with valuing each individual's safety, but I do not wish for you to remain in this middle-man position, Your Majesty. We are fully prepared to fill that role with diplomats who decide to be couriers. — Is this man you have spoken of the president of Crosswall?"

"When I've had my say with everyone my plan be tu inform them oov ya and thu help ya've offered; allowin' those who truly wish tu see this thru take that step oov commitment on their oon. How wood ya like me tu convey what ya would be doin'?"

"I think it best to have some of it written since it is a bit lengthy, Your Majesty" Destan glanced at a small device on the one table.

"Ey. Wood be a help, that it wood." Majesty Presley felt for the device and offered it. "But nare ya feel obligated to put down anything bein' oov compromise. Do what be fittin' tu ya and doon't be a-tall worried if ya make some oov if 'werdy'. I be understandin'."

Destan began typing as he explained, "Our main duties are to ensure — to our absolute best — the physical safety of those who hold power and wish to push the Syndicate out of existence. Once their commitment and other information are secured, we see to it that they have face-to-face contact and coordination with the individuals who will act as their personal body guards and points of contact to us; what I will make sure you have for yourself before the week is over. While we do everything humanly possible to ensure their safety, there is an inherent risk that can never be negated by any means; this caveat extending to their loved ones as well. We've yet to have anyone as high up as those as you are speaking of found out, thank God for that, but as we get closer to this all coming to the forefront things may change. We've trained and prepared as best we can, doing our best to also prepare those we protect, but there truly is no way to tell for certain how the Syndicate and their deep entrenching will react… or how quickly. … Each person will work within their government exclusively for the time being as we lay the final groundwork for what we have called Total Eclipse. They will have 'some' names of others within their government who are partisans — as well as all persons to completely steer clear of — and they will have updates as to when what phase will begin. This attack has to be as systemic and methodical as possible to prevent a major outcry, but it is going to be fought not just on the political front. I'm sure you're well aware of this reality. There's been no indication for 'negotiations' with the Monarch so we're prepared."

He continued typing for a while after he finished and then added, "At the end I've put my direct contact line. As family, I want you to have as much contact with Calli as possible."

"If-in this here plan fail fer what-er reason, I be formally givin' ya two my vow as thu ultimate power oov this country: thu protection n' safety here within these walls." Majesty Presley gestured around him.

"I know this be still hard fer ya tu believe, but trust me when I say ya 'do' have family here who loove ya, Callimay. I know there be in the past and will contin-ya tu be backlash froom certain members oov thu family, but I woon't-ne let them oostracize ya like this." *Noot er again.*

"Thank you." Destan took a large sigh of relief as he sat back.

The rhythm of their conversation appeared to come to a grinding halt. No one said a word, but it appeared as if Majesty Presley was not concerned in the least.

Callimay felt uneasy, as did Destan, but he had a better handle on things in this type of situation, "Is there anything else you wish to discuss, Your Majesty? I know this was rather brief and somewhat of an info dump."

"I be apologizin' fer my stillness. I was enjoyin' yer company that I be forgettin' everything else," the smile on his face growing even more. "I know what ya stated was brief, as ya say, but knowin' less is goin' ta be more in a time such as this oone. I have what I be needin' but'll request information I feel be necessary. And as far as everyone else? I'll be fulfillin' my duties as I've vowed and then'll make necessary details available tu them soo things can-e progress as they oot tu."

He was the first to stand, Destan taking Callimay's hand and rising as they were given this stern, hushed warning, "Make sure ya speak tu 'new' oone boot Haggis er myself — Aleck be how he wood-ne introduced himself, boot he fore'er be Haggis tu his ole' father — aboot this. Being neutral fer soo long has made some oov thu family lazy with their speech n' relations. I don't-ne want tu jeopardize anything. Ey?"

"I completely understand."

"Coom 'ear, my wee Callimay."

"I'm coming," she jerked a bit and then took his hand.

"Ya be welcome home when-er ya be ready, Callimay Everlyn." He said tenderly as he felt for her face and patted it before embracing her. "Ya be welcome home tu yer title oov Princess if and hopefully when ya decide ya be wantin' it. It be waitin' fer ya. 'I' be waitin' fer ya. I've been lookin' forward tu this moment e'er since I foond oot ya were my granddaughter. I got only tu meet ya a handful oov times before ya were lost, but I knew ya tu be a very special lassie. I missed ya soo and am singin' praises tu have my bonnie loove's namesake back; oh what a joy that bring tu such sorrowful oov a loss. I just be sorry ya doon't-ne have thu family ya shood; tu truly know thu loove yer father, mother, n' brothers had fer ya an-ne other. … I can't-ne, nor any oov yer other family, substitute fer yer parents er siblin's; I know that. There be a hole that'll ner be filled and I doon't-ne try tu pretend this be able tu wash it away. — Destan told me Trever be also alive but his situation be tryin'. I grieve again fer them all as well as ya and Trever; especially fer ya my wee lassie and thu strain it be to know yer brother be alive but not. Doon't-ne loose hope, lassie. The boond he had with ya will last fer eternity. It only be tangled and frayed at thu moment. … I remember as if it were yesterday: his carryin' ya to-and-fro around that very ballroom; showin' ya oof tu all yer clan with yer mother and father en-toe — them worried half to death he wood be droppin' ya. He spent a good fifteen minutes describing ya tu me as he took my hands soes I cood 'see' what he was talkin' aboot. That alone is proof enough fer me: I cannot-ne believe a mind can be broken tu thu point such a loove as that can be forgot. God woodn't-ne be faithful if that were tu happen."

"Oh grandfather," she cried as she buried her face in his chest. "I'll be home soon. I promise you. And I pray it's with Trever, too. … Whether it is to stay? Destan will need to decide. He's my husband and my head. Wherever he leads me in The Lord I'll always follow."

"I woodn't-ne expect new other answer." Majesty Presley smiled as he stepped back. "Safe travels back. I be contactin' ya soon."

"I look forward to hearing from you." Destan stepped forward and shook his hand. "And thank you. Thank you so much for what you've done for Calli. It means so much to me knowing she's got somewhere to go if something does go wrong, Your Majesty."

"Just see tu it that doesn't-ne come tu that." Majesty Presley replied as he gripped his hand.

℈

Aleck was a bit nervous as they came out, almost pushing them down the hall until they rounded a corner. This drastic switch wasn't lost to either of them; something was up.

As both of them were about to take extra precautionary measures, Aleck stopped. They looked around and found they were at the veiled portrait. She fought so hard, but when Aleck took a rose from a nearby vase and handed it her it was more than she could take.

"I felt yer longin' tu linger earlier and oonted ya both tu have a chance withoout any oov thu 'others' seein' ya. — Dalvin was a good man he was. A stroong-willed and honest brother, loovin' and carin' husband, and an involved and strict father… ey. And yet he be a bit of a pushover when it came tu ya, lassie. He looved ya dearly and shed a rare tear when thu blessin' tu give ya moother's name was given."

Her hands shook as she reached to take the flower, Destan helping her lay it among the other flowers and candles that were scattered on a small table under the portrait.

Callimay's voice cracked and strained as she labored to say, "Did… did you know me? I mean… d… 'do' you know me?"

"Ey, lassie." His eyes smiled as he nodded. "And it didn't-ne take me boot a second tu recognize ya: thu spittin' image oov yer mother when she was yer age, ya are. Ey. … Why I—"

A door opening somewhere down the hall prompted Aleck to break up this family reunion and time of reverence; rushing them down the hall and to the door they came in.

Destan activated his beacon the moment they got out of the meeting to let Chicane and Fidus know they were ready to go, so by the time they got to the door everyone was on their toes.

There was a moment's pause between Callimay and Aleck: her dying inside to know more and it appearing him knowing this and wanting to help as he could. But this just wasn't the time. Whoever it was that he had to keep them away from was obviously coming their way.

"Stay safe, my wee lassie." Aleck took Callimay and held her close for a brief moment.

Something about the way him and her grandfather spoke tugged so hard on her; as if she was remembering things in a way. And yet it was a tug that was empty: there was nothing to tug on. Oh what torture this all was, not knowing!

Destan took her hand, smiling as Chicane went ahead to the waiting chopper: *We're gonna make it, Calli. I know feelings are fickle and there are so many questions you have about your family and such; but this right now? This meeting? I can't help but feel like everything is so much clearer and concrete. The Syndicate 'will' be done away with, Elder 'will' be taken down, and we 'will' have the life we both want… and it'll be 'very' soon. … Now let's get back and get things rolling.*

ℬ

The weather hadn't changed, but it now felt like it were sympathetic to Callimay; the rain trying to keep her there so she could talk with Aleck. But for as much as it tried, it wasn't going to detour those flying from getting them back to Gastonia.

After she'd come to terms with everything, Callimay nudged Destan.

Hum? He replied, sounding content.

How long has Chicane been a Veil?

Three years. Why do you ask?

Is he naturally the nervous type? I mean I don't remember him acting like this while we were flying out.

Destan's relax frame slowly froze as he started glancing around: *No. No, he's not that type. In fact his cool — almost cold — demeanor was specifically why he was chosen.* *Why are his boots so muddy? He hasn't stepped foot off pavement since we left Bulwark.* "The lightning sure isn't any help, is it, Chicane?"

"You can say that again." He responded as he snapped to; nodding outside, "Just miserable."

Calli, we may have to jump. Destan's voice did a one-eighty as he gripped her hand; Fidus alarmed by what was said as well.

What! She tightened her grip on his arm and leaned against it.

"Doesn't seem like there's much room between us and the canopy, huh, Fidus? Storm must be picking up again."

"Less and less it looks like." Fidus nodded as he leaned over and put his one hand on the hilt of his knife. "Not what we had planned at all. I'm hoping we make it back before it settles in. Do you want me to—"

"But you know? Traceur would've loved this." Destan continued, his eye contact with Fidus a form of communication in and of itself.

"This might have even been a bit extreme for h—"

"What do you think, Chicane? You know Traceur best. Would he enjoy this?" Destan cut off as he tugged on Callimay so she'd scoot closer; him having one leg practically out the opened door. *I got you.*

209

"I've gotta agree with Fidus on this one. The rain wouldn't sit well with him, Doyen. He never likes his track to be unstable like this."

In one swift movement, Fidus whipped one of his Kopis knives out and thrust it against the intruder's neck as he sneered, "Who are you!"

The young man lost it.

This response was so jarring Destan stopped himself from jumping; them listening to the young man's whimpering words that came out in between sobs, "I'm just doing what I was told to! They said they'd kill me and my family if I didn't! Please! I have a wife and two little ones!"

"Likely story." Fidus gritted his teeth.

"No! Stop!" Callimay shrieked as she grabbed Fidus' arm. "He's telling the truth! His wife's name is Edna and his two children are twins who aren't born yet. There's a picture in his right back pocket."

"How did you…" The young man asked dumbfounded as Fidus frisked him, eventually finding the picture.

Those up front asked for an explanation, but Destan assured them things were under control and to keep going. He then took a deep breath and turned his leery focus to the young man whose eyes were bugged out as far as humanly possible, "Alright, who threatened you?"

"The Syndicate. — Please… I don't want to, but I have to so my wife and children don't die." The young man started to cry as he took a gun out and pointed it right at Callimay.

"Don't do it Fidus! No!" She yelped as Destan threw himself over her; her not at all afraid as she assured her husband it was alright and reached out to the young man, "I know you won't do it. You don't believe this is right. Just let me have it. … Please. … Edna wouldn't want you to. … Now. Tell me why the Syndicate threaten you? I want to help, but I can't until you tell me why."

"I'm a Derelict." The young man wept as he buried his head in his quivering hands. "They somehow found me and gave me this as my only alternative to… well, you know. — I was so careful! So was Edna. I… I don't know how they found me."

"What happened to Chicane?" Destan snapped at him, furious more with what the Syndicate did than his bowing to their threats.

"I'm just trying to keep my family alive. I'm sorry." The young man wailed his confession; tears streaming down his face.

Let me talk to him, Destan. The last thing you need to do is get angry right now. "Is he dead? Did you kill Chicane?"

"I don't know, honestly. It all happened so fast, I—"

"Where did it happen?" Fidus questioned, his Kopis still readied.

"Right where he was: by the door. No one was around. He thought I was just a servant so I was able to sneak up on him." The young man explained as he took the picture from Destan. "They're all I have left in this world. My family threw me out when they found out. I've been living on the streets ever since. Only by some crazy misunderstanding did I even 'meet' Edna and— oh please help us! Please save her, she's blind and was so scared when I left; save my babies. I don't care what happens to me. I deserve whatever you do since I'm a Derelict and probably killed the one guy, just… just please don't let them die for the wrong I committed. Please!"

"Don't call yourself that." Callimay scolded while trying not to make him feel any worse than he already did. "Doing that is playing right into the Syndicate's hand: they want you to think you're useless and evil. You're not! … You don't have to die so they live. And they don't have to die so you live. No one has to die. We'll help. — Right?"

Her plea for backup was met with more support from Fidus than she expected; his grumbling as he sheathed his knife what she knew to be his agreeance, "I'll never understand: using our own against us?"

I mean I know it's been like this from what Destan said, but… but giving them that option or death? How can they be human!

While this was relevant and disturbing, Destan kept things pointed to the situation at hand, "Where are you from?"

"Y… you're not going to kill me?"

"No."

The young man froze. How could someone say that after what he confessed? But truthfully his confession was he didn't know, so how could Destan go to that extreme without concrete evidence.

"Where do you live at? Is that where they're holding your wife?" Destan repeated in a calmer tone; his anger washing away.

"They told me he was going to stay there at the house. I hope they didn't take her, it's almost her time. And with it being twins—"

"Tell us where you live." Callimay did her best to keep him focused.

"We have a little shack just north of Trawnvane about ten miles. It's not much and it's a ways off the road, but we've made it work." The young man explained as he tried to point, his hands almost convulsing. "The man said he would stay there with my wife until I got back with proof that you were both dead. — If I don't come back before sunrise he's going to have his dog kill my wife and babies."

Justice Wan? But I thought I—

You never made a headshot, Calli. They can be thrust through the heart and still make it. The computer's in their brain and 'that's' what keeps them alive. "What's the proof he wants?"

"Your wedding bands… umm… st… still on your hands." The young man sounded disgusted as he took out a pair of heavy plyers.

"Well… let's give them to him." Destan replied as he shrugged.

"What!" Fidus gasped as he whipped his head over.

What do you say, Calli?

We can't leave without at least trying. Shadows never abandon those who need them. We protect our own.

Destan smiled as he patted her hand, turning to the young man as his voice sounded stern, "Do you trust us to keep you as safe as we can? I can't make guarantees, but I can promise we'll do everything to get you, your wife, and your children to safety."

"I'll trust anyone willing to help my Edna and little ones." The young man begged, hands interlocked as he shook them while dropping to his knees. "I… I know I'm weak, I just—"

"You love them." Callimay comforted, her eyes glassy as she bit her lip. "It's hard to see the ones you love in danger; you feeling trapped and unable to do anything to help without having to make some 'deal with the devil' as some say. Don't give up. They need you. They need you to be the strong man you've always been capable of being. This is one mistake. It doesn't mean you can't make amends."

𝕾

The second the helicopter touched down, Destan and Callimay left with the young man. Fidus objected but Destan stood his ground. Yes, Fidus knew they both had abilities, but he didn't understand. He didn't understand how Callimay was able to know if someone was lying. Yes, people who were "good liars" could fool her; and that was a reality she knew about from early on, but this young man most certainly didn't strike either of them as someone capable of such deception; not while under the amount duress he was.

They sent the young man on ahead; them following at a distance to his car he had parked by the rail station. It was odd to be where they were not that long ago; the circumstances not much different.

Once they saw what car it was, they stuck close to anything that would be cover — helping them become as much like shadows as possible. This stealth ability was executed so well that the young man just about jumped out of his skin when he heard the back door open; even though he had been watching the whole time for them.

Being scared already only made the young man on the brink of losing his mind… but he knew he had to try. Running or not doing anything would mean his wife and children would die. They at least had a chance now. He just had to keep himself together long enough for their only chance of survival to get there. Just long enough.

Now that all he could do was wait, Destan was able to process what happened; seeing his father's work more and more evident in Callimay. It was her who caught the substitution in the first place! In a way, she was beginning to outpace Destan; or he just wasn't paying attention like he used to. The former wasn't bad, but the latter was: he couldn't afford to let his guard down for one second.

And then that made him remember what Canary said about her not wanting Callimay to become a Shadow at all; and so he felt remorse for dragging her into this. Yes, she was excellent at doing what she was being trained to do and was getting stronger and stronger with each passing day; but at what cost? He knew it was her choice to stay, but he didn't want her to acclimate so well that she would "lose" Callimay and "become" Liaison. Destan knew it was easy for him to slip at times and knew how much it hurt her when he did.

"I love you," she whispered in his ear.

I love you too. Holding up okay?

Kareal is getting worse, so my guess is we're close. … Are you sure you'll be able to handle the keeper 'and' him at the same time? I don't want to you to have something happen with your heart be—

I'll make it. Believe me. I'm comfortable with situations like this.

But not with that monster you now have, she reminded as the car jolted a bit as it turned onto a gravel road.

Destan gripped Callimay's hand from the jar and began to see the fear creep into her eyes. He knew it was in part due to what Kareal was saying to himself, but when it boiled down to bare bones he knew: *If it 'is' just the one who stayed behind like Kareal said, and it's in God's will, this will be done before it even starts. Just keep your eyes open and trust your gut. — Dear Lord, give us Your wisdom and strength to help this family. Give us Your protection. In Jesus name, Amen.*

Kareal got out and took the bag he had; his nervous nature actually helping them avoid being found out. If he had done what he planned to, what normal person wouldn't be affected by it? And then Justice Wan — as Destan was hoping — would be focused on a frantic person rather than his surroundings. The belvedere being thrown off? Not so much. But all he needed was a second. One, solid, second of surprise.

It's Justice Wan, alright. Destan growled as he took surveillance of what it looked like inside the house. *Kareal's almost there. You ready?*

She took a rather shaky breath and nodded: *The confusion and chaos is good. Right?*

It's all to our advantage right now. Just stay focused on your detail.

Justice Wan was quick to order the belvedere to attack regardless of this all happening, but Callimay got to Edna much quicker. She put up her barrier and turned to check on the young woman who looked to be in pain and utter shock, "Edna? I know you're scared and you don't recognize my voice, but I'm here to help. Kareal asked me to. I need to get you out of here. Can you walk?"

"I… I can't." She wheezed in agony as she cried out in pain.

Callimay raised her voice to help drown out the chaos around them, "Just try to take big deep breaths. Can you do that? … Here's my hand if it helps. Just try to take big deep breaths. Focus on my voice as much as you can. It'll be alright. Just breathe, Edna. In. Out. … Good."

Seeing the look on Callimay's face and hearing the cries from Edna made Destan aware of a "tiny" detail Kareal forgot to mention — there was no way their original plan was going to work. His tries to catch the belvedere off guard weren't quick enough — it obviously learned from its bout with Callimay. But he wasn't about to give up: *I just need you to 'stay put' for a few minutes.*

It looked like the irritation of this belvedere's ability to rebound and learn was starting to get to Destan — this throw being "way" off target — but he grinned. It was quite intentional, in fact: the throw pinned one of the creature's feet to the floor. And so now with that danger "contained" he switched his focus back to Justice Wan who has shaken off the surprise left cross. The struggle was intense even though it was short, but Destan wasn't debilitated like he was last time; his size and agility worked in his favor like they would have the other time had he been able to function.

He knew the belvedere would go to whatever lengths it needed to free itself and obey its keeper, so Destan called Kareal over.

But he hesitated, seeing how much pain Edna was in. Destan tried his best to keep from lashing out since he understood how he felt, but being in their situation? This wasn't helping, "Kareal! I need your help. … Now! She'll be alright. Come on!"

Once he was sure Justice Wan wouldn't cause a problem, and just as he started to turn around, Callimay screamed, "Destan watch out!"

Following that sharp sound was a weak yelp from the belvedere before it hit the floor, reverting to its white color.

Destan whipped his face up as his breath came back to him and saw Callimay standing there, still in a stance of follow-through; one of her spikes embedded in the belvedere's skull, "De— your face!"

The moment she got that warning out he felt the splatter line from his left cheek up across his nose to his right temple start to burn. He ran outside and threw himself to his knees; clawing at the ground to get a handful of mud.

Knowing his emotions were climbing, he sat there and forced himself to listen to the calm, deafening rain and thunder. His posture started to soften as he sighed… until lightning flashed: *Just can't catch a 'real' break, can I?*

Trever ran over and asked if he was alright. He nodded and groaned as he worked to stand up, raising his head so the pouring rain could help wash off the mud still on his face. Trever started to ask something when they heard a shrill scream come from the house.

They darted in and saw Callimay following Kareal to another room. She turned when she heard them thunder in and ran over.

"What's wrong?" Destan asked worried as his eyes darted back and forth; him still wiping mud off his face.

"Edna's gone into labor. — Trever? Oh good. Call for a medical transport. Now!"

"Where are you going, Calli?" Destan asked confused as he grabbed her arm after they heard Edna scream again.

"I don't know if they'll make it in time. She needs help."

Once she left, Destan went over to Justice Wan who was just waking up and gripped him by the arm as he jerked him to his feet, shoving him against the wall, "You were 'so' worried about your own child for so long, but someone else's child apparently means nothing to you. Did you ever 'truly' care about Hyra? Really? No one can be 'that' bias. … Can they? Are you?"

Justice Wan didn't say a word.

Destan contacted Fidus and told him to pick a team and send them to take Justice Wan in for questioning. Fidus asked for a short brief and so Destan gave him the good — and concerning — news. By the way Callimay was running around he wasn't even sure if things were going as well as he suggested they were.

At one point she ran up to him, not caring she was interrupting his conversation and asked if he had any kind of tracker she could use to monitor Edna's vitals. He paused for a moment as he put the phone down, but shook his head, "No. I can ask Trever if he does. — Calli? What's wrong?"

"I don't know, Destan. … But I know something is." Her voice was terrified to even say that much; her taking off when Edna screamed.

He stood there for a few moments trying his best to figure out what might be wrong when he heard Fidus calling out. He picked up the phone and started to explain, his tone becoming more doubtful.

As he looked over, Destan saw the belvedere as well as the "mess" in the room. It finally registered, "Oh! Fidus. Have the team that's coming bring a containment unit for a belvedere. … Yeah. … There's a medical team on the way so just make sure they're aware of how they approach. … Good."

Trever came back in as soon as Destan hung up and told him the medical transport was about a half hour out, "Better contact Fidus and let him know, Emissary."

"Got it."

"By the way, do you have a monitor on you?"

"No, sorry. Tetralyn's was in for repairs so she's got mine."

With the ETAs for the transport and Veils being so close together, Destan and Trever moved the furniture so the belvedere wouldn't be seen, "If the team doesn't arrive first you'll need to take our 'guest' out back. And then unload your 'open' weapons." *I should take my veil off, too.* "No need to prompt unnecessary questions."

"No problem," Trever's voice sounded cruel as his eyes narrowed; him gripping the handle of his drawn knife as he gritted his teeth and glared at Justice Wan.

Not too much later Destan "heard" Callimay panicking. There was no way the transport would get there before the babies did and she didn't know what to do — she hadn't figured out what was wrong and she'd never don't this before. He began pacing the floor, not sure what else to do. He could hear what Trever was saying to himself but kept his cool. Trever didn't know it was a hot topic for Destan… let alone he didn't even know Destan could hear him.

Edna cried out in pain for almost a good fifteen minutes and then it felt like the world itself was holding its breath. Destan whipped his head up with a fearful look and waited.

Before the minute was over he could hear the cries of a baby just as loud and clear as anything else he'd ever heard in his life; their voice allowing the world a brief reprieve. Destan could also hear the joyful, yet sorrowful, words of his wife; him having to fight to stay positive: *You're doing so well, Calli. You 'can' do this. Don't give up.*

While she didn't respond he knew she heard him.

A few minutes later — Edna still crying out the entire time — a second baby's cries could be distinguished. This reassurance that the babies were alright was so welcome, but it also took so much out of Destan; him collapsing onto the nearest chair.

Not but a moment later both he and Trever saw lights outside and heard voices. Trever popped up and bulldozed Justice Wan into the mud room before coming back. While he just stood in the doorway at first, he snapped to and told them where to go; Destan too distracted to do anything.

Trever asked as he walked back, seeing his commander still slumped in the chair with a hand covering his face, "You alright? Is it still in that slow burn phase?"

"I'm… just thinking, Emissary." He sighed as he clasped his hands in front of him and leaned forward, looking at the floor. "That stopped a while ago."

A minute or so later the door opened and Callimay staggered out, reaching for something to steady herself on. Destan ran over and caught her, them hearing the soft cries of the babies. He whispered as he stroked her hair, sounding choked up, *You did so good, Calli. I'm 'so' proud of you.*

She gripped his shirt and cried: *That was so hard, Destan.*

One of the transport members came out and made sure to praise her for the amazing job she did under the circumstances; asking her if she had any training. It was a second round of shock to find she had none, but they smiled as they remarked, "There are some things women just naturally know when push comes to shove. Kinda amazing."

It didn't take them much to get the babies ready for transport, but they had to take extra precautions with Edna. As they wheeled her by, she reached out, trying to find Callimay, who took her hand. She managed to smile as she thanked her for everything. Callimay collected herself and told her she hoped her and the babies would be home soon.

"Thank you so much." Kareal said breathless as he stumbled over to them. "I… I just don't know what to… I'm so sorry that I—"

"Fear can sometimes make us react in ways we wouldn't ever dream ourselves to be capable of." Destan calmed as he put his hand on his shoulder. "And when the woman you love is in danger it makes things even more difficult to keep right and wrong in the correct place. … I can only imagine children in that situation as well."

"What's going to happen to… where is he?" Kareal asked in a scared whisper as he nodded to where Justice Wan had been.

"He's in the other room for very obvious reasons. He'll be taken somewhere where he won't be able to do this again; and he'll pay a debt for what he's done. — Oh. That's right: this is Emissary. He's going to stay with you and get you to the closest Safe Haven once you're able to leave the hospital. … That is if you want to."

"I don't know how— why did you help? I mean after everything I did. Is that guy even alive?"

"Barely, but he 'is' alive." Destan sighed; and then added as a note of caution, "Everyone deserves a second chance when they've noticed their wrongs and are willing to repent and make things right. Take hold of this second chance you've got and make it count: for good."

"I promise I will."

"If this doesn't let up any, you 'may' not be leaving for Bulwark anytime soon." Trever commented as he opened the door.

"I doubt that'd detour Sentinel from trying, but we'll get back when we get back. Make sure to get with Tetralyn about accommodations."

"Will do." Trever's demeanor shifted to a much more casual smile as he took Callimay's free hand and squeezed it so she'd look at him. "See ya later. Y… ya did great. … Take care."

ℬ

The other Veils finally showed; them handing a set of keys to Destan so they could go on. While he never let the thought of staying behind for a cleanup cross his mind — belvedere cleanings were beyond long and tedious — things were different.

But it really had nothing to do with the cleanup. Destan couldn't help but remember what happened last time he let something like this be taken care of by others: Toreon slipping through enabled him to do so much damage with his "comeback". There was no way he was going to let the same to happen this time with Justice Wan — giving Elder the chance to "fix" things so he got out prematurely.

Callimay sat and watched, a hollow shell. When they finally left, the drive was silent and somewhat depressing. Processing what happened was going to take time; and there was that pit in Destan's gut that knew she wasn't going to get the time she needed.

When they were run to the jet she didn't feel like she was the one who was making her body move. But the second she came out of that "out of body experience" she crumbled to the floor. Destan gathered

219

her into his arms and did his best to soothe her as he dragged himself to his seat for takeoff. — Sure enough, just like he thought, Rocher wasn't about to let the weather stop him from getting them back.

Everyone was confused and a couple almost scoffed out loud at Callimay for reacting like she did. Destan was furious they would think such things without even the thought of asking what was wrong. But, then again, this cruel treatment wasn't "that" surprising.

He held her the whole way back, taking her to lounge and away from everyone for as long as possible; reminding her he was there and it was alright to cry. And yet she kept apologizing for begging him for his attention and affection when she knew he was in pain too.

"You're not begging me, Calli." He hushed as he rocked her, leaning his cheek against the top of her head. "I want to do this for you. And believe it or not, just being able to hold you is all the comfort I need right now. It's okay. Just cry, Calli. It's okay."

<h1 style="text-align:center">~ 12 ~</h1>

Not even a second after they stepped foot into Bulwark, things went from depressing to downright insulting. Everyone was thrown into a tizzy of sorts with Justice Wan arriving and Chicane being in such serious condition — Kareal "really" caught him off guard — but what happened to Destan and Callimay specifically was uncalled for: they were "greeted" by Elder who told him to report to Deep Dark while he told her that she needed to get her preliminary run research completed and approved for her first run that night.

Neither of them expected to pull a two-day shift, but in light of "who" was talking to them and acting the way he was they pushed their emotions aside. Callimay knew she couldn't fall a day behind; it was imperative she get done as soon as possible. And then Destan was Doyen. Even though Elder had pretty much stripped him bare of his authority, he was still held responsibility for everything; and being present was never a bad thing with what was going on.

They said rushed goodbyes and took off, each trying to get as far away from Elder as quickly as possible.

ﬄ

It wasn't the easiest thing to explain since she didn't know what she needed to do, but Callimay fumbled through it good enough to get her point across. Synchronizer grumbled to himself as he rolled his eyes, slapping the table as he handed her the paperwork she needed.

She scurried to a desk and started looking at it: *Oh dear. I...* *Destan? ... Destan can you hear me? ... Destan I—*

I can't right now, Calli. I'm sorry.

A… alright, she sighed as she slumped over the papers.

An overwhelming feeling of judgement washed over her, Callimay jumping when she saw Synchronizer standing over her, "Oh! I… I'm sorry. … Am I doing something wrong?"

"What do you need help with?" His gruff tone didn't budge as he crossed his arms.

"Well…"

If her fumbling before caused him to be this gruff, what in the world was he going to do now! She felt so lost she was ready to give up, and understandably so: she wasn't expecting this. But, she tried to be realistic — were runs always a planned thing? No.

But then again, performing a run wasn't something she knew how to do; that's what this part of her regimen was all about: *Why was this happening! … I mean I 'know' why, but 'why'! Why can't I~ Just keep going, Rose Petal. You can do it. Yes, it's not Destan helping you, but at least you have 'someone'.*

ℬ

Four torturous hours passed, Destan finally able to get out for a few minutes only to find Callimay was sent to her drop off point. He was livid when he asked Synchronizer who authorized her to leave without her trainer, "Why did you let her go!"

"Elder said you gave your approval and would see her after," the signed paperwork snapped as he thrust it toward him.

Destan ripped it out of his hand and took off, Synchronizer griping to himself as he went back to his work.

And things just "had" to go from infuriating to insulting; Elder stopping him, "And where do you think 'you're' going?"

"I have a trainee starting runs. I am 'required' to be their subject for the first month per—"

"Gathering Night is more important." Elder's eye narrowed; his tone beyond condescending. "I sent her with Traceur, that's good enough."

Well at least you sent Calli with her. Destan said a bit relieved, but didn't let it show as he shook the paper at him, "Don't 'ever' let me find that you've lied like this again."

Then I won't let you catch me. Oh the stupidity of this child. If he would listen to himself.

"Forging my signature? What in the world did—" *Cool it, Boon. Let's not lose it and make things even worse.* "Even you know that alone could get you thrown out of the Veil. But we both know that's not enough, don't we? — As stipulated and duly voted on: I'll be relieving Traceur and sending her back to get an update on Chicane. He sh—"

"You can get that information from Mender as needed."

"I've done what I'm supposed to do with 'your' little snake. And I'd think you'd want some time alone with him to talk things over or make him pay for his mistake. — The Veil won't be able to do any more until we find out the Syndicate's contact within Brigon's royal castle; which is what we have a half dozen Veils doing right now. And when we do find them it's up to the royal family to decide whether or not we take them down or they deal with them. — Then as far as the meeting with Majesty Presley? That's been conveyed quite clearly to everyone. … I've more than fulfilled my portion. A leader is supposed to oversee from a generic and overall perspective unless requested to become involved in details. Micromanaging from the get-go does no good; and you seem to want me out of the loop on things, not involved. Or do you? There must be something you want me to fix for you. Or are you just flattering me? — Would it kill you to make up your mind!"

He started off and then stopped, turning back as he kept his burning anger stoked, "The Veil even gave me the waiver for this first month to fulfill the duties of trainer; no strings attached. You know that better than anyone since 'you' were the one who tabled it as such. There was nothing said earlier to indicate that changed. Lying to Synchronizer doesn't fix your slip up there. I'm going, Elder. You can't stop me."

"I don't think you have a choice, Doyen. Your power is hanging by a thread. This defiant act will just cement what I've been telling them."

"I don't get you, Elder. You assumed power and responsibilities that just aren't yours and yet when things go wrong — because let's face it: anything you do tends to lean in that direction — you always peg me as the fall guy. Like I said: I'd think the less I'm involved the happier you'd be. Baleck was happier with Mr. Freigh being casual and aloof about everything and it worked for ten years that way until you decided to push the envelope. — I'm done letting you bend and break me, Elder." Destan gritted his teeth as he stopped millimeters from jamming his finger into Elder's chest. "Remember: power doesn't originate from one's position. It comes from their reputation and the gained trust. I'll concede you're capable of twisting people's minds due to doubts they have, but there is 'no' way you're capable of destroying people's deep-seated trust and love for each other… Trever Presley included."

You would think all of these hints at Destan knowing what Elder did in the past would cause him to have "some" kind of reaction in the negative sense; but a depraved mind that was basking in the evil it loved really couldn't… which made Destan's skin crawl.

"What 'are' you talking about? Why would I need to break you?"

"I assure you, I will make you pay for everything you've done to Calli, her family, 'and' mine."

"It seems you've done more damage to her than anyone else has, Doyen." Elder smirked, shaking his head as he worked to suppress his evil laughter. "I haven't laid one finger on her."

"We both know you have. Stop playing coy with me you devil."

"Let this fantasy go, Doyen. Stop letting a dead man fill your head with lies."

"I don't have the word of a dead man. I have your own confession in ink — Harmon."

"I highly doubt that, Doyen."

Not even using his real name fazes him. What 'kind' of evil is he! "You keep living 'your' fantasy, Elder, and you'll find that reality has been biding its time. You can't make this façade last forever. Your time is running out quickly. I promise you: it is."

☧

Part of him wanted to run the entire way there — or even jump — but tapping any ability at the time was going to be nothing but a recipe for utter disaster. And yet even using his own, natural power it didn't take him long at all to get to the drop off point. Destan checked his watch as he took a deep breath, smiling, "You're relieved, Traceur. I appreciate you bringing Liaison to the drop off point."

"But I was told—"

"Elder neglected to recall the vote 'he' put forward that gave me this liberty: no changes happening since I got back." Destan calmed as he put his hand out. "Chicane should be out of surgery. I want you to go check on him; and when he's able to, get his debrief. We need to make sense of this mess last night."

Oh thank you. "Of course. ETA is four-fifty." Traceur nodded and then checked her watch; just her overall look showing she was pleased to be released.

"What's the plot?"

"Runs in and out of the demarcation zone." Traceur said hushed as she pulled him aside. "I'm not sure why Synchronizer didn't catch that. Liaison told me he never said a word about it. He was pretty put off when I showed up, but why would he do this intentionally? It's going to cause headaches left and right with her coming in and out like that. We could even miss an actual breach! That's no good-willed joke."

"I'll call them and take care of it." Destan assured, pleased that she was able to see things and question them.

"Very well. Godspeed."

After contacting security and putting in a top command withdraw on barrier trips —only at the points he saw from Callimay's paperwork — he strolled over and did his best to put everything aside, "Ready?"

"Why did they send me with Traceur?" Her voice quivered as she gripped his arm. "You promised me you'd be—"

It's Elder, Destan sighed as he pulled her to him. *He's just flexing the power I've let him take. But I'm here now. It's alright. I'll be right beside you this first month. I've made sure of that and he's not going to have a leg to stand on if he wants to try and change it.*

How much longer can we wait? It seems impossible since he's had this ability for twenty-some years. But add to that the fact he's getting stronger each day? I just— it's like he feeds off your anger. It scares me so much. And then after what all those things we read—

Calli... he sighed; his expression morphing into more of a puzzled look than anything. *How do you know that?*

He's very open with himself about praising his 'work' — how he manipulates others. It's a game to him; one where his only competition is his past exploits. And then your anger? For one thing it bolsters his confidence; but then it's like he's addicted to seeing you like that. Like it's some drug fix or something. Like he described the pain was at first.

After what he was able to do to you those couple times— don't do it anymore, Calli. He reprimanded her even though he sounded more terrified; taking a deep breath as his eyes softened and he changed the subject, "It'll be alright. This is your first run. You're a quick learner, yes, but this is your first time putting everything together, okay? If you start getting overwhelmed, tell me. I don't want you getting a migraine on top of everything. I know the first couple times are challenging for you. With what happened the past day I'm ready to jump in and help."

"I… I just wish you would have been the one to help me with my paperwork. Synchronizer wasn't the least bit understanding."

"Well I think part of that was Elder, but I won't deny he's one of those, 'since I can do it then you better be up to my level from the start' types. He's been doing this for so long he doesn't know how to start at square one. — Now I can understand being like that with those who don't want to or don't care to learn, but those don't make it this far. — I've tried to get him moved, but no one wants to take his place. Which begs the question if that's actually true or Elder has some reason f…"

"Just promise me you'll sit down and explain everything so I know what to do. I've gotten so used to you knowing how to explain things to me that it's hard to make others understand. I'll probably start finishing what you say, but 'doing' it rather than just talking about it—"

"I'm your trainer, remember? We'll have a debrief after each run."

She looked off in the distance, her wringing her hands, and then whipped around and asked, "I know you said this is putting everything together… but did you mean 'everything' everything? Like combat?"

"Just focus on now, Calli. Run. We'll talk about that stuff later. — Priority number one: keep your subject close." Destan paused, trying to be serious but let a small smile jump out when he heard what she said to herself. "Priority number two: become a shadow. Priority number three which is kinda more like two-a since it's so closely tied: move like a shadow. This first run is to see how well you can follow your planned path while being quiet and as close to invisible as possible. Many times variances occur without an issue, but there are times where you have to be able to follow a plotted path to the millimeter; being able to follow your run exactly as you envisioned it is vital. The Syndicate's been very devious as of late planting trips and even a couple webs through 'high traffic' areas." *Another one of Elder's doings I have no doubt.* "Thankfully we've found them before anyone was hurt. — If there are any notes on maps or other papers at any time during these two months: do 'not' brush them off. They're there for a reason."

"Understood, Doyen." She nodded as she put her hand up to her ear. "Liaison checking in. … Subject is ready, no variances necessary, moving out in sixty."

As he anticipated, Callimay was a nervous wreck about doing everything right this first time to make him proud. At first she was only making small mistakes which were really of no concern whatsoever, but the longer they kept going the more those tiny errors compounded.

Destan finally had to stop her and sit her down.

"I'm sorry, Doyen." She cowered and turned around, clutching her arms across her chest. "I know I messed up. Not even the smallest thing is forgivable in this all. I know."

"Cal— I'm not mad." He soothed as he reached out and put his hands on her shoulders; backing off when she flinched. "I… I know you're upset from what happened with Kareal and Edna. I know it's not easy to bounce back from that. Believe me."

She whipped her head up, eyes wide as she struggled to get a single word out.

He smiled as he continued to calm, "For as calm and cool as I may 'look' I'm not ready for this either, on that front. Part of that persona is the way God made men, but just because we 'look' alright doesn't mean inside we are. … You know that better than anyone, Calli. I know you do. Sure, I'm a 'pro' at pushing emotions out and acting like nothing's wrong, but I also know I tend to push them onto you if I'm not careful."

In a fit of absolute terror, she gasped as she gripped his arm, "I wasn't trying to make you think that I—"

"That's not what I m— Calli just listen." Destan did his best to word what he was trying so desperately to say so she'd understand. "You're not me. Not when it comes to bouncing back and dealing with this all. And the fact is I don't want you to be me. … Geez! I don't even want to be me at times when I do the stupid and idiotic things I sometimes do."

"But I have to be able to function no matter what." She cried as she ripped the earpiece out and threw it away. "Sometimes things happen."

That was 'supposed' to help. You know? Make her at least smile if not laugh. "Callimay." Destan turned her around as he kneeled down, the edge in his tone catching her attention. "You 'do' function when you know it counts."

"When!" She snapped back she pulled away and shook her pointer finger in the air. "Name me one time I didn't spaz out and mess everything up; doing nothing but making things a million times worse for us and even getting Dakoe killed. I always do something stupid; thinking I'm helping when I'm not! I'm an idiot in that sense because I have no true sense of danger! What about when I broke into Deep Dark? Was I functioning then? Didn't it 'count' then? How can you say I can get my act together when it counts! Stop patronizing me. It's just another way to lie!"

Now he was starting to get frustrated — who wouldn't when they're accused of lying — but seeing the fear in her eyes kept him from going that extra step. She truly wasn't mad at him. She was scared she would fail and she'd have to leave: making him choose between her and finishing what his father and her mother begged him to. Everything in her was raw and on edge; she wasn't thinking clearly.

Her challenge did sound reasonable with this in mind. And yet it didn't take him but a couple seconds to remember a handful of times she held her own under immense pressure. And it wasn't that she was completely daft when it came to sensing danger, it's just that she knew she needed to help the person right then; and the only way she knew to help wasn't always the safest thing to do. Destan bent over and picked up the earpiece, putting it on his belt before he crept over to his distraught wife; resting his chin on her head as he soothed, "Just think back to yesterday, Calli. You noticed something was wrong with Chicane. And you thought enough to bring it up in a way that didn't tip him off. Then when he had a gun to your head you didn't flinch? Do you remember that? 'I' was the one spazzing out; so was Fidus! You kept yourself so calm and collected when we were going to Hougle and even while we were there. 'You' saved me from the belvedere. And then when you had no idea what to do but knew you had to help Edna? … I know so much of it is fuzzy to you, but when we were at your mother's you reacted without thinking when we were fending off those few men and didn't see the others behind us. You didn't think twice when you cut your hair to get free; even though that sent you falling almost two full stories, not knowing if I was ready to catch you or not. — You're terrified of heights and yet you knew you had to get away and that was your only option; plus you trusted I would be there. — And what about when you saved my life from the belvedere and Justice Wan at the Society? When I said I couldn't drive you didn't hesitate; booking it from those Falconers who were on our tail. ... Then there's the time you were hanging off the ledge at Bulwark: you didn't give up. You hung on and waited for me even though Elder was doing everything he could and you were beyond exhausted. — And let's not forget that infamous moment when you thundered into Deep Dark. Even though you did neglect the warning and wisdom of others, you stepped up to the occasion in an altogether different and amazing way. It didn't matter what anyone else in the room said — you weren't going to back down. Your red roots burned like a solar flare that day. I have 'never' seen a woman stand up to Elder and call him on the carpet like that; no one has. ... That's quite the resume but I'm not done: you fought Baleck and Ginger, Calli. You fought them without my help; and you won both times. I mean, you were so calm that I thought you were Dakoe when we were at the plant. You stood your ground against Hyra that whole time even though you'd never been in a situation like that. All you did was what you knew to keep everyone safe. You didn't kill Dakoe. You didn't. Please stop blaming yourself for that, Calli. You never met someone like her so you had no clue Hyra was a live wire and wouldn't listen to reason. Dakoe made his choice; and he chose to save you. I... maybe this isn't the time to say it, but I know you two had feelings for each other at one time. I do. And I have a feeling you might be trying to justify your feelings while pushing them away at the same time."

"I... I mean..."

"Yes, I felt the jealousy of a husband for his wife for the first time when I saw him talking with you... but that was actually my feelings toward him; partially because he appeared to be better at comforting you than I was. But I have 'never' doubted your love and devotion for me. Never. I know it's possible for the human heart to care for more than one person without confusing the care toward a spouse to that of a dear friend. I know you were devastated when he died. It's okay to feel and show that sorrow. That doesn't mean you're cheating on me."

This wild swing totally caught Callimay off guard, but at the same time it was helping her let go of something she'd been holding on to for so long, untying a knot that was, in a way, beginning to strangle her.

"I can't help but think he respected the clear line he could never cross because we were married. And so that's why there's no way I can see him blaming you. If he ever got the chance to say something before he died I'm sure that's what he would've said: it wasn't your fault. You did everything you could to save him. He made that choice because he loved you and didn't want you to die."

While this made her relive the memory of what he said to her and made her heart hurt so much, being reminded it was okay to feel those emotions — that it wasn't a sin — reminded her how Destan was learning. He was growing. He knew her needs were different from his. And he reminded her that he trusted her.

Even with this all, Destan wasn't quite finished; he wanted to make his point crystal clear so she'd learn to trust herself like she had before this all started, "Then there was that first time, Calli. There was that first time I saw your inner strength you reserved for critical moments. You ventured out alone — 'a-lone' — and followed that sleazebag of a male to see what he was up to. You put yourself in the worst kind of danger but you did it anyway; albeit maybe unknowingly to a certain extent. — Do you realize what Toreon could have done to you; let alone what Baleck would have if he found you! … Calli? You 'are' strong and focused. You step up when you're needed. And you follow it through to the very end. It's just that you're 'conditional' when you do it. And that's fine. It shows that you know how to roll with the punches: enjoy life when you can but deal with issues when you have to."

Destan paused and lifted her chin while wiping her face, "Oh Calli. Why are you crying? It is because of what happened last n—"

"I… I'm just mad with myself." She grumbled in between sobs. "I'm f… failing miserably. And I d… don't know why! I 'know' what I'm supposed to do. Why can't I just 'do' it!"

And so there was a sudden moment of confusion for Destan: another emotion was tied to her reaction of crying. But instead of just staying confused, he began to understand this was a training exercise for him; he was being reminded of his need to be patient with her and learn to understand her on an ever-deeper level.

"You're not failing, Calli." He comforted as he pushed her hair away from her face and then framed it. "If driving and physics were any precursors — which I know they were — this isn't a surprise at all. This is your first time which means it's not going to be easy… like I said before we started. 'And' you're still reeling from what happened. You're trying to push it aside to be tough like me, but you're not able to. Deep down you know this isn't the real thing; that you don't have to focus. It's alright. You only learn by doing… and sometimes failing."

He took a step back and glanced around, taking a deep breath as he took her hand and kneeled, "Elder's just trying to overload the two of us so we'll give up. I do 'not' want him to win this battle. He's won one too many today. — Dear Lord? We come and ask that You will give us Your strength right now. We thank You for Your deliverance earlier and ask that You will continue to be with us as we continue in this fight. Help us to continue to follow Your lead. It's in Your precious Son's name I pray, amen."

"Amen," Callimay whispered as she leaned her head against his chest, her heart tugging at her so hard.

There was a much needed period of silence. Both of their hearts soaked it in and began to heal and recharge.

"Let's go back to the drop off point and do this again. I'll explain things as we go like I would've during your plotting. Okay?"

She nodded, a sob jumping out.

Destan put in the earpiece and relayed the changes to the observer as he took her hand and started off.

When he found out who the observer was, he stopped; sounding more than irritated, "Fidus, why are you on observation duty? I told—"

"Synchronizer's shift ended halfway through her run. Traceur isn't back yet so Elder told me to fill in."

"Why are you let—" He began arguing; groaning as he reached over to Callimay when he spiked. "I told you to delegate, not take over."

"I— Traceur's back." Fidus avoided, static sounds filling the mic.

"What's the issue, Doyen?" Traceur asked concerned as she got on the line. "Why isn't Liaison on the com?"

"We're rerunning the plot. I'm going to show her since I wasn't with her during her plotting." His tone smoothed as he started off. "It's my fault," *more like Elder's,* "this run failed so I'm giving her a pass."

"No reruns are allowed, Doyen. You are well aware of that." Elder spoke up. "Do I need to give you the code reference for it?"

"What about the code where a trainee is never to be without their trainer?" He snapped back, trying not to spike again. "She's at a major disadvantage coming into this because of what 'you' decided to do. I was not there during her plotting like is 'required' so I wasn't able to explain to her at the time what would be best. — Something we 'both' know Synchronizer should've done. — That's an order, Elder."

There was mumbling on the other end of the line before Traceur said, "Give me the green light when you're ready to start."

"Give us ten minutes to get back to the drop off point."

ॐ

Destan had to coax Callimay the first bit, but once she was calm — him reassuring her everything was fine and neither of them were going to get in any kind of trouble for what he was doing — they picked up the pace and were back to where she planned to start.

She knew these were to test her ability of being silent, so it confused her that Destan was talking so much: *You can just talk to me like this.*

"It's okay." He smiled as he stopped and kneeled. "Now look here at the way the land 'looks' compared to what is on the map; what you decided to do."

The fact was, her plot started out with such precision and accounted for everything she needed to. But, as was usually the case with trainees on their first run, the longer she thought about things, and the fact Synchronizer was no help, the more her plot became careless, sloppy, and at one point Destan pointed out it was dangerous and totally avoidable, "Now. Let me get this out before you start apologizing: you started out so well. You 'do' know how to do this. Your circumstances while doing this; things piling on top of another just overloaded you."

"But I know I can't—"

"Now don't start that again." Destan put a finger to her lips. "You're just starting. Didn't I just say most trainees do this exact thing on their first run? — And Elder forgot a failed first run isn't even considered a real fail. — I mean, how many times did you kill Wolf before you were comfortable driving?"

Silence.

"Well?"

Her eyes started darting back and forth, sounds coming out of her mouth in mumbles but no actual words.

"And what about the common gas law? How many 'weeks' did it take for you to remember that your moles weren't always what the chart said: you had to account for subscripts?"

"I still wouldn't remember." She rolled her eyes and shook her head. "I really can't remember any of it now. … What?"

He stared at her a bit longer and then nodded on, "That's the whole point! Some things take longer to learn and you sometimes choose to only remember what you think is important. — Not everything is easy. This all is 'deep' stuff. Not surface-level fluff. And this is your first run. Your 'first' run. … Finally making sense now?"

It took a few more seconds, but then her eyes lit up, "Oh!"

"Oh is right." He gave her a quick peck and then started off again.

They finished the run using her plot for a while and then switched to the most preferred one.

It was so wonderful to have this kind of "hands on" learning, but deep inside Callimay knew this wasn't the time for it. Destan did say he wouldn't get in trouble, but never said he wouldn't get flak from Elder: *I hate being a pawn in his game. If he were going to do something I wish he'd just do it! ~ Speak for yourself. He wants us dead! Dying isn't on my to-do list right now. ~ That's not what I meant and you know it. It's this tug-of-war he's playing with Destan. At times he's trying to use me as the rope, in a manner of speaking, and then others I'm the person on the other end of the rope.*

And add to that the fact she didn't stay with the other trainees in her "class" while not training and was now almost a half a year ahead of them now even though she started three months later? Talk about resentment and being labeled a teacher's pet! Oh, but that's not all. It just keeps getting better. She was Destan's wife; still seen by some as a hindrance to him and his role.

At the end of this depressing and worrisome tunnel was this: regardless of what he said, she was still kicking herself about messing up. This blunder made him stick his neck out for her and as Elder saw it: "bending" the rules for her even though Destan pointed out it was technically allowed. He was holding up so well, but she could feel things were getting to him bit by bit. If this dragged out much longer he might not survive.

Was that Elder's plan, now? Drag this all out until Destan wasn't able to stand it and Callimay wasn't able to bring him back?

Destan continued to talk as they went along; showing how this was putting her training of geography, meteorology, astronomy — even the physics she couldn't remember — horology, as well as the basic anatomy and physiology she had to learn into practice. Of course he reminded her if she didn't notice it wasn't a big deal; time and practice would bring it all together, and once it did come together she wouldn't even think of them as individual aspects.

At one point he shifted and was a bit more generic. He explained her endurance and parkour training were going to be some big points to work on: adapting those two skills in particular to the point where they would make her look and move as close to a real life shadow as humanly possible. Combat training would be the last thing added; and by far it was the part Destan was dreading most since he wouldn't be right beside her most of that time.

Hearing all of this brought back the realization that Callimay forgot how everything she was learning was meant to go together. It wasn't like "normal school" where each subject tended to stand on its own. Yes, there were those subtle crossovers, but history was history and physics was physics. Linking all of her classes into one was almost mind-melting. It showed once again how the tiniest of details could make the biggest difference. Another level of understand began to fall into place; it clicking for her why Destan started out being so serious — not tolerating her jokes, even as harmless as they were.

~ 13 ~

Right on schedule, Destan heard back from Majesty Presley at the end of the week with more great news. As he suspected, and not a shock to either, the president of Crosswall was the only one refusing to commit; asking for a week to think it over. While it wasn't a flat out "no," his willingness to even listen was promising!

It was a momentous day for the Veil. This flood of new energy spread far and wide, everyone jumping back onto Destan's side; all but abandoning Elder. While Elder still had the ability to exert what was still a strong level of control over them, he couldn't twist this in their minds. This wasn't Destan telling them or some isolated incident happening that they had no concern about. This was the king of Brigon — the country they'd been trying to get ties with for decades — as well as other governmental leaders around the world joining the fight.

Destan was beyond overjoyed to see the world map become more and more black; and yet he wished his Calli could have been there to see it… to see what "her" work had done.

Sb

When he got back, Callimay was so confused as to why he was so happy. At one point she was scared Elder was doing something: *He usually just comes back and holds you as tight as he can, not saying any word, let along smiling! More times than not he wants to forget it all.*

"No need to worry," He rubbed her hands as he worked to get her attention. "In fact I'm like this because he got schooled 'so' bad by your grandfather. Here, give me a second, he wanted to talk to you as soon as possible."

"What on— hello?" She fumbled as she put the phone to her ear.

It was so wonderful for Destan to see Callimay's face light up as he spoke to her. She was almost like Rose: fidgeting and squirming in her seat as she listened to him tell her the good news.

⚜

But even with that wonderful news Destan was given a rude reminder the next night that his "mission" was far from over. Fidus and a small detail of Veils brought him a box, asking if he wanted the Veil officially assembled or not.

His face showed a split personality almost; him fighting with which way to go. He let go of the leather and sighed, "Go ahead. It— 'she' needs to be given her official parting memorial."

"That will be done when Liaison joins us." Fidus added a slight correction after the others left.

Thanks for that vote of confidence… but I'm 'not' looking forward to that day for that exact reason.

As was the Syndicate's "kind" custom with any Veil they discovered, they sent the shredded veil home. No one ever figured out how they got it to known drop off points, but Destan had a very good idea, now.

In keeping with what always happened prior, it was Destan's duty — while in front of the assembled Veil — to speak of her and place her veil alongside the other veils of those who gave their lives.

While doing it wasn't going to be easy because Canary's execution was still fresh on his mind, there was something else which made him so hesitant. Its home was going to be right beside the last veil: his father's. There were now two screaming reminders of the two who gave their lives to protect the woman he loved with his whole being as well as pleaded with him to finish what they started, but beyond their control, were unable to finish.

And then add to that the shell of a human being they fought against outliving them and free to smirk and belittle their "meaningless efforts" to take away his power? The fire inside him was kindled once again.

He was hoping with this shift in favor his rekindled drive to bring up the accusations would come to its required conclusion. It was his prime opportunity with the Veil assembled like they were. He would have an upper hand in showing his proof against Elder and with the emotions people would be feeling it was his best shot at being believed. It was now or never. Hopefully it would be enough of a jolt to catch Elder off guard.

But something kept him from doing it, that fire inside wasn't doing what it had always done before. Why?

Fear, plain and simple.

Fear? But of what?

It was fear of losing the only physical piece of evidence he had left: the journal. How could he give that over; the last thing both Canary and Destry worked so hard to protect? If he lost that what leg did he have left to stand on?

Perhaps what Destan dreaded more than losing the journal was the weight of what he would ask be done. When it came down to it he was not asking for just an expulsion vote. Canary made that very clear; the fear and anger in her eyes haunting him. Elder had to be placed on trial for crimes against the individuals he vowed to protect, conspiring with the Syndicate, and breaching security measures which put countless lives at risk. He "had" to be given the mandatory sentence of capital punishment for his treason and the more than one dozen murders he was responsible for — let alone his multiple attempts on Callimay.

It was easy to see why his zeal could be so easily curbed, and yet the thought of Elder finishing his twenty-some-year task of finding and murdering the now young woman he hated with his entire being? This brought into focus his totally depraved nature that was nothing but a fast-acting poison of mankind that needed to be snuffed out right then. He had no remorse for what he had done and was doing. Nothing short of death would make him stop.

❦

Callimay had a couple slip-ups in her next few runs, but no fails. Things started progressing like she knew she could; it appeared the first talk was the encouragement she needed.

In an odd and humorous turn of events, they would get into debates about what was best prior to starting and sometimes would end up at odds for an entire run: *Those red roots from her father, I tell you what!*

That woman just~ Easy, Boon. Just let it go. So she wants to take the ledge route, it's low tide and calm… like she said. ~ But why risk it when you don't have to? ~ You talk about 'her' red roots? If anything you'd have blonde ones, so where's this fire 'you' have coming from? ~ What's that got to~ It has everything to do with it because it has nothing to do with the color of her hair!

Even though she was mad enough to not "talk" with him, hearing these types of conversations helped her understand more where he was coming from. And so even though she was bound and determined to do it her way she began to be less combative when he made suggestions: *He's still your husband. ~ I know. … It's hard. I'm supposed to be the one in the leadership role and yet he's my trainer 'and' husband. Who thought this was a good idea to have him train me? ~ Oh land sake, Rose Petal. That has nothing to do with it. ~ Oh no? ~ Well you're still alive, aren't you? Who's to say that if it would've been someone else that your little accidents would've ended differently?* "Destan?"

"Huh?" The edge in his tone tried its best to stay hidden.

"I… I know you just want me to be safe, and so you—"

"I need to be willing to trust your judgement more, Calli." His heart won, his voice tumbling into regret as he sighed and rested his hands on her shoulders. "Yes, there are times you need reminded that there are those who know more than you and their suggestions need to carry some weight; but when it comes down to it you're completely capable of doing the right thing. … And I 'know' you are."

~ 14 ~

During the last month of her run training she was instructed to always be ready for anything. "Any" thing. She was on her toes as it was with Elder, but knowing someone held hostage by him could pop out of nowhere? It's no wonder she was exhausted after each run. Her mind was almost mush now and so were her muscles.

After the first run of a week-long test — one of her best to date — she still found some points she could correct. Since her second one of the week was running the exact same plot, she was happy she'd be able to "fix" those areas and do better.

She pranced up to Destan as he came out of the observation post, grinning as she clasped her hands behind her, "Bet you thought I didn't notice those few slipups, huh? I sure did a good job this time, didn't I?"

"Oh you did a job of it, that's for sure."

"F… fail? What!" The paper crunched as she gripped it.

"Calli just calm down."

"But I fixed what I did wrong! How could I fail tonight if I passed last night!"

He tried to keep pace as she stormed here and there, but then he let her go. As much as he wanted to tell her this phase of the regimen didn't allow any feedback on failures. The trainee was doing mock runs as if they were a Shadow and so being in a more difficult level, "they" had to figure out what was wrong: *She'll get it. Let her sleep on it and come tomorrow she'll get what's going on. ~ I hope so. ~ Oh come on, boon. It's just one failure. She's passed them all up to this point without even one demerit. A couple warnings, yes, but come on. I know, I know, this 'not explaining' is a rough adjustment, but just give it time.*

239

~ If time were only something we had. And what am I supposed to do if she 'fail' fails? ~ How in the world could she fail the exact same way five times in a row? … Im-pos-si-ble! She's not stupid. Come on, Boon. Have faith in her!

ℬ

Day six came and beyond what Destan thought possible — what he actually believed to be impossible — happened: she failed four runs straight! One more fail meant she'd be done for good. He was faced with the fact he needed to make up his mind what he would do and "do" it no matter what.

He was able to observe her that night and kept praying nonstop that she'd realize what they were trying to get her to do; what this entire week was testing her on.

After a few hours and not seeing any movement or having any kind of contact whatsoever, Destan decided to go looking for her.

"You don't think she passed out do you? I know she was so tired and frustrated yesterday."

"No, Traceur," he stopped at the door and picked up a paper. "No I don't think it's that."

"Then has she figured it out and just not said anything?"

"I am praying she's just sitting in a tree somewhere crying because she's kicking herself for not noticing," he took an agonizing breath as he shook his head. "Try to get her once more."

"Alright," she sat down and linked into the com. "Liaison? What is your status? We're unable to detect you. … Liaison? — Nothing."

While he could tell her emotions weren't all over the place and she wasn't screaming for help, this void of communication still worried him: *Calli? … Calli answer me!*

Not wasting any time, he took off to where she was supposed to be. He called out a few times but there was no answer.

At one point he cleared a bolder in the most graceful of ways and then immediately hunkered down since he knew he was at the drop off point. There weren't any signs of a struggle as far as footprints go, but something didn't feel right. Destan glanced around for a bit and then up; seeing her fiery eyes, her ready to throw a spike, "It's just me!"

"Oh," she backed off and sat back down on the limb where she must've been this entire time.

"Why are you still here? And why didn't you answer me?" His whisper was fighting to stay quiet and calm.

"You said we weren't supposed to 'talk'. Remember?" She glared at him, and then huffed as she rubbed her temples in frustration, "And as far as me not going anywhere… this is ridiculous! It makes no sense. I run perfect runs, take down each and every obstacle and trap I come across— and let me add that pinning and running from Scaffold, Sidewinder, 'and' Firefly multiple times so I didn't have to fight them 'is' allowed. You told me so. So explain to me how I fail each and every time? And 'four' times in a row! It's like I'm being set up to fail; like I'm not supposed to run."

"So, you're here because you're mad?" Destan asked rather worried as he crept up to the base of the tree. *Come on, Calli. I know you're in pain right now and beyond exhausted, but please… think! Listen to yourself. Come on. You can do it.*

"Yes," she growled as she snapped a twig; throwing it down to her left and disabling a trap.

"Oh."

"I thought you were supposed to be the best runner?" Callimay rolled her eyes after she came out of a perfect roll out when she hit the ground; rubbing her head a bit as she quickly steadied herself.

"What do you me— are you alright?"

"I saw you the whole way. Even with the tree cover I—"

The abrupt silence scared Destan, "Calli, what's wrong? Does your head hurt that bad?"

"I… I'm fine." She said a bit dazed as she patted his outstretched hand and walked a bit past him; looking out at the landscape.

He stood there and waited, still worried but now on the edge of his seat: *She did it! ~ Just say it, Calli. Tell me why you can't run. Come on.*

"I 'am' supposed to fail." She mumbled as she shook her finger at the plotted course with determination; almost gasping as she turned, her eyes wide, "The moon! It's full! Even with the best tree cover we can't hide. It's impossible. Cloud cover would need to be thick to help;

or fog. … I… I wasn't supposed to run at all the past four runs because it's been close to clear the past four nights: clear! — I'm such an idiot!"

"You learned the lesson, though. And that's the most important thing." Destan smiled as he handed her the paper he brought with him. "Congratulations, Liaison: you pass."

"That's what those last four runs were for?"

"That's what the last 'five' were for."

"But I passed the first."

Destan didn't respond with anything but a raised eyebrow.

"Something was diff— it was cloudy that night!"

"Exactly. … Moral of the story, as they say, for this week? Even if you're given an order you've got to pay attention to your surroundings. We get weather reports, but you know how reliable they can be at times. You have to be confident enough to make a judgement call that defies your orders when your safety is at stake. It can make runs so much longer, but being alive is the most important part." He paused as she slouched and started to turn away. "What's wrong? Do I need to go grab you some medicine? I'll carry you back s—"

"I took the max I can; it's just not working tonight. And I think we both know why. … But I really can't put 'all' the blame there. I… I just wasn't paying attention the past couple days." She sighed as she turned so her back was to him. "I was seeing my failures as nothing more than pushback from those who don't like me; I didn't stop to think 'I' might be the one who was wrong. I got cocky about my ability to do this. I'm sorry, Doyen. I didn't even realize until I saw you—"

"Calli. I don't blame you for thinking that way. Not now I don't. I was worried for a while, I admit, but what you said makes so much sense. There have been 'way' too many things like that happening — that aren't supposed to — to make you react like you did. I get it. It's alright. You figured it out and that's all that counts. Okay?"

She groaned a bit, but sighed, "Alright."

"And you 'are' good at this. Very good. Just keep it in perspective."

⑁

Knowing how she reacted to negative comments right now, Destan knew it best to not tell her about the whole failure thing. Her migraine she had lasted a total of three and a half days. She didn't need any added stress that could cause those miserable daggers of pain to stay flared. But this wasn't an easy thing to keep from her. He had to ask someone for advice before she found out; so he got with Redje and Tabitha, "I don't want to start hiding things from Calli again and make things like they were before."

"You know she can do it." Tabitha encouraged. "Don't lose faith in her. If she notices you're on edge or something's 'off', obviously tell her. But if she doesn't, let her do what she's been doing. I really believe that wakeup call about 'the enemy' has triggered her to use 'all' her senses and training like she's supposed to; as it has in segmented ways this entire time. She's just got to balance the caution with her confidence."

"There's nothing wrong with confidence, but it can make that slow shift to arrogance if you're not careful." Redje agreed. "I think this was a major wakeup call for her so it won't be an issue at all. … And this is just me, but just saying that to inform her about a possible outcome? Don't put more on her. You know she's already stressed out."

Destan sighed as he leaned back in his chair, "She's had migraines almost every day for the past couple weeks it seems like. Just as she starts to get over one another flares. And with her senses being in overload right now with watching every tiny little thing I'm sadly not surprised. … To be blunt, I really don't know how she's made it this far with only making that one major mistake. She kept on top of every trap and decoy sent. I— just pray for her. I 'really' don't know how she'll make it through her overnight runs if this keeps up. She's 'got' to get her rest; keeping her eyes closed in a dark and quiet room while she doesn't move is the only thing that works for these kinds of migraines."

"What about the treatments Lance gave her?" Redje leaned forward a bit and put his interlocked hands on the desk.

"She got one earlier today. It's sticking for now but I just don't know. He told me they might get to the point they wouldn't work because of her ability. Either that or her body will become 'immune' to the help they can give — kinda like an addiction if you will. Neither of us want to get to that point, so he's only giving her one when absolutely necessary. It's killing me to see her like this, though. I understand more what that pain she's going through is like and I just can't stand it."

"She waited until she just couldn't take it, didn't she?" Redje asked.

"Yeah." Destan sighed as he rubbed his face.

"Well, maybe give her a sweet reminder about taking care of herself through this all." Tabitha suggested as she jerked a bit and put her hand to her baby bump. *Practice what you preach, I know, Benjamin.* "With her getting less sleep she really needs to watch herself. Not having sleep can cause so many other problems, you know that. So help her remember. Be an example for her to follow."

It was a rather rude reminder, but one he knew he needed, "Thanks again for getting up so early."

"Whatever we can do to help." Redje put his arm around Tabitha, smiling as he nodded.

"Rej? Maybe this isn't the time, but you said something a while back about Aldred Hilston? It's been what feels like a lifetime ago, but—"

"Oh, that's right!" Redje recalled as he snapped his fingers. "I saw him at the office. Popped up out of nowhere and wanted to act like nothing changed… at first. We went out to lunch and when the topic of you came up… well, he—"

"You don't think he's—"

"That's what I'm worried about. Looking into that, though, is a bit above my 'paygrade' so to speak."

"I'll get someone on that last night to see if there's anything to find out. — Did he say anything about where he was?"

"Still over in Agroos Union as I understood it. At least that's the only place he mentioned."

Then why in the world was he in Kerogen? "Okay."

"Just remember, Destan," Tabitha interjected, trying to keep things focused. "Callimay comes first. Talk to her and ask her what she needs help with. Remind her you just want to help and you love her so you say things you notice. Doyen's been doing a fantastic job up until now. Keep it going. We're both pulling for you."

While this comment didn't wash away the endless pit of questions about Aldred, it did help him see he was beginning to drift, "Thanks. I 'am' noticing a big change and I'm so glad about it. I— Calli's done, I'll talk to you later."

"Tell her we all said hi." Tabitha smiled as she waved.

"Take care and I'll get with you later about Aldred." Redje did the same and then hung up.

Calli?

There was a short moment of silence followed by a depressed voice moaning: *I could 'so' use a hug right now.*

What's wrong! He jumped up from his chair.

I'm so cold. It's the one and probably 'only' thing I can't seem to adjust to. — Now don't worry, I passed. Sorry about my wording. I'm just half frozen and can't think quite as clear as I should.

Destan groaned as he dragged his hands through his hair: *You're sure you're alright?*

If you mean, 'do I have frostbite', I'm fine. No worries there. If you're asking 'can I stop shaking' or 'will your teeth stop chattering'? Then no, I'm miserable. I know this ensemble is supposed to be insulated and the foot beds have some type of special pressure point stuff in them, but it's not helping.

There are some who aren't helped by the acupuncture points, so don't go thinking you're crazy.

It's alright. She half chuckled as a deep shiver ran through her. *I'm just complaining to keep my mind off of shivering. I'll be fine.*

Are you back at transport?

Just getting in now. … Ah. So warm. We're… we're supposed to be back in probably two hours. Maybe three.

She sounded a bit better, so he kept encouraging: *I'll be waiting for you. Try to get as much rest on the way back as you can. And make—*

It's okay, mister worry wart. I'll make sure I get back alive.

I love you so much, Calli. … And I really miss you.

You didn't sleep much, did you? It sounded like she was smiling.

I could be all puffed up and not answer that at all, but I know better: I'm running on fumes too.

Well, we'll 'both' get a good night's rest tonight. … I miss you too.

Just one more week. Then I'll be with you again for your final.— How's your head?

It was longer than he wanted, but she finally answered in a groggy tone: *Bad pressure and I'm dizzy if I move too fast, but no 'real' pain.*

Well, get some rest. I'll meet you at the lot.

~ 15 ~

Finally! So much hard work and perseverance that led to this day was about to be repaid in full; the one they thought wouldn't come: the first day of her final, three-day run. It was going to be a plot that spanned roughly one-hundred eighty miles; each day consisting of two, four-hour runs through an array of terrains: *Just three more days. If we can hold on to this for just three more days then it won't matter. There's nothing new about this. ~ Just keep calm and focused. If we can keep a migraine from flaring that's a major win. ~ Don't I know it. It would make everything so much easier.*

As Destan rolled over to say good morning, his phone vibrated. He ignored it at first, but it went off again and again… and again. Not happy to know something was wrong, he grumbled as he threw his hand over and ripped it off the stand: *I just 'knew' you'd get your nose out of joint. What is it n— oh no. You've got to be kidding me!*

"Destan what's wrong?" Callimay all but gasped as she ran over.

"I don't know if this is some sick joke Elder's pulling or the actual truth. — Why are you up?"

"What's is it!"

"Your grandfather's been trying to contact me all day… we might be losing half of the leaders we started with."

"What!"

"I… Calli, I don't—"

"Stay," her voice dug down deep and stood its ground, her eyes quenching the fear that was trying to escape. "Do what you need to."

"I'm not backing out now. I can't! This is Elder's doing, it's got to be!" His face followed her as she marched over to his desk.

"I 'know' this isn't what we had planned, but neither is losing half the support for Total Eclipse. We agreed its success is more important in the long run. Surely I can get Rocher or Auditor to go."

Fighting the anger, Destan popped up and followed after his bold wife, turning her toward him, "I'm not letting this get between us. I won't let Elder do this. I won't dare leave you alone only to lose you."

Callimay grabbed his arms and said with a level of determination he'd never seen before, "I'm 'telling' you to stay. Regardless of Elder's involvement you 'need' to be present. The last thing we need is him getting his grubby hands into this pot. I'll be fine. I can watch Rocher or Auditor to make sure he's not doing anything to them."

"This is three days that I won—" the phone rang again.

"Who is it?" She whispered, hearing a muffled voice on the phone.

He hushed her with his hand as he started pacing the floor, "Yes Majesty Presley? I apologize I didn't respond so— oh. I. See. … They 'all' did that on the same day? … I will get out there as fast as I can. … Unfortunately, she— wait! I'll see if she can. … Yes. I will contact you right before I leave. … I will be sure to. Goodbye."

She was wringing her hands and fiddling with the hummingbirds in her sleeves the entire time, jumping in the second he hung up, "Well?"

"You may not have to worry. He said he wanted to see you as well, so maybe I can pull what I did last time and get you a waiver to go."

"But I thought waivers were put down as—"

"Ugh! You're right. It'd been written off as a failed run. And you don't have any to spare as it—"

His immediate response of clapping his hand over his mouth and letting his eyes bug out caused her to ask, "What do you mean, I don't have any to spare?"

"I…" Destan slammed his fists on the desk as he tossed the phone. "Calli? … If you fail this you're done. Five and you're out. No retries."

"But I— oh wait," her tone fizzled out. "I remember now."

"What do you mean by that? How did you know? I never told you." Destan asked shocked as he whipped his head to look at her.

"Synchronizer told me. Well, more like he lectured me on it when I had to do everything for my first run. Guess I don't retain that type of instruction well, huh?"

"Calli, I…" he hung his head and clinched his fists.

"M… maybe this is a bit ill-timed. But…" She said a bit choked up as she hesitated to reach out to him. "Remember what our dream is, Destan? That a big part of that happening is Total Eclipse working? I know it's nothing near what either of us wants — and I'm not saying it's gonna be easy — but… but sometimes you have to be willing to go through short, hard times to get to the finish line."

It was working. As slow as a sloth sliding down a sap-coated tree, but it was working: he was taking it in stride and seeing what she was trying to do to help. The major hindrance was the fact they didn't have much time to work with.

"I know you're stressed out. Everything was probably planned this way. But we can't just crawl into the corner and accept defeat. God wouldn't put us in any situation we couldn't make it through. I 'know' He wouldn't because He said so. We've just got to find the way that He has ready and waiting for us. We've got to look, and look hard."

He knew on all counts she was right, but he had to vent about the thing he should have taken care of that last time; now seeing he was swayed and lured in by this false lull and quiet, "What if Elder's doing this to get me away from you? What if he has poisoned everyone's minds just to release them once I'm out there and so my going would be for no good reason at all? I can't just leave you! You're worth more to me than all of this. We don't 'need' this to live happily together."

"I… I 'know' there's that possibility." Callimay sighed as she let her hands slip off of his and fall to her side. "I never denied it."

"I should've finished him off long ago." He hissed under his breath as he flopped onto the seat and buried his head in his hands. "What is wrong with me! I keep hesitating every time an opening comes. It's as if I really don't think he'll do what he promised to do to you!"

"Destan. Destan, please look at me." Callimay pleaded as she kneeled beside him and ran her fingers through his hair. "How can I help? What do you want me to do?"

"I… I don't know," his flustered voice quivered as he looked over to her. "I… I just don't know."

"W… well. You know the basic plot, right? … How many high-risk danger points would there be?" Callimay asked as she tapped the top of the desk and then opened the drawer and took out some paper and a pen. "Where would the 'best' places be for blind traps or ambushes that you know Elder could place easily?"

If something did happen while they were apart she needed this so she was ready to take on whatever Elder tried to come at her with. Her thinking to ask this and putting everything else aside was showing him she was ready to take her place beside him. That she "could" handle the stress; what he'd told her not that long ago. So, he took a deep breath and picked up the pen and used it to type on the keypad; giving her a look as he glanced up: *I 'could' get in trouble if 'someone' were to twist this around, but… we're supposed to be as wise as serpents, right? — You're in a type of danger no other trainee has been in. So it's my 'duty' to tell you what I know. If someone finds out and starts giving you a hard time about it, tell them to talk to me. Got it? … The first run segment in the gorge is going to be a prime target area since it's so open while being so restrictive: it'll look and even feel safe, but don't fall for it.*

That's the place southeast of here, isn't it? Callimay questioned as she watched him pull op the holographic map while jotting down a few things on the paper. *Why don't I just run down the middle following the creek?*

No one's ever even tried that. And no, you can't just bypass the gorge altogether. You've got freedom in this run, but not that much.

Then I'll do that, then. She smiled, explaining when she saw the look on her husband's face as he stopped and turned to her. "Look. Elder wouldn't be expecting it and so he wouldn't use it as an ambush point. I need to plot this run like no one else has; possibly a little risky or downright stupid if you want to word it that way. It'll give me the best fighting chance to steer clear of anything he might try. And I'm not supposed to put in a pre-run plot anyway; it's supposed to be me doing it on the fly, right?*

Y-ea-h? But, there are actual Syndicate webs around this area, Calli. You've 'got' to be careful about 'winging it'.

Where are they?

He looked around, as if he expected someone to pop out of the closet or such, and then zoomed in on a certain area where an icon with three parallelograms stacked on top of each other was: *The ones we haven't been able to disarm are on the south side.*

Are you sure? Is that all of them for the entire plot?

I'd remember the web I almost lost a— now don't get all emotional on me. I said 'almost'. He made a face at her as he dropped his pen; and then pointed it at the symbol. *This is all that would be in your direct plot path for the first day. Do 'not' get that crazy, understood? — All these symbols on the map are webs we know about. They're all razor wire so it's impossible to see them.*

"Almost," Callimay smiled as she took a small disk off her belt.

"Huh?"

"There's this thing called powder makeup. You've seen me put it on before. It looks like powdered sugar in the air. Traceur told me to carry some with me so I could find them. Whatever metallic additives they use to make this specific brand is attracted to it. She got some for me to carry; a glitter-laden type that will help me even during a new moon run — like this one will be." *And I've always got the belvedere.*

He sat back and let out a small smile as he looked at what was in the disk, but sighed and shook his head: *I don't know. With how far they start out from the gorge you won't be able to reach him.*

"It'll work. I know it will." Callimay tried to encourage as she dropped to her knees.

"Who am I going to get to go with you?"

"What about Traceur?"

"I need her on observation post. I trust her to know if something's going to go wrong and get you out. She's strong-willed, so—"

"Who's going with you?"

"Rocher and Enforcer at least." *I 'should' make Elder go, really. ~ That's not a bad idea. You could keep an eye on him. ~ But then again what good would that do? He can still reach anyone here.*

"Destan?"

"I guess I could— he 'might' not be able to. I don't think Mender has cleared him yet."

She could tell his thoughts were jumbling and he was rambling, so Callimay started throwing ideas out, "How about one of the trainees? I'd think they'd be the most difficult for Elder to man—"

"No! First off it's not allowed and second off there's not one of them I'd trust with you. — Now what are you doing?"

"I… I was going to call Redje and ask him if he—" Callimay froze as she looked and saw the anger burning in his eyes.

But, they began to brighten and soften as he stood and put his hand out, "Let me do it."

"It's dialing right now."

"What's up?" Redje sounded chipper when he answered the phone. "Find anything out?"

"I don't know if you'd be willing to, but there's a huge faction forming in our support that I have to see to immediately; and as it 'just so happens', today's the start of Calli's final run. I need someone to take my place I can trust."

"Like 'now', today?"

"Yeah, great notice I'm giving, I know."

"Elder?"

"Most likely."

"Give me a sec…" Redje put his hand over the mic. "Tabby? Tabby Bae, can you come here?"

"What?" She tossed the kitchen towel as she scurried over.

"Destan? Can you say that again for Tabby?" Redje requested as he turned the speaker on.

"There's a huge faction that's forming and I've gotta fly to Brigon to take care of it. Calli's final run starts today and you know this is her only shot. I wanted to ask Rej if he'd be willing to be her subject since I don't have anyone else I trust to be with her."

Silence.

"Look, I… I know this is so last second, but…" Destan tone spiraled into defeat; this lack of response feeling like his answer.

Tabitha clapped her hands over her mouth as Redje put his arm around her; her whispering as the front door opened, "You've got to."

"Terra and Uklo won't be back until tomorrow. I don't want to leave you alone that long." He shook his head, though he looked pained to say it. "And I don't know if Baron is able to fill in, yet."

"We promised we'd be there for them." She pleaded as Rose climbed up and sat next to her.

"When we could, Tabby Bae."

"If this fails we lose everything and they most likely lose the chance to have what we've got right now." Tabitha begged as she gripped his arm. "Baron said he'd have our backs and it's only one night. Maybe Mr. Utree can even help for a few hours. I'll come so you don't have to worry and so I can do what I can to help observe. Callimay needs someone she can trust there as well. Zelpha can watch Rose for a couple days or at least overnight until the Utrees can pick her up."

"I gets two stay which Mammy?"

"Shh, Sweetheart."

"Destan… I…" Redje tried to weigh everything as fast as he could and still make a wise decision.

Rose perked up as she bounced, "Desan!"

"You need to be quiet, alright Sweetheart? This phone call is very serious." He said calm but firm; the sight of his daughter looking terrified making his mind up for him. "We'll drop Rose off with Zelpha and get there as fast as we can."

Destan looked at Callimay and began to smile; his voice almost quivering, "Thank you so much. I'll let them know you're on your way. — But are you sure you want to make the trip, Tabitha? … Alright. I'll let Calli know. God bless you two. Thank you so much. See you soon."

"What?" She asked wide-eyed as she laid her hand on his chest, not trusting the half that she heard.

"They're both coming. Rej agreed to be your subject and Tabitha said she'd be the other trusted pair of eyes and ears to watch you."

"Leave now so you can get back sooner. I'll stay with Doctor Gerould until they're here."

"But Elder could—"

Callimay calmed as she brushed the side of his face with the back of her hand, "There's nothing he can do to me without me knowing it. Not now, anyway: migraine-free and no concussion flares. You know that. Just keep yourself safe for me. Let Doyen do what he needs to and don't let that monster inside of you wake up."

His voice was agonized as he pulled her close, it muffled by her hair, "Lord? We come before You to ask that You guide us over these next three days. Please give us wisdom and clarity so that we can see when temptation is in front of us, and look for the way of escape. Be with Calli. I pray it is in Your will that she have no pain these three days and she finishes this with the outcome we are wanting. Help my trip to be productive and be over in a day. … But we always pray that Your will be done; and that whatever it is, You would strengthen us to continue on and be faithful in all things. It's in Your Son's name I pray, amen. … Calli? If you ever, and I mean 'ever' need me; know I'm never going to be so busy or preoccupied that I can't stop whatever it is I'm doing to talk."

Unable to keep her moment's realization to herself, she almost giggled with excitement, "Just think: the next time we see each other I'll be a Shadow! And then I'll be just a vote away from always being by your side."

"Always my ray of sunshine. You're such a blessing. … This never gets any easier — leaving."

"It… it's not easy on me either. I'm just trying to keep things in perspective and look for the good. Please try for me. Just this one, last time. Don't stop praying. I won't."

There was what felt like an eternity where nothing was said, and then Destan whispered as he gave her a kiss, "Love you. Godspeed C—"

"Don't you dare say that!" She shrieked as she grabbed his collar and shook him.

"Wha—"

"That's the last thing Dakoe told me before he died." She sobbed as she gripped his veil. "I… I know it's not— please just don't say that."

"I…" he tried to find words; taken aback by how one word could cause such a violent reaction. "Calli? I didn't mean to— Calli look at me. … I'm sorry. — Stay safe. Is that okay?"

"Stay safe." She bit her lip; still fighting off sobs.

"I'll let Lance know what's going on and to expect you."

"Alright."

Destan paused as he opened the door and looked back. She looked as if she were about ready to cry again. He gripped the door handle, struggling to not run back and scoop her up into his arms.

Callimay closed her eyes and sighed, trying to do what she could to help the two of them make this hard time easier — turning her back.

He shut the door and leaned against it. He just couldn't imagine Elder not being responsible; not even Redje could!

God? Please don't let this effort of his work. Please don't let him take my Calli away from me. Please, God. Please. Just give us the strength we both need to make it through this. It's in Your Son's name I pray, amen.

Destan felt Callimay so close and sighed as he groaned: *I don't know if I can do this. ~ Yes you can. Three days; just like her conditioning. And she'll be with Rej, Tabitha, and Traceur. It'll work out. Have faith. … If you don't go now, she's gonna come flying out of that room crying and begging you to stay. Step up and be the leader she needs so she can help you the way you need.* *Calli? I know you can do this. I know 'we' can do this. Hopefully it won't take me the whole time and I'll make it back in a day. … Calli?*

Sounds good.

After a few moments, working through hearing her desperate voice, his tone deepened: *Don't leave the suite for a few minutes. I need a couple to fill Doctor Gerould in.*

Alright. I love you, Destan.

Love you too. He paused, his voice sounding so grieved; him trying to drag himself along. *It's just a couple days… and you're going to have those we trust close by. I've got to remember that. I've got to remember that and pray. Pray. Pray. Pray.*

ᚼ

Those few minutes felt like a lifetime. And yet she was glad to have time to gather herself and accept what just transpired. Things were going to be a challenge as it was; this all added on top was going to make her job of being aware of her surrounding that much more important. If Elder didn't do this — which let's face it, is close to impossible — this all happening was still playing right into his hand.

After double-checking what Destan jotted down, she turned the computer off and burned the page.

She shut the door but held onto the handle, it somehow making her feel safe; the moment she let go a wave of shock and fear washing over her. Callimay closed her eyes and took a deep breath before taking that first step… the hardest one.

254

As she rounded the corner she saw Elder a little way down the hall. She kept her head down and followed behind the small group; hoping he wouldn't see her: *Just keep going. Stay calm.*

His cruel voice boomed as he stepped in front of her, "Where are you going, Liaison?"

Without missing a beat, she replied, "Reporting to Mender per Doyen's orders until the substitute subject for my final run arrives."

"Doyen assigned you someone else? When did this happen?"

Oh pl-ease. ~ Why did you offer that extra information! ~ I... I don't know! ~ Well you stuck your foot in your mouth now. Better finish chewing it. "Yes. It was just about twenty minutes ago."

"Why?"

"Something of grave importance came up, he told me." *Why bother asking, you know 'I' know and I know 'you' know.*

"Well, Mender is speaking with Doyen right now so I will wait with you until he returns." Elder's eyebrow kept a doubtful edge to it.

Callimay knew he was already in the air and Doctor Gerould was in the medical wing waiting for her. She didn't want to have it out with Elder right then so she did everything she knew to keep herself calm and collected, "I appreciate that but I will wait in the medical wing. I am sure you have more important things to tend to."

"What important things?" Elder threw his hand against the wall.

"Something important must be going on with all of this traffic and Doyen assigning me someone else." *Could we 'not' do this right now?*

"What traffic?" Elder looked around... no one anywhere in the hall.

But... then that means... this was all a setup! All those Shadows were being manipulated by Elder. ~ Either that or he slipped back in somehow. ~ I would have known, though! I know things are out of whack right now, but— "Well, I guess the group I was with gave me a false impression of the gravity of the situation; though there must be something since Doyen reassigned me."

"You know, Liaison," Elder warned as he stepped closer, making her pin herself against the wall. "Knowledge can be dangerous. Too much makes you vulnerable to leaking said life-threatening information."

"That is why hierarchy is in place within an organization such as the Shadows: to compartmentalize and make sure the least amount of individuals know compromising information." Callimay gulped as she tried to stay as far away from him as possible.

Calli? What's wrong? Why are you so scared?

"Your hair is much shorter than I remember." Elder grabbed a loose lock of her hair and rubbed it between his fingers. "Did you get tired of having to take the time to make sure it was properly styled? Or did you have an 'accident' again?"

"Some things are done out of necessity." She tried not to loose it from this brash invasion of her personal space. "I think I see Mend—"

"That's impossible."

Calli, what's wrong!

She tried to keep her voice from begging as she tried to keep him at arm's length, "I'm just going to go wait in the medical wing. Doyen looked very concerned when he left. I don't want word to get to him that something is wrong when it isn't."

"Oh, stop already." Elder snapped as he grabbed her hands.

Calli!

Heavy footsteps stormed up to them, someone placing a strong and heavy hand on Elder's arm as he pulled him away, "Is there something wrong, Elder?"

"Just a spot check." He shoved Callimay back and stepped away; taking a deep breath as he cracked his neck.

"Alright," Doctor Gerould replied rather confused as Callimay wheezed and took off for the medical wing. "Any word on when Doyen might be back?"

"Not as of yet. When will you be reporting back?"

"In a few hours, probably. Rounds need to be made and a couple of the trainees have come down with something."

Calli talk to me! Destan pleaded as he gripped the armrests.

I... I'm alright. She finally replied as she tried to catch her breath, curling up in a corner of an unlocked room.

What happened?

It's okay now.

Callimay Rose you better— please tell me, Calli. Please.

The air was drenched with tension as he waited, her tiny voice wheezing: *Elder... he... he reminded me of what Toreon would do.*

What!

When Toreon grabbed my hair the one time—

Destan jumped to his feet and looked back in the direction of Bulwark: *Did he do anything?*

No, she let out a shiver of a deep breath. *Thankfully Doctor Gerould came out.*

I should've walked you down there myself.

It's fine. She sighed as she leaned her head back against the wall.

You're sure he didn't do anything?

I'm sure. He just grabbed my hands and kept after me to tell him everything I knew as I tried to keep him at arm's length.

Destan raked his hands through his hair and then dragged them down his face, sounding irate: *He had 'no' right to even think— you're 'sure' he didn't do anything? You can tell me, Calli. It's alright. … Calli? Calli, do I need to come back?*

Just… go on. I'm okay. Don't stay longer than you have to, though. — Doctor Gerould's back.

The few Veils with Destan were all eyes and ears now, so he stepped into the back lounge before continuing: *Rej just called a few minutes ago and said they're on their way.*

She got up and following Doctor Gerould who was asking her the same things Destan had, still talking to Destan: *I'll make up the lost time, don't worry. — Where are you, now?*

Just about at the edge of Ferdinan. … I still can't believe—

I'm alright now. He didn't do anything. I just… it just reminded me was all. I can tell Elder's crawled back into his hole in Deep Dark.

I don't know why I didn't just give the journal to the Veil after favor swung in my direction.

Elder would have capitalized on it as you manipulating situations for your own good. The last thing we need is for him to ever get his hands on that journal. … Where did you put it?

Somewhere 'he' can't even find it. It's safe. Destan assured, and then jumped in thought: *Don't forget you've got the Big Fella.*

He couldn't have gotten to me in here.

Belvedere's are programed to do anything — 'any'thing — to get to their keeper if they're in distress, Calli. Don't assume that a bulletproof, reinforced doors that are hidden to naked, untrained eye will keep him from you. They're strong creatures as it is, but he's an alpha. He's ten times smarter than his smaller counterparts and stronger than any man alive; even me in my heightened state. *I oughta know. ~ Let's not say anything to her about almost dying, shall we? No need to get her panicky about things like that.* *Do you have your computer?*

Of course I do. I always keep it r— it's gone!

When do you last remember having it? He ripped his off his belt and started working.

I double-checked before I headed over. I did! I promise! Callimay defended as she looked around her. *I never heard it fall off and I—*

Elder. Destan grimaced as he started working on his computer in a fury. *He's trying to decrypt it right now.*

What part? The whole thing?

The unnamed push command I put on it for the belvedere. If he figures out what it is he'll be able to find him.

Has he?

No.

Well just move it to another computer so I can—

It's not that easy, Calli. The belvedere has to be synced for me to get the right coding imputed for it to go on any other computer. I can't just copy and paste it. It's gotta be completely deleted.

She gasped as she stopped dead in her tracks: *But then—*

"I know!" Destan yelled; then calmed when he realized he was spiking: *I… I know, Calli. You're going to lose your only leash you have on the belvedere. And… I'm too far away now for mine to work.*

She started crying as she stumbled back, Doctor Gerould ushering her into another room and leaving her alone for a bit.

It took her longer than she expected, but she tried to keep herself quiet when she heard someone else's voice in the next room: *It's only until you get back. And if things go well you won't be gone but a day, maybe a day and a half… right?*

There was a deafening silence for a few seconds, Callimay venturing to ask though hating to: *Did you fix it?*

He sighed as he let the computer fall into his lap: * I've set it to do a factory reset. He won't be able to find him. — Did you get breakfast?*

No.

Destan's scolding sounded more like a desperate plea. *Calli, you're going to be up for the next three days… running and on rations. You 'need' to eat something.*

Doctor Gerould just asked me and is going for something.

Take care of yourself, Calli. I don't want to come back and need to take you to the medical wing first thing. So eat something good… and a lot of it.

This start in another direction helped Callimay keep it going. They both needed to get their focus on something a bit more positive: *Are Traceur and Tabitha going to take turns? I can't see Tabitha making it that long with as far along as she is and her blood pressure still having fits at times.*

They'll switch off every eight hours. — Make sure you plan your intervals so you're in maximum cover during the day. Rej hasn't run in a while, but he shouldn't have a problem keeping up with y— umm, I didn't mean that. *There you go putting your foot in your mouth again.* *Keep your contact with Tabitha and Traceur to an absolute minimum. Now as far as I go: remember you can always talk with me.*

She chuckled to herself about his "slipup" and then replied: *This makes me think back to when we left the Society: you staying up for three days. I never thought in my wildest dreams I'd ever be able to stay up that long and actually function.*

You're so nervous. Oh my Calli. ~ And you aren't? *It had been a while.* Destan reminisced, almost sounding like he was chuckling. *I can without a doubt say I've 'never' had a subject sleep on my lap during a recovery run. It was a completely different experience.*

Well I'd hope you hadn't!

<h1 style="text-align:center">~ 16 ~</h1>

Over the next couple hours, Callimay and Destan talked off and on until it was time for him to see what in the world was going on and how to fix it. That transition happened just when Doctor Gerould said Redje and Tabitha arrived, so he held out and waited for her to say she was with them before he "left".

Seeing her dear friends' faces made the uncertainty and fear of everything wash away as much as possible. She ran up and gave each of them a hug, her voice trembling a bit, "Thank you so much. You have no idea how relieved Doyen was when you agreed."

Tabitha held on a bit longer, sounding choked up, "We're so glad we're able to help. You've done so much for us."

"I feel like we've been the ones—"

"We better get to it. You've lost quite a bit of time already." Redje interrupted at he looked at his watch.

Everything came flooding back as to "why" they were there. As abrupt as it was she needed that push; Callimay nodding as she turned and headed for the chopper.

❦

The first stop came quicker than she expected; Tabitha's tone and line of questions with Traceur of the serious type Callimay has never seen from her. Redje helped her out and spent a minute with her, handing her a small bag before jogging back.

He "felt" leery and suspicious as he got back in the chopper and she couldn't blame him in the least. With what he knew now about Elder and why Destan left, she knew it wasn't in any way easy for him to leave his wife and child alone… and rather defenseless. She thanked him again and again as well as reminding him she'd keep an eye on the two of them; hoping that would somehow help him.

He appreciated her doing what she could and lightened a bit; though the remainder of the trip he was silent.

When Callimay felt a slight falling sensation, she closed her eyes and gripped the railing closest to her: *This is it.*

A firm and yet tender hand rested on her shoulder, her looking up to see Redje's encouraging smile, "You've got the first new moon, Liaison. You have more going for you than maybe you know. I'll see you soon."

"Be careful."

He nodded as he patted her arm, "You got it."

Even after that encouragement, Callimay began to worry. She was all alone. Yes, her fear of heights had waned quite a bit, but that wasn't really the issue she was having. She wasn't familiar with those flying. In fact she didn't recognize them at all: *Oh I wish I could talk with Destan. He'd know who they are. … God please give me Your strength right now. I know this all is very physical in nature, but You know how much this can impact Destan and me. Please watch over me, watch over Redje and Tabitha, and watch over Destan. Keep Your hand on us as we're apart. And please let the plans that Elder has be foiled to Your glory. It's in Your Son's name I pray, amen.*

She opened her eyes and let out a sigh of relief; a huge weight taken off her shoulders in a way.

❦

Callimay ran through the warnings Destan gave her one last time and then hopped out of the chopper when they made it to her drop off.

As she had been doing for the past couple weeks, she took a moment to "listen" for anyone nearby and then made contact with the observers for clearance to begin.

Traceur gave her a starting time and confirmed her drop off point as well as where she would be picking up Redje; along with other details. Callimay remembered Destan and her talking about her losing time, but when she looked at her watch to figure out how much run time she had left she realized part of Redje's hesitancy was how daunting the task was going to be. As she looked out the mountain that marked her near halfway mark appeared to shrink into the horizon: *How in the world am… I'm gonna have to outpace a belvedere to even 'think' about having a shot at doing this! ~ Well you won't if you never start, Rose Petal. Stay focused and keep your mind clear.*

She took one more look around and then kneeled down; taking a long, slow, deep breath as she opened her eyes. While this change in determination that became evident was what she always saw in Destan when he would "turn on" his Doyen side, unknown to her, she had picked up this trait — her eyes losing their sparkle and gaining a dark, burning focus.

The plot she ran to get to Redje was short and simple: *Check this first task off as a complete success. ~ One down and three days to go.*

"Just take this one step at a time." Redje whispered as he grabbed her wrist. "I'm right here."

They started on a plateau for a little bit; making sure to hang right inside the tree line. With the new moon everything was coated with layer upon layer of thick black. Add to that the higher winds? Callimay saw her failures as a blessing. Had she run last week, she would've had to contend with the moon even though it would have only been a waning crescent. It was completely clear then with no wind at all.

Now? As Redje said: she had more going for her than she realized.

About two hours later they started their steep descent into a ravine that would eventually open up into the wider valley. The area resembled more of a gorge than anything; but groveling over the technical name wasn't something Callimay cared much about even though Destan was pretty adamant about it being a gorge.

Something hit her odd as they continued on, Callimay having this feeling scratch and claw at her of someone watching. That and fog started rolling in so her visibility was being cut dramatically. She made sure Redje was keeping up — she couldn't lose him for any moment or it'd be an automatic fail and she couldn't allow him to be the one to find a trap… be it planned or not.

Finding holds on the way down into the ravine — or gorge — was easy where she decided to go; several large trees with their roots jutting in and out of the clay-like soil working almost like stair steps. She gained confidence with each step and was picking up the pace when she felt something strange pressing against her arm. Callimay looked up and saw it was some type of string, panicking: *Don't move, Redje!*

He slipped a bit from being startled, but did as she said while surveying the area himself.

She took out the powder she had and blew across the top of it, making sure it was pointed in the direction she wanted it to go.

Sure enough, it was a Syndicate line. She blew some all around her and revealed a web of lines that extended farther down. Redje nodded and then pulled his hood over his mouth, "Confrere calling observation post for an alarm, over."

"Go ahead, Confrere. This is observation post." Traceur fumbled to hit the com button and woke up her computer.

"Syndicate web in the gorge about… twenty feet from the top. In direct line with the tree line, west end. Lock onto Liaison's coordinates since she's in the web." Redje kept on as he nodded to Callimay.

They both heard a muffled slam, Traceur gasping, "Is she alright!"

"I'm fine."

A web? That wasn't on any paperwork I got. Let alone we 'never' let a trainee encounter one. … This… it makes no sense. We just combed that area yesterday. Traceur took a deep breath and then replied, "I'll send in a team to quarantine them and see if they're safe to remove."

Redje helped Callimay back up to where it was safe and then they scaled around to the far side to finish their descent.

Time marched on, her making another metal checkmark when she was on level ground. She made sure Redje was down and safe before taking a quick surveillance of the area. The feeling of being watched was gone — in fact it left the moment she found out she was in the web — but the fog was getting thicker. Callimay knew it would only get worse the farther they went. The first step she took reminded her of stepping on wet sand under shallow water: her foot sank in. She heard a faint tick and jumped back, pushing Redje to the ground.

Sure enough, she'd set a trap off.

Callimay spent a few more moments scanning the ever-decreasing area of visibility for any other traps and then continued on.

It was treacherous for the first half hour, but then things began to level off. The high sides were becoming farther and farther apart, and they were beginning the last descent into the larger portion of the gorge. It frustrated her that she could only see fifteen feet in front of her, but that was better than the four-foot radius she had earlier. The frustration was more with the fact she wasn't able to move at the pace she needed to… which made her deadline that much more impossible to achieve.

Now she was wishing she just had the moon to contend with. She looked straight up and saw the small portion of visible sky directly above her that was spackled with stars. One in particular seemed to glisten even more than the others: *Oh, Mama. I need help. Lots of it.*

She closed her eyes and worked to remember how the map Destan showed her looked, being able to faintly hear what had to be the waterfall located at the extreme southeast end. Callimay motioned to Redje and started off.

While she knew why she was taking this "drastic" detour, Redje was beyond confused with her choice: *Umm, Callimay?*

What is it?

What are you doing?

Taking precautions, Redje. Just taking precautions. I'm not heading for the webs. Destan showed me where they were.

When they got to the creek she understood why it was never chosen. The creek bed itself, as well as the clear area around it, was nothing but beautiful, black pebbles. Yes, the creek bed had sand as well, but being a Shadow meant making no noise. — Well, as close to that as humanly possible. — This was nothing short of a sure fail if she tried it.

But Callimay smiled as she motioned to Redje. … Excuse me, what?

What seemed so impossible a half hour earlier now began to look doable. The fog was her friend. She remembered how fog suppressed noises over long distances; especially high-pitched ones — the main type made by running through water.

They'd been running for close to four hours at this point and Callimay knew she'd need to start thinking about where to stop before long. While the fog made sure she hadn't covered nearly anywhere the sixty miles she needed to, this small break was helping her keep her thoughts positive.

Redje knew she was pushing it to try and squeeze as much distance as she could out of this first run, but even he was getting concerned that she wasn't thinking when the sky began to change color. And yet before he said something she stopped and started working to find him a spot to hide.

Having a meal with another man, and alone with said man, was odd… borderline unnerving: *It's Redje. He's not going to do anything. Just do what you've been doing: keep an eye on him and Tabitha.*

This unsettled feeling wasn't something only she felt, and yet Redje had it for an altogether different reason; but he never showed it so Callimay could physically see it. Listening to him she wished she was capable of letting two other individuals talk to each other, but she did what she could: *Tabitha?*

She did her best to keep from falling out of bed: *What's wrong!*

I'm sorry! I… I just wanted to ask how you were doing. Callimay sounded frantic as she kept climbing up the tree to her spot she chose to spend the day.

Oh. She sat back and took a moment to catch her breath. *I'm doing alright. How are you two?*

We're fine. Just got settled for the night. *That 'still' sounds so odd.*

Tabitha took a drink and then laid back down: *I'm really tired, so I'll talk to you later.*

Alright. She grunted as she pulled herself up to the last branch and gripped it; taking a moment to scan the area before saying anything: *Redje?*

Have I ever said how disturbing that is? No offense. He tried to be light-hearted.

No, but I'm not surprised. I talked with Tabitha and she said she's doing alright. Really tired, but doing alright.

There was a few moments of silence, Redje finally replying: *Thanks. I don't know if you understand how much that helps.*

It's the least I can do, and… in a way I do understand.

Their conversation went on for a bit, but it was easy for Callimay to tell Redje felt like he could rest easy now. This tugged at her a bit; her wondering how Destan was. But then she remembered what was going on and called in her status: *Land sake! I almost forgot!*

Traceur sounded concerned, but understood with everything being thrown off she was struggling to remember finer details. In fact, in light of what all happened Traceur was impressed.

As she took surveillance of the area, she noticed the fog wasn't burning off. If anything, it was getting worse: *I could run now but am I 'allowed' to since I checked in? I can't see anything which means no one else could see me either. … Right? … I just, you know, all that time I lost— ugh! There's 'got' to be a way to make up that time without failing the run, or worse yet: killing me or Redje in the process.*

She sat there, hashing out her options; still clinging to her desire to go. The thought of getting more time in was so tempting, but she couldn't afford to fail this run. … Then again, if she didn't get back in three days she'd fail anyway.

Callimay shimmied down after checking the area once more, sounding urgent: *Redje? We're moving out.*

He sat up and rubbed his face: *What do you mean by that?*

We've got a blockade of fog and it's getting thicker from the sunlight, not thinner. I've 'got' to capitalize on this.

All he could do was sit and stare. He "wanted" to say something, but knew he wasn't "allowed" to.

I don't have time to be careful. If I don't get back in three days it doesn't matter how well I do everything else. … Please trust me. She sounded desperate as she hit the ground.

I won't argue with that. Lead on, Redje sighed after he shook his head a bit to wake himself up.

They made it to the pond in just over two hours. It went against everything Callimay had been taught up to that point, but how could this fail! Any distance she could gain was a win; each step a thumbed nose at Elder and a stamp of proof positive to the Veil she was worthy.

Once they made it to the pond, Callimay slowed down. The fog was horrendous: *If Elder knows that I'm still moving he could 'so' use this to his advantage. ~ Well, just standing here will make it worse. ~ Right.* *Let's keep moving, Redje. Umm. Is what I'm doing cheating? Me talking like this, I mean.*

You never asked Destan?

I did, but I wanted to get your input on it. I don't want to have you participate in something you think is wrong.

Well, you're supposed to be as quiet as possible and there's nothing that outright says you can't talk another person, so no. He half-laughed as she motioned for him to slow down. *Something not right?*

She crooked her head and froze, closing her eyes to help her focus: *There's someone nearby. They can't 'see' us either but they've got some trap set up so they can figure it out.*

What kind?

I don't know. She pursed her lips; gripping both of her Seaxes. *Stay low and try to just step where I do.*

So you don't think this is just a normal encounter? He sounded concerned as he reached for one of his knives.

Callimay started breathing heavy as she tried to keep the fear in herself at bay: *No. Something's most 'definitely' not right about this.*

We can stop and—

We're in the open! We've got to move. This fog won't last forever.

Don't panic, Callimay. Redje took one of his double shadow knives out; scanning the area. *We 'will' get out of this. There's two of us and only one of them. Right? … Good. Now can you tell where they are?*

This shock was making her lose her collective nature she'd trained so hard to gain; him grabbing her arm and looking her in the eye: *Callimay you 'can' do this. Reach out. See if you can find them so we know where they are. Tell me where they are.*

Hearing that sent shivers down her spine: *Oh God please don't let this end like it did with Dakoe!*

Callimay!

There was fear in his eyes, but so well hidden by the fire in them that it took her a moment. She bit her lip and worked to listen carefully: *I… it seems like they're above us.*

Probably on the ledge to the south, it's the best place. Redje looked up and then reached out and took her hand. *No one needs to know about this since this has nothing to do with what you're supposed to do. It's eating time, but I'm not willing to take a chance. I made a promise to your husband and I fully intend on keeping it. Come on.*

It was hard to force herself to go "toward" this type of danger, but she took a hard swallow and followed.

His willingness to run like the wind without any concern scared the living daylights out of her, but he explained when she kept pulling back on his arm: *They won't expect us to go straight at them. The traps they set would be in the direction you were supposed to go. And I know for a fact we never set traps for trainees out this far because it's too far out of the way. — I need you to keep an eye on my six, alright?*

She nodded and whipped around as he started climbing, taking her Seaxes out and gripping them until her hands stopped shaking.

The wait felt like an eternity, but Redje finally said: *Okay, I'm up on the first level. Your turn.*

As quick as a flash she holstered her knives and flew up the rock face. Not being able to see where she was going while climbing made her feel safer in a manner of speaking. The fog was still thick enough that she never felt more than two feet off the ground; as if it would catch her if she slipped and fell.

He took her arm and helped her up, glancing around before looking her in the eye: *Okay. There are four more of these to go before we get to the top. I'd like to get above the person, but we're gonna be pushing limits with the fog before long. We'll inch our way up like this as long as we can. Alright?*

Two more "flights" up was as far as Redje dared go for the sake of her run. While this area wouldn't be monitored directly, if they noticed something they would check and then that'd be it once they recognized who it was. While not the most desirable place to be if it came to a combat situation, Redje knew they were safer there than on the ground. He kept in the lead, knife in hand the entire way; glancing up and down to see if he could catch a glimpse of anyone.

As they crept along, the fog began to dissolve as quickly as it flared up; it dangerously thin: *This is a good spot, Redje. Let me take over.*

You sure?

They're gone. I don't how they left this quickly, but they're gone.

It baffled him how she could know that, but Redje was willing to trust her: *Guess they gave up because we were taking too long.*

Get some rest.

Are you sure you're alright?

She rubbed her face and sighed: *I'll let you know if I hear them.*

℈

Callimay wasn't completely satisfied with the ground they covered, but it was almost double what they would have had she not pushed on. And in spite of what they had to deal with she really couldn't complain at all. Sure, it bugged her to no end about the mystery visitor; but something told her it wasn't the last time they'd come snooping around. And it was odd she couldn't recognize their voice: *Well, if you think about it, this shouldn't surprise you 'that' much. Elder does have the ability to reach anyone, so who knows who that was! ~ It almost sounded like a woman's voice. ~ Strigidae? ~ I pray not.*

While she could've kept on this thought for the entire day, she knew that wasn't going to help her keep focused on the task at hand. It'd keep her awake, yes, but not focused. So, she fought to think about what was going to be something constantly changing: plot this run like no one else has or would.

She'd been keeping a constant eye on Redje and Tabitha, but could now tell she couldn't reach far enough to talk with Destan: *I wonder just how much range I lose with three channels open. Maybe that other person didn't 'leave' like I thought they did. ~ Let's not overthink things too much. You could still reach Tabitha and she's quite a ways off. ~ True. … Which now begs the question: that person must either be able to fly or they've got a vehicle close by. ~ You mean Ingrid? I'm fairly sure you would've known it was her. ~ True. Her voice. I would've recognized it. Thanks. I needed that encouragement. ~ Anytime, Rose Petal. ~ Hopefully Destan will be free for a little bit. I 'really' need to hear his voice. ~ But don't 'offer' information. ~ Oh believe you me, you don't have to tell me that. The last thing he needs is that added worry of knowing Elder really is using this chaos to its max potential.*

With that settled and things stable, she broke off Tabitha and Redje only to find Destan was a wreck: *Where were you? I've been trying all day to get to you. Are you alright?*

I'm keeping tabs on Redje and Tabitha… and I just remembered that causes me to lose range. I'm sorry.

269

The pause in the air felt like Destan was face-palming; and his tone sounded like it, too: *Oh. Right. I forgot, too. — How are you?*

Wait. 'You' were trying? But you should've been able to.

Well, maybe my mimicking ability doesn't reach as far as the real deal, if you will.

Who knows. She shrugged as she glanced around.

So. How are you? His voice almost cracked.

Keep it together and simple. *Still in one piece! Did find another Syndicate web when we got into the gorge.*

Where!

Right as we started getting in. I almost sliced my arm on it. 'Almost' being the key word like you love to use. Callimay stressed, part of her finding it interesting to be in the same position Destan was on a few occasions. *Though it wasn't cutting my ensemble. It was just pushing into it and against my arm. I actually felt—*

'Please' be careful. Where are you at?

At the far edge of the gorge.

Why only there? You should be—

Fog. It's miserable. And then I lost five hours by the time Redje and Tabitha got here.

Destan sighed, dragging his hands down his face: *Well…*

At least I was able to make up some ground by running during the day. She sounded rather proud.

You what! Calli how could you risk that!

Easy! I can barely see my hand when I stretch it out in front of me, Destan. I 'did' stop when it started getting light out because I was expecting the fog to burn off. … Well, it didn't. It made it worse. So, I fought with myself for a while and finally decided to make up some time. It wasn't as much as I wanted but I couldn't get out of the gorge or we'd be seen. — And I did end up running down the creek. I remembered once I got there that fog dampers higher-pitched noises.

You're doing it, Calli.

What's wrong, Destan? Why are you sad?

That tiny part of me that's terrified of you being in the type of danger I'm in all the time? I've gotta be frank: it wants you to fail. Now it's not that I 'really' want you to—

I understand. Callimay calmed in such a loving tone. *This all has flared so many emotions that it's hard to know exactly what to believe at times. … Wait. Why are you up?*

You're up.

Destan, please get your rest.

I'm still keyed up about what's going on here, and then with you not next to me… I just can't, Calli. He beat the pillow, frustrated.

What happened?

Well, Elder's not going to make this an easy fix; I'll tell you that. The ones threatening to back out say they were promised this would be finished within a month of them signing on. Well… we're just about there and you know good and well we're not ready.

You never promised them that! Callimay fumed as she gritted her teeth, noticing the fog around her was receding at an alarming rate.

I know I didn't and so does your grandfather. Which means it 'has' to be Elder doing this. But… I can't push back even though I am right and have Majesty Presley's support. If I do they'll back out for sure. And we can't move ahead until Elder's been— I just don't know what to do. I know I'm tired so I'm not going to really be able to think, but I just can't, knowing you're so far away from me. This is all my fault. … I'm being depressing, huh?

She sighed, trying to cover her worried undertone as much as she could: *I love you so much, Destan.*

I love you too, Calli. The edge in his voice beginning to fade, him finishing after a minute or so: *Your grandfather told me to be sure and let you know he said hello and he wishes you every success.*

Tell him I said hello as well and thank you for the encouragement.

I miss you. He almost grimaced.

I miss you too, she felt his emotions beginning to rise quickly. *Destan? Destan, I need you to calm down. It's okay. I get it: you're tired, frustrated, and lonely. I am too, especially after today. This is a perfect storm for you to— just close your eyes and rest. I… I'll try to touch base with you right before I leave. Okay?*

Alright, he said a bit relieved, and even more tired.

Goodnight, Destan. She faded to a tender whisper.

Goodnight, Calli.

~ 17 ~

Before long she relaxed and started to find little ways of keeping herself entertained and occupied as she kept watch and waited for sunset. She was grateful she was able to sit and watch things without becoming stir crazy, but it sure did help that she wasn't going to be waiting the entire day. And after the adrenaline rush she had toward the end? Hopefully that quick burst of energy wouldn't come back to bite her later on. And hopefully she wouldn't need to expend another one at some point.

All the fog burned off by late afternoon. Callimay looked back at where they'd been and got a good look at how the creek was a horrible place other than the noise factor. Any amount of moonlight would have reflected off the water and given her away since there was scarce canopy coverage in large areas.

Taking one more scan as darkness enveloped the area, she climbed the tree a bit more to see what she was in for that night. It looked to be pretty easy for a bit, which made her a bit nervous in a way, but then there were a few hills and one of the mountains of the Badlang Range they'd have to get over.

Callimay knew they'd be getting into colder terrain and this was going to probably be the hardest stretch for her. It made her think of her last cold weather run and how her motivation was to get back to Destan's arms. She sighed, knowing that she couldn't use that this time. Well, not as an immediate reward, anyway. Being outside leading up to that point — it being cooler overall — did help take the edge off, but she knew good and well it was nothing like what was waiting for her on the top of that mountain: *Don't give up now, girl. You'll get back*

272

down to somewhat warmer temps and be just fine. ... *Destan? Destan, are you awake?*

No response.

A sigh lingered as she got down to Redje, gently jiggling his arm to get him awake: *Confrere? Confrere, wake up. It'll be time to go in—*

"Rose… go back to bed, Sweetheart. Mama needs her rest." He shooed her hand away; still half asleep.

"Shh!" She clapped her hand over his mouth, startling Redje so he flipped her over and had her in a chokehold.

"Callimay!" Redje gasped in a whisper when he finally woke up; her clawing to get away from him when he let go. "I'm so sorry."

It took her a minute to settle down, but she reached in the pouch on her leg and handed him a small bag: *I'm okay now. — Here's your ration. We'll move out in a bit once you're ready to go.*

Redje nodded in thanks: *Doing alright? Any new visitors?*

So far, so good in that area. She rubbed her temple.

He opened his mouth but didn't say anything since she shimmied back up the tree.

As she got back up to her perch she heard a tired voice: *Calli?*

There you are. I was just about to try again.

About ready then? Destan asked as he yawned.

Didn't you get any sleep?

He laughed, yawning again: *Yeah. I just got up is all.*

Oh. She trailed off, trying not to say what her heart was crying.

I miss you, Calli. And I love you so much. One day closer. — Are you going to be able to make the mountain today?

This shift in conversation helped her get back on track: *I better or I might as well quit. I'm hoping to get out of that terrain altogether by the end of the today. That should get me pretty close to where I was supposed to be in the first place.*

Just… don't run yourself so much that you can't focus.

Oh, you're not worried about Redje? Callimay began to laugh.

Why? He's always making fun of how he's so much better than I am. Let him prove it.

Callimay smiled as she started back down: *Now you're ready for the day. I'll talk to you when I can. I really should check on Redje an—*

Remember: there are two passes up the mountain. As tempting as the northern one is, don't take it. Yes, it's on the correct side but it's got more traps and isn't a straight shot path; AKA — it doesn't save you any time. And the other way also has a shortcut… providing Elder didn't bug it somehow.

You mean the one I missed last time? I couldn't see it, Destan. I tried to find it. Really I did.

You know where it's at. It didn't move. He encouraged as he kept on getting ready. *Redje is one of the very few others who know exactly where it is, so he won't question you if you stop to look for it.*

Pardon my constant asking, but I'd prefer you to tell me rather than Elder lecture me: isn't that cheating?

You're supposed to find the fastest way. And you're supposed to use all the tips and tricks that your trainer gives you. You aren't supposed to hold back information just so you look good. Not telling someone something that could save their life does your ego no good. — I've benefitted from others being transparent about 'tricks of the trade' to the point they saved my life a few times. — Redje isn't going to 'show' you it. You still have to find it by yourself.

If you're supposed to tell to help, then why are there so few who know where it is?

We don't run official runs there, and so even though it's been passed along to others, not everyone's found it and there's never much down time to actually go out for a 'casual' run to show it.

Oh. She over exaggerated. *It's time for me to go.*

Just be careful. And watch yourself.

I promise I will. You watch over yourself. Please. I can't lose you.

I promise, Calli. — Now if you need me just let me know. And… and if you 'need' me? I… I don't know how many jumps it would take me, but I'll get there as fast as I can.

I'm praying I don't need that. She shivered, trying not to think about what could happen; finishing on a lighter note: *And neither is Redje. He said he made you a promise to keep me safe and he intends to keep that promise.*

I'd never doubt him to. Godspe— I mean, be careful, Calli.

Stay safe, Destan.

❦

She had a bit of explaining to do when Tabitha asked why there was a discrepancy in her coordinates from when she last checked in. But unlike what she was expecting, Tabitha sounded very impressed with her decision… even though she never said it outright.

Redje looked better — not as focused or serious as the last time — and was comforted to hear his wife's voice; him ready for the trek ahead of them for the night.

The fog began to creep back into the gorge as they finished the last little bit of climbing.

Out of nowhere, she got a bad feeling when they were on the ledge where Redje suspected their mysterious watcher was; switching direction without notice and heading up a steeper section that would land them up top much sooner but would be in an area that was still clear of where "normal" runs would be.

Callimay disabled a couple "planned" traps in the outer portion of the first wooded area, but was becoming jumpy the longer they went with nothing. And by nothing that means not even an owl screech was heard, let alone footsteps of another human: *Now what's your plan, Elder? ~ Well he probably wants 'us' to make the next move. And by that I mean mess up. ~ So what you're saying is calm down. ~ Yes.*

Even though the canopy was thick, Callimay could tell clouds were moving in. The wind picked up even more so it sliced at her face — a snowstorm was brewing. It got bad enough that she stopped a bit short of where she planned to for the first run of the night so she could "bundle up": *How can you even call this thin thing warm? ~ Well, it's better than nothing! ~ 'Nothing is better than nothing', how can you be serious? ~ Just be quiet.*

Eating rations was a shock to Redje's system, but this slight inconvenience was worth what benefit was going to be gained. He was beyond impressed with Callimay; even when she was frantic at the one point. It would've been so easy for her to give up and let Elder have his way so she didn't have to risk being hurt, but she didn't. All she needed was help. She hadn't been in that situation before and needed to know she wasn't alone: *She recovered so well. I just hope she keeps this going. It's super tight, but if she takes the shortcut I 'know' she can do it. … I pray she knows where it is. And I pray what I did doesn't trigger a full-blown migraine. I was such an idiot.*

Once they were on their way again, it only took a few minutes to reach the next tree line. When they got there, all of the air in the area was stripped away.

Callimay stood frozen in disbelief all the while knowing precious time was wasting as she tried to figure out what to do. There were two sets of foothills that led to the mountain. If she would have only stuck a bit further south they would have been under tree cover the entire way even though it looked to be more rugged terrain — stupid clouds. Where they were was an open plain to a few easier foothills. There wasn't time to deviate to the other route, but recalling Destan's advice she knew she had to get to the south side of the mountain. So, she decided to cut a diagonal path across the plain.

But this all presented another problem. Sure, it was the new moon, but it was "so" open. There wasn't even a rock that they could hunker behind if needed.

Callimay?

I… I know. Let me have one more minute. She whipped her head around, trying to find something that could help her decide what to do. *Think! ~ That's the problem! You're 'over'thinking this, Rose Petal. It's pitch black. Cutting across it will limit your exposure and you'll be able to see anyone nearby. ~ But a sniper would have an amazing shot. ~ Well you sitting still right here is equally as 'open' and nothing's happened. Just go!*

She signaled and took a deep breath as she hunkered down and rushed out into the open; her instantly having this feeling of being "exposed" wash over her. It almost got to the point she needed to scream to get it to leave her.

As it turned out, the plain was a field of overgrown grasses that hid them. — It just looked like a flat and unprotected plain from that far off! — This was a great opportunity for her to make up for her delay and the last little bit of lost time she was still trying to cancel out; she just had to watch her footing. Redje was right with her so she pushed herself as much as she dared.

They were over halfway into their run at this point for the night and Callimay couldn't bear the thought of having to stay anywhere on the mountain; and yet it was something that was a real possibility… if she didn't find that shortcut.

"Traceur?" She put her hand over her mouth as she kept going. "What are the weather conditions up on Mt. Velo?"

"Umm…" she stalled as she looked for the data. "Looks like there's a squall up there right now. And then right after that a pretty sizable blizzard is supposed to move into the area. It's about an hour and a half out, northwest of your current position. There's about two feet of snow on the paths as is. It's projecting another four feet will be added in the next twenty-four hours."

Lovely. Callimay gritted her teeth as she fended off a shiver. "Then we'll just have to outrun it."

"Are you sure that's wise?" Traceur asked concerned. "If you get stuck up there—"

"As long as we're off the mountain before it hits it'll be fine. There's no snow down here now and the blizzard may lose its breath before it gets here."

"Keep me posted on any changes and what's going on."

As they came down the second foothill, Callimay paused to give Redje a chance to switch his ensemble over so they'd be able to make it through the colder temperatures easier: *Sorry I didn't do this sooner.*

It's alright. She shrugged off, though part of her was getting worried. *If he's starting to forget simple things that means he's worried about something. ~ Maybe it's just Tabitha and the baby. ~ Oh how I pray that's the case.*

It was tempting to double-back to the northern trail with the news of the weather coming in, but she stopped when she remembered what Destan said. And yet she couldn't shake this feeling Elder did something to the shortcut so it'd be deadly to use it. But the only way to find out was to go with what made the most sense for immediate safety.

So, to the south it was.

While the first seven miles were easy enough, she had to really slow down as they got farther up. Callimay was frustrated, but tried to keep herself focused on something positive so the exhaustion she was beginning to feel wouldn't be fed by her emotions. This reminded her of when Destan and she were at the cabin when they went for a walk up to the lake.

In what was a rather anticlimactic fashion, they made it to the area she'd been told the shortcut was in. After taxiing herself so much the last half hour, stopping to look for it was a necessity… in two ways. She struggled to focus so she could remember exactly was Destan said, her scared for a split second: *You can't get stuck up here. Neither can Redje. You'll both freeze. ~ Stop it! It's fine. Just a few more minutes. It's here somewhere. Like Destan said: it hasn't moved.*

Redje knew what she was doing and was baffled that she couldn't find it… he knew she was right where it was at. But that wasn't what baffled him: *Where is it? The snow does obscure it, but not like 'this'. What's going— Elder?*

Right before she turned to keep going, she noticed what looked like a rock in the snow about ten feet to her right. As she pushed the snow aside, she noticed it wasn't a rock at all: *Is this it?*

Redje jogged around her and leaned over, looking in the small hole: *Maybe a secondary entrance but no, this isn't it.*

What's that supposed to mean?

The shortcut Destan and I know is supposed to be back here. He backtracked and started digging snow out.

What are you doing! I can't—

Something's not right, Callimay. It's never buried like this, even in this much snow. Someone's buried it on purpose. He refused to stop, the determination in his voice becoming edgy. *You and I 'both' know we've got to find it or we won't be making it off this mountain without a rescue unit. So come on, help me.*

They spent a couple minutes, endlessly digging into what turned out to be nothing. He didn't scare easily, but Redje was becoming very curt: *It's supposed to be right here! These things just don't move.*

Well, Callimay dragged herself back to where she first thought it was; her dead arms somehow strong enough to keep pulling snow away. *Let's just see what this is.*

As she pulled more back, it looked just big enough for her to get in. — There was no way Redje ever would. — She wanted to give it a try, but she knew she couldn't lose sight of Redje for a moment while they were on the move: *If I could just see inside! ... Having Destan would be such a perk right now. ~ No kidding.*

Knowing why she hesitated, Redje reminded: *Go! Like last time, this has nothing to do with what your actual run is supposed to be.*

But if we get separated, Elder—

Go! Redje pushed her in.

She yelped as she slid down for a bit and then tumbled into a wall. It took her a few moments to shake off the hard hit and orient herself, thankful her head didn't make any direct contact.

Being in a place where she couldn't see her hand was terrifying, but the fact she could stand in the area baffled her. Was this part of the tunnel? This couldn't be an animal's den... could it? — And what animal would it be if it were!

Callimay felt around, part of her scared someone was in there waiting for her, but she couldn't feel anyone but Redje nearby. The floor was what you would expect any "natural" floor to be, but as she turned back toward where Redje was — so she thought — she started getting colder. And then she felt snow on her face: *You've gotta be kidding*— *Elder, so help me... stop it! I don't know how you snuck past me but you're done. This tunnel is wide open. Redje's probably standing right in front of me. Get out, you devil! I won't play your game and let you hurt Redje or myself! Now leave!*

Sure enough, the snow they cleared wasn't really necessary: *He's been blocking my view of this the entire time. Where is he hiding! ~ Get Redje first and 'then' take care of it.*

What in the name of!

Come on! She grabbed his hand and took off as fast as she could.

Once in a bit, they stopped and were both wheezing as they worked to catch their breath and try to warm themselves: *I thought you s—*

I'm sorry! Callimay whimpered as she started to cry. *I don't know how he did it. I never felt him.*

Redje calmed, the edge that was so sharp in his tone before vanishing: *Is Tabby okay?*

I... yeah. Yeah. Yeah, she's fine. — Look I'm so sorry. I... I don't know why—

We're okay and that's the most important part. And I know for a fact what I did earlier didn't help your head any. If anyone's at fault it's me. — Is there anyone else nearby?

She wiped her eyes and then focused for a moment: *No. No, not that I can tell. — Maybe me opening multiple channels is making this harder; telling where Elder is.*

Then just watch Tabby. Redje gripped her shoulders. *Please, Callimay. Whatever you need to do to keep her safe, please do it. If something comes up and I need you, fine, but not until then.*

Hearing the amount of fear in his voice was something she'd never heard before. In a way it scared her: *A… alright.*

While taking a bit longer to recover was something they both preferred, they had to keep moving. This area was a perfect place for an ambush.

Callimay was expecting the tunnel to just be a bypass that would end about the same elevation on the other side, but it was taking quite a bit longer and the downward slope started to become steeper.

Having this extra time away from the elements hit Callimay hard: *Thank you so much for telling me, Destan. I don't know if I would've made it over that with the wind and amount of snow there was. — And thank You, God, for letting me find it. Thank you for giving me Your strength to fight so I could see what was really in front of me.*

When they got to the end, Redje helped her clear the snow again. She was in utter disbelief when she saw where they were. That tunnel was a direct line from about two-thirds up on the eastern side to the base of the mountain on the western side! Callimay wanted to giggle and jump around, seeing how much ground they'd made up — and that they would be back under the canopy when the blizzard hit — but she couldn't waste the time she'd banked.

"Any update on that blizzard, Traceur?"

"It's dissipating." Tabitha answered.

"Oh. I didn't realize what time it was."

"No worries, Liaison. It's slowed, so accumulations are high, but the wind is all but gone from what I can see. Where are you at?"

"Already past the mountain."

Callimay could feel her smiling as she replied, "You found it?"

She looked back at Redje who shook his head furiously, not going into the details, "Eventually, yep."

The discussions he had with Destan from time to time took on new meaning now that he was witness to how mature and Godly Callimay was at handling these situations. With all she was faced with in just over twenty-four hours, the fact she was still pushing like she was, should push anyone's doubts about her away. She truly was a Veil. Everyone needed help and encouragement — every Veil he knew had those moments — so nothing in that area could be used against her.

They were running close to the edge of the tree line again and she didn't stop when the snow picked up. He could tell she wanted to move farther into the forest and keep going when it was just beginning to get light out, but he also knew her better judgement would stop her.

For him, this run was more exhausting than the previous day's. In fact, Redje was so exhausted he didn't eat his ration for the evening.

She made sure to cover their tracks as best she knew and then took her lookout station. And then as she went down her mental checklist, she called in to let Tabitha know she could stamp her coordinates for the day, "Are you sure you're going to stay put, child?"

"I 'want' to keep going, but Confrere's tapped out. ... I..."

What is it, Callimay?

Something happened today that's got me really worried. Now we're fine, but Elder sent a little calling card in the form of blocking our view of the shortcut tunnel for a bit. Maybe I shouldn't say anything, but—

You're sure you're alright?

Redje's never said otherwise.

Is that all you think he did? Tabitha's voice quivered as she looked around her, clutching her necklace.

All that caused us any problems, yes. Callimay bit her lip, but finished: *I think the problem was I was trying to watch you 'and' Redje and couldn't detect Elder like I could before. To be safe, Redje told me to only watch over you. ... I'm sorry I said anything. I guess I'm just desperate to have someone to talk—*

No. No I'm glad you told me. — And don't blame yourself, you obviously didn't know that would happen. Let me know if something else happens, okay?

~ 18 ~

She stared up at the thick, buff-colored clouds that were showering the ground with their white, frozen presents; like a child in a float at a parade with an endless supply of candy to hand out. In a way it was hard to imagine it was already December. Being at the Nest made her feel like she'd just been through winter; so how could it possibly be that it was already winter again? And then on top of that it was almost impossible to realize she was doing this: her final run. What she'd worked so hard for was finally here, and yet she had to admit she didn't think it would actually happen… in a way.

Watching the tiny crystals sway back and forth somewhat hypnotized her. Her legs were exhausted and she was starting to struggle against her constant yawning. She shook her head and looked around, making sure to keep a watchful eye; her "real" combat encounter still hadn't happened.

A few moments later, her still thinking on this, a rustling noise from behind her caught her attention. She braced herself against the tree and had a throwing knife ready to go: *Here we go. ~ Just keep calm.*

Out of the undergrowth bounded a small gray-haired rabbit. He twitched his nose and ears quite a bit before going back inside. Not but a second later a few others braved the cold and came out of their warm hiding place and congregated under another tree.

After a short "briefing" it looked like, each went off in a different direction; staying there for quite a while before returning one by one; their little mouths stained bright red from the yummy fruit they found.

Callimay smiled and watched them scurry back into their little home to get warm again; her settling back down only to see someone perched in the tree straight across from her. It took her every ounce of self-control to keep from screaming. Her hands were almost convulsing from her internalizing her reaction; it impossible for her to get a good hold on her Seaxes as she got behind the trunk of the tree for cover.

Something else flew past her peripheral on her right, but dare she look? In that moment all her training went out the window, all her focus and composure were lost. She felt as if she were in a horror movie and she was trapped by those who wanted her dead.

The same thing happened yet again, so she worked to pull her attention to the side… only to find another individual in the other tree beside her: *What! Two! Destan never said anything about there ever being two at once!*

She looked back and the first person was gone: *Oh no. Where did they go! I wasn't paying attention! Oh gosh. I… I can't do this.*

Being in the tree made her feel trapped, so the only thing she could think to do was get down to the ground. But as she started, she saw a hand reaching around her.

Grabbing the first blade she could, Callimay swung around in wild fear and stabbed the person in the shoulder with a spike.

Or at least she should have: *Where did they go! They were right here! ~ You don't think! ~ Oh please no. This isn't what was planned. ~ Not another jumper!*

While things were spiraling out of control, she at least remembered there was someone she was supposed to protect. She checked to be sure the place she put Redje wasn't touched: *Oh thank goodness. … Now where in the world did they disappear to?*

Whenever she watched any kind of suspense movie she was the one to roll her eyes and scold the main character for neglecting to look up when they lost track of the person sent to kill them. The amount of fear she was feeling helped her understand why they never did it — a very realistic representation.

And yet she had to look up. She had to find where they were. She couldn't run. And if they were above her they had a tactical advantage.

Hoping to catch them off guard, she whipped her head up and threw another spike.

Nothing.

I can't stand this! Where are they! Stop playing with me like this! … Oh if I could only yell. ~ Listen. ~ What? ~ Listen! Use your ability and find where they are; if they're anywhere nearby.

This moment of clarity was a major boost. But doing that only made things worse: there wasn't a soul within her somewhat lessened range — whatever that was. It got her to thinking: *Maybe my problem is that I can't handle watching someone else 'and' myself. … But I don't want to abandon her. ~ She's asleep right now, you 'need' to know if Elder's playing with you!*

She clinched her fists as she bit her lip, almost wanting to scream in anger as she cried out: *Elder! You sick, evil—*

I told you there was no way to beat me. His mocking voice echoed in her mind. *You 'are' strong, but 'not' strong enough. You'll 'never' be strong enough.*

We'll just see about that. Callimay thrust the spike into the tree, focusing like she did before to push him out.

The next thing she knew she opened her eyes and found she'd fallen out of the tree. She scurried to her feet and looked around, relieved that Redje was still safe and she was indeed alone. Her right side was really sore as she reached up for the first branch, her wheezing and wincing as she fell down and curled up: *Oh gosh what did I do! That hurts so bad. … Ah! I… it's so hard to breathe!*

Tears hated to, but icy streams starting flowing down her face.

And then she felt someone: *Why now! Why now of all times!*

Callimay moaned as she worked to listen so she could figure out who it was she was up against.

It was Enforcer. He couldn't see her, but she was a sitting duck where she was and the shape she was in.

In a flurry of semi-composed thought, she scanned the nearby trees. There was one that was her best shot as far as staying hidden and the one she had the best shot to trap Enforcer by.

Had she not seen this done before and knew it was him by listening to him, she would've sworn Enforcer was a real Falconer — he had the bracelet on that switched his ensemble to its white counterpart. He blended so well with the snow… but not with the trees.

But he wasn't stupid — holding steady for the past five minutes.

She had to figure out how to lure him three trees to the east. Still in an immense amount of pain, she pulled herself to the other side of the tree and glanced around, looking for something — anything — she could make noise with to attraction him to the other tree; which would also throw him off as far as where he thought she was.

Oh please work. She held the spike to her lips and then threw it.

Snap! It hit its target dead on.

At first she wasn't sure he reacted, but then she saw the snow kick up behind the tree directly across from her: *Just one more, come on!*

Callimay slid over to get a better angle and then threw another one behind and to Enforcer's right. He shifted a bit to look, but not as much as she was hoping.

Time crept on. And as far as she was concerned this stalemate could continue all day, but she had to get him down before Redje woke up… and before one of Elder's minions decided to show.

Just when she was about to have another moment of sheer panic — as if they'd planned this out to help her — three of the bunnies she saw earlier were on their way back.

And as it turned out, their den was right on the other side of where Enforcer was.

They bounded along, stopping and sitting up as they sniffed the air for a bit; them darting back from where they came when they realized they weren't safe.

This sudden movement prompted him to switch positions, falling right into her hand. So much of her anxiety washed out when she saw where he was. She took a deep breath and then let three hummingbirds fly at once, them landing like they always did: dead on bullseyes.

Enforcer was completely blindsided, which worked more to her advantage as she crept over and clipped him from behind.

It took just as much out of her as it did him; her side just about killing her with its stabbing pain and restricting her breathing.

"I'm sorry," she whispered as he looked up, only to see her boot.

While he wasn't completely out, she was hoping he was dazed enough so she could tie him up and disarm him.

Close — oh so close — but not quite: *Why did I think just one hit would do it? Idiot!*

She rolled away as he reached out to trip her, Callimay throwing a couple more hummingbirds so both his arms were pinned to the tree.

While it was true her level of strength couldn't compare to his, the throwing knives she used required more finesse than brute strength; so the lack of the latter right now wasn't a major factor. She winced as she got to her feet, grabbing her side as she repeated the same apology; using the hilt of her Seax this time.

Once she had him tied and his weapons moved to a safe place, she called in, "This is Liaison calling in a takedown. Single male. Due north of last coordinates by… fifteen yards."

"Was he armed?" Traceur asked in a calm tone.

"One silence breaker, one large doubles, a half dozen sticks, and four broad wings."

"Location?"

"Last given for subject, south side, five flights up."

Traceur smiled as she jotted down a couple notes, "Got it, Liaison. One gun, double-sided standard knife or short sword, six spikes, and four large throwing knives. … Are you alright? You sound pained?"

"It's alright. I'll make it."

While it was a comfort to know this part was over, the disturbing fact that Elder was still able to reach her was enough to make her a nervous wreck. And then her injury? Let's just say someone who can't breathe easily starts obsessing with the fact it's hard to breathe.

Destan? She grunted as she struggled to pull herself up to where she was going to stay.

Calli! How are you doing? Where are you? Did you find the shortcut? What's the weather like?

As you would say, 'so many questions'!

Calli, you sound so tired.

Well, being as how I just finished taking Enforcer down, I am.

There was a pause, Destan sounding worried: *Planned?*

The way Traceur sounded, yeah.

He took a deep breath and said relieved: *Well thank goodness that part's done for you. — Where are you at?*

When I talked with her, Tabitha said I'm just ten miles short of where I 'should' be. We're well past the mountain. Callimay yawned.

What can I do to help you?

Tell me everything is going well on your end… if it's the truth.

We're making progress: almost half have come around. Your grandfather is most concerned about the president of Crosswall pulling out no matter what we do. He hasn't gotten back with us even though we've tried him several times. Him and then Indalla, Faberton, and Quimbergo are really pushing back. And as it turns out, they're all hot spots for the Syndicate since they're the countries surrounding Crosswall — and Indalla is just a pain as it is. So, in short: things could be better but they could be a 'whole' lot worse. … But…

His not wanting to finish his sentence worried her: *What?*

That means I won't get back until you do. I'm sorry Calli.

I accepted the fact you wouldn't when you told me last night what was going on. It's alright, Destan. Just keep working. They'll come back around. I know they will.

What would I do without my ray of sunshine?

You'd be lonely and bitter. Callimay laughed, hissing a bit as she grabbed her side.

Well I thank you for your honesty. Destan exaggerated, thankfully not picking up on the pain she was in.

You know I'll always give you that if nothing else.

So, Destan started, changing the subject. *I take it since you're off the mountain you found the shortcut.*

Even with Elder trying to keep it hidden. *In the nick of time, I might add. It wasn't easy to find. I'd guess there was a good two, maybe two and a half feet of snow up there already. The wind was horrible and a blizzard was moving in. … And I was about frozen.*

Are you in the blizzard right now?

Yes and no. It's died down, thankfully. And I was able to warm up while in the tunnel. I'm just glad that part's over with. … Well, that and the combat portion. It 'is' just the once, right?

Supposed to be. Destan sounded rather cautious.

She suspected as much, so she moved on: *How are 'you' doing?"

I've had a few moments where I've had to leave and really work to get myself calmed down, but I'm catching it and making sure to walk away and do what I know to fix it. Your grandfather's been great about helping. — It's been interesting this hop-scotch movement: I haven't slept in or met with your grandfather in the same room once. In fact I just got settled into a new room. Campbell— you remember him, right? Well he showed up about a half hour ago and rushed me into this new room. … For a neutral as they are, they're 'very' aware of how to keep things secretive. Even from family members in the same residence. It's really amazing to see.

Callimay sighed as she looked around: *It's snowing here.*

It's snowing here too. Destan echoed as he looked out his window.

I don't really know why, but it makes me think of you. She smiled as she looked up, snowflakes clinging to her eyelashes. *I miss you.*

By this time tomorrow we'll be back together again, getting actual rest, Lord willing.

I can hardly wait. … So when do you think you'll be back?

Hum. … Probably right before you get to Bulwark. At least that's what I'm praying for.

So, are you going to sleep or do you have to stay up?

I've gotta get this all straightened out first. It's easier to get in contact with everyone during the day. For some reason normal people sleep at night. He now sounded light-hearted and somewhat happy.

You don't say. She exaggerated.

They don't know what they're missing. But, to each their own. — You sound better.

I feel better. She rubbed her side. *So much better now that I've heard your voice.*

❧

This stretch was especially hard on Callimay. Even with her skirmish against Elder and then Enforcer, she had quite a bit to go… while doing nothing but watching. She couldn't directly see Enforcer, so she couldn't even make funny faces at him. — She saw him a few times and he struck her as the "big brother" type who was easy-going but able to flip in an instant. Almost like a fusion of Trever and Destan.

The storm stayed all day and there was about a foot of snow on the ground now; but this was just in the wooded area which was shielded by the trees. There was going to be at least double that amount in the clear areas. Callimay knew the rest of the track was relatively simple as far as the terrain went, but this snow was going to make things hard. She really couldn't run in it. It frustrated her: knowing she was so close to finishing and had the easiest part to go, but knew it was in jeopardy with this added roadblock

And yet, with every bleak situation there had to be a silver lining. This one had one. One and only one. It was going to get darker much quicker. — Which, if it was only going to be one good thing, that was the best one to have.

Redje looked rested and ready to tackle the day when she got him up — him knowing where he was this time. He smiled when he saw Enforcer and went over, checking how Callimay tied him up before releasing him. She had a moment of fear creep in, but seeing his smile made that fear fly away. She motioned to where his weapons were and then waved as he got ready to leave, motioning toward her head as if to ask if he was okay… him winking as he waved back.

Home stretch. You've got this. You're so close. No slowing up or backing down now. Just do what you want and need to; and remember to not worry about me.

Thanks. Callimay smiled, and then let Tabitha know they were leaving in a few minutes.

There were several areas that were high-traffic for animals, so Callimay opted to stick to those as much as possible when they were heading in the direction she needed them to. They did most of the time; and it also assured Callimay there weren't any traps she would have to be worried about — her arsenal of hummingbirds and spikes were just about depleted.

She was able to zig-zag through wooded areas to help make it easier for her to run, but it was making her track longer. And yet if you were to calculate her speed as compared to the distance, it was faster in the long run.

Redje had to slow down a couple times actually so Callimay was in front of him, that being her clue to stop the first run. Her legs were past being exhausted at this point and her side was stinging her with all it had. But she knew she couldn't give up.

You okay?

Unable to keep it from him, she said: *I fell out of the tree toward the beginning of the last watch.*

Redje's eyes bugged out as he jumped to his feet: *How!*

Elder. Who else?

You mean he—

No. He wasn't there. It was nothing but an illusion, thankfully. — It's okay. I'm sore but I'll live. She winced as she sat down.

Knowing this made him stay up with her; him refusing to take any rest when she was hurt and so close to finishing: *This isn't 'cheating' and I'm pulling rank on you.*

Glad to have the company and the pain eating away at her stamina, she couldn't resist.

They started up before long, Callimay not wanting to rest too long or she wouldn't be able to keep her legs moving. It was a rough start, but her muscles began to remember the feeling and started ignoring the nerves cries for help.

Before long the snow vanished. It started to get warmer and Callimay could begin to smell the salt in the air. The only thing was… she knew she was starting to lose her cover because the clouds had moved out and so the sun was going to make everything visible that much sooner: *You're almost there, Rose Petal. Just a little bit more. ~ Why couldn't they've lasted just 'that' much longer! Why!*

As with all final runs, the finish line was the barrier around Bulwark. Callimay had to check in when she passed a checkpoint landmark that was discussed prior to her leaving so security would know she'd be tripping the sensors soon, and where.

She was getting frustrated, knowing she wasn't running nearly as fast as she needed to or could. Add to that the emotions she could tell Redje and Tabitha were feeling — both were extremely nervous? It spelled out nothing but: she was running out of time fast and wasn't there yet.

Callimay started to recognize the area and remembered this was part of her first run where Destan showed her the location of the barrier. All she could think was to grab Redje's arm and take a diving leap for where she knew it was.

~ 19 ~

As she opened her eyes, everything looked blurry and appeared to begin spinning. The second she blinked and things became clear everything rushed back. Callimay heaved from being out of breath, hissed from the pain, and couldn't bear the thought of looking to see the look on Redje's face. She could hear his tone was raised and he was talking to Traceur, but she couldn't understand what he was saying.

All of a sudden she heard as clear as could be as he shook her arm, "Callimay? Callimay I've gotta go. Tabby's not doing well."

"Go!" She yelled as she opened her eyes and practically shoved him away. "I'll be fine."

Redje nodded and took off toward the helipad.

Nothing else mattered to Callimay any longer; his desperate eyes searing an unforgettable image in her mind. She reached out to Tabitha but Elder wasn't anywhere near her. She checked Traceur and then asked out of breath, "Traceur? What's wrong? … Traceur?"

A few seconds passed, a serious voice with a hint of fear replying, "Helpmate's blood pressure spiked sky-high. She's got a splitting headache, upper abdominal pain, and to say she has to labor to breathe is a conservative estimate. I'm worried she's going into preterm labor."

Dear Heavenly Father, please be with Tabitha and the baby right now. Whatever caused this problem please let it leave her. I thank You so much for her and what she's done for me; please let her have relief from this and let the baby not be hurt. Keep Redje safe while he is on his way to them. It's in Your Son's name I pray, amen.

Nothing was said for a while, but then Traceur's relieved voice come through, "She told me to tell you she's already feeling better. She's lying

291

down right now and drinking as much water as she can. … Let me ask you something: are you a thrill-seeker?"

"N… no?"

"That was the most heart-pounding finish I've ever witnessed." Traceur gulped, taking a giant breath as she finished, "Wow."

Callimay got to her feet and looked around, dragging herself to the nearest tree and flopping behind it so she was hidden from the sun's rays, "Re… request for results?"

"I think 'cliffhanger' would've been a better title for you, personally. But I'm sure you have good reasons for picking Liaison."

"I'm sorry?"

"Doyen will have to sign off on everything — so just keep that in mind — but I don't see any reason why he wouldn't. Small formality away, but get used to being called Liaison. Welcome to the Shadows."

She looked out, not believing what she heard, "I did it?"

"With three seconds to spare I might add. You completed the run faster than anyone else I've ever seen. Good job utilizing the fog and shortcut to your advantage." She praised as she leaned back in her chair; saying in a hushed tone, "Little known fact: the fog forms quite regularly but I've only known a handful of trainees who actually took advantage of it — I wasn't one, but I know Doyen was. And you're the first to use the creek bed. The fog is something I know Doyen looks to see if it was capitalized on. And then that shortcut? That's the other thing Doyen looks for specifically when he knows the trainee knows about it. — In my opinion? You're Veil grade. I know I'm not supposed to say it, but you've got my vote. Congratulations again, Liaison."

It still refused to sink in. She did it? She really did it? After all Elder tried, and the fact she started so late, she "still" beat all the odds and came out on top? She actually beat Elder, as it were? She made it back to Bulwark safely?

Time felt like it paused for a while; her trying to wrap her mind around what happened. She started wandering back to Bulwark, her body ready to collapse. It wasn't that far, but her legs felt like each step was the entire one-hundred eighty mile run all over again.

As she looked up from the spot where she fell, she saw her husband standing not too far off. Without a second's hesitation she scrambled to her feet and ran to him, "Destan! Did you hear! Destan I did it! I made it! It's all over now!"

She slowed as she got closer, noticing he wasn't running to her and he didn't look happy at all. — That should've been a huge red flag, but by the time she realized what was going on it was too late. He kicked her feet out from under her, her not able to react fast enough to keep her head from smacking the ground.

It took her a bit to come to; Callimay moaning and yelping as she rolled back and forth, holding her head, "Why did y— Fidus?"

He leaned over, getting in her face and sneered as he yanked her arm, "Get up, Liaison."

She fell over herself as she tried to get to her feet, wincing from the pain, "What?"

"You're supposed to be ready for anything. You've done fine with Doyen, and tricked Enforcer better than anyone I've seen, but I have to see how you 'really' perform."

"But my run is already done? I've graduated. What revenger are you looking to take? Why!" She stumbled as everything started spinning.

"No one is 'ever' safe until they're 'inside' Bulwark. Have you forgotten your training? … That seems to be somewhat of a common error: even Challenger made that same mistake." Fidus warned as he took the offensive.

Elder? Callimay's eyes widened as she fought to fight through the borderline vertigo she was experiencing; grimacing as she took as much of a defensive stance as she could handling with the flood of pain she was dealing with where she smacked her head. *What… what did you do to Destan's father?*

For as much as she wanted it to be a shadowboxing match, with Elder controlling Fidus she knew it was going to be nothing but winner take all: a death match. She tried to reach out to Destan, but the pain was too much for her to focus while trying to keep Fidus at bay.

In those few moments of confusion, Fidus laid another critical, open punch without any restraint.

Once she came to after crumbling to the ground, she gasped for air as she rolled over and tried to get up, only to be grabbed by the throat and pull up; her feet flailing.

"Fidus… please…" she frantically tried to pull his arms away, her eyes wild with fear as she clawed and clawed to get him to let go

"You need to be able to fight anyone. We have Narks in our ranks if you didn't know. Just last week they killed ten of some of our best Shadows in Aridigobe. But I guess Doyen didn't bother to tell you that, did he?" He almost laughed, him refusing to let go and dodging her strikes at his face. "You've got to fight through the exhaustion. Come on, Liaison. Don't let it only take two hits to take you out. Fight!"

A few seconds passed, her still fighting but making no headway. He shoved her back and let go; her coughing and hacking as she tried to breathe, "You're weak. And you're making Doyen, Mender, Sentinel— you're making us 'all' weaker. I should've had you killed that day in Kerogen and not listened to them."

"Stop it!" Callimay said infuriated as her buckling arm tried to stabilize her effort to get up. "Destan's. Not. Weak!"

Nothing but a sudden burst of energy swept through her and gave her a perfectly clear mind — sometimes anger did that. She drew one of her Seaxes but slammed the handle of one of her hummingbirds as hard as she could against the side of Fidus' face. He stumbled a few steps, his expression showing utter shock, and fell; her helping by putting her boot on his chest and pushing him back.

"You don't even have regard for the Shadow's code of direct address." Fidus hissed as he threw a strong arm out to catch himself; him wiping the blood from his temple. "You have no right to be here."

"Elder, let him go," the fire in Callimay's eyes burned brighter than ever as she braced for Fidus to come at her again. "Quit using others and just fight me yourself!"

❦

Destan's flight was delayed due to weather conditions so he was just now landing. He was nervous the whole way, but kept that faith in his wife: he knew she could do it. And he knew his best friends would do everything they could to help her.

As he got off he saw Redje carrying Tabitha across the apron.

"What's wrong?" Destan ran over and asked, seeing the worried look on Redje's face.

"I just got too worked up is all." Tabitha admitted as she smiled, hushing Redje. "I got up so I could watch Callimay's finish but wasn't ready for the thrill of a ride that it would end up being. All that strain did a once-over on me and Benjamin so my blood pressure spiked and I started having pseudo contractions. I'm alright now. I just— oh dear."

"Benjamin, huh?" Destan's voice grinned; his eyebrow raised as his eyes sparkled.

Redje sighed as he threw his head back, "Oh great."

"I'm sorry," Tabitha tried to appease.

"Well, well, well. You're having a boy!"

Tabitha sighed, upset she let it out, "Please don't tell."

"I promise." Destan nodded as he raised his left hand and gave the Shadow signal; then asked concerned, "So, she's alright? Clean finish?"

"Three seconds to spare." Tabitha nodded.

"Where is she?" Destan asked as he looked around. "Did she just head back to the suite? I'm sure she's wiped out."

"She was at the demarcation line when I left her." Redje recalled. "That was probably… oh, a half hour ago?"

"You left her!" Destan's eyes began to flash as he jerked back. "You promised me you wouldn't leave her!"

"I'm sorry, but when I heard Tabby's voice I couldn't— Destan!"

He didn't stay to hear Redje's explanation and at the time it really didn't matter; him sprinting off toward where Callimay would've been. He tried calling out, but she wasn't responding. And to add to everything she wasn't where Redje left her.

"Calli!" He continued to yell as he looked for signs of a struggle.

But all he found was one set of footprints that didn't have any indication of being in distress. He started to calm, but then heard what sounded like shrill screams. He took off and soon found Fidus and Elder standing against Callimay; her dangerously close to the cliff.

"Fidus!" Destan bellowed as he ran toward the two of them. "Fidus, stand down!"

"Leave them, Doyen." Elder scolded as he drew his cane sword and laid it on his chest, Callimay taking the offensive against Fidus. "I assure you, Fidus won't let it go too far. Just far enough to see what is truly in her. To see if she truly has that capability in her."

You want her to 'kill' him? Just how sick are you! "I'm giving you a direct order, Fidus. Stand. Down!" Destan yelled as he dodged Elder and bolted; reaching out to grab Callimay's hand.

She'd been fighting Fidus with most of her efforts being defensive following that first burst; the strain of her injury letting his efforts put her in the dangerous place she now was in. But she — like Destan reminded her that she had so many times before — found the positive: her ability to adapt to her opponent's style made it easy to find their weak point. This moment she had now was what she had been waiting for, so she ignored Destan and found her opening, laying Fidus out and pushing her Seax against his throat.

"Calli don't!" He shrieked as he tried to take her knife away.

While it wasn't surprising that her initial response was to fight even him — he knew she was so frantic she didn't know who to trust — the force and power she used to get her knife back startled him. And the fire in her eyes terrified him... he almost felt as if he were looking at the monster inside of himself, him crying out: *Calli! Calli what did he do to you! Don't do this. Please.*

Right as she went back to him, Fidus began belly-laughing as he looked at Destan. Elder began clapping in a slow and exaggerated manner as he sauntered up and congratulated, "Very good. You may stand down, Liaison."

"What!" She shrieked in disgust as she shoved Destan aside and ran at Elder, her Seax still drawn. "You dirty, filthy, sum—"

"Calli!" Destan gasped as he grabbed her arm restrained her.

"What do you mean, 'stand down, Liaison.'?" She fumed as she started to fight Destan. "Fidus is the one who started it. He's the one who is supposed to be told to stand down. I was just doing what I was supposed to: defend myself."

"You're tired, Liaison." Elder chuckled as he patted the air in front of him with his hand. "You must've forgotten you lunged at Fidus. 'You' initiated this all. That one hit obviously messed with you."

"No I didn't! I thought he was Destan and was running over to greet him. I wasn't initiating anything! I didn't have any weapon drawn!"

Destan pulled her to him, saying something in her ear so she'd stop fighting him, before eyeing Elder, "Alright Harmon, you've gotten your stupid challenge. Now back, off! That's an order. Go back to your hole and stay there until I call for you. … Now!"

"You are right, 'Destan'. I 'did' get what I wanted… and I believe even a bit more." Elder nodded, the crooked smile and gleam in his eye bursting with pride. "I will see you in a week, Liaison. 'If' you make it."

"Good job, Liaison." Fidus said a bit winded but sociable as he put his hand on her shoulder. "Your bluff at the beginning was flawless and your ability to f—"

"Leave." Destan demanded as he grabbed his wrist and threw it away. "Don't make me tell you, what, for the sixth time? Go get the Veil assembled, I have news."

He looked stunned as he took an extra step back, standing like a stunned statue for a bit before replying, "Very well."

"Calli, are you alright?" Destan asked not but a second later, him terrified as he put his hands on either side of her face.

"I'm alive." She crumbled to the ground and grabbed her side, her hand still clinging to the Seax she kept drawn this entire time.

"Calli!"

She started coughing and gasping for air, a deep furrow in her brow from all the pain she was being flooded with. Her free hand trembled in a violent manner as Destan took it in his, her body's reserve of adrenaline gone.

Everything became still for a moment as he pushed her hair back and lifted her chin so she was looking at him. A couple cuts and a black eye marred the face he'd been missing the past three days… and then he saw marks on her neck.

Destan was flustered, him trying not to cry, "What c— how? I…"

"It's… not… your fault," she shook her head, trying to take a deep breath but only managing a wheeze.

ᛞ

The air inside Bulwark was so thick and tense you could've cut it with a knife… but no one was around. Was this tension coming from Destan alone? And the silence that was in the air; it was as deafening as one of Callimay's bloodcurdling scream. What was supposed to be a happy reunion — celebration of victory — was drowned in the looming expectation of doom and destruction. What did Elder get that was "a bit more," than what he was hoping for? What happened? And why was Callimay so bent on killing Fidus?

While it was nice to be alone with his wife at the time, it did make the trip to the medical wing that much longer. He was trying so hard to be so careful, but each step made her moan; her coughing bouts making her reach up to her temple as tears fought to keep from falling.

As he rounded the last corner Traceur and Doctor Gerould were walking toward them, talking. But when they saw the two of them they ran up, "What happened? — Traceur? Go get Auditor."

"You got it."

Destan hesitated, waiting for Traceur to leave before he answered, "You know who."

"This is beyond ridiculous. … Let's get her back so I can see what needs to be done." Doctor Gerould grumbled as he ushered him on.

ℬ

"Well, she doesn't have a collapsed lung like everything hinted toward; but she 'does' have three broken ribs. … I'm shocked her skull and cervical vertebrae are clear of any stress fractures — that hit she took was brutal — but I'm not about to complain." Doctor Gerould took a deep breath and walked over. "She needs something going for her."

"Excuse me?" Destan picked up on his hesitation.

"S… she has another concussion."

"What!"

"I thought you said it was Elder? I looked at the footage and it was Fidus who fought her."

"Remember? 'Abilities'? … It's hard to understand, I get it. And what he's capable of is about as terrifying and 'unrealistic' as it gets, but please believe me when I say he 'can' do it. Trust me when I say it was him who did it. He just used Fidus like a puppet." His shoulders slouched as he rubbed his face; asking as he looked at Callimay who was asleep, "How bad is the concussion?"

"Her memory's a bit foggy and her conscious state isn't stable. I'm not letting her leave until she is. … She's strong, Destan; but I can't say for sure. That hit she took was on solid limestone. And with the force

Fidus got her down with coupled with him cutting off a majority of her oxygen flow for a minute or so? I just can't give any guarantee. — But at the same time I'm not willing to put my hands up and walk away. She's pulled through worse. Just keep praying. I'm doing everything I know to so she's got the best shot. It's just up to her to fight back."

"Auditor isn't allowed to leave while you're gone. Understand?"

"I've already let her know. Well, actually she's the one who told me." Doctor Gerould corrected himself as Auditor opened the door, giving him a rather dirty look before checking on Callimay. "I'm headed to Deep Dark. What should I say as far as—"

"Fifteen." Destan replied as he kept staring at his wife; and then jumped up and ran over, grabbing Doctor Gerould's arm, "What are her chances? Really, Lance. Tell me. I've got to know."

He knew the mentally-battered young man in front of him needed that reassurance, but it was a complete tossup. Saying one thing or another wasn't going to be a lie, but it wasn't really the truth, "She's strong. Just be there for her and remind her you're there to help her fight. And keep calm. That's going to probably be the biggest help for her. I know that's rather impossible to ask right now, but I know you can do it, Destan. Fight this fight so she can fight her own. — I know it's not the answer you want, but it's the only concrete one I can give you: it's up to her."

When he got back Auditor was busy, working away. She stopped when she saw him and left after she asked if she could get anything.

Callimay was resting peacefully. And yet it wasn't what he knew to be her natural, sleeping rest. He could tell she was sedated. Of course he knew why and agreed she needed it to help her brain heal, but a part of him was starved; starved for her.

The halo device was still on, doing its job of monitoring all of her brain activity. She was hooked up to several other monitors and had an IV running. This all brought to mind a painful memory, but like Doctor Gerould told him: he needed to keep strong, keep positive, and keep calm. She wasn't gone.

Destan noticed there was a second bag hanging for her IV but didn't know what in the world it was for. While he'd seen a couple hanging before in other circumstances, a horrible feeling washed over him. He darted out and called for Auditor, her running over as fast as she could, "What is it, Doyen?"

"What's that other bag hanging?"

While she didn't brush him off, he could tell by her taking a deep breath as she closed her eyes that he was overreacting.

"It's Heparin — a blood thinner. In fact it's the same type you had after your surgery and similar to your blood thinner medication you were 'supposed' to take for the two weeks after." Auditor explained, sounding a bit displeased as she eyed him; as if she knew he hadn't been faithful in taking it like he was supposed to. "Mender wanted to ward off any possibility of her having any type of stroke because of the other injuries she sustained."

"Stroke?" Destan's voice cracked, his eyes bugging out further.

"She's not having one right now and I am of the opinion she won't. In situations like this we always make sure the worst case scenario is warded off in every way possible." She put her hands out to calm him, her voice still level-headed but caring and kind. "Now. Do you need anything else?"

"No." Destan replied a bit shaky. "Thank you."

He rushed back over and sat on the edge of the bed, taking her hand in his. Beside them on a nearby chair was her ensemble that had been folded with perfect attention to detail; her Seaxes on top, and boots — cleaned, polished, and reloaded — beside the chair. Destan reached over and took the knives, reading what he had engraved on them. What was implied weighed on him so much: *Why can't he just come after me, Calli? How much more of this has to happen? I know you're not unbreakable, untouchable, or immortal. I 'can' lose you. And no matter how much Elder loves toying with us and playing his heinous game… his goal is for you to die. Drawing it out like this — eating away at your strength bit-by-bit — is beyond cruel. In a way it feels like… if it were possible: it is beyond evil, even.*

He then took his wedding band off and looked at its engraving: *I've got to quit acting like I can control him and there'll be this 'perfect time' to catch him off guard like every physical battle I've had before. … I can't control him and I can only make the best of the circumstance I'm in at the time. This is more than a physical battle.*

And yet the more Destan thought the more he couldn't help but think how scared Elder must be of Callimay. He's waited for over two decades without letting go of his hatred but the second he thought he found her he sent person after person after her, using them to rid the world of her. When she confronted him in Deep Dark he actually had to bow to her even though he didn't want to. — Even that day showed his fear of her. He waited until she'd run for three days, was emotionally unstable, physically exhausted as well as injured… and "still" had someone else fight her.

Even though Elder shoved all of Destan's proof aside last time, he wouldn't be able to refute his own writing. It was in ink… it couldn't be altered. There wasn't a doubt in his mind that Elder knew he had it; but he still took every precaution to ensure it was safe until he needed it. — He now knew the time had come to surrender it. It finally clicked in his mind: his father and Callimay's mother didn't sacrifice their lives just so he could hide that book forever. He had to use it! If he lost it, then holding onto it wasn't going to do any good: if they weren't going to believe him there wasn't anything he could do to convince them.

On a different, yet still related topic, Destan saw her empty belt and remembered… the belvedere! He'd gotten so caught up in everything else that he forgot to check on the creature: *It's still puzzling why Elder would do that. ~ He needed every safeguard she had stripped away. ~ Which means whatever he had planned he did that last day of her run. There's no way Fidus was it. ~ Oh I wish I knew what all happened. Something 'must' have! I… I know she made it through alright — Rej would've told me if it were something major — but maybe it was while she was on guard.*

After a few moments, he took her other hand in his and squeezed it as he silently wept: *God? My Calli needs help. She is strong because You made her that way but she doesn't have the strength to get out of this on her own. And I by no means have the strength to keep going by myself. I need her… and most importantly we both need You. I know what she has in her now from what my father made helped her the first time; please let it help her again. Please. I can't lose her. Please, God. I need my Calli, my ray of sunshine… my precious jewel. Help me be the man I need to be; push the fear aside and 'do'. Help me be wise in my decisions and reflect You to those around me in how I handle this. I pray these things in Your Son's name, amen.*

Destan leaned over and gave her a hug and kiss; making sure to move her as little as possible. He could feel her heart beating and the soft rise and fall of her chest as she breathed and it was a comfort to him: while she wasn't awake she was still there: *She's a fighter.*

☧

After lingering a bit longer, his emotions soaking in as much of a recharge as they could, Destan stepped out and waited for Auditor to get in the room before he left. He reminded her to not leave for any reason until he or Doctor Gerould got back and to not let anyone else in. She confirmed the order and that she understood, and so he left.

Like he'd grown accustomed to, he switched over to Doyen mode and marched to Deep Dark; but this time about ready to rip Fidus apart. He knew it was Elder manipulating him but he was strong-willed like Destan; he could've resisted a bit more than he did… if he did at all. — And yet him thinking that reminded him; he stopped at the door to Deep Dark and stared at the handle: *What am I thinking? I haven't got a leg to stand on? I… I even let Elder do the exact same thing to me. ~ And Calli didn't blame you, did she?*

His hand didn't let go of the handle, him starting to shake in both regret and anger. In a way he felt Elder had to be laughing at him: if he dared try to blame Fidus, Elder could slap his own mistake in his face. Was there no way to win against this debased man!

☧

The debrief for his trip didn't take too long since things returned to their stable state: he was able to keep everyone — even the president of Crosswall — on board. Destan could hear Elder's inner laugher as he spoke and had to shut off everything so he couldn't hear the despicable monster revel in his victorious mission. At least that portion of it was.

It was easy to tell Fidus was leery; him being extremely submissive to every order given… even suggestions or comments! Knowing what he'd planned to say made him feel even worse. And then it hit him how he treated Redje. — It appeared he had a million little messes to clean up like he did in Brigon. — Destan asked his best friend to do what was impossible: keep someone else's wife safe when his own wife and child were in danger.

He dropped everything that moment and contacted them; making sure to find out if Tabitha was indeed doing alright.

Redje was a bit perturbed, but kept his cool. — Who wouldn't be a bit put off in a situation like that? — Destan didn't blame him at all and in a way he wished Redje would chew him out. For some reason he felt he needed those words to give him a work over; let alone he knew he deserved it.

But Redje refused to lash him when he knew Destan was doing it to himself already. No matter how much he was given permission, he refused to be the one to put more on Destan's shoulders. He'd obviously come to his senses and realized his fault. — Not to say what he did was a sin, but it was must definitely a major learning and growing moment for him.

Once the conversation ran its course in its own time, Destan came back to everyone else. In that short time something major happened: there was this blatantly obvious rift between Doctor Gerould and Elder. But it wasn't a rift like Destan had with him; no, this one was different. Doctor Gerould was avoiding him like he was some carrier.

Of course the reason wasn't hidden to Elder. — How could it be? — He stormed up to Destan, confronting him about earlier.

And yet Destan wasn't about to have a thing to do with his whining; him growling under his breath, not even looking to see who it was, "Don't even try to start, Elder."

"You're shielding her, Doyen. You can't expect to be able to protect her all the time. She has to be able to defend herself."

"What do you think the last three days were? When I'm not around, yes, I agree, she needs to be able to defend herself. Well she did it, didn't she?" Destan whipped around as he gritted his teeth, almost choking on his words that voiced agreeance with Elder's statement. "What do you think her taking part in the regimen was for? … But like I've said before: if I'm around she has no need to be the one who takes the burden of being the protector. It is 'my' duty and responsibility as her husband and I 'gladly' bear it. 'Glad-ly'."

"I hope this rude awakening the country leaders sent you has opened your eyes to the fact you cannot keep waiting for her."

"Once she's cleared she gets her beacon and then stands before the Veil a week later for the vote. So, what… that's just another three weeks speaking in reasonable terms? Our original timeline was always Newgenary. You 'know' that. Nothing's being put on hold for her. And seriously? Without her we wouldn't even 'be' ready to go next month. Without her speech that convinced Majesty Presley to get Brigon to join there's 'no way' we'd be able to even 'think' of moving. I think it best for you to remember how much she's helped the cause without truly be a part of it: without her we would've had to move everything back to who knows when!"

Elder rolled his eyes as he scoffed, Destan still not done yet, "Let alone the fact our current trainees won't be ready for at least another three months. If 'any'thing is going to hold us back it's them. … And who approved the new class? Wasn't that 'you'?"

"Oh come now. You really think she was able to do 'all' that?" Elder smirked as he shook his head. "Through just one tiny, childish 'story'?"

"You 'know' she was and you're terrified of her because of what all she's been able to do." Destan slammed his fist on the desk, catching a glimpse of Doctor Gerould in his peripheral; clearing his throat as he finished, "I know I said this already, but I'll give you one last chance: your reign of tyranny is coming to an end. And I think it's sooner than you're willing to admit."

"You seem rather… 'cocky' about this all, Doyen; repeating such slanderous statements again and again. Just remember who 'really' has control here. Fidus was just a precursor — a 'preview' — if you will, of what's waiting for your 'precious Callimay' if you keep this up. Don't hold the notion you have any chance against my full and unleashed capabilities." He stepped closer, hissing through his teeth as he eyed him, "Don't push me… 'boy'."

"You threaten her once more and I 'will'…"

"Will what, Doyen? … Now really. If you're going to threaten my life you need to be a little bit more committed. Like this: I'll 'die' before I let that Chameleon slip out of my grasp again so she lives to see Total Eclipse." Elder roared as he turned to everyone, and then laughed when no one noticed. "You're pathetic concern and value of life has no place in this world. How can you even 'think' to compare with my power?"

Destan was shaken by this, but there were four individuals who he could see a different expression in their eyes; albeit it no more than peripheral glances. Fissures were forming in Elder's hold on some. He didn't know how or when they broke through, or how much they could withstand, but it did give him some hope.

The lack of response irritated Elder, him gripping and twisting Destan wrist, whispering as he smiled, "Still hurts, doesn't it? The sting of a feeler never does go away, does it? Just like a concussion or a broken rib never 'quite' heel."

He gritted his teeth and kept himself composed, his eyes burning with the brightest green color imaginable, "Or the love of a brother for his sister."

Finally. It worked, he'd found a soft spot that he could start pressing on, "Oh please! How could something so trivial be so strong? There's no possible way for Trever Presley to 'ever' think of that Chameleon as his flesh and blood."

Elder let Destan's wrist go, Destan shaking it a bit as he began to smile, "Ginger had the same issue. Your work was superb... but lacking. You couldn't find that winning combo. You couldn't recreate what Ingrid had done naturally: sever all emotional ties to family... all for the sake of selfish gain."

"I'll die before I ever let such a pathetic emotion bring this world to its knees." Elder's face began to change as he started growling.

I've got you now. Destan's eyes narrowed as he appeared to give a honorable bow to Elder — as was the custom of Commander's culture that he knew — finishing as he stood and looked him in the eye, "Your wish is my command. Death it is... for 'you'."

Though his willingness to fight back was admirable, there was a balance he needed to keep when he saw the look on some Veils' faces. Destan needed the support of them in this all. The looks on the faces of those who overheard could only mean one thing, and that was "not" what he needed — total shift back to Elder's side: *Just 'had' to be big mouth about it all, didn't you? ~ I wasn't 'that' loud and you know it. If Elder 'helped' them earlier, there's no way he didn't just now. ~ Yes,* but don't pass the buck on this one, entirely. You still said it. You didn't 'have' to.

Destan grumbled with himself for a while longer, jerking his chair out as he sat down to look at the few papers that were on it. A smile washed over his face when he saw what they were: Callimay's run reports. While he wanted to sign off on them without reading, he was curious to see what Traceur and Tabitha recorded… hopefully find out what happened that last day.

It wasn't the first-hand account he was dying to know, but still, what was recorded amazed him. How she was able to do what she did in the time constrain she was under? And then to actually beat Fidus afterward with the injuries she had? She truly had all the earmarks of a Veil. And if he was willing to concede — which he was — her run was even better than his; and hers was more treacherous and longer.

"Traceur?" Destan asked as he saw her walking by, him looking back at the beginning of the run. "What ended up happening with that Syndicate web?"

She froze mid step and replied after looking around, "It… was removed. By what the team found, it was placed in a rush. I had them leave pictures and pieces of it in the lab for you to look over."

"Why?" Destan asked a bit confused as he got up and followed.

Her brow began to show the etchings of her inner angered, worried feeling as she walked with him, "You know I've investigated many Syndicate webs. I've learned the signatures of so many trappers I know what to look for. … Well, this one just doesn't add up at all. It was in a low-traffic area, the web's overall structure was sloppy, the anchors weren't current Syndicate grade — they're at least ten years old — and then the wires themselves? Well, just look at them for yourself."

He leaned over the microscope, picking it up as he said shocked, "Dull? They never—"

"Exactly!" Traceur shook the anchor she picked up; glancing around before finishing in a whisper, "All that aside, this was the clincher: these anchors were in 'wet' cement. They had to of been placed 'just' as Liaison started her run. It's as if someone knew exactly where she was going to be. Granted, dull ones don't make much sense as far as being a true trap—"

"But if it was put up in a hurry the person couldn't risk cutting themselves." Destan started examining the other pieces. "And if they were in wet cement they could've easily been mistaken for branches since they'd have some give. … Which means had she put any weight on it she would've fallen to her death."

"W… what you brought up concerning Elder? It wasn't a fantastic lie?" Traceur grabbed his arm, sounding and looking terrified. "What you said is true about what he did? Is that why you had Confrere and Helpmate brought in? And is that why you only allow certain Shadows and Veils to be alone with Liaison… well isn't it?"

Destan looked around and then turned the com off in the room before he began to hem haw, "Traceur…"

"Liaison's accidents… they weren't accidents! What I heard earlier wasn't some sick joke of Elder's… was it! Doyen tell me!"

All along Destan trusted Traceur's strength and will, but in this moment he didn't want her to take his side like this. He needed her to lie low and blend in. But he knew her personality too well. How was he going to stop her? Or at least keep her zeal at bay?

"He's trying to take you down but in an indirect way that no one else will see! 'He's' our Veil Nark we've been looking for the past year! The one Canary got word to us about!"

"While it's true he is the Nark she told us about, the reasoning as to 'why' he's doing what he's doing… that's one thought. But— Traceur? You have 'got' to keep this quiet. Make this disappear. Well, for now anyway. All the evidence needs to come out together. A shock-and-awe reveal is my best shot to make this stick like it needs to."

"Alright. … Doyen?"

"Yes, Traceur?"

"You mean she knows? Liaison that is. She knows about what we're doing and Elder, too? That's why she's being targeted. … Isn't it?"

While having a comrade who was completely on his side was a breath of fresh air, this hesitancy on his part started to make sense as far as being a red flag: *This could be a ploy of Elder's.* "It's more complex than that."

"Tell me, Doyen. Let me help you!" Traceur asked under her breath, almost sounding desperate.

"Please understand I 'do' appreciate your willingness to jump in, I do. I always have. That's why I chose you. But as far as this goes — for right now — I'm not saying another word." Destan's tone found its perfect balance of being firm without being sharp. "Just… just keep going as if nothing's changed. And don't start digging around. We've lost at least two Veils and who knows how many Shadows and innocent civilians trying to get to this point."

Why are you waiting? Why didn't everyone believe what you presented? Why didn't I! … What's happening to us, Doyen!

It was just as likely that Elder anticipated the web being found, but Destan couldn't keep from hoping he was getting "sloppy" like Traceur said. I mean he did get him to crack pretty easy just now. Had his laying low actually paid off better than a frontal attack earlier on?

When he got back to his desk, he signed off on all of Callimay's run paperwork; a smile on his face as he added a note at the bottom, placing his "recommendation" — which was an actual order — about her appearing before the Veil a week after receiving her beacon.

This was so wonderful, but the only thing was… when was she going to be able to get her beacon? Doctor Gerould didn't mention anything about a timeline of any kind. And she still wasn't out of the woods yet. Destan looked back at his signature and then over to his left hand, collapsing in his chair: *You've got to make it. — Please, God.*

❦

Once the remaining debriefs were finished, the evening was long, uneventful, and calm. — After all that upheaval and stress he was glad to have this break. — But this void let his mind focus on Callimay; his thoughts of worry and concern fueling his drive to "disposed" of Elder.

But, hour after hour of thinking and worrying soon led to a new dawn that shined as if to say there was still hope. He did the best he could; it wasn't his fault this happened… even with his procrastination weighed in the balance. Sometimes bad things happen no matter how careful you were. Evil finds a way no matter what. It's a cancerous disease that will feed on itself if it has to until it finds a food source.

There was a short meeting he had and then came the long walk to the medical wing. For some reason he didn't want to walk in and find her like he left her; his heart just couldn't take that "rejection". And yet, when Destan got back, he saw Auditor laughing as she talked with… Callimay? He ran in, his heart pounding and him out of breath, "Wh… when did you… are you alright?"

She smiled as he wrapped her in his arms, answering slow and labored, "About ten minutes ago… maybe? — I'm so glad to see you."

His voice cracked as he nestled his face against hers, his eyes stinging, "Thank you, God. Thank you so much. — You have no idea how glad I am to see you. I missed you so much, Calli."

"I missed you too."

After a few minutes, him finally grasping this was real, "Do you really feel alright? I mean—"

"I'm fine until I move my head. Then I'm really dizzy and light-headed; even a bit nauseous."

"Which means you will be spending the night." Doctor Gerould interjected as he came in. "When did you wake up, Callimay?"

"It'd be about fifteen or twenty minutes now. Round about? — What happened? What's the big fuss?"

"I didn't tell her." Auditor shook her head as she got up and handed something to Doctor Gerould.

"Thank you. — Well, for whatever reason, Fidus started treating you like a Nark and laid you out on an uncovered area of limestone. Since you weren't three months out from your last concussion, and your head took the brunt of that quite substantial one, your brain relapsed as well as compounded your concussion symptoms. You've obviously made it through the first, largest battle, but your body needs as much rest as it can get; brain tissue isn't resilient like your skin is when you scratch it. — I gave you a sedative to try and help give your body a head start healing, and from what I'm seeing it's working."

This answer sounded positive, but then again, he could be softening a huge blow for the two of them. And so Destan and Callimay waited for him to look at the paperwork and finish what he was saying.

"Give this to Neurosan and let them know to come in about, oh, twenty minutes?" Doctor Gerould mumbled as he wrote.

"Alright." Auditor took the slip, nodding as she read it. "I'll be back as soon as I can. … That is unless you need me somewhere else."

"Chicane should be in for his physical in a few minutes." He glanced at the clock, checking it against his watch. "You can go get things set up in room five."

Watching the two of them talk with each other was rather strange. There was always this tension between them. And yet they were never at each other's throats or rude. While this was something Destan had come accustomed to seeing and thus ignored, Callimay could tell it was becoming stronger; Doctor Gerould and Auditor had a deep rift that had never been resolved… and it was slowly eating away at their ability to even look at each other now. Well, it was eating at Auditor. Not to say Doctor Gerould wasn't changing, but he only had an initial moment's flare of it and then it was as if nothing were wrong.

He waved her on, not bothering to see it wasn't him she was waving at; him clearing his throat as he finished, "It's completely baffling to me. But, then again, I don't truly understand all of what your serums are capable of. Destry did an amazing job of compiling information about it but I don't understand half of it because it 'is' missing useful clinical information. — All that aside, though, I understand everything I'm seeing now; and I see nothing but good. I just want to be sure this isn't a placebo. And before you ask, Destan: yes, you can stay. I would prefer she not move her head much if any for another twenty hours. That'd put her right at a day out from the incident and I'll be able to accurately see how her brain is doing."

"Maybe this is jumping the gun, but how — if any — would this change her beacon placement?"

"That's right! I got the official word a little bit ago that you finished your final run successfully, Callimay. The highest congratulations are in order. It was a miracle, but one I knew could happen because it was you. — As long as nothing changes there should be no complications with her being put under general anesthesia, if that is what you're asking, Destan. — Whenever you feel you are ready after I clear you I can get the team together for your beacon placement."

A wave of reality crashed into Callimay, her finally recalling what brought this all on, "Oh. Okay."

~ 20 ~

Her eyes fluttered open, it plain to her something was off. The lighting in the room was harsh, a low hum rattled in the air, and there was a smell that she recognized and yet couldn't quite place. Add to that the fact Destan wasn't holding her left hand and Callimay was at a complete loss as to where she was and what happened: *The last thing was… I fell out of the tree, right? ~ Well don't ask me. I don't know. ~ Thanks. … The rabbits came back and then I saw— no, no that's not right. I remember Fidus laughing. Someone was trying to kill him. … Right?*

Trying to move helped the rest fall into place. — Pain was capable of doing such things. — This tidal wave began to overwhelm her, each breath being more and more of a laborious task. But then she felt a strong hand holding her right hand. The pain reminded her not to move, and so all she could see out of her peripheral was what looked like Destan passed out in the chair beside her.

So, with that heart attack averted, she laid there and waited for him to wake up. Although the longer she was aware of him holding her hand, the more she realized how tight he was holding it. It got to the point Callimay was concerned enough that she did her best to reach out to see how his emotions where. … They weren't out of control in any way, so at least it wasn't caused by that: *You know what I think? I think he just doesn't wanna lose you. ~ Okay now I'm going to cry.*

The finer details of her fight with Fidus began to come back and she was troubled by one thing he said. She knew it was Elder talking through him, but what did he mean when he said Destry made the same mistake thinking he was safe by just being inside the barrier?

That all brought to mind a kind of regret she felt too often, it seemed: Callimay began to regret not being able to help Fidus realize Elder was manipulating him. And yet, would what she did for Destan work on someone who didn't have abilities?

And then all of a sudden her thoughts ran to why Redje left so suddenly. Were Tabitha and the baby really doing alright!

"Just relax, Calli." Destan rubbed her hand as he yawned. "They're all fine."

"I… I'm sorry I woke you."

"Don't ever — 'ever' — be sorry if you wake me up, Calli." He sat on the bed and brushed the side of her face. "How are you feeling?"

"Perfectly fine as far as my head goes. Of course if I move that's a different story. But maybe that's just because I moved so fast. I wasn't sure what was going on when I woke up so I tried to get up and, well, you can guess what happened. — My legs are as dead and as heavy as anything. I absolutely hate running in snow. I can do water, rocks, and even thick grass; but snow? I'd rather just sit it out and wait."

"Well, you won't have to worry about running anywhere but into my arms for at least a month. … And even then I'd probably just run to you so you didn't have to move at all."

"Such a softy."

"I have my moments," he grinned as he kissed her hand. "So! You want to tell me how it went? Or do you still need some time?"

Her eyes became drenched in fear, her first thought one not what he expect: * Fidus didn't break my ribs. I… I did.*

He knew there was more than just that left-field bombshell, but didn't bother responding with more than a half nod, half shake.

Elder… he… I guess when I open more than one channel he's able to slip in. The last watch I had he had me seeing Shadows all around me. Her voice quivered as she clasped her hands together. *I finally figured out it was him and forced him out like I had before… but I blacked out and fell out of the tree. At least that's the only thing that makes any sense — I came to on the ground.*

Is that all he did?

Oh heaven's no. Callimay rolled her eyes, exaggerating the disgust she had. *He had more fun with me and Redje than I think he ever did with you and me. — He actually sent someone out to the gorge. They set some kind of trap at the northwest edge, but Redje and I didn't bother trying to find it.*

Who was it?

I don't know. We tried to get up to them but it was day and so we could only go so far up before being seen… and they just vanished. They must've had a vehicle close by. One of my crazy thoughts tagged Ingrid as the person for a minute, but I know her voice.

There was a pause, Destan feeling her emotions continuing to churn: *I take it there was something far worse?*

The one that shook Redje the most was when we were up on the mountain. I was looking for the shortcut and he didn't understand why it wasn't where it was supposed to be. I thought I found it, but it was such a small hole. Since things were getting borderline dangerous with the cold, and after what Elder had already done, Redje told me where it was and started helping me dig. — Nothing. We found nothing, Destan! — We went back to the other place and he had me go in by myself. I stumbled around for a bit but started to feel the cold wind. — There are some things Elder can't block. — And so I pushed him out and was able to get Redje free of him as well.

It was hard for him to not say anything, but he sat there, biting his tongue so she could get it all out.

I didn't tell you this when we talked at the time because what could you do? Even taking massive jumps, it would've burned you out to the point you wouldn't have been able to do anything, Destan. Callimay tried to explain, working to calm him. *Redje doesn't even know about that last day watch and he never told Tabitha or Traceur about the mystery observer or the shortcut fiasco. We were just trying to keep things compartmentalized as much as we could. He knew how much pressure I was under. He actually kept me from flying off the handle when that mystery person showed up.* She clutched her hand to her chest, each breath painful. *C… can we talk about something else?*

He slumped over, sighing as he ruffled his hair, "I… I just—"

Still trying to calm, but knowing she had to say something, Callimay grunted and wheezed, "You're frustrated I was alone for so long and Redje had to pull double-duty. I know. But that's all over now. Maybe a bit scared and worse for wear in some ways, but we're alive. Why don't you go call Redje? Talk with him for a bit. I'm sure he'd enjoy hearing from you since you said you really didn't get to talk."

"I talked with him a bit, but I'll do it when I have a few minutes later on." Destan nodded as he looked at his watch. "I'm going to go in for maybe an hour or so to make sure things are still alright with your grandfather and such then I'll be back. Do 'not' dare think of leaving without me. Understood?"

"Oh there's no question there. Are you leaving right now?"

The sparkle came back to his eyes as he slapped his knees while getting up, "No. After breakfast. What do you want?"

"Something simple… yogurt?"

"Just that? You've been on rations for the past three days."

"I don't want to stuff myself and you know good and well I hardly ever eat a big breakfast. Plus, if my head starts bothering me again the less I have on my stomach the better off I am."

"Okay. Grape nuts?" Destan tilted his head when he looked back.

"Umm… not with my head the way it's feeling."

"Let me go get Auditor or Doctor Gerould and then I'll go get it."

Being able to eat a meal with his wife was a small thing, but it was a special, precious slice of time to him — it was just the two of them away from all the chaos that so much of their life was. And sadly this time was something not very common as of late. This reminded him what he felt for Callimay wasn't only out a sense of duty, it wasn't from infatuation; it was a pure and deep love and desire to be her husband.

She gasped out of nowhere and then tried to laugh; only to have her broken ribs cry foul.

"What is it, Calli!"

"I just," she paused as she hissed yet again. "I just missed my mouth is all. It was 'supposed' to be funny."

He wanted to be light about what he saw, but seeing her in pain kept him from it.

Doctor Gerould sympathized — where did he come from! — but told her she had to keep taking deep breaths as much as she could stand so she wouldn't be at risk of coming down with pneumonia on top of everything else. Her bruises looked a million times worse, but

Doctor Gerould reminded Destan, "Bruises that surface early are superficial. They still hurt like the dickens but they'll clear quicker."

"I'll attest to that," Callimay sighed as she raised her hand.

He looked at her chart and then started working on his computer, stopping at one point; sounding shocked, "I just don't know how to explain this. What the Halo is telling me is— it's as if your concussion has been completely erased. Your brain appears completely normal."

"Is the serums I have 'that' strong?" Callimay started to sit up, but closed her eyes and grabbed Destan's hand.

"Well… hum." Doctor Gerould sounded concerned as he focused in on what the beeping device was showing. "It appears movement triggers what I was expecting to find to flare. These areas are nowhere near as inflamed as they were yesterday — even though it may not feel that way — but they are progressing. … So, in short, you know what this means: lying still is going to be your best therapy, Callimay. I'm sorry I need to do this, but I'm putting you on mandatory bedrest for the next two days, 'min-i-mum'."

"But she 'is' doing better?" Destan looked up, trying to keep positive.

"Oh yes. Very much so. It's what I was expecting — and hoping to find. … I know her staying it's not what either of you wanted to hear."

"We could both use a couple days of rest after everything." Callimay smiled as she patted her husband's cheek. "We haven't had a break in a while so this will force it. Well at least for me. — Not that I really have to be forced to rest."

"Pfft! Oh 'really'?" Destan scoffed as he eyed her.

"Well… I guess my definition of rest can vary at times."

"I think so." Destan chuckled before turning his focus back to Doctor Gerould, "So, is it just best for her to stay here?"

"With the way things spiked when she moved just now; just that tiny bit? I don't want her moving more than that for the time being. It won't be disastrous if she moves every now and again, just keep it to an absolute minimum."

❧

Even though it was the day after she finished, everyone was still abuzz with the news of Callimay passing her final run in such "epic" fashion.

They were astounded by her ability to complete what they saw as the impossible. If nothing else it was unprecedented — no one had ever run the one-hundred and eighty mile track in just two and a half days' worth of runs. "Ever". And her aptitude to adapt and utilize her surroundings to her advantage was second to none. Many Veils voiced their support to Destan, but were careful in how they worded it. — Another pesky code of the Veil that wasn't very "logical", but as it stood, publically voicing one's vote before it was brought before the entire body wasn't allowed.

Amidst this all, Elder was less than thrilled. While his plan to rip the two of them apart "did" succeed, his ultimate plan failed miserably… again. — You'd think he'd take a hint, but it appeared he needed the hard lesson one more time. — She now had the support of an entire organization that he had worked years to control for his own purpose.

Destan's conversation with Majesty Presley was quick, and he was thrilled Callimay was doing alright and had completed her regimen.

Overhearing "completed" coupled with "regimen", Elder came down on Destan the second he hung the phone up, "You do know she will still be required to complete her Veil regimen if allowed into our ranks… or have you forgotten that 'minor' detail?"

Why can't you just go sulk by yourself? I'm not your therapist. "What she needs up front won't take too long and the rest can be done as needed… like we do with 'all' new Veils." Destan stressed, showing there wasn't any surprise or lapse in preparation for her next steps. "And if you want to know: I've already been incorporating such things into her regimen. If you would've truly been paying attention I'm sure you would've noticed."

The lack of an immediate response made Destan chuckle ever so slightly, "What? You assumed I hadn't thought that far ahead? That I was trying to bend rules and put my wife in a place she was completely unprepared for? ... Well?"

There's the cool cucumber Toreon saw so much of. Bravo, Destan.

Elder cleared his throat, trying to regain his cool demeanor, "Well… it's about time you got your mind set straight."

"And I'm glad to see you're realizing I can learn from mistakes and that I 'do' have things — even you — under control."

~ 21 ~

By the end of the two days Callimay was recovered to the point her brain could tolerate simple and short duration movement. Her bruises looked much worse, but she was accustomed to having them and knew how to hide them. A small price to pay for her "freedom", in her words.

"Calli!" Destan gasped as he ran over, her beginning to fall.

She clawed to get a good hold on his arm, crying, "That… 'really' hurt. Land sake!"

"What do you want me to do?"

"Just let me relax here for a minute."

He didn't want to move and cause her anymore pain, but hearing her wheeze like she was terrified him; let alone the fact the position she was in was so awkward. And then it broke his heart yet again knowing there wasn't a thing in the world he could do to actually help his Calli. There was no way for him to take this pain away from her. This cascade of emotions began to feel too familiar to him: this happening just like it did each time before when she was severely injured in one way or another.

What Elder said about him making sure Callimay didn't survive jumped into his thoughts. Each time he did something she became physically weaker. Destan knew that. He didn't know how much more she could take. Her abilities were "cushioning" each devastating blow, but they could only do so much. And really? He could only take so much, both mentally and emotionally. He wasn't invincible either.

And the worst part? Not only did they both know that, but to a sickening level of delight, Elder knew this too.

Callimay reached up and locked her hands around his neck; interrupting his depressing thoughts, "Now, stand up. Slowly."

Her arms shook and her hands had a grip on him like he only remembered for a few other times. Tears dragged down her face as if they were in pain as well. And yet she was determined to fight through this pain.

Once he got her to the wheelchair, her face softened and she sighed as deep as she dared. She looked up at him and smiled as she took his hands; him kneeling in front of her and gently wiping the tears from her face.

"Could I wait a day… maybe two, before the surgery?" Her voice pleaded as she looked over to Doctor Gerould. "I… I know I need to get it done as soon as possible, but—"

"Don't give it a second thought. I wouldn't dream of doing it for at least a week, anyway. And if it takes a bit longer, it's understandable. It's best if you do get some more rest before we do it. Just make sure you keep breathing as deeply as you can. If there's any 'risk' with your surgery, that will be it. We can be ready the day after you decide; so don't worry."

~ 22 ~

What began some seven months ago — a task which loomed over Callimay as something as something she might not accomplish — was now completed. And as she looked back, all the stress, turmoil, and effort endured was worth it. Most trainees had some type of background in combat or tactical strategy to some degree or another. She started from ground zero; and yet was able to become proficient in everything in half the time that was normal for the regimen. And beyond that, she was in an elite group of less than a dozen who showed they had the earmarks of a Veil when in the regimen. She'd proven what Destan and a few others saw glimpses of over the past half year: her special consideration wasn't just a gift to help Destan… she truly was worthy of this honor and position due to her own ability.

Two days turned into a week before Callimay felt well enough to undergo surgery. She felt bad putting things off, but Destan was not about to have any of that negativity, "You need to rest and gain back what strength you can while you've got the chance, woman. Got it?"

Doctor Gerould wasn't at all surprised with the delay and was so supportive when she finally gave the go-ahead.

The day before, during their discussion they had about the surgery, he was firm about Destan making sure Callimay didn't eat anything for dinner that evening… or anything in the morning. Obviously, Destan was confused, "Why is that so important?"

While this inquisitive nature of his wasn't completely foreign when it came to medical things, it was noticeable to Doctor Gerould that his reactions were becoming more and more pronounced because of Callimay. So instead of shrugging if off with a simple, "Because I said so," he explained everything. … But, maybe he could've skipped the whole "death" part so Destan wasn't paranoid. That threw him into a complete micromanaging frenzy of sorts; ordering Doctor Gerould to make sure there was the absolute minimum surgical team members in the room and that he would oversee all the prep work himself, and— this was one of those moments where Doctor Gerould had to kick himself: *Not my proudest moment or decision.*

𝕭

As Callimay turned her head to let Auditor cut back and shave the small amount of hair necessary for her beacon to be properly placed, she told Destan, "Make sure she doesn't take too much."

He chuckled a bit as he smiled, but sounded nervous, "Okay."

I know you're worried, but just remember in order for you to help protect me you've got to be able to notice and realize you have to take care of yourself. You losing control won't help me. She squeezed his hand as she tried to keep smiling. *Don't blame yourself for anything that might — 'might' — happen, okay? And nothing may happen at all. Elder may just sit this one out to make us second-guess everything.*

"Well! I'm proud of myself even if I do say so myself. This was all I needed to take off." Auditor rubbed Callimay's arm as she turned off the clipper and showed her a very small lock of hair. "Let me go check a few things and I'll be back."

"Alright," Destan nodded as he sat down and took his wife in his arms. *I hope nothing goes wrong. I really don't know if—*

Don't hold me too tight! She pushed against his chest, starting to wheeze and moan.

He kept going on and on, apologizing for what he did, but stopped when she took his hand and pulled him back to her. She leaned her head against his chest, smiling, "I love you, Destan."

"And I love you so much more than you'll ever know."

"Are you going to keep these safe for me, again?" She took his hand and placed her wedding bands on it.

"I promise."

"Good morning! Are we all ready to go?" Doctor Gerould asked curious as he poked his head in the room, sounding jovial.

The two of them looked at each other, not wanting to answer.

He continued on, noting the hesitation but trying to help, "Any last-minute questions?"

"H… how long is it going to take?" Destan asked for the fifth time.

"The surgery itself, altogether about three hours. — Trust me when I say I've seen to as much as I possibly could to ensure Callimay's safety. I don't want anything happening just as much as you two don't."

"I… I can't lose her," Destan mumbled as he bowed his head.

Callimay cried as she slipped her hands around his neck and cradled his head against hers.

He would usually excuse himself from such a raw scene, but something struck him, "You know? The more I think about it, the more you two are an example of the ancient moral teaching of yin and yang that Commander spoke of so often: you're so interdependent, unable to function without the other, while being at complete opposite ends of the spectrum. Yes, for short periods of time you can function alone — if necessity deems it so — but you always have the goal of looking toward being with each other again. And you two do things in ways that makes me wonder how in the world you get along at times. … Now I'm not saying this to laugh things off, just to help you think. It's a powerful strength to have: overcoming differences because of the care you have for each other. But your collective fear looks to be overshadowing everything. You sorely need to learn to control it; both of you. You could tear apart your strength if you don't. So don't give up now. — Destan? You know better than Callimay how being brave and strong doesn't mean you're not afraid. That doesn't just apply to missions and such. If anything it applies even more here and now."

Auditor got back and slipped in, standing there this whole time. At one point she dropped the paperwork she had, only to pick it up and dash out of the room.

Silence that was full of reflection flooded the room, Callimay still having a bowed head as she mumbled, "I'm ready."

Doctor Gerould waited for a few moments and then sighed as he looked out the window, "I'll get Auditor and have her bring you back."

When she did get back, her cheeks were flushed and her eyes were glassy. Destan didn't notice, but Callimay was so worried she listened…

only to be shocked and heartbroken for Auditor; now understanding why she acted the way she did those other times.

Able to segment her emotions at that time, Auditor continued working. Callimay took the mesh cap from her hand and put it on, rolling her hair up and tucking it in so it would all fit. Destan snapped his finger as he started going through his pocket, "Oh! Wait. … Here. Why don't you wear this?"

This flurry of nervousness puzzled her at first; and then she started to cry as she took the orange cloth hat from him.

"Outfitter told me that's been the strangest request he's ever had."

It was a snug fit and he was worried the whole time he was going to pull on her hair, but he eventually got all of her locks tucked away in the bright-orange fabric. He smiled as he ran his hand down the side of her face one more time. She leaned forward and closed her eyes, letting Destan give her one last kiss before she left: *All I need now is Mr. Ruff and a camera.*

Which Mr. Ruff?

Ha, ha. 'Very' funny. The living one, silly.

❦

As if she knew he needed this, Auditor pushed the bed down the hall at a crawl; Destan able to walk beside and hold Callimay's hand the whole time. He knew he couldn't go the entire way and dreaded seeing the ominous double doors in front of him with the large red bars on them come into view.

Auditor stepped aside for a moment to let them talk with each other and then waved to the sensor so the doors would open.

Not but a moment after the doors closed, he ran to the observation room and tapped on the glass when he saw Callimay looking around. She whipped her head over, looking frightened; but softened when she saw his face — worried but loving.

The anesthesiologist must have asked her a question, her looking up and nodding before looking straight back at Destan. A mask was placed over her mouth and nose, Auditor holding it while the anesthesiologist pushed the drugs through her IV. Auditor leaned close to Callimay as the white fluid raced down the thin tubing and into her arm, nodding as she took her hand. Destan felt a sharp spike from Callimay, but was calmed when he heard her voice: *Three hours.*

And then I'll see my Shadow. I'll be waiting, Destan put his hand up to the glass. *I love you, Calli. I always have.*

I love you too, De… she drifted off.

With her now asleep, the team in the room began to work in a rather gruff manner; Doctor Gerould and Auditor with a couple other team members rolling and moving Callimay to get her positioned.

Yes, he'd watched this surgery countless times before and knew what to expect, but you have to take into account that he only stayed for portions each time and it was never his wife in there. Let alone her life was in danger through means neither of them could truly control. — There was no stopping him from being startled by every little thing that happened.

They had quite a bit of preliminary work to get done with placing various monitors and such, but before long Doctor Gerould left for a couple minutes while Auditor washed the side of Callimay's neck with what looked like a horrible brassy, sudsy makeup.

His attention was diverted by the door swinging open; Doctor Gerould coming in with soaked arms and walking over to the young woman who had been in the corner of the room this whole time. She offered a towel to him and started chatting as she helped him put his gown and gloves on.

Things were going well, but when they covered her face Destan jumped to his feet. Doctor Gerould looked back when the young woman who had been helping him nodded behind him, startled himself when he saw the look of desperation on the young man's face — reminding him of how he looked when Callimay was in a coma. So, he stopped and mentioned something to the anesthesiologist. The man started moving things by her face; their joint efforts ending with Callimay's left hand completely uncovered and a shadowed outline of her face visible. Destan mouthed "thank you" before bowing his head and slumping back in the seat.

All of the drapes were placed, all the equipment plugged in and tested, and Doctor Gerould seated and ready to go. Auditor came over and started reading things off of the computer she had, everyone in the room stopping what they were doing and taking turns participating in what was the final check to make sure they were all on the same page about what was to be done.

Once that final check was completed, the young woman who had been helping Doctor Gerould handed him a scalpel.

If he was nervous earlier this was more along the lines of terror for Destan. He knew Doctor Gerould wouldn't do anything to her just by himself, but there was no way for him to know if Elder was twisting his thoughts or not: *I should've had Calli help me work on that this past week! It's not like anyone would've noticed. Ugh! Why is it that I seem to be thinking of good things to do 'after' it's too late to do anything?*

He could've gone on and on with this accusing, but something struck him as odd… "very" odd. In fact, it was borderline disturbing: the team was much more serious than Destan remembered them ever being. They were usually casual and chatty with peppy background music playing. Why was everything and everyone so… stoic? — Could you blame them, though? With how Destan just acted and the orders he gave prior to the surgery they knew "something" was going on aside from the fact this was his wife.

Time dragged on, the first hour feeling more like a couple days since all Destan did was sit there; he ever saw much since the incision was so small and on the opposite side from him. But, even if everything was flipped so that side was visible, Doctor Gerould would obstruct the view unless he moved for a brief moment to check something. — Again, not something that perked Destan's interest before as in it didn't bother him one way or another, but his micromanaging, fearful, husband self began to panic due to some of the oddest reasons.

Several different types of instruments were handed back and forth, them all looking barbaric in their own way. And it disturbed him to know his wife's blood was what was on them.

Before long, he could hear the faint sound of a small power drill. Again, it was something he knew was going to happen but one single slip and Callimay's brain could be injured, she could be deaf in that ear, or she could lose nervous usage on that side of her face. All of these risks were exactly the reason why — compared to everything that happened up to this point — the drilling took the longest. None of the "normal" risks were lost to anyone in the room, but Doctor Gerould knew better than anyone about the "real" risk and wasn't about to take any chances.

Finally, Doctor Gerould made mention of a "beacon" to the young lady who had been handing him things. She rolled over to her table and asked for the "implant"; Auditor picking up a small box off of the table she was working at. The two women looked at the package to verify certain details and then Auditor opened it in a special way so the young woman could take it. In turn, the young woman opened the little container she took out and waited for Doctor Gerould to finish what he was doing so he could prep the beacon for placement — he never let anyone else touch it.

After a minute or so Doctor Gerould looked up to Destan and nodded. He turned his beacon on to both send and receive; nodding each time Auditor would hold a different number of fingers up. The frequency was never something chosen specifically for a Shadow, but Destan couldn't help but hear Callimay in hers: it was high and yet soft, a medium repetition that wasn't annoying but wouldn't surrender.

When he was satisfied he gave them the official okay and Doctor Gerould went back to finishing the placement of the device.

This part went relatively quick compared to everything else and soon it was time to close the incision and call it a day. Destan saw the anesthesiologist turn and talk with someone who came in the room with another bag to hang and run through Callimay's IV. — Doctor Gerould liked to give additional antibiotics just after he finished placing the beacon since it was in such close proximity to several sensitive and vitally important structures.

"She's moving," Doctor Gerould glared at the anesthesiologist.

"Go ahead and hang that, Coalesce." The man in his late forties turned and grabbed a syringe that looked like it was filled with milk. "How much time you need?"

Doctor Gerould put down the instrument he had and placed a firm hand on Callimay's bucking shoulder; feeling Destan's eyes of terror watching, "Twenty."

"You've got it."

Sooner is better. … Come on, Torpid!

Everyone in the room began to relax now that things were wrapping up. All the danger was over!

Auditor, who was fulfilling the role of circulating nurse, was talking with the young woman Anticipator — a young woman who was pretty much the most organized and timely Veil in the group. Destan knew what they were doing but never quite understood why they would account for the amount of some things and not others. He'd actually asked Anticipator once and she laughed and admitted even she didn't understand why the governing bodies over such medical codes stipulated that some items — which were smaller than some she was required to count — were omitted.

Those humorous memories popping up out of nowhere were nice, and Destan did want to calm like everyone else… but he just couldn't. He wasn't going to until Callimay was awake and talking with him.

It had only been a minute or so since Torpid gave the small dose to Callimay when everyone froze; all eyes turning to him. The machine she was being monitored by began flashing and sounding a different type of alarm than even what Destan had become numb to; and in addition, he could see Callimay's hand twitching. Auditor ran to the door while Anticipator doused a cloth and threw it over the incision before calling out to another young woman in the room, having her take all the cords off and away from the drapes. She almost shoved her table full of equipment back to the farthest corner while the other young woman took off as quick as a flash.

Meanwhile, a few other people came in with Auditor as Doctor Gerould ripped the drapes off as fast as he could and moved Callimay so she was on her back. Her skin was almost grey and her entire body was quivering.

And then a few seconds later, she went limp.

"What's going on!" Destan panicked as he slammed his fist against the window. "Calli!"

When he slammed his fist on the glass, a couple of the people jerked and looked over at him for a brief moment, but went back to doing what they could to help.

Torpid was irate about something concerning the second bag that was hung for her IV; him shaking the collapsed vinyl bag as a few choice words were exchanged between him and Doctor Gerould. They continued on in this snippy manner for a few moments while never stopping what they were doing; Doctor Gerould now performing CPR and Torpid filling and measuring drugs in syringes — injecting each into Callimay's IV as fast as he could.

Auditor was busy linking a small machine to the monitors Callimay had on. She wasn't severely rattled until Torpid showed her the bag. He shook his head as she asked something and then handed her the bag and pointed to the door. A couple individuals rushed over when Torpid called out, Auditor saying a few words to them before stepping back, bumping into a man who was busy keeping a record of everything that was happening.

As if it couldn't get any worse, Torpid threw his hand out to point at Destan, beyond annoyed with his commotion, and then shook the same hand at Auditor and the door.

What was going on! This was chaos!

Unless the individual watching knew medical terminology and the way a code was conducted, their reaction couldn't be anything but what Destan's was. All he could see were angered doctors, nurses who couldn't stand still, and his wife looking like death itself. He knew her heart had stopped and she wasn't breathing; he "did" understand that much of what was said. The antibiotic she was given had something to do with it, so it seemed.

Destan hadn't stopped pounding on the glass this entire time; now hyperventilating and zoning out. And anyone with half a brain that knew what he now dealt with knew what was happening: he was making a free-fall into frenzy mode. If they didn't bring Callimay back soon, the least he would do was shatter the window. Worse case? … Let's not get there!

With the next blow of his hand against the glass, it snapped and cracked. At the same time he unclenched his fist just enough to let Callimay's rings fall out. They fell end over end, making quiet, high-pitched "plink" sounds when they hit the resin-coated floor. Destan jumped back, looking at the three bands of precious metal and stone as they rolled around, finally coming to rest. He could hear her voice from earlier, telling him to keep himself safe so he could help her, and see her face. That moment of pause gave him enough of what he needed to stop this endless spiral. He looked in the room and saw Callimay with the small group of highly trained professionals working to save her.

As if blindsided, Destan dropped to his knees. He was out of breath. His hands and arms shook violently as he threw them in front to brace himself as much as possible.

But, for as much as he knew how to calm his emotional storm, something wasn't right. He could only get so far. It was like he was hitting a wall; but not a wall he put up.

Why can't I— Elder! Destan grimaced when he realized he could hear his voice. *Get out! I'm not letting you control me. I'm not going to let you use me to hurt Calli. Never again! Leave!*

Elder obeyed, apparently feeling he'd done enough. — Destan didn't "force" him out like Callimay could. — It was terrifying, though: how his anger and fear were being twisted. He was "too" close to harming those who were working feverishly to save the woman he loved! He collapsed on his side, still heaving as he clutched his left hand that was seizing: *Oh please not this too. Not now!*

🕉

Things continued in their serious, quick, and yet level-headed manner — less that short exchange between the two doctors at the beginning. Auditor was only gone for two minutes when she came in and told Torpid, "This wasn't clinda, it was four-percent unbuffered lidocaine."

"What! That bag had—"

"I know," she shuttered as she handed him a similar bag. "I prepped this myself."

Torpid grumbled as he snatched the bag off Callimay's IV to spike this one.

This all caught Doctor Gerould's attention, him sounding winded as he threw his gown and gloves away, "What did she say?"

"Liaison was given four-percent unbuffered lidocaine; 'not' one gram of clinda. And to add insult to injury: Coalesce left the line wide open." Torpid rolled his eyes and shook his head as he looked back at Callimay's chart and wrote something down. "I've told that kid I don't know how many times to never have it wide open."

"How in the…" Doctor Gerould trailed off as he looked back to where Destan was supposed to be; speaking in a grave tone, "Where's Doyen? Did anyone see him leave?"

"I… I don't know." Auditor replied timid as she whipped her head around. "He was—"

"She's coming back." Torpid interrupted, noting the sudden change in the monitor flat lines.

"Stay here." Doctor Gerould put a calming hand on Auditor's arm, speaking in a hushed tone. "I've got to find him."

He threw the door open, ripping off his mask as he rushed down the hall. While his first thought was he'd find Destan right outside, he realized if he wasn't coming to Callimay he was going to look for the source of what, or in this case "who", orchestrated this near-death experience. — What number was this one? — And so, knowing Deep Dark was the only other logical place, he wasn't going to check the observation room. Thankfully the door was glass and he saw him on the floor, "Destan!"

The door slamming against the wall startled him, "What!"

"Is it your hands again?" Doctor Gerould asked as he helped him to his feet.

"No. Not now. It… it's nothing now." He stretched his hands out again. "How is Callimay? Why aren't you in there with her?"

"She's beginning to stabilize so I came looking for you. … I was concerned when I didn't see your searing gaze burning a hole in us." Doctor Gerould ever so slightly dropped a hint; switching his topic when Destan refused to answer, "It's going to be at least an hour before she comes out. We've got to be sure she won't relapse."

"What happened?"

"Someone switched her antibiotic with another drug. Now, in small dosages it does nothing but numb the skin and surrounding tissue for small procedures; it can also help when the heart is beating too fast or not normally. But when a dosage of that strength and amount is given — and in such a short time span — it shuts the central nervous and cardiovascular systems down."

His eyes flashed as he began pacing, raking his hands through his hair, "But why wasn't that caught, Lance! I thought you sa—"

"So many drugs are suspended in water without adding any color so there is no way of telling them apart by just looking at them. It's always been premixed and wasn't something Torpid or myself considered a problem area. And having someone else hang a bag isn't uncommon practice. Granted, Torpid didn't check to make sure the IV wasn't wide open like Coalesce is known for, but there would not have been any way for him know they were switched." He defended, trying to keep things calm; putting his hint a bit more obvious this time, "I'm glad I found you. I was concerned when I looked up and you were gone that'd you left to find Elder."

"He promised me she'd be dead by the end of the month." Destan leaned against the sill of the window. "And I almost helped him."

"No one else heard the threat, did they?"

"No one ever does, Lance! You know that." Destan hissed as he gestured to those in the other room. "He's able to put up a false view to everyone so I'm seen as some kind of lunatic obsessing over my wife and wanting him dead for no reason! Even if people would've heard him talking they would've heard what 'he' wanted them to hear. I can't touch him with any of that!"

"But something tells me you've got what you need to convict him." His eyes narrowed as his tone became serious; him flipping once again when Auditor came up to the window, "I'll be right back."

"Okay." Destan sighed as he looked in desperation at Auditor who looked like she was smiling; trying to calm him.

ℬ

Doctor Gerould didn't stay very long. He spoke with the entire team for a few minutes and then left; someone else closing Callimay's incision and dressing it. They didn't need much draping so Destan didn't have to worry about not seeing her face this time around.

"Worked out that she wanted it implanted on her right side." The fatherly voice of the man Destan came to respect, commented as he walked over and stood next to him, gripping his shoulder in support.

"It did," he bowed his head, leaning heavy on the sill. "About what you asked… *You listening? … Good. I've got more than enough but I don't know if the Veil will support carrying out the penalty. They may just want to turn him over to the Ferdinan government like we've done with Narks in the past. But we both know he'd just weasel his way out and run to the Syndicate. His abilities are too far advanced and he's so twisted and evil I don't know if there is any saving him. I don't want to kill him, but at the same time, he sees no value in life of any kind. He's got to be stopped before he takes another life.*

"Well, if it's any consolation: I know who brought up the bag and I'm going to go ask them what happened. Though, from what you've told me 'they' may not have any clue about the switch."

Like Emissary! Destan whipped his head up and gasped; everything starting to fall into place. *Remember when Emissary came back the day Calli was poisoned and said everything was gone?*

That he didn't find anything and then went to talk with the patrol even though the video feed shows a very different story altogether?

All this time I thought he was collaborating with Elder. — Well… he is, but I don't think he 'knows' he is. After what he said I— why didn't I realize that sooner! I've said it so many times and yet… it's 'all' Elder! It's 'got' to be! That's the only logical conclusion. No one's truly against me, against Callimay! They only have some resentment because I bucked the system because of her; but without Elder it would've never been this bad.

Then how are you going to get the Veil to accept your evidence if he's got everyone wrapped around his finger? Doctor Gerould asked as he turned to watch what was going on in the room, folding his arms across his chest.

I don't think Elder's influence can erase the truth in what I have to present. Plus I've discovered a few who are breaking through his hold.

"I found them! You were right about everything!" Traceur blurted out as she ran in the room.

She stopped dead in her tracks when she saw Doctor Gerould.

"It's okay, Traceur." Destan calmed as he nodded. "You can speak in front of Mender."

There was still hesitancy, but Destan repeating what he said gave her the confidence she needed; her handing him a satchel, "These are extra anchors and wires just like the ones I showed you!"

"I told you—"

"I wasn't about to sit by idle when I knew I could help. — They're exact matches to everything else. I checked them five times each."

"Where were they?"

She glanced around and then answered in a hushed tone, "Hidden in Elder's quarters."

"Traceur! You could've been killed!"

"Saving the lives of thousands like Chicane is more important to me, excuse my boldness." She bowed her head, though her voice was as firm as ever. "This is why I'm a Veil. I'm supposed to be willing to put myself in danger's way for those who cannot with any true hope of survival. I did this with full knowledge of the consequences that could have come upon me and may still be lingering."

Destan couldn't be upset. He knew how close Chicane and Traceur were and how she'd sacrificed so much already for his safety. Their sibling bond, in his opinion, was as close as you could get to the love of a husband and wife.

"You're 'sure' they're the same?" Destan questioned as he took one of the anchors out and examined it.

"Positive. Even the cement is the same composition."

"Put this with what you found in the gorge. Keep it out of sight."

"Affirmative, Doyen. … If I can ask, is Liaison alright?"

"She is now." Doctor Gerould nodded.

"Okay," she sounded worried when she saw the cracked window. "Let me know if there is anything else I can do to help, Doyen."

He nodded as he gave her the Shadow signal, "You're dismissed."

Traceur nodded, returning the signal, and then left.

"Wait! Traceur?"

"Yes, Doyen?" She turned back as he ran up to her.

"Thank you for doing what you did. You didn't have to."

"You know I like living on the edge. That's why you chose me." Traceur reminded as she grinned, tossing the satchel over her shoulder. "I know this is dangerous, but that's not going to scare me away. Things are at a tipping point anyway. Might as well get used to it."

I don't know if you realize how dangerous this is, Traceur.

~ 23 ~

It was beyond relieving to know Callimay was safe from Elder's latest attempt on her life, but Destan oftentimes wouldn't get much sleep — and hardly no rest — because she would breath so shallow; sometimes to the point she would begin wheezing. Each time he would wake Doctor Gerould up in a panic, only to be reminded each time that was going to happen, "We naturally breathe shallow when we're asleep, Destan. But because of the broken ribs she has her body is over-compensating to prevent pain. As long as she keeps making a conscious effort while she was awake to take deeper breaths, keeps hydrated, and gets rest she'll be fine. — Now 'you' need rest as well… as do I. Goodnight."

One night, though, he was wide awake for an altogether different reason: he heard someone's beacon going off and it wasn't one he recognized. And yet he did.

He rolled his eyes at himself when he took the time to actually think about it. Since he always had his beacon set to receive when he was asleep, he forgot to consider there was a drawback to that now: *That 'never' crossed your mind, huh? ~ Obviously. … I still say her beacon frequency sounds like her voice; I don't care what you think.*

Destan reached over and was careful to only press enough to trip the activator so it'd turn off. Callimay moaned a little but thankfully didn't wake up.

ß

With the looming deadline he was now unable to put off, Destan forgot a very important, personal day. When he got back to the suite he found

333

a fancy dinner ready and candles lit. Callimay had an outfit laid out for him and was busy in the kitchen when he plodded over. She ripped her apron off and flew to him, "Oh good! You got back early!"

"What's this all for?" He sounded upbeat but surprised when he saw she was wearing her black dress.

"Ha-ha. Very funny. I forgot and so now you are." Callimay joked as she gave him a kiss. "Now stop playing with me and get changed."

"I'm not."

The brutal honesty in his eyes and voice hit her hard for some reason; her letting a depressed sigh linger as she fought to be positive, "Oh. … Well? … Go change. Maybe you'll remember. … Go on."

He started to say something as she let go of his hand, but groaned as he hung his head, "Okay." *What 'is' today? It can't be 'that' impossible for me to figure out. ~ Well I'm all ears.*

Beating himself up about this wasn't really helpful, him catching himself before she said a word: *I know, Calli. I'm working on it.*

Nothing was clicking until he came out and saw the calendar on his desk. It hit him like a tidal wave: *December twenty-fifth!*

He ran over and swept her off her feet, "I'm an absolute idiot. How could I forget today? Happy anniversary, Calli."

"I knew you'd remember," she almost giggled as she laid her cheek against his.

This flamboyant apology was sweet, but she was still extremely sore; and yet she pushed it aside because of how happy she was. They'd been through so much pain — literally and figuratively — their first year of marriage. It only reminded her that they made it through so much but were still pushing ahead to win this fight.

ℬ

They enjoyed a relaxing and private evening and then come "morning" after Assembly, Destan left to check on a few things. As he came in the room he had a set of keys dangling from his hand as he smiled, telling her to put something warm on so they could go for a drive.

Her face lit up and she bolted; her getting back in record time so he wouldn't have time to change his mind. The two of them kept that pace until they got out to the border lot.

Destan tore out of there, grinning like they'd just left their wedding. The air was so light and free; neither of them caring where they went. All they wanted was to be with each other.

When he stopped the car it turned out he "did" have a plan all along. He did a few checks and then got out and opened her door. She could hear the low roar of water; whipping her head around to see what was the mist-coated top of the waterfall in the gorge.

"What are you doing?" Callimay asked rather puzzled as he glanced up at the moon and then down to the waterfall as he walked around.

"Just wait," he smiled as he motioned for her to come to him.

He turned her to face the falls and waited.

And waited.

And waited.

"'For'…" Callimay egged on after a few minutes.

He whispered in her ear as he leaned his head against hers and pointed, "That."

She ran a few steps forward, fumbling to say anything when she saw the bow of pastel colors in the mist, "I… I've never seen— how!"

"Short version: it only happens when the moon is full and if a bunch of other things add up; blah, blah science stuff that you'd probably say is over your head." Destan wrapped his arms around her and rested his chin on her head. "It's so foggy out here so often that it's rare. But it worked out this month. Like it?"

"It's amazing!" Callimay said breathless as she gazed at the moon rainbow that arced over the waterfall, becoming more and more vivid as seconds slipped by. "How did you know it would happen tonight?"

"Well, I wasn't 'exactly' sure, but Traceur told me she saw it last night while she was out on drills with the trainees. … Are you alright? You're shivering!"

"I'm just a little cold." She tried to keep her teeth from chattering as she smiled.

Destan sighed as he ran to the car, "What am I gonna do with you, woman! Why don't you have your coat on?"

"I didn't know I was going to be out this long."

"Here," he twisted his frowned lips as he offered her the coat. "I don't want my Chameleon freezing to death."

Seeing his carefree nature pop out tugged at her heart in a way, but it also gave her comfort, "I'm so glad you're doing better. You've been so distracted and frustrated the past couple days that I was getting pretty worried."

"I know; I have been. I'm trying to keep— no, I'm not gonna say a word about it. I'm not gonna let it invade our little slice of together time. … Do you want to see something else?"

"Now I feel bad that the only thing I had was food."

"Oh, Calli. Come on. If you hadn't done that it's likely I wouldn't have remembered… I'm ashamed to say. — You gave me more than I could have ever asked for. This? This is just something I threw together last second."

"Doctor Gerould believes we're yin and yang, but I just don't agree with that." Callimay chuckled as they started walking. "I think we're so much more alike than we are different."

"I think it's because we complement each other so well that we forget the differences."

"True. … So, what is it you have waiting for me?"

"It's not too far a walk from here, but don't worry," Destan stopped and picked her up. "I'm not going to make you walk when you don't have to. And as an added tid-bit of fluffy talk: I've actually missed carrying you around just to carry you."

"Remember the first time you carried me?"

"How could I ever forget? Your hands were ice-cold."

"I said I was sorry!"

"I didn't mean it that way. I was just starting to list different things about that time. 'You' interrupted me. — Like how your hair smacked me in the face and you apologized for that. Smelling your perfume. Being able to hold you close and protect you. Just knowing you were still alive. … I still remember those things and yet somehow I forgot our anniversary. Pretty rotten priorities I have, huh?"

"Now, Destan. Don't start." Callimay scolded as she patted the side of his face.

In a sudden shift, this wave of terror sprayed over Callimay like the fine mist they were coming to. She now couldn't help but think about the "mystery observer" she had during the first part of her run; how they must have parked close to where her and Destan did. Even how this ledge they were on forked so it also headed in the direction of the northwest end. Were they still around? Were they even real? Did Elder make her think that there was someone?

Unlike that figurative mist, the actual light mist in the air whisked her away to another memory: the mansion. The only major difference was the one she felt here was much colder because it was from freshwater that came off the mountains. And yet making that connection made her realize this must be another place Destan spent some time at when he could. For some unknown reason she couldn't help but notice he was drawn to water, be it the ocean or a lake… or in this case, a waterfall.

Enjoying this peaceful time and place, Destan strolled along; skirting behind the waterfall and setting Callimay down in what turned out to be a small cave. He told her to stay put until he got some light.

She heard him grunt a few times as it sounded like stone was rubbing against stone. A few moments later a thin column of moonlight burst into the cave. Callimay had to blink a few times, but adjusted and saw he'd pushed out a stone ledge to divide the water.

Destan smacked his hands and then rubbed them on his pants leg, laughing as he answered her unheard question: *The falls is 'thin' — if you will — right here. I'm not 'that' strong.*

As he came over and took her hand, they sat where they could see out: *This is why you'd stand out by the cliff, isn't it? The mist and roar of water is your safe place, isn't it?*

It's one of the very few things I've found that'll drown out the stinging memories of being in a burning, collapsing home with your parents you never get to see again. … So now the big secret's out. He smiled as he put his arm around her. *But I must say, the real deal with you is so much better than the substitute alone.*

So this waterfall is the real deal?

Yes and no. He looked thoughtful as he stared out into the night.

I'm not meaning to—

*I know you're not. Don't worry. — The mansion was the first place I began to notice the calming nature of water, but that place reminded me too much of my parents. So even though it helped it wasn't a place

'I' could view as safe and separate. The mansion still had a hold on me. And I didn't like how it felt. … Does that make sense?*

This burst of open, raw discussion wasn't something Callimay was about to stop: *He's in a safe place. Tell him you do so he'll go on.* ~ *Why?* ~ *His emotions feel so much more stable and calm. I truly think he 'wants' to talk about it. Just support and encourage him… but don't push him.*

Well, when I began my regimen I tried the beach but that wasn't much different, really. It wasn't until I came out here that I felt… well, I felt safe. I felt free. — Rej actually immersed me down at the base of these falls, so Spiritually it was where I 'was' set free.

Don't you 'dare' cry. ~ *Why not? He'd expect me to.* *I love you.*

His smile continued to grow as he brushed her cheek, wrapping her in his arms: *I love you more."

ß

They were able to stay "much" longer than she was expecting. Destan's phone never went off and he wasn't fidgety or anxious about getting back. While the conversation never went back to his parents and such, they still talked for a little about spiritual things before sitting in silence and holding onto each other until he decided it was time to go.

All of this was an amazing change in pace for the two of them… let alone a total reversal as far as emotions go to what happened a year ago. They weren't running for their lives from people they didn't even realize were after them for much different and deadly reasons. And then to have Destan open up again like he did?

With each step he took back up the path toward the car, Destan's strides became slower and his emotions revealed he was concerned about something. He stopped short of the car and had Callimay face him, "I don't mean to be a downer after this all, but… I 'really' don't know what to expect day after tomorrow."

"That's the day you picked for everything, isn't it?"

He sighed as he rubbed her hands, "It's the safest time to do it."

"We're stronger when we're together," she assured as she put her hand atop his. "And even though he 'has' caught us off guard on a couple occasions, we 'are' able to defend ourselves unlike everyone else. We 'can' stop his attacks. I know there's a huge question about how everything will go, but what you've said? Everyone's supporting you — supporting us. Yes, it 'could' be a ruse by Elder, but I don't think it is. Maybe I'm a bit too optimistic but I hate thinking the worst all the time. … Is there anything you need me to do to help?"

"I'm probably just being pessimistic." Destan sighed as he dragged himself over and opened the door. "And you're right: we 'do' have an upper hand no one else does. You more than me, but I understand what you mean. Just— don't charge in like you did last time. I'm not saying lay down like a dog and let them treat you like dirt, but just—"

"Be calm and follow directions."

"'My' directions. Fidus will be the one leading the vote since he tabled it, but 'I'm' the one who's in control of everything. Alright?"

"Yes, Doyen." She snapped to attention and nodded, then tapped her fingers at her side before grabbing his wrist, "Thank you for tonight. I know you probably are going to get in trouble with Eld—"

"I don't care what he thinks anymore. Almost everyone else has admitted you aren't some kind of symbol of rebellion by me against them; you're not this little play toy I have and show off when I want to only to throw away when I'm tired of you. They're actually beginning to understand I married you because I wanted a wife. I married you because I was lonely. I married you because I loved you. And I married you because I 'do' want a family. There are still those who haven't gotten with the program, but they just complain and grumble because they don't have the happiness I do. I truly think they're jealous. — Elder's different, but then again, it is kinda the same deal with him if you think about it. Deep down I do want him to repent of everything he's done and chose to do the right thing… I just don't know if there's any soul left in him to save. It's like he's allowed it to be devoured by satan entirely. But maybe I'm wrong. Maybe he 'will' come around. It wouldn't be an easy thing to believe in the slightest, I'll say that much."

"We'll just cross bridges as they come. And pray."

"Without ceasing," Destan nodded and then gave her a kiss.

Callimay replied as she slid her arms around his neck so he could twirl her around a few times, "We're gonna make it. This 'will' work. Leaning and trusting in God is going to get us through this."

~ 24 ~

It was amazing what one day's worth of joy could do for a person. Callimay was beyond nebula nineteen; her nothing less than her happy, bouncy self when Destan got back for dinner the next night — the night before she was to go before the Veil. She felt a few spikes from him, but figured it was just normal Elder stuff.

But she couldn't have been more wrong. He was irate. She tried to broach the subject to find out what was wrong — he always did his best to separate "home life" and "work" — so this was a struggle for her: *Let's face it: tomorrow is do-or-die day. He's giving up the book his father and your mother died protecting. … Kinda ironic they had to protect an evil man's book instead of 'the' book, but anyway! ~ What you're saying is I should lay off and let it rest. Am I right? ~ Precisely! He's just getting himself worked up. Keep things calm for him like you always do. He'll settle down in time.*

With it being winter, their "night" was quite a bit shorter which made the wait much more bearable. Getting as much rest as she could was the best thing to do, but she couldn't bring herself to drift off until Destan finally did… which was at about a quarter past three.

In an effort to start their day off right, she popped up early and got breakfast ready. — For only getting three hours of sleep she felt really good. — She saw movement as she finished setting the table, pretty much skipping over as Destan rolled out of bed, "Good morning!"

"Morning," he grumbled as he rubbed his face.

She smiled as she sat down and ruffled his already messy hair.

"Just stop, Calli." He pushed her hands away. "I… I just can't. Not right now."

Well land sake! He's just as bad as he was last night. ~ Well let's not make it worse by making 'other' things worse. ~ Oh gosh! You're right! She sat back and folded her hands on her lap, bowing her head. "I'm sorry, Destan."

"Calli, it's not— it's got nothing to do with that. … I… I got… I got this note from Fidus yesterday and I haven't been able to think about anything since."

Keeping her inquisitive self under control was no easy task, him taking his sweet time to find the paper and handing it to her. It snapped as she unfolded it, the words contained just as abrupt and harsh.

She struggled to understand what the silver ink on the black page meant. It said she had to challenge Destan or he had to challenge her before she could stand before the Veil. In no uncertain terms, it said the spar they had was not enough and her final run could not be approved without it.

All I did basically doesn't mean a thing without this stupid little add on? Are you kidding me! After all I went through to get to this point! This can't be happening! "But I don't understand. I thought—"

"Yeah, I did too. But when I saw it on the paperwork I was hoping they'd forget about it after what you've done multiple times. I don't blame Auditor, she was right to flag it. 'I' wasn't the one you fought."

"Why does it matter 'who' did it? Haven't I—"

"Calli, please!" Destan pleaded, trying to keep himself from getting mad at her. "I'm just glad it's me. Elder was one vote short of being the one who would be your opponent. And before you say it: I know his bid to be your opponent goes against why he refuses to let your final run gain approval. But when does anything evil does 'truly' make sense?"

All the air was ripped out of the room. She wheezed a bit before taking a hard swallow, whispering as she braced her ribs, "What!"

The fear drain every last ounce of color from her face and destroyed her emotionally. She'd been held back on technicalities the entire time but with Auditor getting all of her clearances and— how could she do this to her! Now Callimay felt like she did at the beginning of this all: it felt like everyone she had come to trust — Auditor in particular — had betrayed her. Yes, she and the others had "help", but: *Destry withstood him for years and didn't have any 'help'! Why can't she open their eyes and see this even just a little! It's obviously possible. And she's a strong woman! I just… I don't…*

Who cared who it was she fought! She won: Fidus, Destan, Baleck, Ginger, … even Elder himself. And don't forget those during each run she had. She bested them all.

Elder, that's who cared. This was what looked to be his last hold on her. His last chance to keep her out of Deep Dark. And what a time to bring it out.

Unwilling to be the instigator — still trying to find a way out of it on some other technicality Elder didn't consider — Destan danced around the issue as much as he could; but only ended up making things worse, "We should've never gone for that drive the other day. I should've known better there was something off about it all. It was too—"

"Why would you say such a thing!"

"Elder had complete control of everything going on for almost an entire day, do you realize that? Us leaving was what he wanted, Calli! He might've even been the one to plant that seed in my mind… 'and' yours! Do you realize that!"

"But we needed that time."

"Don't you see, though? He got me to think it was a good idea; he took something that was in-and-of-itself a wonderful thing and used it against us!"

"Why do you think he couldn't do it with you around?" She stormed away, so angry at this point she began to cry.

"Because he's slipping. I know he is. And if he was willing to be honest, he'd admit he knows I do. But since he won't, he needed me away so he didn't have to worry. Somehow he can't control me if I'm face-to-face. And I've noticed there are a few who are starting to break free from his hold. … He 'knows' he messed up 'big time' with that web he had put up for your run. He 'knows' that satchel of his is gone and there are others who are taking my side; questioning whether or not he is the devil we know him to be."

Not wanting to lose the last person she trusted, tired of fighting, Callimay asked, "Well… what do we do about it?"

And then he sealed the coffin, so to speak. Instead of making amends and being supportive, he forced her to make the decision he should have, "Emissary's supposed to be the observer and he's always early. I'm sure he's ready to go right now."

Why in the world would he say something like that! Keep it together, Destan! Stop slipping and stabbing yourself in the foot!

This whirlwind wasn't doing anything but build and cause more friction between the two of them. In fact, this was probably what Elder wanted all along. She sighed as she flopped down on the bed, bowing her head, "When do you want to leave? And where are we going?"

Push now came to shove. He said he wanted to get it over with but now that he'd been forced into that corner, "I know you've done it already. I even told Elder to sign off on it since he witnessed it. You shouldn't have to do this."

Destan fell to his knees in front of her and leaned his head against her knee, him yelling at himself for not figuring something out in time. And then on top of that, he wasn't being who he was supposed to be. He wasn't protecting his wife like he promised he would.

Callimay leaned over and ran her fingers through his hair while trying to calm him. He was more torn up about this than she was. She was just in shock. When she thought about it, she knew he was only battling with himself — Doyen against Destan — to do what needed to be done while keeping her safe… which right now was for her to be by his side in the Veil.

They couldn't wait any longer. She had to get this done right then so they could get to Deep Dark and expose Elder for who he had been all along. Waiting was only playing into his hand. No one could sneak up on either of them if they stayed inside Bulwark and were in the combat room. But then again, if something "did" happen to Destan and the person locked the door, she'd be stuck with no way out. — The locks in Bulwark could only be overridden by those who were of equal or higher seniority. Right now? She was the lowest on the roster. — If they were up top she'd be able to get away and the belvedere could get to her sooner. But then there were countless places someone could hide. She could sense them, but if they were snipers it wouldn't matter.

For each logical argument for either place she found one just as logical against it. She caught herself — overthinking this wasn't going to help — and blurted out, "The Green Guard, fifteen minutes, Doyen."

"Calli," he squeezed her hand, his voice cracking.

*Elder wants us to put this off. Total Eclipse is supposed to start in just a couple weeks! We have no time to spare. — And like you said, you're my opponent, 'not' Elder. I know you won't lose it like last time. And really? Our spar was going just fine. Just… please don't throw me to the ground or try to choke me. Doctor Gerould would kill you if I got another concussion and I can't handle the memories— I've experienced you choking me once before and I do 'not' want to do it again. Please."

She's stronger than I feel I 'ever' give her credit for. ~ That's not true and you know it. — Now come on, Boon. "I promise."

ℬ

They got up top as the last hint of sunlight vanished. Callimay gave Destan a kiss and then tried to leave to take her position. He held on as tight as he dared, unwilling to let her be where he couldn't see her.

But you can. Use what your father made for you for the purpose he intended it for: protect me.

If it were ever possible to see that mental lightbulb pop on, she saw it in his eyes right then. Destan knew the danger that was there so it wasn't possible for him to be surprised.

And so with that they prayed and then parted ways.

She found a nice spot and sat down, knees curled to her chest and eyes closed; blocking everything out so she could listen. While Destan was as quiet and fast as a real shadow could be — if it were humanly possible, that is — she was still able to tell where he was since she could "feel" him.

Before long she heard rustling: *He's still well within the tall grasses behind us. Ready? ~ No.*

The rustling continued and started to raise questions in her mind; her laughing as she shook her head and shifted so she was sitting on her heels: *Are you 'trying' to give yourself away? Seriously! I can hear you so well I could throw a spike right at your left foot!*

Her joking scolds apparently did not good, the rustling continuing for a little bit longer before it all of a sudden stopped. He was standing behind her, about thirty feet away. He was breathing a bit hard but Callimay knew he was nervous.

The breeze that had been so soft vanished as if the ensuing violence scared it. All that was left was a silence full of anticipation and fear.

Neither of them moved an inch, that desire to not do this still pulling at both of them.

A few minutes passed and nothing happened.

I… I really don't want to be the one to— I'm the one who started this. Couldn't he at least do— "Trever!" Callimay gasped as she turned and nearly fell over. "What are you doing here?"

He reminded as he rolled his eyes, "To observe… 'remember'?"

"I'm sorry. Emissary." *Silly nut! Why'd you do that?* "Wouldn't be much use if someone wasn't here to witness it, huh?" She shook her head as she turned around, trying to keep things light. "You know you really are a brute, stomping around like that. You need to learn to watch where you tread so you're quieter."

"Thanks for the tip," he threw his back against a nearby tree.

"How are Kareal and Edna?"

All she got was an irritated scowl all but tattooed on his face.

Callimay bowed her head, "This isn't chit-chat time."

A second round of silence began; it feeling more and more awkward as the seconds ticked by. Now knowing he was her real brother — the one who had to have seen what happened to their family and still was able to save her life… and willingly sacrificed himself to keep her safe — she wanted to say something to see if it might wake him up.

Well, almost.

Ten minutes passed and Callimay couldn't hear Destan at all. She tried to talk to him but it was as if he were asleep.

Her heart started racing. Something was wrong. "Very" wrong.

Then it dawned on her: *Trever was— 'is' Elder's little minion!*

Why was he so late? Destan said he'd be there already. Why did he come from the same direction Destan was supposed to? And why didn't he question why Destan hadn't shown up yet? He did nothing but stand there and tap the handle of his one knife.

Speaking of which, the handle looked like it belonged to a modified Karambit… the type of knife Callimay hated the most. It was extremely short with an awkwardly shaped blade and equally awkward handle, making it a melee weapon rather than the standard, precision type:

Why am I surprised? I mean it 'does' make sense that Elder would have him choose something so heinous. … Are you still in there, Trever? ~ If we only knew a nickname we called him by.

Keeping a low profile and paying attention to every move he made was all she could do until she figured out what happened, "Did you happen to see Doyen when you were headed this way?"

"No, why?" He shuffled his feet and took hold of both knives.

"Don't you think it's been an extremely long time?" She rose slowly, trying to be nonchalant about everything she did. "I know there's the whole 'element of surprise', but it's been what, ten minutes?"

"Oh, I think the element of surprise has been used to perfection." Trever replied as he began to grin. "He's not coming, Liaison. Doyen can't help you."

"What did you do to him?" She demanded as she drew her Seaxes.

"What I was told to and of course gladly did. There's only one way to handle a Nark and that's to dispose of them."

While her knee-jerk reaction was to reach out for Destan to see if he was indeed alive, she knew he was. It's just wherever he was he was unconscious, "Don't do this, Trever. This isn't you. It's Elder."

"You're telling me to stop and yet you're the one who drew their weapon first. Fidus was right about what happened after your run. — Sorry I ever doubted you. — I'm just defending myself at this point."

"Trever, stop!" She pleaded as she let her knives fall and put her hands up. "Trever, it's me. It's Callimay. You're little sister. Please try to remember. Don't let Elder keep doing this to you!"

"I should've taken out a bet, Elder was right again." Trever began laughing as he drew his knives and pointed at her with one. "He swore you'd try something like that at some point. Gotta say you pulled that one out pretty early, but you're new to this all."

"But that's not true! Canary was your— 'our' mother, Trever! Don't you remember her?" Callimay tried not to cry, her heart breaking from this brash rejection. "Don't you remember our family? That our father had a thick Scot—"

"Canary was nothing but a tool, a Nark… just ours. Why do you think they waited a week before executing her?" Trever questioned in a furious tone as he tried to scare her by faking a run at her.

What he did startled her, but she didn't move, "What do you mean? She died in her home after she made sure Destan and I were safe."

Now I 'do' regret not taking out bets. "Canary was executed in front of the entire world on television. Of course you won't remember it because I overheard Doyen talking with Mender about how it was the reason for your initial concussion: you were 'so' hysterical after seeing her die that you ran out of the Nest and ended up buried in a snowbank with a gash in your head… wiping out your memories of the event."

She didn't have another broken rib, but nonetheless she could barely breathe. Callimay stumbled back a few steps as she framed her face and looked at the ground, utterly shattered, "She was… executed? A… and I saw it?" *Destan's nightmare! Thinking 'I' was ex— he was seeing me where she was!*

Trever had enough with waiting for her to do something; he lunged at her with full force and no restraint — just like Fidus.

By the time she came to her senses, she understood Elder was doing everything he could to keep her from focusing and defending herself. And it was working: her Seaxes were too far away and she didn't have any spikes or hummingbirds. — In a challenge, both individuals were required to use whatever weapons they had on them at some point. She was an excellent markswoman with a throwing knife and spike, but she didn't want to risk Destan tapping his ability at any point and that making her throw one she would forever regret.

He got her with a glancing blow of his elbow, but thankfully missed her with his blades.

Callimay screeched when she hit the ground — landing on her side — but gritted her teeth and scrambled to get up.

His second pass was easier to dodge, her controlling her landing and ending up much closer to her Seaxes. She glanced at them and then him, making a dive for them.

It was obvious she needed to keep on her feet to spare her ribs as much stress as possible, but the range of strike Trever had was wide enough she really needed to build space between the two of them to protect herself. But if she hit her head she'd be completely defenseless.

Perhaps the only saving grace in this shock-n-awe turn of events was the very blatant fact that Emissary's fighting style was forceful and… well, downright sloppy. It took her no time at all to notice how he left himself completely vulnerable half the time in between strikes. And while Callimay wanted to get his knives out of his grasp without resorting to punching him to get him to loosen his grip, she realized he was extremely strong; almost like when Destan was tapped into his ability: *You've 'got' to understand he isn't your brother. He won't 'play fair'. Not with him allowing Elder to have free rein. ~ What if I did the same thing I did with Destan and Fidus? ~ I don't know that it really worked with Fidus. He didn't act any dif— watch out!*

After a few more rounds, Callimay finally found the strength to do what she needed: she loved her brother so much that she had to keep him from doing what she knew he never wanted to… but it wasn't enough. She had to actually draw blood for him to think of slowing down, let alone stop.

She cried as she tried to find an opportunity, the tears of sadness becoming those of anger as Trever continued to belittle her "weakness" when it came to fighting someone.

Her ability to use both of her hands so well made her a bit of an enigma when it came to her fight style. It was extremely easy for her to distract her opponent, so she drew the lonely hummingbird she forgot was still in her shirt sleeve when he wasn't looking and stabbed him in the side with it.

It helped, but that little of a blade was only going to pause things for a minute or two. He cursed at her as he ripped it out and threw it away, hissing as he snatched up the knife he dropped — a perfect opportunity wasted! No!

That was now a tender spot, but she knew he'd be careful of it from this point on. So their fight was going to require her to be strategic… and she was going to need to react faster in those conflicting moments.

Even with the injury the amount of power and strength he had far exceeded hers in this weakened state; she couldn't fight the way she wanted or needed to. She wasn't the best at it because every other time she panicked and kicked, punched, and clawed her way out of those holds; but she understood you could use someone's strength against themselves in such situations. You just had to know how to redirect the force so it hit them and not you: *Use it now so you don't end up in—*

"Quite avoiding me, you little—" Trever swung his arm behind him, slicing her right elbow with the edge of his blade.

She screamed as she dropped her one Seax; him laughing as he watched her fall to the ground and grip her arm.

This taunting fueled the anger burning inside; she hated when Elder twisted the person's mind to that point. Callimay threw her knife into the tree beside her and pulled herself up, screaming as she ran at him.

He stumbled back and looked at her wide-eyed; her ripping his knives out of his hands, "Stop it, Trever! Stop it!"

While this was a jolt, he still snickered, "Oh 'come' now. Really?"

Callimay threw his knives as far away as she could, ready to grapple when she caught a glimpse of Elder in the distance. And if that wasn't bad enough, she saw the gleam of his cane sword from the moonlight. Her focus darted back to Trever and made her realize she was alone and without help.

The look of crazed bloodthirst in his eye — showing no fear — made her blood run cold. And so dodging was all she dared do at this point. Aside from the fact she was starting to breathe hard — her ribs starting to bother her — she knew if she showed her weakness he'd mercilessly batter her weak point similar to how Elder had Destan do: *Maybe he doesn't know what happened. He just got back today. Right? ~ It'd be kinda stupid for Elder to 'not' tell him. ~ Oh, that hurts.* *Destan? Destan can you hear me?*

Sore, exhausted, and desperate, she kept trying reach Destan; but each time there was no response.

Elder was slithering toward them like the vile snake he was, basking in seeing and hearing her spiral into absolute terror: *Destan please!*

All of a sudden the three of them froze and looked to the west. Someone or some"thing" was thundering toward them. She was the first to calm; knowing it was Destan in a full-on sprint. So when Trever was on the ground the next second she wasn't surprised. But as soon as she calmed it dawned on her — she screamed as she bolted toward him, feeling his emotions spiking through the roof: *Destan! Please! Let's just get out of here! Let Elder go! We need help!*

"No you don't." Trever grimaced as he grabbed her ankle; him struggling to his feet. "You're mine."

Callimay cried out as she hit the ground, her grabbing clumps of grass as she was dragged away from her husband.

Trever grabbed her in his bear-like hug, aggravating her broken ribs to their limit, "N… o, Trever!"

"Don't think we'll be going out on a double-date," he hissed in her ear as her eyes began to roll back.

He laughed as he let her unconscious body fall to the ground.

Feeling the pain she passed out from wash over him, Destan let the frenzy mode overtake him. After jumping and pommeling Trever, he jumped back for Elder; bouncing from one ability to the next as quick as he ever had.

But much to his surprise, he wasn't able to lay a finger on Elder. It was as if he were able to anticipate his every move. Destan got more and more furious and then realized: *Get out, Elder!*

Having a little bit more control over himself, he did the unthinkable: he got himself to a somewhat stable point and did what he could to shut off every one of his abilities. He even threw his only weapon down; heaving as he taunted, "Fight me like a man, Elder! No abilities, no aids, no backup, no weapons… just 'you' and me. … Or does the thought of doing your own dirty work appall you?"

"It's been so long, though. I don't know if I 'can' do that." Elder belly-laughed, eventually dropping his sword. "But why not indulge the ignorant youth of today and do things in their frivolous ways? … Though, to fight man-to-man I would need a man for an opponent. Don't think for one minute that 'you' could consider yourself one."

"I'm more a man then you'll 'ever' be… and probably ever was. — Case in point: after the incident with Kareal and what I found out about Ginger? I did some digging into Syndicate operatives and those odd trafficking reports we were getting for about five years."

"Oh?" Elder asked curious, folding his arms across his chest.

"Over half of them are lefties. And from what I could gather earlier this week, they didn't join willingly. I don't understand how that was missed… but then again, you 'do' have your ways."

"I was doing them a service… 'especially' Ginger."

"You took it upon yourself to go as deep and dark as what many governments in the past have: prey on the one thing people fear —

death. They'd do anything — turn in a loved one or kill them — if it meant they would live. That's not 'doing them a service'. That's finding free labor in fear of their own lives so you can pad your pockets with blood money, keep yourself immune from any prosecution of any kind, and have control over more people than most people could imagine."

He scoffed as he let out a sigh, shaking his head before resting his full gaze on him, "Most of them came to terms with it. And some of them are our best operatives. They're not in fear any longer. They enjoy the work they have."

"You even consider yourself a Syndicate member. … What in the name of— what are you doing, Elder!" Destan clinched his fists, doing everything possible to keep calm. "You've always spoken about helping those who were oppressed. That was why you started working with Commander in the first place. Was that just a cover, a front, for you to gain power so you alone would be in control?"

"You're beginning to see the light, slowly but surely."

"And my father was going to blow your cover before you had cemented yourself so nothing could touch you. Or at least he found something you couldn't dispute regardless of your hold."

"He was a pesky thorn in my side that was up to no good." Elder snapped back, his eyes narrowing.

"Let me take a wild guess: you murdered Commander, didn't you?"

"Oh, I do believe you're beginning to assume things now, Doyen."

❦

When Callimay came to she couldn't move; she could barely breathe. It wasn't easy to keep calm knowing the situation she was in, but flipping out wasn't going to help either.

As she calmed her lungs and chest slowly unlocked the bands which were holding her hostage; thought it wasn't as much as she wanted. She could manage wheezes, but it was something at least.

"It's about time," Trever grunted as he stood and tapped her side with his foot.

Callimay sounded hoarse as he kneeled beside her, "Don't do this."

"Are you seriously begging? — Such a coward. — A Shadow 'never' begs for their life. They die with their dignity and secrets."

"Trever!" She barely got out, trying everything she knew to get him to let go of her neck.

His hold on her was even stronger than Destan's when he was in frenzy mode.

Somehow in this madness she noticed what looked like a burn mark on his arm: *It can't be! Trever has abilities?*

Keeping panic at bay wasn't going to work now that she was almost certain his strength wasn't his own, natural strength. She clawed as his arms, trying to reach his face, "Trever, it's me, Callimay. Please stop!"

"Quit lying to me, Nark!" Trever bellowed as he tightened his grip. "I have no family but Elder."

Her hysteria was at critical levels. She could feel, and even hear, everything in her neck begin to crack. Her ability to think and move was fading.

But with the last bit she had, she cried in a hoarse whisper; tears streaming down her face, "Trever? It's me… Everlyn. I'm Everlyn. I'm your little sister. Please, Trever. Don't… don't do this. I know you don't want to. You let Elder do this all to you so I wouldn't die and I can't thank… thank you enough. Please don't help him now."

"What did you say?" Trever paused as his eyes bugged out.

"I… I'm E… ver… Everlyn," she whimpered as she kept pulling on his hands; hoping she had enough left in her to pry them off.

"Everlyn?"

She hit the ground hard, gasping as she held her throat, "Yes."

"Ever… Everlyn?"

There was this moment of stabbing silence. A war had started that only three individuals knew about. But was this last ditch effort enough to get him to turn around?

Not willing to risk anything, she used the last of her strength to grip the handle on one of her Seaxes; her almost dropping it as she pulled her arm close to her face. Any number of words along the lines of terrified, mortified, petrified, and horrified would be a perfect picture of her emotions and expression. Then seeing Trever stagger around, mumbling to himself? She gripped her Seax with both hands and held it in front of her; still trembling and unable to truly breathe as she started to cry.

"Wha… what's going on? Who is… why am I…" Trever stumbled back a bit; wincing as he grabbed his temples. "What is— ah!"

He passed out, falling to his side, and was motionless for a while; but soon, mutters began to come from where he was. Trever worked to get himself up on his hands and knees, shaking his head. Nothing he said made sense and the way he was acting scared her even more — it reminding her of Destan when Elder twisted his mind as well as how those cliffhangers she saw on the videos, this being how they would act right before they went insane.

The mutters turned into mumbles, Trever knocking his fist on the ground now. Most of what he said still wasn't recognizable, but there was one word he started repeating, "Everlyn." What sounded like other names started popping in here and there as questions, even some sounded like city names, but he kept coming back to that name.

She yelped as he slammed his fist on the ground and yelled out, her not hearing what he said, "What have I done!"

Just then he and Callimay heard what sounded like a second heard of horses stampeding toward them.

Bursting through the low brush was the belvedere. The creature spread his feet as he lowered his firm stance, scanning the area for the source of what caused his keeper this much harm; him sucking wind as it were and then growling. His glowing face was scratched and cut, his glistening, metallic blood streaked across his face.

Without any prodding, he ran straight to Callimay, laying down when he got beside her; whining.

"I know, Buddy. I know." She whispered as she managed a faint smile, shrieking in a broken voice as she gripped her throat, "Don't! It's Mama's alpha!"

Trever was fear-stricken as it was, but to see the glowing creature react to Callimay's word as if to obey? The belvedere whipped his head around looked up at him, jumping to his feet standing over his keeper. He growled for a moment and then whimpered and whined after he shook his head and pawed at his face.

"It's just Trever, Buddy. Go help Destan. … Go!" Her hoarse voice crackled like an empty chip bag as she pushed the creature in the direction she wanted him to go.

The belvedere still didn't want to, but took off after a second command and shove. He thundered over and latched onto Elder's right arm, allowing Destan to have a moment to get himself together. Elder reached inside his veil and took out a spike, not hesitating or worried about what he needed to do to free himself.

Destan recovered quickly and jabbed Elder's elbow, finally bringing him to a knee, "You always rebelled against the number one rule of runs: always carry antidote. It has literally come back to 'bite' you. — Leave him alone, Big Fella."

He grunted as the creature let him go and stood guard; an evil grin growing across his face as he lifted his good hand, "Why bother when everyone else has it?"

Seeing three bottles of the black liquid in his hand made Destan glance at his belt which was the worst thing he could've done; Elder using that chance to blindside him with a left-cross.

⍚

Trever, meanwhile, called for medical backup and then tried to gain Callimay's trust so he could help. Memories were beginning to flood him in an overwhelming manner with each passing moment; him just starting to realize who Elder was and what he was doing to her.

But all of her pushing him away wasn't solely because she was scared. She kept pointing as she whimpered, "Destan. Help. Please!"

Seeing the determination in her eyes, Trever did as she said.

Elder had taken the antidote and reached for another spike when Destan got to his knees and tried to orient himself. The belvedere had launched another attack, unafraid even though he had a spike in-hand.

Trever snatched up Destan's dagger as he kept running, pushing Elder's hand out of the way before he thrust the twisted blade into his chest; hissing as he put all his weight on him, "Die you filthy demon."

Elder gasped as he stumbled back, a death grip on Trever's arm as he tried to say something; his eyes flooded with fear as he collapsed.

While spitting at him gave him some pleasure, a few second later Trever grimaced and winced as he dropped to his knees. — Thinking the spike was for Destan, he stabbed himself with it so Elder couldn't use it.

Now that he had his bearing, Destan scrambled to his feet… and then paused. Part of him just couldn't believe Elder was gone. Killed by the boy he'd raised and trained to do whatever he said. His focus then shifted when he heard labored breathing, "Emissary?"

"I'm fine. Help Everlyn." He nodded toward Callimay.

Similar to how he felt when he was standing over Toreon and remembered her, Destan's body instantly froze. He looked to his right and then bolted; ordering when he saw the belvedere, "Watch him."

It mystified Trever to see an alpha follow Destan's command, let alone see a fellow Shadow be so calm and trusting of one. This was a Syndicate tool! And an alpha!

The creature barked at Destan and turned, staring down Elder who was motionless. He then glanced at Trever and barked and whined as he sniffed the air. Trever reacted the only way he knew when there was a belvedere nearby; ripping the spike out of his hand and getting ready to throw it.

Just like he did at the Nest, the belvedere cowered and whimpered.

Trever was even more mystified. He knew for certain a belvedere never cowered from anyone but its keeper: *Wha… why is it acting like I'm its keeper! What in the—*

Since he lowered the spike, the belvedere looked at his hand and yelped and then looked back at Callimay and let out a howl; appearing to do what he could to explain he was friendly and protecting both of them while still obeying Destan's command.

"What 'are' you?"

ॐ

"Calli? Calli look at me." Destan said winded as he slid on his knees next to her; trying to hide the fact he gripped his side.

You're okay? Oh good. Her quivering hand brushed against his chest and then fell to her side.

His heart shattered when he saw the state of his wife; what she had to endure at the hand of her brother. The fact she was a alive looked to be nothing short of a miracle.

He leaned over her as the moonlight vanished; a low rumble and the wind picking up as ice-cold drops dove for the ground. Destan knew she needed help, but Doyen shut down. Husband Destan won out and yet didn't have a clue of what to do; him stammering as he tried to think of what to say, "C… Cal— can you talk?"

Her lips began to buckle as her eyes watered; his awkward question a relief in a way: *Not now. It's hard enough to breathe.*

"Oh, Calli. I—" He jerked a bit as he caught a glimpse of a group running toward them from the direction of where Elder and Emissary were. "There are others coming. I've got to get you—"

She fumbled to, but gripped his arm as she calmed: *It's the medical team, don't worry. Trever called for them.*

"He called you Everlyn when he told me to check on you."

If I hadn't remembered he only called me by my middle name… I 'know' I'd be dead right now. She shuttered as she took his hand and held on for dear life.

Destan looked back and saw Trever sitting there, the belvedere still looking back and forth between him and Elder. It dawned on him the medical team didn't understand about the belvedere, "Big Fella!"

His ears instantly perked and tail began to wag, all one-hundred and seventeen pounds of computer floof thrilled to be allowed to come back to his Callimay. But he stopped and as if to ask Trever to come, ran a couple circles around him before romping over.

"You've gotta go." Destan ordered as he pointed in the direction of the Minka.

The creature looked but whined at him as he looked at Callimay and then back to Trever.

"I'm here now. You need to leave." Destan repeated.

"Go, Buddy. I'll be fine." Callimay found enough strength to say.

After glancing back to Trever, the belvedere took off. It wasn't as fast as he would've liked — Destan knew they'd seen him even though he wasn't glowing — but the creature wasn't in danger; they wouldn't be able to keep up with him. But now he had to explain things.

Trever dragged himself over and dropped the dagger before he fell to his knees.

"Is he dead?" Destan asked.

He shook his head as he almost hissed, "While I admit I was a little high, he needs to be there in that much pain for a 'good' long while. I'll be sure to take care of him in a bit." *And believe me when I say I'll enjoy that.*

"Just let him be. I'll take care of everything." Destan warned.

Trying to act like he didn't hear what his commanding officer said, Trever asked, "Everlyn? Everlyn, are you okay? I mean…. I know—"

She barely nodded as she offered her hand; that all the movement she dared make.

"I'm so sorry. I… I didn't I… I don't understand h—" Trever began endlessly rambling apologies when they heard the voices of the others.

"We're over here." Destan motioned as he stood up.

The team ran over but it was instantly clear to Destan and Trever that something wasn't right, "Where's Mender?"

"You're all under arrest for conspiring with the Syndicate and attempting to murder a member of the Veil." One of the men said as another knocked Destan to his knees and cuffed him.

"What!" Destan asked dumbfounded as he looked back, seeing them do the same to Trever. "What are you talking about? I've been trying to tell you all— don't touch her!"

Callimay screamed in a similar fashion to that blood-curdling tone as one of the men grabbed her by the arm and jerked her up.

"What are you doing! You're no better than a Falconer, treating an injured person like that! It doesn't matter whether or not you think they are a spy." Destan scolded as he flashed his eyes at those around him. "That's not how we do things! Now where's Mender?"

"I'm here." Doctor Gerould said out of breath as he pushed his way through the ring of Veils gathered. "Doyen is right, Chicane. Even if they are Narks they deserve to be treated as humans."

He gritted his teeth, no one saying a word…. and then growled as he gestured to the man who was holding Callimay, "Let her go."

"Fine," the man hissed as he just about shoved her down.

"W— are you 'trying' to kill her?" Doctor Gerould fumed as he ran and caught her. "Chicane! What has gotten into you?"

The small group turned when they heard growling and saw a glow in the air behind them. A few shouted as they drew spikes, "Belvedere!"

Not flinching one bit, he bulldozed through them; snarling and snapping at them the entire time but not latching on.

Once in he sniffed at Callimay he then stood over her before bearing his teeth at the entire group.

For some reason this defensive character puzzled them to the point they didn't throw one spike. — Apparently their curiosity was perked; or their fear outweighed their training.

"Doyen!" They all heard a strong woman's voice call out; the group turning to see who it was as her voice lowered to a harsh whisper as she stormed up to one of them, "Chicane! What 'are' you doing?"

She shoved him, after which he tried to be subtle as he eyed her, "Let me handle this, Traceur."

"I'm a Veil as well… 'and' your superior. I'm telling you to stand down. I can explain everything."

"Oh. So you explain this?" One of the men spoke up as he stepped to the side and pointed to the glowing dog creature.

Chicane scoffed as he rolled his eyes, "Please enlighten us." *I can't 'wait' to hear this one.*

"I… what in the— Liaison!"

Figures. "Take the belvedere down and then bring the three of them in." Chicane rolled his eyes and kept on; pausing when he realized, "And Traceur? Since you're wanting to take control by pulling rank, go gather the rest of the Veil. We've got a trial to hold."

"I— how in the world are you all— Chicane what is wrong with you?" Traceur rambled in disbelief as she looked at the creature that refused to leave Callimay; scrambling to find a way out of this, "Fine. I'll take care of the belvedere… 'and' Doyen. Since Fidus isn't here the most senior Veil should do it."

"Fine," Chicane whipped around and headed back; him trying to sound stern, "Mender? Make sure you see to Elder first."

Doctor Gerould grumbled under his breath as he forced a nod, then turned to Callimay and started into his triage, "Can you still breathe?"

"Barely," she whispered as the belvedere whined and nudged her arm with his nose. "Buddy, please s—"

"Come on," one of the other men snapped as he grabbed Trever and jerked him up, shoving him along.

The belvedere whipped his head around and snapped at the man, stalking over and doing what he could to get between the two of them.

"I'm… I'm alright." Trever hesitated to answer, still confused.

The creature cocked his head to the side and stared at him as he walked away, then looked over at Destan as if asking what to do, "Just stay with Calli. Trever can take care of himself."

"Doyen, what is going on?" Traceur asked in a hushed and critical tone after everyone else left to tend to Elder. "Why in the 'world' do you have an alpha?"

"It's Canary's." He looked back as Doctor Gerould picked his wife up, causing her to cry out in pain. "Calli!"

"I'm sorry, but I need to get her back right now, Destan." Doctor Gerould sounded borderline panicky as he adjusted his hold on her. *It'd be a miracle if she doesn't have a collapsed lung.*

"I… well… go. Just… please don't leave—"

"I'll make sure Auditor stays with her."

"Thank you. — Well, that means' you've gotta stay with me, Big Fella. I'm sorry. No one understands yet and it's for your own good. I can't afford for Calli to risk losing you."

He whined and yelped after her as he stood beside Destan, his feet doing a record-breaking foot-fire shuffle. And when she vanished from sight he began hopping and pacing back and forth, clawing at the ground as his ears and nose kept searching for her.

"What do you mean: 'this alpha is Canary's'?" Tracer gripped his arm, still furious this was all happening. "How do you know that? And if that's so, it shouldn't be obeying 'you'. I've stuck my neck out for you! How could you betray us—"

"Link into him. Calli, myself, and Emissary are his keepers. You can tell Calli and Emissary were in the programing from when he was originally coded. I was added the night we met with Canary."

"You what!"

"She secretly requested to meet with me, and my father left me strict instructions to get Calli to her. It's a huge, long story that'd probably come across really messed up if I tried to tell you right now."

"But why would Canary make Liaison and Emissary defaults at the same time? And what has Challenger got to do with this all?"

"To answer your first question, they're her children. Canary's real name was Lanta Presley. She's their biological mother."

"Presley?"

"Not so loud!" Destan hushed as he whipped his head around; now speaking in a whisper, "Majesty Presley is Calli's grandfather."

"Wait. Hold on a second. How do you know all this?"

"Like I said, Traceur: it's a jumbled mess of a story in a way." He paused, hoping she wouldn't press him right then.

Not willing to back off, she stared him down as she crossed her arms in front of her.

"Basically Canary left all the documentation necessary to prove who they both are. And if I'm being totally up front, so did Elder."

While he left much to be answered for, it was enough for the time being, "The evidence you have! It just doesn't incriminate, does it?"

"Well that's one way to put it." Destan bobbed his head as the creature came over and laid down next to him, puffing his lips out in disgust as he continued to sniff the air. "I know it's not fair, Big Fella. Believe me… I know."

"Where have you kept the belvedere hidden this whole time?"

"The Minka." He admitted, him fidgeting as he watched how the belvedere became more and more irritated. "Please, Traceur. I promise I won't run. Just undo these cuffs so that I can put the block back on so he won—"

"Just wait," she hushed as she watched something on her computer screen. "I've got to download this first and then you can."

After a few minutes, Traceur undid the handcuffs and let Destan put the block back on the belvedere. He told him to go to the Minka, him bolting back into the trees as the moon's light was blocked by another fast-moving storm.

And so, with that taken care of, Destan put his hands back behind him and let Traceur cuff him.

Is this really happening? Can a belvedere be good? And why does Elder want Liaison dead? It's not like 'she' did anything. Well, not knowingly. … And why in thunder was Chicane being such—

"Traceur?" Destan kept quiet as they walked back. "Don't blame Chicane. That wasn't him."

"He's been acting like this more and more lately. You know that." Traceur huffed as she started kicking at the stony ground — her not even questioning how Destan knew what she said — the small pebbles flying into nearby puddles. "He changed for no other reason than his own selfish ones and it's not right. I've tried so much to get him to see that he's—"

"It's because of Elder; he's manipulating Chicane. I know it doesn't make sense but remember what I was talking about earlier? There's information in the evidence that points directly to Elder having abilities — he's able to do things that a normal human being can't."

"What's that got to do with Chicane, though?"

"Elder's able to manipulate people's thoughts. And he does it in such a way that they have no idea. Chicane's been one of the reluctant ones concerning Calli from the get-go, correct?"

"Yeah. But—"

"Elder's using his reluctance and amplifying it."

"Then how did 'you' know if no one knows he's doing it?" Traceur cutoff, immediately noting a discrepancy.

"I have abilities too, Traceur. So does Calli. — Yes, those rumors were true. — We're both able to sense him. I don't understand all the science behind it or how to explain it, but we can." Destan tried to get as much information in the open as he could before they got inside. "I know the belvedere probably makes it hard to believe, but believe me when I say I'm telling the truth."

"The only moment I truly doubted you was when I saw the creature. But now? Yeah, I'm still mulling it over, but it's making sense. Well… as much as a crazy, twisted, extreme series of events can. … I'll do whatever I can to help, I promise."

"Just have that video feed you downloaded and what I told you to hide, ready. Okay? And… try not to stand up for me too much. If they think you're siding with me they might put you in custody too. I 'need' your eyes and ears free to get things done and to keep an eye on Calli."

Traceur nodded, taking the hint and pushing him to start walking.

⅏

Every back turned to Destan as he made his way through Bulwark. His first reaction was to be irate, but then again, he "did" have quite a bit of explaining to do aside from what happened with Elder.

361

"Anything else to declare?" Enforcer's brow wrinkled as he finished patting Destan down; not finding one blade on him.

"Would you even believe me if I told you I had my dagger at one point?" Destan rolled his eyes.

"Fair enough." Enforcer took out a wand and turned it on.

After the scanner found nothing, even Traceur found it baffling that he would dare go up top without any type of blade when it wasn't a recluse deep op: *He hates that dagger. Why would he only have it?*

Enforcer opened a door and shoved him into a cell, leaving him to begin begging forgiveness for his wrongs while the Veil was assembled.

The room was dark and rather musky; by no means inviting. — And a testament to the fact: someone wasn't doing their job. — He was expecting to be in solitary, so having a cellmate in his brother-in-law was a bit awkward now that Trever knew who he really was, "Did they do anything for you?"

Trever sighed as he half smiled while shrugging his shoulders, "No, but it's not like I'll die from it... right?"

"Traceur?" Destan whispered as she unfastened his cuffs. "See if you can get someone to come look at Emissary."

She nodded her eyes so no one else knew.

"And... and see how Calli is doing."

Her eyes began to soften and water; her head bobbing once.

It was nice that the door couldn't be slammed the way it was designed, but Enforcer sure looked like that's what he would've done if it were possible. Destan chuckled to himself as he sat down, Trever asking, "So is the belvedere dead?"

Destan shook his head.

"Traceur?" Trever asked a bit confused.

Trying not to let prying ears know much if anything, Destan only nodded. — Traceur and Doctor Gerould appeared to be the only ones left who believed him... well them and "hopefully" Rocher; he needed them where they were if for nothing else than to keep Callimay safe.

It wasn't but a few minutes later that Traceur showed up with some first aid supplies; tending to Trever's wound herself. She was upset no one was willing to come, but was beginning to understand how much pull Elder still had.

He glanced to see if anyone was watching, then scooted closer as he whispered; his voice trying to be positive, "Did you find Calli?"

"Yes?"

His eyes widened with fear, his whisper not really quiet any longer, "What is it?"

"T… they won't let Mender touch her until Elder's stable. And the shape he's in I don't think he ever will be even though he's continuing to hang on somehow. Auditor's been able to do some, but Liaison needs more care then one person with close to no resources is able to give."

"But she's alive?" Destan tried to find a thread of hope to cling to.

"And asking for you constantly."

Oh Calli. Destan grimaced as he bit his lip and threw his head back, doing everything he could to not lose control. "Traceur? There's one other thing I need you to get for me."

"What?" She asked wide-eyed as she whipped her head around.

"Ask outfitter for my new ensemble. Keep it with what you have."

Even Trever was baffled by that comment; Traceur pausing her winding the bandage on his hand before answering, "O… kay? I will."

Once the door was shut, Trever sighed, "So, Elder's our Nark, huh?"

But no one was there!

What in the— how did he get out!

The only thing he could do was wait. He wasn't about to say anything and get Destan caught. But how in the world did he get out? Trever didn't even remember seeing him get up.

Muffled shouts started breaking through the numbing silence; a feeling of boiling anger and tension sweeping under the door. He hoped that it was just someone seeing him out and reporting it, but the door soon opened and a limp Destan was tossed in the room.

Trever jumped to his feet, getting his hands in front of him, and rushed to check him.

Destan was alright, but it took a while for him to come to. At first Trever relaxed, but when he saw his left hand started to shake and seize — hearing him grimace — he obviously was concerned.

By the time Destan actually woke up, he was in so much pain it was all he could do to ignore Trever's well-meant concerned questions. He'd dealt with this so many times, but this time was different. He knew he didn't have Callimay as his backup any longer. Whether he wanted to or not, he had to work through this all on his own… and pray that Elder — if he was still alive — wouldn't use this golden opportunity to sneak in.

It was an excruciating seven minutes for both of them, but his hand finally released and he collapsed onto the closest bunk. He won. Now he needed rest: *She's okay. Lance got in to see her so it'll be okay. ~ I wonder if she's able to talk, still? ~ Worth a shot,* *Calli? Calli are you there? … Calli?* *Well, it's better that she rests.*

"You okay?"

"Yeah."

"What's with the stupid grin, then, after what just happened?" Trever thumped his boot. "And how did you get out?"

"I'm just… looking for Calli." Destan sighed as he sat up.

"Al… right?"

"We can communicate without talking. Kinda like having built-in phones in our brains. It's just… when one of us is in pain or asleep it's hard to make and keep a connection."

Still confused and wanting answers to a more pertinent question, Trever raised his eyebrow and narrowed his eyes.

"Would you believe me if I said I have the ability to jump from one location to another?"

"Oh pu-lu-eeze. You can think of something more believable than 'that'." Trever rolled his eyes; his scoffing voice exactly what was expected. "Teleportation. Good night. — You're a Veil. You can just do things like that. … So is this just some technique that you've learned? That's gotta be it. And it's some secrete Japanese one, isn't it?"

As Trever leaned forward toward the end, Destan couldn't help but notice he recognized the mark on Trever's arm. Yes, it was dark in there, but not "that" dark: *Hum. I wonder. ~ Oh wouldn't that be a laugh if 'he' had an ability after badmouthing and laughing it off like this.* "By the way, what's that on your arm?"

"You know, I really don't remember." Trever turned his elbow, showing the scar and where Callimay got him. "Well that one I know exactly who did it and that I deserved it, but this thing here? I've got a couple tattoos but this thing isn't one I asked for. And the location of it?

I just remember waking up one morning and it being there. Come to think of it, there are others pretty much all over me. That was the morning my muscles ached like none other. They don't hurt now or anything like that: nothing contagious. Just annoying as y'all get out."

"Wait. You don't remember?"

"Last thing I remembered was going out to the Society to check on the recovery mission of the bodies." Trever thought back as he looked toward the ceiling. "And the more I think about it… I don't even remember driving back to town."

"Have you noticed anything… well, 'different'?"

"Like what?"

"Oh I don't know: say you're able to teleport form one place to another or something like that." Destan half joked.

While he was all for a good joking match, Trever could sense a very real and serious truth being suggested, "What it is, Doyen? Do you know what these are?"

"I think so. Let me see it closer."

"Then tell me!" Trever demanded in a raised tone; shoving his arm out and almost clocking Destan in the head.

He hushed him and waited for a minute, then rolled up his pants leg, "Calli and I both have those scars; albeit ours aren't nearly as 'fresh' as yours. — They'll fade pretty well, don't worry. — They're from the process you undergo to gain abilities. … You said they're all over you?"

"Yeah." Trever sounded bewildered, him staring through him.

Destan thought for a minute and then asked, "H… have you noticed that you're any stronger?"

"How in the world do you know so much about this?" Trever's voice starting to sound irritated.

Just then, his handcuffs snapped. He jumped back and stared at his hands. Those were carbon steel cuffs that he popped like a balloon!

"Ah. Irritation. Makes sense, really. While you might not exhibit it consciously, underneath I've always known you to be irritable." Destan nodded as he sat back. "And it sure looks like you have Sinew."

"Huh? What? Sinew? What's that got to— what are you talking about? What's going on!" Trever's eyes darted back and forth.

"To answer your earlier question: the reason I know so much is because my father is the one who made the serums that give people heightened abilities. He never intended them to be used the way Elder started using them, though. — As to what's going on? If the last thing you remember was being at the Society then there was a jump in time and those scars 'popped up out of nowhere'? I don't see how it could be anything else than a memory wipe done after you were processed while at the Society. … Now 'why'? I guess to give Elder an advantage against Calli. Enforcer didn't end up killing her in Kerogen; and let's face it: he wouldn't have and no one else capable of making that shot. I do have heightened strength but she was still able to beat me. Fidus couldn't account for her adaptability and so he failed. With three fails just in the last what… three months? Elder couldn't let that happen again. So he made sure you — his little personal minion — were ready."

"What kind of evil and twisted person sends out others to do their dirty work? At least the Syndicate uses their own. … Okay, so they use the Sisterhood too at times, but this is one guy! What's his problem!"

Destan kept his voice low as he growled, "I wish I—"

Light streamed in the room, Destan having to shield his eyes.

There was a detail of Veils with Traceur and Fidus in front.

"It's time." Fidus' voice boomed as he crossed his arms in front of him. "Emissary? How did you—"

"Just cuff me and get it over with." Trever replied as he thrust his hands out.

ക

The group which surrounded them marched at a slow, methodical pace down the hall; a constant thumping rumble reverberating off the walls. Destan kept his head bowed, going through all he could think of as far as making his defense "believable".

Catching out of his peripheral Trever being shoved, he looked up and saw they were going past the medical wing. One door opened and he caught a glimpse of Callimay — Auditor was rushing out of the room looking worried and beyond nervous.

Calli?

No reply.

God? Please, 'please' help Calli. Destan begged as he was shoved by Chicane and Enforcer.

He overheard Trever talking to himself about breaking free, so he warned: *I need this undivided time with the entire Veil. It's the last shot I have at taking Elder down that I've been trying to get for months. I'll have my opportunity to give defense when we get in there. Unless you have some secret medical training, there's not much you can do to help Calli, anyway. … I've learned that lesson, finally.*

Trever whipped his head over and looked at Destan in fear.

This is one of my abilities, Emissary. I can hear what you say to yourself and talk with you. So if you have anything to say to me, just 'think' it. I'll hear you.

One?

The serum I have allows me to gain abilities. This one I'm using right now is actually Calli's.

The bewildered look on his face seemed to paralyze his voice — inner one included — and apparently his legs; him needing another shove to remind him to keep moving.

♲

He'd never been in this room and was almost scared when he stepped foot into Deep Dark. — Trever knew the punishment for anyone who wasn't a Veil and stepped foot in this place. — It wasn't anything like he expected it to be. Though, what he "was" expecting to find wasn't something he put much thought in, either.

All the voices were hushed as soon as Destan's first footstep hit the balcony floor. Practically every person turned to him with utter disgust and contempt. If anyone dared strike a match in the room, it was quite possible that the air would explode. Had Traceur, Rocher, and Doctor Gerould not been there, his task would've been near impossible.

Wait. Doctor Gerould was there?

Why aren't you with Calli? Or at least in the Wing? He was infuriated as he locked eyes with him.

She's stable, now sedated, and on pure oxygen. It didn't take much for her body to respond like I wanted it too. She should be going for her scan here any time now so I know how severe things are. — I didn't leave until I knew she was alright. I think 'you' need more help. Especially after your little 'escapade' you went on an hour ago. How—

But Auditor was running around—

She hasn't gotten with me so it must be some med she forgot and didn't want to leave Callimay alone any longer than she had to.

The group left the two men — who by the looks on everyone's faces were already condemned — in Traceur's custody.

"I think everyone is aware of what has happened." Fidus said in a loud and clear tone. "These two, plus the addition of Liaison, conspired to murder one of their own."

"That's a lie!" Trever yelled.

Emissary? Stop! That's an order. Destan tripped him; his eyes burning a hole through him.

"I think the video is very clear." Fidus turned to a screen where the surveillance of what happened came on.

As much as he should've expected it, Destan was still furious. It was just showing Elder and Destan… not Trever and Callimay. Nothing about what happened leading up to this was shown. Talk about being bias! This lack of "full disclosure" was made worse when the belvedere came into the shot followed by Trever; everyone voicing their anger.

Traceur? Don't spaz out. Just trust me. I need you to hack into that and put up what you took from the belvedere. I know it's something we try never to do, but I need you to stop this skewed view of what happened out there right now. Destan looked out of the corner of his eye back to her.

Her eyes got wider than dinner plates, but she took a hard swallow and did as he said: s few seconds later, the video feed glitched. Canary showed up on the screen as if she were talking to everyone.

Fidus yelled for someone to trace and stop the hack, but Doctor Gerould stepped up, "It is Canary, one of our own."

Rocher stepped up in defense; others finding the courage to agree.

Unwilling to let the control of this situation shift, Fidus refused to back down; but seeing Canary's face and listening to what she was saying? He begrudgingly took his hand down and looked away.

This video was when Canary first got her belvedere. — This video was over ten years old! — While it was good to get their attention,

Destan knew they needed to see more recent recordings. They had no time to wade through insignificant footage like this.

But then it skipped to her filming the video for Callimay.

I edited it. I skipped through it earlier, honing in on key phrases and facial recognition.

Good job, Traceur.

Seeing Vashti on the screen and hearing how they addressed each other left everyone in total shock. No wonder Majesty Presley was so strong in his support as well as his constant mentioning of Callimay whenever he called!

And piling it on, the feed switched to a phone call where a coarse male voice said a Veil — Challenger — had been taken down. She asked who did it, the male on the phone laughing in a low rumble as he said "he" did it.

Everyone recognized that laugh: it was Elder!

The evidence was welling like a tsunami as the feed cut to the belvedere. It took a moment to understand why Traceur included this, but it proved the creature was friendly: the point of view they were in during all these videos was from him. To this, a wave of comments of hushed sorts rolled over the room.

It skipped again to a meeting with Toreon's parents: the Monarch. This seemed like a strange thing to include in Destan's opinion, but he trusted that she put it in here for a reason.

And so she did, the air was ripped from the room when a familiar voice was heard. Elder was known by his same title in the Syndicate! — Beyond sickening.

Oh wait. It gets better… for Destan. Everyone gasped and looked at him when Elder started spouting off about information concerning runs and individuals who were found to be left-handed; both high-standing and "average" individuals! In addition to that, he mentioned "instalments from the Society" at one point.

Destan wanted to hear more of that clip in particular, but it would have to wait. What was showed next had Rocher fit to be tired; him grabbing his sword. It was an "older" clip: Elder reporting he had eliminated Mrs. Jackman and would make sure Destan didn't stand in their way.

A terrified hush fell over the room as Rocher yelled out and started storming out of Deep Dark, held back with some difficulty by the joint efforts of Doctor Gerould, Fidus, and Enforcer.

It skipped at that point to a conversation Canary and the Monarch had with Baleck. Toreon, the Prince, was even present; and this is where he was told by them that he'd be attending and become the leader of their new group of Falconers they called "Elites". — This hit a nerve with several in the room, them whipping their heads to look at each other… some running off after being nodded to.

By this time Destan knew everyone had seen more than enough, but he video skipped to clips from when Mr. Freigh was being interrogated, what Canary did to get in contact with Destan, and then their meeting; it then going dark.

Fidus looked at Destan in fear as did everyone else; no one daring to say a word or move now. In some terrifying way that none of them understood, they'd all been played like the finest of an instrument by the most heinous and yet cleaver of a player that ever lived. The Pied Piper couldn't begin to compare to this performance which led to such a deadly end. He'd twisted them to see things his way for years upon years. Each new group of trainees which came to help and give new life to the group were placing themselves in the palm of one who wanted them all dead. He'd been destroying them from the inside little by little, letting his stench of hatred and treason steep until it infected every individual there… even Destan admitted he was infected as well.

They began to let the reality that Destan's earlier proof was real and his accusations against him concerning Callimay weren't overreactions to his wife's accidents. Every single, solitary thing surrounding Elder and his connection to the Society and the Syndicate was true.

While he knew almost all of this was true from the original evidence he had, Destan had no idea the belvedere held it all. That cyborg dog that was seen as a Shadow and Veil killer was the most valuable creature on Quidoria as far as they were concerned. — If the Monarch ever found out where he was there was no way they'd do nothing to make sure he was destroyed.

He really didn't need the other evidence now. This relief made him beyond angry with himself, though: *You mean I could've risked giving the journal over without losing everything? … How stupid could I be, not even thinking the Big Fella had half of this information? I could've saved Calli so much pain!*

"I know this is all a shock to you," Traceur stepped forward, putting her computer away. "I was completely floored when I went through this footage at first. — Yes, I was the one who did that. — But I think you can see why. Veils? Think back to something you did that just didn't feel like your 'true' self reacting. Think. It still doesn't make complete sense to me either, but trust me on this one. Think back. … I hope we all are mature enough to see it and humble enough to admit it. Maybe some more than others, but I can honestly remember a handful of times when I made a decision that right now I know 'I' never world. — This evil man has worked for longer than some of us have even been alive to get where he is! It sounds so much like Commander caught on, but Challenger and Canary were the first two who were able to actually fight back. They got so close but Elder was able to rip them apart and thwart their plans; him apparently believing that by doing so made him safe. And things did sit idle for so long like he wanted… until a miracle happened. One we never knew we needed but the powers that be did. Doyen and Liaison met and found the clues to start digging. I don't know what prompted them to, but I am beyond grateful for their sacrifice. He's tried to tear them apart and we've let it happen, Veils! 'We'! We're to blame. Again and again he's attempted to kill one or both of them and what did we do? Those weren't accidents, Veils. Those were planned efforts to commit nothing but what is cold-blooded murder. Those discrepancies in the videos those couple times Liaison had scares? … I think you know where I'm going with this. — We have broken the only code that really is of any importance to Shadows and Veils: to protect the oppressed and fight those who seek them out for their lives."

"I know this is enough for prove why Emissary, Calli, and myself did what we did; but I had no idea about this video. The proof I've been holding onto — trying to find the perfect opportunity to give to you — was what my father died to get and Canary sacrificed herself to ensure I got safely." Destan explained as he nodded to Traceur, an edge still in his voice since he was angry at himself. "I'm sorry I never trusted you, but with what Elder could do I had no choice but to hide this and treat you all as the enemy to some degree. … This evidence was something two Veils died to protect. I couldn't let it fall into his hands and risk losing what I saw as my only hope of exposing him."

Traceur undid his handcuffs and handed him the ensemble. He reached in and found the hidden zipper, pulling out the white leather book he'd come to hate so much. — It was indeed the perfect hiding place for Elder's journal. Everyone knew Destan was adamant about how he would "never" get a new ensemble.

"This book contains all of Elder's personal accounts of what happened from when he gained his abilities up until what had to be the night before he murdered my father." Destan declared as the pages whipped and snapped from him shaking it above his head. "It will help fill in some gaps, but believe me when I say I won't fill all of them." *I'm sorry, Rocher. I wish those details were in here.* "I have no idea when he first joined the Syndicate. I do have my suspicions though… he was with them first before coming to the Shadows. — If you will amplify the sound from the footage of us fighting, you'll find more confessions from him. He's been selling out left-handed people for years; giving them the choice of death or becoming a worker of whatever sort for the Syndicate. And from what I heard on the one clip, some even have abilities: those anomalies Canary warned us about and the trafficking tips we'd been getting that were 'odd'. Don't take my word for it. Look at the footage and read this."

"Elder's been working nonstop since Liaison's come to Bulwark to eliminate whom he saw as his worst enemy. I think it's evident from previous information given to us that he tried years prior as well; but here he had a full arsenal of 'trained' people he could utilize." Traceur walked over and picked up a box. "These are all pieces of the web we took down from Liaison's final run. Nothing about them was right and the team that worked with me I'm sure now has the confidence to say it: old anchors, dull wires, wet cement, sloppy arrangement. It was set up right before Liaison got there… which means someone targeted her specifically. I found the exact same items in Elder's personal quarters not even two weeks later. I don't know if he placed the web himself or twisted one of us to do it, but that's not my point. I'm of the belief he fabricated this whole uproar with the faction that occurred the first day of Liaison's final run. He was trying to get them apart so they'd be weak and vulnerable. … He almost won, wouldn't you agree? — This 'ability' business may seem fantastic and all a ridiculous lie, but we all know of the rumblings that can still be heard of what happened during the infiltrating recluse op in Faberton during their civil war: how people were being modified and weaponized. I have full assurance the book Doyen hold contains the answers we may still have on that front. Though we may not want to know the depths to which Elder was capable of molding the very fabric of our own individual morals — I know I shudder at the thought of it — we must be willing to accept this and make amends for our sins."

In that moment of silence, someone pounding on the door caught everyone off guard. Those up by the door opened it and there was Auditor; she was severely beaten and out of breath.

"Sophia!" Doctor Gerould gasped as he ran up to her.

"L… Liaison." She tried to get out as she fell into his arms. "They … took, her."

"Who?"

"C… Chi… cane an… and Coal-esce."

Traceur unlocked Trever's handcuffs so he could follow Destan; them racing up to Doctor Gerould and Auditor, "When did it happen?"

She took a few more moments to catch her breath before finishing, "About five minutes ago. — You've 'got' to find her! Her trachea is fractured. She's got eight broken ribs and both her lungs are showing hemopneumothorax. And then she's got full atelectasis in both lungs. I had just gotten back with a trach kit when I found them with her."

Yeah, that medical stuff sounded terrifying, but what did it mean!

It's worse than I thought. 'Much' worse. "She's going to suffocate if you don't find her quickly." Doctor Gerould clarified.

That's all Destan needed to know. The doors slammed against the wall as he bolted for the medical wing. Trever followed but had no idea where to go to start looking. And really, what good was running going to do?

Destan tapped Toreon's ability to see if Chicane and Coalesce were anywhere nearby, but…

Nothing.

"Emissary? I need you to call Nexus and get her to scour through all video feeds to see where Chicane and Coalesce took Calli."

Just like the last two times, the video feed had been altered. They were visible in the room with her and in the medical wing but vanished when they got in the hall. No one could get a fix on their homing signals so they were left blind.

And yet could this be a devilish plan perpetrated by them alone: *How strong is Elder that even— did Trever not get him? Was 'that' all a lie! ~ You don't think~ If Ginger's still alive...*

The two men met down in the detention quadrant. After sharing his concerns, the two of them raced back up to the medical wing.

During whole this time he kept calling and calling, begging her to respond: *Calli! Calli, can you hear me? Even if you're in pain you've got to try. ... Please!*

Finally! She answered in a weary, pain-ridden tone: *Destan?*

Trever ran into him, not expecting him to come to a sudden stop on the stairs, "What is it?"

"Shh!" *Calli where are you?*

I... I don't know. It's dark. ... And... and I can hear the ocean. — Destan? I can't breathe very well. It hurts so much.

I know Calli. Just hang in there. He tapped Trever's arm and headed toward the south side entrance. *I'm coming.*

It's so cold. She kept babbling on as she moaned and inched her fingers around her to find some clue. *So cold that I can't shiver. And my hair is wet. Why would my hair be wet, Destan? Am I sweating that bad? — Where am I? I can feel water with my hands. Did I fall in a pool? Is there even a pool in Bulwark? I know the mansion had one, but I don't' remember seeing on here. It would make sense, though.*

While hearing her voice was a comfort and the details she was giving gave him a really good idea where she was, the fact that she wasn't able to focus — she was starting to become delirious from the lack of oxygen. Destan tried to narrow his search further, but couldn't use Toreon's "and" Ingrid's abilities at the same time. Toreon's only worked when you could see; seeing into something dark was no help. And Ingrid's could only amplify what he already saw.

As the two of them got outside, Destan called back to Trever, "She's in the labyrinth. And wherever she is, the tide's rolling in."

They raced through the shoot into the labyrinth but right before they got to the combs the passage was full. Destan yelled in a hysterical voice: *Calli?* "Calli!"

The volume of his call jerked her into a somewhat better conscious state, her now starting to cry when she realized: *Hurry, Destan. There's more water in here. I… I don't know how much longer it'll be before I'm covered.*

"How's your swimming?" Destan asked as he ripped off his veil.

"I'm no fish, but I can hold my breath and beat feet." Trever jumped in; gasping as he came up.

Once he worked off the shock himself, Destan ordered, "Take the left side. She's in one of the upper coves. If you find her, get her back to Bulwark the fastest way you know how. Let me know when you can. — And remember: just think. I'll make sure to be listening."

"You've got it." Trever nodded as he took a deep breath and plunged into the ice-cold water.

It was almost high tide now so Destan knew they had no time left.

And it also dawned on him that getting her out was going to be something only "he" could do since she wouldn't be able to hold her breath for any amount of time: *Emissary?*

You found her!

No. I just remembered something: Calli can't hold her breath. If you find her, tell me which comb you're in and wait. … Which means keep count!

O… kay?

Just trust me!

Destan, hurry. Callimay pleaded; her now sobbing as she tried in vain to push the water away from her face. *The water's up past my ears. I—*

Trever and I are looking as fast as we can. Please just try to stay calm. I know it's hard, but just keep talking to me.

He popped up in another empty comb, slamming his fist on the floor of it as he heard Trever: *Doyen this is going to take too long. She can't have that much time left!*

The only thing left he could think of — and what he probably should've done first: *Lance!*

What is it Destan? Doctor Gerould jerked back, now trying to catch his breath.

Lance? Get Nexus to hone in on Calli's coordinates.

I'll get right on— oh no. She's not wearing her ensemble, Destan. He looked over in the room she had been in. *It's not on her.*

You've gotta be— Destan fumed as he took a deep breath and dove back under.

Precious seconds slipped through their fingers, them both trying to figure out a way to find her faster. And then it came: *Wait! I forgot! Callimay has the new style of beacon. They contain a homing chip.*

Find her! Destan sounded frantic.

I've found her, Doyen! Hurry! She can't breathe! I'm in the second to last one on my side. "Everlyn? Hang in there, sis." Trever panicked as he gently picked her up.

Only her mouth and nose were above water at that point. She was shivering, convulsing, and gasping; her skin pale and lips starting to look blue.

Doyen!

Destan burst out of the water and scrambled to take hold of Callimay and Trever.

"What are you doing!" Trever tried to shake his grasp.

"Trust! Me!" Destan flashed his eyes before looking in the direction of Bulwark. *Get back to the Wing, Lance. We're on our way.*

It took a few seconds longer than he hoped, but Destan made the jump and landed them in the main area of the medical wing.

Trever ripped his hand away and scampered back into the nearest wall, understandably terrified.

Destan… Destan, I can't breathe. Callimay cried as tears streamed down her face, her eyes staring at him with almost a death stare as she clawed to hold on to him. *Destan help me! Make it stop!*

He clutched his chest as he tried to keep from passing out; his emotions ready to burst wide open.

Once the pain and dizziness passed, he picked up his wife and staggered over, kicking in the bay door closest to him. He stumbled over to the bed and did his best to not fall on top of her, his breathless cries for someone to help evaporating as fast as he could get them out: *Where is everyone!*

Out of nowhere Torpid ran in and told him Doctor Gerould sent him. Destan didn't want him touching her, seeing what happened the last time he did, but he had no choice. If nothing was done in the next few moments Callimay "would" die.

"This is going to hurt, Liaison. I'm so sorry." Torpid opened a small box and took what looked to be a dagger out of it.

"What are you doing!" Destan yelled as he reached out to stop him.

"Emissary… Sentinel— help me!" Doctor Gerould called out as he tried to keep Destan back.

"What's wrong with you, Lance!"

"He's gaining access to her airway, Destan! It's alright!" He fought to keep control of the hysterical young man. "This 'will' help her. He's not going to kill her. I promise you! Let him do it!"

Callimay looked to be unconscious at this point, but Destan could hear her screaming to herself… and him. He just couldn't take it, all but pounding his fists on the sides of his face, "Stop hurting her!"

Trever got a good hold on him and pulled him out of the room, giving Torpid and Doctor Gerould room to work. They needed to get her stable enough so they could make the mad dash for surgery. — The same thing that happened to Destan in Berchshire.

A couple others rushed over as they pulled her out, hooking her up to some monitors as they went; their voices clear but not yelling as they said certain words and phrases that made no sense to Destan at all. He broke free from Trever but ran to the observation room.

The first thing he saw was the broken glass from where he'd lost it last time. Seeing it made him take a deep breath and make sure he didn't repeat his near deadly error.

And so the substitute for anger was feeling. The feeling of cold. Feeling his soaked clothes bind his every movement. Feeling his heart still pounding in his throat.

He folded his arms across his chest and stood there, fighting off the chill of the ice-cold water and trying everything to calm his mind so his heart would follow suit.

Trever came in not too much later, his face beet red, "I… I'm sorry, Doyen. This is all my fault. I'm ready to accept the punishment for a—"

"It wasn't you, Emissary. Don't you get that?" Destan didn't move except for a shake of his head as he kept an ever-watchful eye on Callimay and what was going on.

"But I was—"

"Just shut it, Emissary!" He yelled as he slammed his fist on the wall; then paused, "I… I'm sorry." *Deep breath… or two.* "Don't blame yourself. You didn't know. And with what Elder did for so long there really was no way for you 'to' know. You truly thought what he said to do was right. He'd trained you to. And if you don't mind me being up front: I know that all too well myself. He got to me and 'I' almost killed her myself."

Since he was mumbling the last part, Trever didn't hear it and wasn't about to ask him to repeat himself. He began to ask as the door opened, "What's going to happen…"

They looked back and saw Fidus with a few others, him asking rather reluctant, "Is she?"

"They're still working so she's alive." Destan nodded to the room, rubbing his face as he turned back.

Conducting official Veil work in front of a Shadow wasn't code, but Fidus was about ready to chuck them all out the window; the anger in him burning white-hot, "We've heard from everyone except you."

While most would've needed some context, Destan knew exactly what he was asking for. He stared in the room for a moment then closed his eyes as he sighed. Fidus was about to ask again when Destan opened his eyes — them full to the brim with determination — and replied, "Take him off. And now. He's murdered two Veils — as well as the former Commander of the Shadows — taken responsibility for the massacre of my wife and Emissary's family, attempted on numerous occasions to murder her, trafficked countless left-handed individuals for who knows what purposes... and only God knows what other abominations. He's shown no remorse for what he's done. … Proverbs 28:17 seems rather fitting here. He has others' blood on his hands. He has openly admitted he is a fugitive and thus deserves no help of any kind. He's never shown he has any intention of repenting of what he did. If allowed to be around anyone who can't 'see' him, he'll only manipulate the situation or person to get what he wants. There's One I 'know' he can never manipulate. And I think it's time for him to take responsibility for what he's done since he has condemned himself — before God Himself."

He looked back as if to ask what the vote was. It wasn't an outright yes/no answer, but he understood when Fidus nodded, "So be it."

The group left, leaving these two, half-frozen, drenched, and exhausted men alone yet again.

Saying what he wanted to might not have been the best idea, but Trever needed confirmation of what Destan said earlier, "Now what?"

"Now? We wait and pray." He groaned as he sat down, not taking his eyes off of Callimay.

ℬ

Trever stayed with Destan the entire time Callimay was in surgery. It was altogether nine-hours of gut-wrenching waiting, waiting, and more waiting. And then afterward she was taken to a special unit where Destan wasn't allowed in to see her for a few more hours.

While the fact he was still slightly hypothermic was most likely the cause, Trever couldn't help but notice Destan's hands were shaking. He left for a while, not saying a word; finding him right where he was when he got back, "You need to eat, Doyen. I'm not sure if this is—"

"Destan."

He put the sandwich back in the bag, looking puzzled, "Huh?"

"My name's Destan. Destan Nevrille." He repeated a bit louder as he turned and offered his hand. "Not that it's probably much of a shock with the blowup of news that happened a few months back, but… well, we're family. Might as well start calling each other by our real names since we're stuck with each other for life, right?"

Being open and conversational was something Trever never thought Destan was; and especially in this type of situation. Quippy at moments, yes; but this? He almost didn't know how to respond, but eventually took his hand and gave it a firm shake, "I'm sure you already know mine because of Everlyn… but I guess even I don't know my 'real' name. At least I'm not sure."

"Believe it or not Elder copped out there. Your real name 'is' Trever. Trever Sebastian Presley." Destan paused when Torpid walked out of the room. "H… how is she?"

"I've never seen anything like this," he shook his head as he looked back at Callimay. "With as little oxygen as she was getting for that amount of time? She 'should' have been dead by the time I got to her. But whatever is in her brain, whatever special buffer she was given for other purposes, it's like it paused time: I can't see that she has 'any' permanent brain damage. And logically speaking she should with as blue as her lips and fingers were. I know some of that was due to the water she was in — in fact that probably helped stunt the damage — but I've never seen anything like this. It's nothing short of a miracle."

"What about her neck?" Trever asked concerned.

"She'll have that brace for a while and the fractures she sustained? There's not too much that can be done right now. Her body has other issues to focus on right now. They'll check her in a week or so to see if anything needs to be done about it. She's young enough that the bone may heal itself since the fractures were hairline ones. — Now the only 'bad' thing might be you notice as a permanent thing is a change in her voice. Mender was able to repair the damage, and by another miracle I put the trach over one of the internal lacerations, but it 'will' affect her voice. How much? Time's the only thing that'll give you that answer."

"Why does she have those tubes attached to her sides?"

"They're to evacuate air and blood from around her lungs. I don't know what happened, but I've never seen someone with eleven broken ribs. I thought five was a high number when you came back from Indalla that one time. But this?"

"How is she going to be able to handle that kind of pain? When she had the three that was hard enough on her."

"She has an epidural line in right now which serves to block her sense of pain in that certain area. With as many as are broken, she's going to need that line to stay in for at least the first week. And while it's in she won't feel her legs—"

"I get it: she's going to be here for a while." His shoulders dropped as he bowed his head. "How long will she be sedated like this? Can I go in to see her now?"

"She won't be awake for the rest of the day if that's what you're driving at." Torpid shook his head as Auditor and a couple other nurses came out. "But seeing as how all their and my work is done, it looks like she's all set and ready for you."

Destan nodded and then went in. He looked back and motioned for Trever to follow, but he shook his head, "You need some time alone."

"She's asleep." Destan almost managed a chuckle. "By the way, what's in the bag?"

"Lunch, breakfast— whatever meal you want it to be." Trever still sounded concerned; him not wanting to intrude.

"You got something for yourself, right?"

"Oh sure, but—"

"Then come on," Destan managed a corner smile as he jabbed his shoulder. "I doubt we'll wake her up."

"Doyen?"

"Huh?" He stopped and turned back.

"Are you alright?"

"This is a technique Calli would use when she was really nervous: diversion. I'm hoping it helps keep my emotions in check for right now. Plus I'll admit I do need someone to talk to."

"What do we do now?"

"For now? We wait. … And try to relax. Thinking of what's coming up has put some things into perspective: what we just went through has got to be the worst of it. Not saying it's smooth sailing here on in, but I don't see how there could possibly be anything worse than dealing with Elder. Messing with people's minds, all the while enjoying them being at war with themselves even? It's a kind of battle I pray no one else has to fight ever again." He flopped onto a seat and sighed.

❦

Come Saturday, Fidus was able to get everyone, Veil and Shadow alike, that was able to even think of doing so, assembled. Much to his initial objection — and other Veils — Destan informed the general assembly of what the Shadow's true mission was to bring to light what Elder's traitorous acts were threatening. To say this left the trainees and newer Shadows speechless was spot-on accurate.

"None of us signed up for this blindfolded and totally naïve." Traceur reminded in her strong yet calming mother tone. "Yes, not everyone knew the underlying mission we have… but is this really 'that' astounding to you? Did you truly think we just existed to function behind the scenes and just do the best we could? To cower away from the heinous evil over us by hiding in special cities and communities? Only doing things for a temporary 'in the now' fix? I don't think any of us thought that for very long. We've 'all' wanted this… for various reasons, but we as one group have worked to make the lives of those seen as evil parasites something to be thankful for. Don't forget we're not doing this for just ourselves. We're doing it for the countless others in this world!"

Some field agents were concerned by the news of the Falconers with abilities, but Rocher stepped in and reminded them that their job by its very nature was dangerous. As long as they didn't act any differently toward those they were around, no one would be the wiser for the time being. And if something did happen, it was something that was thought of and anticipated to be a large possibility.

On the other hand, with that encouragement and blunt reminder, many of the newer Shadows began to take to heart their actual "job", asking what was going to be done about Total Eclipse and how they could prepare themselves… which got Destan to thinking.

And thinking.

Destan spent "days" trying to figure it out; asking Callimay what she thought even though she was still sedated: *We can't really go early… it's only three more days. And you're in no condition to be moved to the Nest. And God forbid me to leave you again like I did.*

If they waited, the Syndicate would jump at any small thing they might suspect and would make things into easier "divide and conquer" battles. But that meant making some recluse ops much more dangerous than they already were. Was that worth it?

But if they went ahead the Syndicate knew what to expect. There's "no" way Elder didn't feed them every detail about Total Eclipse.

Then again, would that give them the element of surprise because they would be doing the very thing "logical" people would brush off as being stupid?

No matter which one he chose, this decision was going to impact the lives of thousands who were under Destan's authority; no including countless others who waited to see if they would have to continue to live in seclusion with a healthy level of fear or not.

❦

Due to what was discovered in Elder's quarters, several Veils and Shadows were immediately pulled from their details regardless of when he would greenlight Total Eclipse. Part of Destan wondered if those they had lost in the past few months could've been saved had he only had the strength to do what he needed to earlier. — Oh what a weight this was on him. — But, when faced with reality, the likelihood of him knowing for sure whether or not his delay would have prevented those deaths? It was slim to none. And he couldn't do this "emergency pull" with everyone. Running and hiding wasn't going to fix anything. At some point they "had" to come out in the open and face the Syndicate: like natural ones, the shadows would have to show themselves. And while he could ask and ask for input all he wanted — some already giving theirs — in the end "he" was responsible.

Again: what an enormous weight of responsibility was on one young man's shoulders. One who was, at that time, praying his wife would make a full recovery from what felt like an endless barrage of murder attempts. Yes, the one who instigated all those attempts was gone forever more, but the consequences of his actions were still there for Destan to deal with.

The End

One last push…
brace yourself.